VILLAINY

EDITED BY
A.C. HALL & PHILLIP HALL

A HALL BROTHERS ENTERTAINMENT ANTHOLOGY

PUBLISHED BY

HALL BROTHERS
ENTERTAINMENT

Cover design by Paul Milligan

first edition, released June 2011

This book is dedicated to storytellers. Heroes wouldn't be nearly as interesting without villains to combat and neither would exist without talented folks who step away from the fast paced grind of the modern world to spend their time creating stories.

READ ORDER

1	26	283	5	38
142	179	77	114	306
217	93	267	147	
70	223		191	
106	236			
259				
298				
169				
249				

TABLE OF CONTENTS

LAST RIDE OUT OF LIBERATION
BY TONY LAPLUME

It wasn't supposed to turn out that way. Anglim glanced over his shoulder, his car wildly veering onto the shoulder, the last of the city passing out of view, and wished to god he'd never visited Liberation. It wasn't even much of a city, he thought to himself, more like an overgrown town, swelled with expectations that had never borne fruit. A population full of failure. Well, it wasn't as if he were going to be just another number in that census. Two weeks was all he needed to determine that.

His troubles had begun soon after he showed up in Liberation, located in the bowels of Texas and settled in the turbulent years of the 19th century. Trouble would have been another fantastic name for a place like that. It was everywhere. Anglim was no saint, but usually he had to look for trouble. This time, trouble was literally no trouble at all. It was a dame, some bad thugs, and a lot of pissed off city workers. Every one of them was looking for it.

To give them some credit, maybe Anglim had the smell of it still hovering around him when he first pulled into the motel parking lot, a seedy place in ill-repair to set the appropriate mood. He'd come from trouble, there was no denying it, but he had been looking to avoid more of it. That had been the whole point of skipping the last town.

The motel's front office was empty when he finally forced the door open, jammed as much on divots from past wars as on its own poor hinges. He rang the bell impatiently, it's true, but he tended to do most things that way. It was his nature. Maybe it made him a conductor. He was no psychologist. He wasn't much for brains in general.

The dame was the one who eventually appeared, wiping her ruby lips, probably from some salacious and not particularly nutritious meal. Anglim heard movement from behind her, some protests, not very serious, practiced. He didn't actually see anything else but her. There wouldn't have been much point. She had a body that could stop a train in full motion. Her eyes were the killers, though. They were daggers handled with expert finesse, always on target, tossed with all the care of a circus performer. She flicked open her registry and threw a set of keys at him. Didn't even bother to ask for money. You don't bail on a girl like that. Anglim understood right away that the city's name was a matter of irony. There wasn't a lot of escaping going on here, at least not the easy way.

He never even spoke a word to her, and Anglim was on his way to his room, which he found to be in general order, if by that it was understood that maybe someone had cleaned up ten years ago. The rates covered about that much, and they were as much as he cared to pay. There was a knock at his door around midnight, just when he was about finished with his gin, and without answering he found it opening, and saw who he suspected the dame had torn herself away from earlier, a burly hulk of a man, pounding his fists and scowling like he was owed something. Anglim was ready to pay, only his currency was a

Magnum, tucked away for safe keeping in a holster beneath the coat he was still wearing.

Liberation wasn't much for words, but it was good for a fight, and that's what this hulk wanted. Either Anglim's reputation was bigger than he'd thought, or he'd been mistaken for someone else. Happened all the time anyway. The hulk moved fast for a man of his size, and before Anglim knew it, there were others to join in. He squeezed off a few welcomes, thinning the crowd, but there were more of these thugs than he was prepared to greet, and he soon had to improvise. Shooting out the light, he was gone before the last goodbye could be heard.

The sirens were on him in a heartbeat. Anglim realized there must have been a setup, but again, for whom, he couldn't have cared. They were in fast cars, and his hadn't been since the last shootout, which he calculated must have been at least three days earlier. Forced off the road, he gave himself up easy this time, looking for a fresh angle, some time to think.

Introduced to the local police commissioner, he said his name was Black Amber, which was true enough, though he doubted his new friend would appreciate his sense of humor. But as it turned out, the commissioner had heard the name before, and wasn't in the mood for joking. He only had one thing to say, and it amounted to a single sentence. Turns out at least some of the locals knew exactly who he was, and what, or some of what, he was running from. No big deal.

On the way to lockup, he strangled the driver and took over the ride, his first new one in four days. It handled curves beautifully, almost as well as the dame, whom Anglim couldn't bring himself to blame for any of his troubles in Liberation. He stopped by the motel long enough to reclaim his things and steal a kiss. She seemed to like it, but there was too much to look at to pay a lot of attention to her expression. Besides, he was gone before she knew it.

He glanced over his shoulder long enough to make sure Liberation was far behind him, and then back ahead of himself again to try and guess where he might be turning up in next. The world was just a sparkplug of possibilities for a man like Anglim, who only slowed down long enough for the next great adventure, no matter the cost. Later, he learned that whoever all the source of trouble in that city really was, Anglim had already killed him, somewhere in the insignificant past. He was, as he always was, a survivor.

BANTAM'S RUN
BY CHRISTOPHER DONAHUE

Kat woke to the feel of needles withdrawing from her arms. Disorientation and a pounding headache welcomed her back to the world of the living. She forced her eyelids open and blinked to clear the tears from her eyes.

It was the usual wakening misery that made being a star pilot such a joy. This time, the pain was compounded by a vague screeching sound inside her head. It was like the sound of a thousand voices screaming. Frozen ghosts screaming for release, her most common nightmare despite assurances that DeepSleep was dreamless.

One more reason to get even with the universe.

Before focusing her thoughts on where she was or what had happened before she went into DeepSleep, Kat looked for the status panel. The red lights indicating an emergency wakening were dark. The few yellow lights scattered among the dozens of greens were on the bottom row, non-critical.

Kat's wits gathered slowly, but inexorably. They were carried on the rolling waves of her throbbing headache. Bantam had awakened her because an operational parameter had been met.

In the piracy business, this could mean that a victim approached, a spy's warning had been received, or their trap had been spotted. At least the months spent in DeepSleep waiting on a victim were ageless time.

On her third try, Kat's numb fingers managed to open her DeepSleep capsule. The transparent lid hissed open, letting in the piloting cabin's chill air. Since there was no emergency, Kat took her time getting out of the capsule and giving the headache and nausea a chance to subside.

She dialed up the heat in her tight, but comfortable pilot's cabin. For most trips, the isolated room was her whole world.

"Ping, from Gamma-21-V," Bantam announced.

Kat snapped her head up to look at the status board. A pulsing yellow light reported a ship was near enough to use microwave scanners on Bantam. The yellow light indicated a reading-level 'ping' rather than the red light 'paint' of a weapons-targeting radar.

"They're coming in," Captain Kryzin announced with a trace of predatory panting to his intercom voice.

Kat, Captain Kryzin and the ship's engineer, Jules, were the only ones awake, assuming Bantam's protocols were operating normally. Behind the captain's, pilot's and engineer's self-sustaining cabins, the passenger section of Bantam closed the vents to the absolute zero of space. This started the slower and less-stressful process of waking the rest of the crew from drugged and frozen zombie sleep.

"Let's see our new friend," Kat croaked.

A screen lit, showing an ugly gray grid-work ship approaching. It was a standard Caliphate design with an engine mounted on a central frame and cross-members laid out for interchangeable modules. It was a far cheaper and more flexible

6

design than Bantam's subdivided, armored shell hull. But the Caliphate design relied on Divine Will, magnetic screens and powered shields to protect the modules. The newcomer's armored crew module and sensor module at the bow were usually the only relatively safe spots on a ship like that. Two weapons modules and a series of nine light passenger modules studded the ship's nearside.

Kat absently stroked the brand mark on her forearm as she studied the ship. Her entire clan had been carried away as human loot on a similar Caliphate ship. The swirling brand on her arm marked her as chattel, for use but never allowed to convert or be sold outside the Caliphate. She could only envy the sheltered childhoods of those she read in the stacks of old-earth books packed into her meager personal cargo allotment.

But the faded brand was a token from many years and a lot of payback ago. She smiled, but it wasn't a pleasant smile.

Glorious Pilgrimage was right where the shipyard spies said the transport ship would be. More than a few pirates had found their traps turned against them, but things looked solid so far. Even so, she wished Bantam's shields could be charged up without tipping their hand to their victim.

"It looks like she's coming in cautiously," Kat rasped into her intercom.

Using only passive sensors, she guessed the newcomer would end its approach around seven kilometers from Bantam.

As Glorious Pilgrimage moved in, Kat hoped the armed transport would only see what Captain Kryzin wanted the victim to see. Bantam's carefully sculpted "hull damage" disguised her forward-mounted heavy laser ports. Invisible grapples magnetically linked Bantam to the larger, frigate-sized ship, Exeter. Molecule-thin panels covered Exeter's real blast damage holes and dummy robots wandered through her gutted hull giving electronic and thermal signs of life. To the observer, it would appear the pirate Exeter was engaged in stripping the smaller schooner, Bantam.

"They're nervous, but very tempted," Jules whispered, unnecessarily.

Catching a pirate in the middle of stripping a victim was the opportunity of every Caliphate captain's dreams. Even after the confiscatory taxes, a captain taking two prizes and delivering pirates for execution would earn enough to start his own commercial line. The luckiest of such captains might buy his way into the comfort of a religious post or an off-world trade minister's position. The lowest, filthiest crewman serving on Glorious Pilgrimage would see enough prize money to buy a dozen girls condemned to the life Kat had escaped at such great cost ten years ago.

From two hundred kilometers away, Kat could hear the saliva drip from the chin of the Glorious Pilgrimage's captain.

"Okay, Jules, we have a nibble," Captain Kryzin whispered over the intercom. "Switch the Exeter's robots to 'caught dirty' and bring our engines up quietly."

Kat settled into the pilot's chair, adrenalin clearing the last vestiges of DeepSleep. Glorious Pilgrimage was a rich prize herself and her captain came in cautiously.

The shipyard spies Captain Kryzin had cultivated said Glorious Pilgrimage carried a full load of "volunteer workers". They were loot from the recently conquered independent world of

New Macao and bound for the industrial hell of Hugo Secundum.

The transport's unarmored passenger modules were packed with victims in the cheapest form of frozen sleep. Workers were the gold-standard of interstellar commerce. Only a prize as rich as two ships and what remained of their skilled crews would tempt the armed transport to come in closer.

Uneasily, Kat realized she still heard faint screaming. She shook her head, letting the reinvigorated headache drown out the sound. The frozen slaves aboard Glorious Pilgrimage weren't even a tertiary concern to most of Bantam's crew.

Captain Kryzin's letters of marque from the Central Committee on Earth authorized him to capture or destroy Enemies of the People (with a share of the profits going to the communists). The letters made Bantam's piracy fully as legitimate as the legalized slavery aboard the Caliphate ship.

The captain also had letters of marque from Stellar Corporation and from Bantam's home port of New Oz to hunt bandits with similar shares going to their ruling corporate oligarchy. The only people the captain did not have a privateering arrangement with were the Caliphate.

That was the main reason Kat signed on to Bantam. She liked adventure and loot, but hated religious slavers even more. A low-rent operation like Bantam suited her perfectly.

Kat charged Bantam's two internally mounted heavy lasers, then diverted power to charge Jules' three dorsal-mounted medium laser turrets. Bantam's power plant only produced the energy to charge one weapon set at a time.

She twisted in her deeply padded chair to ease the kinks in her back, whispering, "Yeah, if it all goes to plan, we'll be knee deep in snuff and flame-stones." The most recent series of underwhelming piracy scores kept Bantam's crew out of debt, but in no danger of drowning in loot.

Glorious Pilgrimage eased in. Her shields were minimal, but her cloaking was on. Captain Kryzin's spies had given him the right frequencies of Glorious Pilgrimage's ECM suite, so Bantam could see the transport with no trouble. Had Exeter been a manned ship, she would have seen a cloaked ship suddenly in so close and brought up shields and weapons by now. The robots aboard Exeter simulated a panicked, amateur pirate crew.

Kat planned to use Glorious Pilgrimage's demand for Exeter to surrender as her own cue to open fire. Instead, Glorious Pilgrimage fired its nearside pair of heavy lasers on Exeter without warning.

Strobing green beams lashed from Glorious Pilgrimage even as the armed transport rolled to present its port-side battery. The beams ripped through Exeter's derelict hulk, shattering two of its five remaining frames. As the roll continued, Glorious Pilgrimage's newly presented weapons modules further wrecked Exeter's stripped engine globe.

Kat let Glorious Pilgrimage's roll take it past the transport's third, "bottom", shield. She fired as the transport slowed its roll. Kat's first shot collapsed the transport's starboard shield and her second pierced its engine module. Kat's weapons board went yellow as her heavy lasers began to cool and recharge.

Jules' medium laser shots slashed Glorious Pilgrimage's unarmored weapons modules open to space and delivered a light rap to the armored crew module. He sent the clear message that Bantam could shred the crew module before Glorious Pilgrimage could roll to present its port shield or recharge its starboard weapons. Glorious Pilgrimage's captain hesitated long enough for Kat's heavy lasers to recharge.

"Be smart, you stinkin' butcher," Kat whispered.

She'd hate to slaughter Glorious Pilgrimage's valuable crew, but the transport's captain had shown his willingness to kill in order to gain a quick and decisive win. After a fashion, Kat admired the practicality.

Releasing the magnetic grapple, Kat nudged Bantam away from Exeter. She gained a clear shot and presented a smaller cross-section in return. Slowed, Glorious Pilgrimage still had a bit of a roll and Kat maintained a clean position to hit the starboard third of the ship exposed by the armed transport's collapsed shield. If Glorious Pilgrimage attempted to reform that shield, Bantam would have time to cycle a full volley into the crew module. At this range, the beams could punch through the module's armor and kill the crew without harming the frozen passengers in the other modules.

"Hot puppies," Jules' voice cooed over the intercom. "Captain, check out her port module seven."

Kat glanced at the screen, but concentrated on targeting in case Glorious Pilgrimage got a fatal case of the stupids.

"Yeah, I see it." Captain Kryzin's voice was husky with an approximation of lust. "P-7 sure looks like a cushy armored passenger module to me. The spies said some imams might hitch a ride back from New Macao along with their first 'converts'."

Kat could practically hear the wide-awake and furious passengers in their luxury quarters. By now the captain of the Glorious Pilgrimage would have been consigned to the same hells as the crew of Bantam. Loyal Caliphate officers took those types of curses seriously.

"Recharged," Jules announced his medium lasers being ready for another firing round.

Kat felt growing relief as the ship's power plant switched to generating Bantam's own trio of shields.

"Imams on-board explains why their captain would pass up the reward money for any pirates on the Exeter and just open fire rather than risk a fight."

Jules liked to psychoanalyze his enemies, a trait Kat felt was usually harmless.

"They haven't dropped their other shields," the captain said. "Jules, tickle the crew module again and remind them who's in charge."

Greed fought with darker emotions inside Kat. Getting the New Macao 'volunteer workers' to a corporate world would be an unexpected mercy for the workers and a nice payoff for Bantam. Delivering a Caliphate crew would pay even better. Depending on who rode in that comfortable module, either their sale to StellarCorp or their ransom back to the Caliphate would buy most of Bantam's crew their own ships.

Having been a branded slave, Kat would happily sling the module and its religious commanders into the nearest star. Some pleasures were worth more than mere money.

"Paint, from vector alpha-9-D," Bantam announced, jolting Kat from dreams of vengeance.

"Damn," the captain snapped, "our friend has an escort. My spy didn't mention that fact or supply its ECM codes. All I see is a destroyer-sized ship coming in fast!"

Kat punched the engines to full power. She brought up Bantam's nose, letting the bottom shield take the incoming shot. The seat's chest straps kept Kat secured as Bantam spun in place.

The passing destroyer blasted Bantam with emerald fire from one of its twin heavy laser turrets. The destroyer decelerated at a rate which had to have its crew nearing blackout, but it still overshot Bantam, Exeter, and Glorious Pilgrimage by a wide margin.

"Bottom shield's collapsed, no other damage," Kat reported.

"Let's be somewhere else," the captain shouted.

Bantam pulled straight away at the vector opposite that of the furiously decelerating destroyer. Jules put another shot into Glorious Pilgrimage, causing its reforming starboard shield to collapse and possibly burning out the shield generator.

Kat angled Bantam to keep her remaining two shields towards the destroyer. Her bottom shield generator shed the heat it had absorbed as its shield collapsed.

After completing a brutally tight turn, the destroyer rushed back in hot pursuit of Bantam. Neither ship bothered with clever maneuvers.

"Someone needs to read the description of 'escort' to that destroyer's captain," Jules said.

"That bastard's too aggressive by half," Kat agreed.

She hated leaving those 'converts' behind, but piracy was a hard business.

"Chewing him out isn't our problem," Captain Kryzin said, "getting him off of our ass is. Jules, are our proximity mines ready to drop?"

"I have two ready to detach, but it'll take me about three minutes to download that destroyer's . . . oh, crap. Captain, I have multiple radar reflections coming from the destroyer. She's launched missiles, eight of them headed right up our tail."

The destroyer was slightly faster than Bantam, but only bad luck would cost the pirates their lead in a pure stern chase.

However, these missiles had roughly twice Bantam's speed. They would overtake her in minutes. Any move Bantam made out of the missiles' path would allow the destroyer to turn inside and reduce the gap between the ships. Bantam could not survive a toe-to-toe slugging match with the heavier Caliphate warship.

"Jules, forget the mines," the captain said. "Kat, drop chaff and prepare for a minimum course shift just in case."

"Readying chaff," Kat answered.

She flipped the switches, injecting microscopic metal flakes into superheated ballast-water mist. When squirted from nozzles near the engines, the metalized mist formed ice crystals. A reflective cloud would spread in Bantam's wake briefly obscuring Bantam from the destroyer, and vice versa. More importantly, it gave the missiles a larger target to spend themselves against.

While Kat cooked up the chaff, Jules fired several shots from his medium lasers. He missed the bobbing and weaving missiles. It was long odds, but worth trying.

"Spreading chaff," Kat said.

She kept her current heading, not wanting to lose ground to the escort if all of the missiles took the bait. The reflective mist spread perfectly.

"Shit," echoed from three throats as only the first two missiles detonated themselves in the metallic haze of chaff.

A quick mental calculation convinced Kat the six remaining Caliphate missiles should be in range before running out of fuel. Even a near miss from those mini-nuke warheads could cause Bantam's engines to go disharmonic and work against each other rather than propel the ship efficiently.

"Veering to new heading of Omega-9-M," Kat reported.

"The destroyer's still with us, but at least our bottom shield is back up," Jules said with resignation in his voice. "It looks like they're settling in for a long chase."

"I didn't come all this way and spend 5,000 lunas on spies just to get chased off," Captain Kryzin growled. "Kat, download orthogonal paths into the decoy drones. We're far enough ahead of that bastard that he can't have a very good lock on us. We'll toss two drones at angles, take a third vector ourselves. Make that bastard pick which of us he wants to chase."

Kat liked the idea. Worst case; the destroyer would decline to chase any of them and return to his damaged transport. It was a lost prize for Bantam, but it beat capture and a short trial followed by a long walk into space.

A branded runaway like Kat would never be ransomed (if anyone would pay) or resold. Unlike most of the crew, she wouldn't get away with simple beatings, either. She checked the charge in her pistol.

While Kat downloaded navigational information and flight orders into the decoys, the pursuing missiles had passed the point where she had expected them to run out of fuel. Worse, they had tracked her new heading and continued closing.

Someone whistled over the intercom.

"Damn, that ship's carrying long-range homing missiles," Jules said. "The imams are finally getting smart and arming their smaller ships with first-rate weaponry. That's bad news for us."

"I'm reading your mind, Captain," Kat said, "I'll dump another load of chaff before tossing the decoys."

She kept her cool as the homing missiles closed in. At this point, Kat wouldn't hazard a guess at how much longer the missiles would run. If corporate colonies sold the Caliphate the latest AresTech missiles they might run for an hour or more.

Kat felt a sheen of sweat forming. The six missiles were glowing specks, but visible on the rear screen. As the old pirate maxim went, any visible missile was too damned close.

Kat dumped more chaff, fired off the decoys and crossed her fingers.

Four missiles expended themselves on the new chaff cloud, one followed a decoy and the last made a tight turn to stay with Bantam. It had almost completed its turn when it lost power and tumbled away on a ballistic arc before detonating itself.

"Those missiles had some legs. I don't mind telling you, I was starting to sweat," Jules voice sounded shaky.

"Sissy," the captain chuckled. "Here's some good news, the other missile burned out before hitting its decoy. The destroyer is going after that same decoy."

Kat dropped Bantam's engine back to a level that should be undetectable to the racing destroyer. At that instant, her decoys did the same. In three minutes, the destroyer would reach the nearly dispersed chaff cloud and be forced to decide its next move. Kat had the decoys programmed to turn their drives back on in five minutes. Depending on the direction the destroyer chose, Bantam could resume her escape, or start a slow trip back to the damaged Glorious Pilgrimage and salvage this day.

"He's staying on the decoy," the Captain whispered. "Head back to Exeter, but go in quietly. Passive sensors only and throttle down the engines before we reach extreme active sensor range."

Of course, Jules had turned on Bantam's cloak. But the system required low shield power, low engine emissions, long range to be very effective. Even then, it was an iffy proposition when approaching an alert target.

The trip back to the Exeter ambush site was nerve-wracking. Kat kept one eye on her engine emissions and one eye on the aft sensors, expecting to see that dogged destroyer roaring in.

"We're almost in range," Jules announced.

"Cutting to 5% acceleration," Kat answered.

"The son of a bitch suckered us," Captain Kryzin said with a tinge of respect in his voice.

Passive sensors were not detailed. But, it was now clear the destroyer had sent a decoy of its own to continue the chase when Bantam had hidden behind the first chaff cloud. While Bantam dodged missiles and ran from a decoy, the destroyer had returned to Glorious Pilgrimage.

"Drift closer. I want a better look," the captain ordered.

Kat's finger hovered over the emergency thrust button. She would punch immediately if the destroyer painted them.

Bantam eased past the destroyer without triggering any alarms. While details were lost, it was clear the destroyer had dropped its shields and was in the process of attaching the imam's luxurious travel module to its own shell.

"Well, gentle-folk, no joy for us today," the captain said.

"Yeah," Jules grunted, "those Martyr-class destroyers can carry two modules on their shell and still make three-quarters speed. They'll grab the crew module as well and head for Hugo Secundum."

"It's not that simple, Captain," Kat said slowly. "Imams won't just leave ten thousand frozen slaves there for anyone to rescue. They'll have their destroyer kill everyone in those modules rather than see them escape. They'll do it for spite if nothing else."

"It's a cold, hard universe, Kat."

"No, Captain. If we let them do it, we really are nothing but bloody-handed pirates. We'll deserve the long walk if we're ever caught. We'll deserve it if we leave those people to die."

Most of the time Kat liked the way Bantam was laid out where she didn't see her fellows face-to-face from the time they launched until they returned to a station. It kept things less complicated. Now, she wished she could look Captain Kryzin in the eye. She stared at the intercom speaker, willing him to agree.

After a short eternity, Jules said, "That's crap, Captain. We've already pushed our luck with that destroyer. We need to get the hell out of here."

Captain Kryzin's voice was rough as he said, "I'm not risking Bantam in a fight against a warship. That's stupidity, not piracy. You joined my crew to be a pirate, not some mush-headed liberator. We're leaving before that destroyer spots us."

Determination flooded Kat. She'd done some questionable things in the past, but none she couldn't justify after a fashion. She knew Bantam and her crew would be cursed if they ran away and let ten thousand people be murdered. If someone had been around when the ship carrying her family . . .

"Kat," the captain said softly, as if in apology, "Bump up our speed, but keep us below detection levels until we're two light-seconds out. I'd love to stick that destroyer captain like he did me, but we're beating-feet out of here."

"Captain," Kat pleaded, "Let's move farther out, turn around and build some speed before throttling back our engines. Our residual velocity can carry us up on him with no engine noise giving us away. His shields are down while they mount that second module."

The captain said nothing, so Kat continued.

"We won't get the complete drop on them, but they won't have time to do more than partially raise their shields and get off a wild shot or two."

"Not worth the risk, Kat," Captain Kryzin answered.

Kat threw the decompression-danger switches, isolating her cabin from the rest of the ship. She furiously typed override protections into her navigational controls as Bantam moved beyond detection range of the destroyer and gained speed for an escape.

Then she turned Bantam back towards Glorious Pilgrimage. She redlined the engines to get velocity up.

"What the hell are you doing?" the captain demanded.

Kat was once again glad they were isolated in separate cabins.

"You know as well as I do, Captain," Jules said. "She's blocked navigation from override, too."

Captain Kryzin shouted and threatened, while Jules attempted to hack into Kat's navigation controls. Kat's attention to her software struggle with the engineer made it easy to ignore the captain's increasingly dire threats. Then, she heard a heavy thump on the cabin door.

She felt the press of acceleration fall off when Jules shut down the engines. Kat still had maneuvering control, but Jules had taken control of the main drives.

Kat smelled the paint on the inside of her cabin door scorch as a laser cutter went to work. Soon smoke began to sting her eyes.

Locking down navigation with a spiral approach, Kat checked Bantam's position. They were still beyond passive scanning range, but would be able to see Glorious Pilgrimage soon if they were foolish enough to use active sensors.

The first hole burned through Kat's door in a spray of molten metal. A few drops landed on her, drawing a curse. The hole slowly elongated into a line. Even with an industrial cutter, it would take time for the crew to force open the door.

The intercom was ominously silent. Either Kat had been cut from the circuit or Captain Kryzin was angry beyond words.

The slow process of cutting through Kat's cabin door continued until Jules announced Bantam was nearly in detection range.

"Dammit," Captain Kryzin growled over the intercom, "Jules, return engines and maneuvering to Kat. We're in her damned fight whether we want it or not."

Then everything was a rush. The destroyer painted them and pushed away from Glorious Pilgrimage, abandoning the transport's detached crew module.

"Heavy lasers, drop the destroyer's port shield," the Captain snapped, now forced to fight for Bantam's life.

Kat had no trouble lining up the shot. The destroyer struggled to roll her starboard side, now sporting the imam's module, out of harm's way.

Kat's shots hammered down and collapsed the destroyer's port shield. This left only its armor against the fire from Jules' medium lasers, but his shots failed to cripple the warship. As Jules fired his third weapon, Kat rolled Bantam to present her bottom shield to the few wildly targeted bolts coming back from the destroyer. None hit.

Ignoring the shouts of triumph echoing through Bantam, Kat ramped up acceleration and swung Bantam around the destroyer in a lazy loop. She searched the active sensor readings, anxious to see if their attack had hurt the warship badly enough to even up the fight.

"Thermal fluctuations from the destroyer, magnetics going into non-harmonic pulsing," Jules said calmly. "I believe we got a solid engine hit."

"Very well," the captain replied, "if nothing else, this bastard won't be running us down. Stay alert for missiles."

"Speak of the devil," Kat said. "Multiple launches, four set to intercept our current heading."

Kat brought Bantam to a tight circle around the destroyer. The newly launched missiles didn't track.

"Quickly, Kat," the captain said. "They tossed those missiles at us before they could lock just to buy time and I'm not giving them any."

A fast pass against a shields-down destroyer was one thing. Bantam was not really a match for a lightly damaged destroyer.

"Here's where your conscience is gonna bite us all," Kat whispered to herself. The display for her heavy lasers was green, they were ready for firing. "Target?"

"Whatever they give us," the captain answered. "Hammer them hard before they get their feet under them. Make'em back off and we might just pull this one out of the toilet. And then I'll settle with you, you mutinous bitch."

The destroyer rolled to present its bottom shield rather than its intact starboard shield and the lasers behind it. Kat hesitated, surprised by the maneuver.

"Of course," she said, "those imams won't let the destroyer's captain expose the side with their module on it."

It took fire from both of Bantam's heavy lasers and all three mediums to collapse the warship's fully-charged bottom shield. Spotty return fire said some of Jules' earlier shots must've hit the destroyer's fire control system. Kat's next course twisted Bantam away after their firing run, giving the destroyer only tangential shots easily deflected rather than absorbed by Bantam's bottom shield.

By the time Kat brought Bantam around for another pass, the destroyer accelerated away from Glorious Pilgrimage. With its bottom shield temporarily collapsed, armor damage under its regenerated port shield and the imams hiding on the undamaged starboard side, Kat wondered what the harried destroyer captain would do next.

The destroyer continued its unsteady acceleration, spiraling away from Glorious Pilgrimage, keeping its port side and heavy laser turrets facing Bantam but not firing before Bantam committed to an attack.

As the destroyer's damaged engines strained to carry the frightened passengers from the battle, Kat decelerated to a path between the destroyer and Glorious Pilgrimage.

"Missiles, four," Jules said.

Kat watched the blips closely. The destroyer's weapons crews had had time to program the missiles. Kat doubted she could outrun them with the starting range so low, but the missiles didn't lock on Bantam. They flew towards Glorious Pilgrimage.

"Lord," Kat said with feeling.

Without thinking, she punched Bantam for maximum acceleration. She entered an intersecting course, putting her in a tight, spiraling roll.

There was no time to spread chaff. Kat had only one thing to put between the transport and the oncoming missiles; Bantam.

The intercom nearly overloaded with Captain Kryzin's cry of rage, cut short as the first missile hit and collapsed Bantam's port shield. The next missile was far enough behind to strike and collapse the bottom shield. The third hit the lightly armored Bantam solidly while the last missile obliterated the flickering starboard shield.

Half of the status screen blazed red. Air rushed out through the damaged cabin door and into the passenger hold, now opened to space. She bit her lip, knowing what decompression and flying metal had done to the crew in the passenger hold. Kat's fist hit the 'all silence' button as she watched the screen to see what the destroyer would do next. It slowed, but remained on a trajectory away from Bantam.

A quick glance told Kat of hull-breaches in the main bay and most systems on emergency battery power. She had killed most of Bantam's crew and would have to deal with the survivors soon. For now, the engines, both heavy lasers and one medium laser turret were still operable.

Kat turned Bantam towards the destroyer and accelerated on a straight line. She shouted her challenge, painting the Caliphate warship with targeting radar.

Bantam lacked the power to shoot through the destroyer's shields and take the warship out with laser fire. The limping destroyer could stop and rake the shield-less Bantam, but not change the pirate's growing velocity. Even as a lifeless wreck, Bantam could cripple the destroyer in the collision the destroyer could not dodge.

That was the choice Kat offered if the Caliphate destroyer continued to slow or turned back. It was all she had left.

Her hands shook as the destroyer accelerated and angled away from Bantam and Glorious Pilgrimage. The enemy ship's new course refused Bantam's challenge.

Kat slumped in her pilot's chair. Residual smoke in the cabin made her eyes tear.

"Lass, you have a world of work ahead of you," Kat said to herself.

The status screen blazed with critical repair demands. Towing Glorious Pilgrimage to a place where the Caliphate wouldn't find it would come next.

The captain would need Kat for a lot of the repairs. He couldn't kill her before Bantam was patched up enough for the return trip. Maybe, after Captain Kryzin sold the transport's new location to StellarCorp, he'd calm down enough to leave Kat penniless, beached and black-listed but alive.

Kat would face that risk, because now she could face herself. The screams in her head stopped and that's all that mattered.

THE REVIEW
BY JOHN E. PETTY

Winthorpe Polander smiled as he put the period to the last sentence of his latest review. "…and to even deign to regurgitate this odious malevolence would be to do too much honor to the culinary criminal who created it, as that would necessitate tasting his vile effluvia one more time. One can only hope that its passage out of the body is more pleasurable than its journey in."

It was a masterpiece, certain to run the head chef at the Wainwright Hotel out of the country within two weeks. How dare that craven cur serve him, Winthorpe Polander, head food critic of the city's greatest newspaper, a shrimp salad that was not precisely chilled to 41 degrees Fahrenheit? Unthinkable.

Polander was well known for his insistence on excellence (although where, exactly, his standards came from, no one quite knew), which meant that he wrote far more bad notices than good ones. Throughout the years that he had been writing restaurant reviews, Polander had gained a certain reputation for his acid-laced commentaries. Readers looked forward to his venomous diatribes, while chefs trembled whenever the arrogant critic walked through their doors. Polander had ruined more than one chef, and closed more than one restaurant, in his twenty years behind the typewriter.

Tonight, however, would be the highpoint of Polander's career. Tonight was the night to which his whole life had been leading. Tonight he would destroy the man he hated most in the entire world.

Paul Montrain, formerly the head chef at the Ritz-Carlton, had recently opened a new restaurant in town, The Crestview, that had been receiving glowing reviews and had become the darling of the city's social elite. Famed for his daring and visionary culinary creations, Montrain had become an instant celebrity, appearing on local talk shows and as guest of honor at charity events. There was even talk of his hosting his own syndicated TV show. He was on top of the world, and that galled Winthorpe Polander.

Polander had hated Montrain since they were students at the Culinary Institute. Both naturally competitive, they had been the heads of their class and natural rivals during their tenure at the school. They had even competed for the same woman, their Sauces and Dressings instructor, Vivian Towers.

Near the end of their senior year, there had been a competition sponsored by a leading hotel chain. The prize was a five-year contract as chef at a major hotel. It was a prize that could easily make a young chef's career. Everyone in the school competed, but it soon boiled down to a duel between Polander and Montrain. To sweeten the pot, as it were, Vivian announced that she would marry the winner.

The battle was intense, with both combatants giving their dishes their all. They were under a strict time limit, with a minimum of three dishes to be prepared in a mere sixty minutes. The rules had to be rigidly adhered to, and both contestants were watched for even the most minor infraction. It was the most nerve-wracking hour either of the two men had ever undergone.

Montrain prepared an appetizer of pan seared foie gras, with gingered pineapple, cranberries, mango jam, and pecans, followed by a Black Angus strip loin of beef and Kobe beef short ribs, accompanied by scallion whipped potatoes in a Madeira wine sauce and finished with a poached pineapple covered in rum cream, served with a coconut sorbet.

Polander offered a chilled Maine lobster salad, with fresh hearts of palm, tomatoes, carrots, avocado, and lemon basil vinaigrette to start, followed by black truffle mushroom soup highlighted with smoked squab. His main course was a delicately prepared pan roasted breast of duck, with duck confit, foie gras, and caramelized pearl onion, drizzled with a dried cherry port wine sauce, and finished by a luscious chocolate tart, accompanied by Chipotle sorbet and passion fruit red pepper sauce.

Finally, the moment of tasting and judgment had arrived. As both chefs walked down the aisle toward the judges bearing their main courses, Polander tripped and ended up wearing his duck. Not only was he disqualified, but a picture of him covered with his creation became the front page of the city's largest newspaper. It was a humiliating moment, one that took him months to live down. Of course, Montrain won the competition - and Vivian - and went on to a successful career as a respected and decorated chef. Polander, on the other hand, never entered a kitchen again, turning his culinary acumen instead into the basis of an award-winning restaurant review column. Deep in his heart, however,

Polander swore that he would someday have his revenge on Montrain, sure that his rival had tripped him to insure an easy victory.

And now that day had come, a day that Polander had been planning for months. Not only would Polander ruin Montrain's career, but he had another surprise in store for the popular chef as well.

When Montrain had come to town, still married to Vivian who was just as beautiful and vivacious as in their college days, Polander had seen his chance. Normally, he would have reviewed the new restaurant within days of its opening, but this case was different. This time there was more at stake here than a mere restaurant review.

Using his vast web of contacts, Polander had gathered a mountain of information on both Paul and Vivian. He learned that Paul had become a workaholic, spending much more time in his kitchen than with his wife. He learned that Vivian was growing restless at being slighted, and that she had begun to express her displeasure with Paul. And he learned that Vivian had started hanging out in the bar at the Renfield, a trendy hotel in the expensive part of town.

Armed with this information, Polander managed to "accidentally" run into Vivian one night at the Renfield. They spent several hours chatting about old times, and Winthorpe did his best to be sympathetic and attentive. Polander had aged well since last seeing Vivian. His salt-and-pepper hair was the most obvious sign of the two decades that had passed, as his trim and athletic build belied his copious appetites, and he could tell instantly that Vivian was attracted to him all over again.

Over the next few months, Winthorpe and Vivian spent more and more time together, although they were careful to be discreet and keep out of the public eye. For all intents and purposes, Vivian was his.

The fact was, though, by this time, Winthorpe could not have cared less about Vivian. He had gotten over her years ago. There was only room for one "most important person" in Winthorpe's life, and that was Winthorpe. None of this was about winning the fair maiden (although he would never tell Vivian that – at least not yet), it was about ruining a hated rival.

And so time passed and Montrain's restaurant become more and more successful, and Winthorpe and Vivian become more and more involved. It was a scheme worthy of Machiavelli, as Winthorpe skillfully played Vivian like a simple trout on the end of his line – alternately reeling her in and giving her some lead - and Polander reveled in his coming revenge.

And finally the big night was upon him. Winthorpe arrived at the Crestview promptly at seven o'clock, the time of his reservation, and was shown to his table for two. Moments later, Vivian joined him. She looked luscious in a sleek black evening gown slit almost too far above her hips, her fiery red hair perfectly coiffed, and her nails expertly rendered in blood-red lacquer highlighted with what appeared to be small yellow flames. For a moment, looking at her, Winthorpe actually experienced a tinge of the old desire that he once felt for the stunning creature who sat opposite him, but the unwelcomed feeling soon passed. She was an object, a thing to be used and discarded, a bit of unwelcome gristle on the plate of Polander's life. Nevertheless, Winthorpe was pleased that she had gone to all the trouble to make herself irresistible (to others, of course). All the better to stick the knife in Montrain's heart just a little deeper, Polander thought.

"Have you seen him yet?" Vivian asked.

"Not yet," said Winthorpe. "I just got here myself."

Although he hated to admit it, dinner was better than Polander had expected. The steak was tender and juicy and cooked to perfection, highlighted with a delicate yet piquant seasoning, and the wine was served at precisely the right temperature. Even the asparagus spears had just the right amount of snap to them. In any other circumstances, he would actually have written one of his rare positive reviews about The Crestview. But tonight wasn't about journalistic integrity. It was about payback for twenty years of humiliation. It was about revenge.

"I can't wait to see his face when we tell him," Vivian said, her eyes sparkling in the reflected candlelight.

"Soon, dearest, soon," Polander promised.

After the meal, Polander had the waiter take his card back to the chef. Just as he expected, Montrain soon appeared from the kitchen, a warm smile on his face, a smile that fell as soon as he saw Vivian at the table.

With a glance, Winthorpe could see that Paul had been pushing himself. He was haggard, and a tic played at his lips. Winthorpe knew Paul didn't deal with stress well. It had almost been his downfall in school. God knows how he was dealing with the pressure of running his own restaurant.

"Hello, Winthorpe," Paul said. "It's been a long time."

"Yes, not long enough," Polander replied, not even looking at the nervous chef.

"Vivian…?" Paul said.

"Oh, cut the crap, Paul," Vivian shot back curtly. "It's over. I'm sick of coming in second to your stupid restaurant. I'm leaving you, Paul. I'm leaving you for Winthorpe."

Polander didn't say a word. He looked up at Montrain and smiled.

Stunned, Montrain turned without a word and shuffled back into the kitchen. As Polander watched him go, he imagined he heard a single sob coming from the chef as he left the room. It was the sound of triumph, the most glorious sound Winthorpe had ever heard.

Winthorpe's review of The Crestview was his most vicious yet. With comments like, "...the disgusting mélange that congealed upon my plate was surpassed in wretchedness only by the noisome glass of viscous fluid that purported to be wine," and "...tasting the so-called creations of Chef (although one is loathe to use that word in this context) Paul Montrain is like having one's teeth drilled sans Novocain: it's unbelievably painful and unpleasant, and, while one is in the midst of the agony, feels as if it will never end." Polander accomplished his goal: within a week, it was announced that the Crestview was closing its doors.

Several weeks later, Polander received an invitation in the mail that bore the return address of the Crestview. Curious, he opened it to see that he had been invited to the closing night of Montrain's restaurant on the following evening. There was a handwritten note on the bottom: "No hard feelings," scrawled in a shaky hand, and signed only with a single "P."

Polander couldn't resist the opportunity to revel in the fruits of his revenge one more time, so he called the restaurant and made a reservation for two. No doubt Vivian would also enjoy the evening.

Later that day, Polander rang Vivian to tell her about the event.

"Wonderful, Darling," she said. "I have to stop by there to drop off some papers but I won't let on that I'm coming, too. It'll be a delicious surprise. I have an appointment with the lawyer at six, so I might be a smidge late, but I'll see you there as close to seven as possible."

The next evening couldn't come fast enough for Polander. This was even better than he had hoped. Not only had he crushed his hated rival, now he had a chance to see him grovel. No doubt Montrain wanted to suck up in the hopes that Winthorpe wouldn't ruin his next restaurant. Fat chance.

Winthorpe entered The Crestview at precisely 6:59 and was promptly shown to his table. By 7:05, he was looking at his watch, impatiently wondering where Vivian was. By 7:15, he was calling her cell phone, and by 7:30, he was ready to start dinner without her.

Stupid woman, he thought. As soon as this evening was over, it was time to end things with her. She wasn't worth his time and his effort now that she had served her purpose. He had more important fish to fry.

The restaurant was sparsely populated. Winthorpe was pleased to see the results of his handiwork. It was rare that he got the opportunity to observe the aftermath of his column's influence. It gave him a perverse thrill and sharpened his appetite.

There was no menu in front of him, and when Winthorpe asked the waiter about his apparent oversight, he was told that the chef was preparing a special menu tonight in Polander's honor. Winthorpe thought this was odd, but other chefs had gone to even more outrageous lengths to curry favor with the great critic. He decided to sit back and enjoy the evening, even without Vivian.

The first course was a liver and kidney compote, served atop a bed of steak tartar, followed by a bowl of rich tomato soup, which had a dark, thick texture that Polander assumed must be the result of organically grown vine-ripened Mediterranean tomatoes grown only in one small district in Italy. Winthorpe smiled to himself, pleased that he had been able to place the peculiar taste. Although the compote was lovely, Polander found the soup a bit too salty for his taste, although he finished the entire bowl.

The main course was a tender filet of beef au jus, accompanied by potatoes au gratin and glazed carrots a la Montrain. Even Polander had to admit that the steak was the best he had ever tasted. Firm and flavorful and seasoned to perfection, it had a lovely taste that Polander couldn't quite place. He had tasted beef all over the world, from Japan to Guatemala to the Australian Outback, but he had never tasted a cut of meat quite like this before. He desperately wanted to ask Paul where it was from, but he knew he wouldn't. His pride wouldn't allow it.

The waiter cleared the table and Polander waited expectantly for dessert. While he sat, impatiently, he called Vivian again. No answer. Where could she be? She had been looking forward to this evening as much as he. Now Winthorpe was angry. No one stood up Winthorpe Polander.

Just then the waiter walked by, and Winthorpe grabbed him by the arm.

"You there," he said, in his most authoritarian manner. "What's going on? Why is dessert taking so long?"

"I don't know, sir," the waiter replied. "Monsieur Montrain is preparing something special. He won't even let the kitchen staff see what it is."

Leaning in, the waiter said in a conspiratorial whisper, "It's very odd."

Now Polander's interest was piqued. What could it be, this secretive dessert? Just as he was musing on the possibilities, the door to the kitchen opened and Paul himself came out bearing a large covered platter. If he had looked bad the last time Winthorpe saw him, he looked downright scary now. Montrain was gaunt and emaciated, his eyes deep-set and hollow. He hadn't shaved for days, and his hair was a mess. He didn't look at Polander, but seemed to stare at a fixed spot somewhere in front of him. The tic around his mouth was worse as well, and Montrain moved with a jerky, hesitant motion. As he got closer, Polander could see red splotches all over Paul's white chef's coat, which was odd, as Paul had always been one of the most fastidious men Polander had ever known.

As Montrain reached Polander's table, he placed the enormous platter in front of his guest and stood there, fixedly staring at the wall. He was beginning to make Polander uncomfortable, so Winthorpe finally said with a smirk, "Sorry to hear that you'll be closing, Paul."

"Yes, I'm sure you are," Montrain responded tonelessly.

"I'm sorry Vivian didn't make it tonight," Polander said, attempting to goad the chef one more time. "She would have enjoyed your final meal."

That remark got a reaction. Turning his head slowly, almost robotically, Montrain focused on Polander for the very first time, with dead, empty eyes that still managed to hold a savage look that chilled Winthorpe to the bone. It was the look of a twisted, desperate man, a man with nothing to lose. Montrain's crooked, deranged smile – the smile of a madman, Winthorpe thought – made the hairs on the back of Polander's neck stand up.

"Oh, Vivian didn't miss anything," Montrain said through tightly clenched teeth. "She wouldn't miss dinner with you for the world. And it wasn't my final meal, it was hers... and yours."

Montrain pulled the domed cover off the platter with a flourish, revealing Vivian's head, an apple wedged firmly between her teeth, staring at Winthorpe, a pleading, helpless expression on her dead face. Arranged around her head were her fingers, all ten of them, like little white carrots equally spaced around the platter.

"She was here for the appetizer," Montrain said, with an insane, sing-song quality to his voice. "That was her liver and kidney, and wasn't that a lovely steak tartar? She was here during the soup, too, that fine blood-based soup. Tangy, no? And wasn't that a yummy filet? All Vivian, you know. And here she is, joining you for dessert. She knows how much you love your food. Say goodbye to Winthorpe, darling..."

Polander was stunned, unable to move. He felt his throat constrict, at the same time that the contents of his stomach struggled to be free. His face turned purple, and he grabbed at the table, tipping it over with a crash of glass and metal. As he rose from his chair, desperate for breath, Paul saw everyone else in the restaurant staring at him, shocked into immobility by the horrific

36

scene playing out before them. Vivian's head, now on the floor, stared up at Winthorpe, although whether her final look was mournful or accusatory, Polander couldn't tell.

Polander took a single step towards Montrain, who removed a long-bladed knife from beneath his chef's coat. Without a word, Montrain lunged at the man who had ruined his life, and plunged the knife deep into Polander's chest. With a gurgle of surprise, Winthorpe sank to his knees, then toppled over sideways to lie motionless on the restaurant's floor.

As the life ebbed out of Winthorpe Polander and he listened to Montrain cackle insanely, seemingly far, far away, he was surprised that he had the presence of mind to be appalled by his final thought: that he had gotten more pleasure out of Vivian as a meal than as a girlfriend.

THE BLACK RAZOR
BY PHILLIP HALL

The Black Razor crouched in the shadows of an alleyway. He watched the thugs, crack dealers, and killers walk in and out of the old run down Harrison Hotel across the street.

It used to be a nice place until the South Rockhaven Stranglers showed up and murdered the owners. The police didn't have the manpower or the firepower to do much about it. Slowly the entire five block area became a no man's land with the Harrison serving as the gang's headquarters. Everyone knew to stay far away from the Strangler's turf unless you had an army backing you up.

The Black Razor stood and stretched his legs, then straightened his clothes. He still hated dressing up in the themed black outfit. He had gone through several versions of his costume including tights and a cape. He learned quick that tights were uncomfortable and capes may look cool but slow you down. He finally settled on solid black combat pants, black combat boots, black long sleeve form fit shirt, black gloves and his black mask. He especially liked the mask because the material formed to his face but let him breathe, see and hear perfectly. Any onlooker merely saw a blank face and head. It was even creepy to him when he looked in the mirror. The only thing missing was a watch. He hated not having a watch but it really didn't fit with the whole super villain theme.

Satisfied that he looked the part he strode from the dark alley and headed for the front door of the Harrison. As he approached, a burly man carrying a military issue machine gun stepped forward.

"Hold on a second," the door guard said.

Black Razor continued walking until he stood face to face with the large man. He watched the guard nervously clench his assault rifle tighter. He smiled under the mask, happy that even this hardened beast of a man feared him. He stood there silently until the guard finally spoke up.

"Uh... you're the Black Razor, right?"

"Yes," Black Razor replied in a low evil voice.

The guard quickly stepped aside to allow entry into the hotel. As Black Razor strode past the guard swallowed hard then said weakly.

"You can go right up Mr. Black Razor. Garrett is waiting in the master suite on the top floor."

Black Razor stepped into the open lobby of the hotel. He walked towards the elevators with a commanding air about him. Several thugs and dealers quickly moved out of his path. He shook his head, remembering how many years of his life he'd wasted in this building. It felt like yesterday, even though it had been years since the day that changed everything; since he found his mission and the means to carry it out.

He came to the other side of the lobby and reached out to press the elevator button when he heard someone come up behind him. He paused before hitting the button.

"HEY! You think because you're some fancy super villain that you can walk in our house without paying your dues?" a hardened killer shouted as he approached Black Razor.

"Dues?" Black Razor asked.

"Yeah, your freaking dues man! Now pay up or pay with your life," the killer said.

Black Razor burst into a fit of evil laughter. The killer, standing only a few feet behind now, began to grow angry.

"Turn around here you freak! No one's gonna walk in here and dis me, the Slasher!"

Black Razor stopped laughing and there was silence in the lobby. Slasher pulled a large hunting knife and readied himself to attack.

"I paid my dues a long time ago," Black Razor said under his breath.

"What's that freak? You got something to say to me? You turn around and face the Slasher head on!"

In one swift move the Black Razor spun around and called on his power, then completed the spin facing the elevator and pressing the up button. As the doors opened, Slasher's head rolled from his shoulders. The rest of him collapsed shortly afterward. Black Razor stepped into the elevator, turned around and smiled. Everyone in the lobby was frozen, staring at him. He held his hand out to keep the elevator from closing and addressed the entire lobby.

"Anyone else need me to pay my dues?"

After a few seconds of silence he let go of the door, allowing it to close. The elevator only took a moment to arrive at the top floor. He stepped out to see a skinny well dressed man waiting there.

"You are the Black Razor I presume? My name is Mr. Filmoore and I am Garrett's accountant," the skinny man said nervously.

"The South Rockhaven Stranglers have an accountant now?" Black Razor asked in a shocked voice.

"That is correct. There is a lot of money changing hands, especially with deals like the one we'll be doing tonight with you," Mr. Filmoore answered. "Now if you'll just follow me to the master suite, Garrett and Mr. X are waiting."

Mr. Filmoore turned and led the way towards the suite. Black Razor shook his head in disbelief. They arrived at the door and a violent looking man stood guard. He held up his hand to stop them.

"I've got to check the boths of you for weapons," the guard said.

Mr. Filmoore held his arms out and the tough patted him down thoroughly. Then he moved over to the Black Razor. There was a tense moment as the Black Razor stood unmoving. Finally he put his arms out to the side. The guard patted him down but found nothing. He turned and knocked three times, then opened the door.

"Two coming in. Filmoore and Razor. Boths of 'em clean," the guard yelled.

As they entered the suite Black Razor could see Garrett and Mr. X sitting in the large living area ahead. He let Mr. Filmoore lead the way. Garrett stood and smiled. He walked past his accountant and stood in front of the Black Razor.

"Whoa man you are way bigger than you look on the news. I'm Garrett, the leader of the Stranglers. Come on in and have a seat," Garrett said as he gestured to an open chair across from Mr. X.

Black Razor walked over and sat down. He stared at Mr. X, instantly taking a dislike to the man. He watched as Garrett sat and Mr. Filmoore walked over to stand next to him.

"So let's get this show on the road shall we?" Garrett stated more than asked.

After short negotiations over the price of C-4, all three men stood up. Garrett shook hands with Mr. X, then watched as he left to retrieve the explosives. Garrett turned and extended his hand to Black Razor.

"Well it's been cool doing business with a super villain but I'm sure you'll be on your way to retrieve the money now," Garrett said.

Black Razor looked at the hand offered to him and laughed. Garrett pulled his hand back and anger flashed in his eyes.

"Let me explain something to you. There are only two ways I extend my hand to a man. One is in friendship and the other is to pull the trigger to kill him. You may be some tough super..." Garrett said angrily but was cut off.

Black Razor shoved him backwards, knocking him violently to the floor. Mr. Filmoore started to rush over to Garrett when Black Razor focused his power and formed a long black katana blade. He stuck it right against Mr. Filmoore's throat, stopping him in his tracks. Garrett scrambled to his feet but didn't make a move.

"What the hell is this man? I thought we were doing business here," Garrett shouted. "And where the hell did you get a sword from?"

Black Razor laughed again as he reached up with his open hand and removed his mask. Garrett's face instantly lit up with recognition.

"Johnny?" Garrett said, then squinted to look closer. "Johnny Goldman, is that really you?"

Johnny smiled, then laughed before replying.

"Yeah man, it's me."

Garrett laughed out loud, instantly at ease.

"Oh man, it's been what, like five years since we seen you? So you're the Black Razor," Garrett said, then laughed again. "And here I thought we were dealing with some psychotic murdering super villain."

Johnny smiled, then flicked the katana, killing Mr. Filmoore in one swift motion. Before Garrett could react, Johnny focused his power and formed a black dagger to replace the katana. He pounced on Garrett, knocking him into a chair. He put the dagger to Garret's throat, then leaned in close to speak.

"Garrett, you are dealing with some psychotic murdering super villain."

***

"Detective, we found it over here," a uniformed officer shouted out across the lobby.

Detective Frank Carmon walked over and looked behind the
fake potted fern where the officer was pointing. There lay the
head they'd been looking for.

"Yeah that must belong to headless guy number seventeen by
the elevators," Frank said. "Make sure crime scene gets some
photos of the face before they bag it."

Frank had been a homicide detective in Rockhaven for
fourteen years and had seen a lot of murders but this was the first
time he'd seen an entire hotel full of them. Forty-two bodies so
far and every last one of them members of the South Rockhaven
Stranglers. He'd seen enough and headed for the front door so he
could get away from the smell of death.

The Detective stepped outside and had to walk around the
body of what used to be the door guard. He watched as a crime
scene tech removed the military issue rifle that hadn't even been
fired. Frank shrugged and walked several blocks away until he
could no longer smell the blood. He took a deep breath then
reached for a metal flask under his coat. He unscrewed the cap
and went to take a drink when it suddenly disappeared from his
hand.

"What in the..." Frank squeaked.

As he stared at his empty hand in disbelief a giant hulking
figure appeared before him. Startled, Frank took a step back and
went for his gun. Finally he realized that standing before him was
Power House, the leader of the Guardians of Earth. Frank had
only seen super heroes on the news. Now standing face to face
with the most famous super hero of all time he couldn't help but
think of how ridiculous the blue and yellow skin tight outfit

looked. Power House held up the flask. It looked like a toy in his massive hands.

"Drinking on the job is like riding a horse blindfolded into oncoming traffic. Never a good idea. You should be solving homicides, not drinking. You are an example to your fellow officers and to the civilians big and small. You..." Power House spoke but was cut off.

"Yeah, yeah spare me the lecture. What's a big time super guy like you want with a small town fish like me?" Frank asked sarcastically.

Power House screwed the lid onto the flask then pinched the top, crushing the metal together. He handed it back to Frank then responded.

"It has nothing to do with you and everything to do with the case you have on your hands. Hawkshaw arrived at the hotel within three minutes of the first 911 call that came in to your dispatcher. Since it took Rockhaven PD forty-five minutes to respond, he had plenty of time to process the entire hotel from top to bottom. I assure you the response time is something I intend to discuss with the Mayor and Chief of Police. I'll let Hawkshaw explain the rest."

Frank saw out of the corner of his eye someone appear next to him. He jerked his head around to see Hawkshaw standing a few feet away. He wore a mask that covered the top half of his head and flowed down into a large cape that drug the ground. Frank knew the famous super hero detective well from the four books and three manuals he had written on crime fighting. All of them were required reading for police detectives.

"From my findings in the hotel, we are dealing with one killer. He is a super villain with the power to somehow make knives and blades. His physical abilities are also super human. I believe him to be somewhere in the range of 5'11" to 6'1". Weighing approximately 190 pounds," Hawkshaw said flatly.

Frank stood with his mouth wide open and shook his head.

"How the heck can you know all of that just by looking at the scene for forty-five minutes? It takes at least three to five days for crime scene to get that much info."

Hawkshaw shook his head before replying.

"Let me briefly explain. One person because I found the same tracks in the blood and carpet throughout the entire hotel. The method of killing is the same on all victims, knives and swords. I counted forty-seven dead bodies and thirty-six of those had different types of blades used to kill them. Thus the super power to make or summon blades. It is highly unlikely he could carry thirty-six different swords and knives on him. I figure his height because the first slice he took on thirty-one of the bodies was at the neck and they are perfectly level. So his out stretched arm would've been perfectly level with their necks," Hawkshaw explained.

Frank spoke up and cut in to Hawkshaw's recap.

"Yeah but wouldn't that mean the guy was taller than them?"

Hawkshaw shook his head.

"No, all the tracks show him wearing heavy combat boots that would give him an extra two to three inches on his real height. So now you can see how I have derived my information," Hawkshaw said.

Frank nodded his head, piecing together what he had seen at the hotel and everything Hawkshaw had said. It all fit and made perfect sense. Power House stepped forward and placed his hand on Frank's shoulder.

"Listen Detective, if this super villain is crazy enough to cut up a hotel filled with killers, dealers and worse, then he won't think twice about harming civilians or anyone else that gets in his way. Hawkshaw has agreed to hang around the city and see what he can come up with. You just make sure your men know he'll be prowling around the area at night," Power House said. "Oh and Detective, no more drinking on the job. You've got to sober up so you can soldier on."

"Okay. Thanks for your help I suppose," Frank said.

He turned to shake hands with Hawkshaw but he was gone. When he turned back to Power House he was gone as well. Frank scratched his head.

"No one is gonna believe that I got to meet the two biggest super heroes in the world and they're both schmucks," Frank said.

***

Johnny sat on the edge of his bed and finished the last drink of whiskey. He dropped the bottle on the floor among stacks of trash, clothes and other debris. He could barely keep his eyes open but looked over at the table across the room. He smiled seeing the three large duffel bags on it. One held two-hundred and fifty thousand dollars and the other two were filled with enough C-4 explosives to level a city block. He lay back on the bed and laughed. After a few moments he reached over to the night stand, trying to retrieve a photograph, but instead found his Black Razor mask. He held it up, staring at the unique fabric. Finally he tossed it across the room, then grabbed the photo. He stared for a long moment at the picture, then spoke.

"I may not have taken the path you wanted me to but I never stopped loving you Mom. Tonight I completed step two of my plan to get revenge on the Guardians of Earth, soon you and Dad's souls can rest and maybe mine can too. Goodnight, mom."

He dropped the picture on the nightstand and drifted off into a drunken sleep.

***

Hawkshaw stopped in an alley seven blocks from the Harrison Hotel. He had made slow progress tracking the villain. He used the optical scanners built into his mask to follow traces of blood that had been on the assailant's boots. They led to this darkened alley. He immediately smelled death and readied himself for anything. He plunged into the darkness and found a brand new SUV parked there. He approached cautiously and could see blood dripping from the driver's side. Hawkshaw opened the door and out fell a man who had been killed the same as all the others at the Harrison.

He inspected the vehicle and determined that the man had come from the Harrison to get a bag or box with heavy contents from the backseat but was attacked from behind. Whatever had been in the SUV was gone now. The only luck Hawkshaw had was that the killer had tracked through this victims' blood, refreshing the trail. Off he went following the almost unseen trail.

He looked up at the sky and could tell by the lightening of it that dawn was coming soon. He knew that he couldn't do much during the daylight hours so he headed back for the time being.

"Justice can wait one more night," Hawkshaw said as he disappeared back into the shadows.

**

Johnny was up and frantically rushing around his apartment.

"Where is that dang mask!" he yelled. "I have to have it."

He continued tearing through piles of old clothes and trash. He was already in full Black Razor get up and only needed the mask. He found it near the bed and pulled it on. It smelled of day old pizza and liquor but he didn't have time to do anything about it now. He held up his wrist but there was no watch there. He cursed to himself about not getting a watch that would go with this outfit. He knew he had overslept as he walked by the TV and saw the 11 o'clock news was on. He watched as the newscaster talked of the massacre at the Harrison Hotel the night before. They switched to a reporter talking with Power House. Johnny listened as the reporter praised the Black Razor for wiping out the Stranglers. Power House spoke of justice for everyone, including the South Rockhaven Stranglers. Johnny kicked the TV and screamed.

"JUSTICE! You'll get yours soon enough."

He stormed to the table and swung the two bags of C-4 over his shoulder. He walked to the door and put his hand on the handle. He paused for a moment sensing something wasn't right. He couldn't really put his finger on it, just a bad feeling. He took a deep breath and stepped out into the empty hallway, turning to lock the door to his apartment. He slid the key into one of his hidden pockets then stopped and listened, but heard nothing. He sprinted down the hall to the stairs. He had a date with the Rockhaven Police Department that he intended to keep.

***

Hawkshaw found himself standing outside of an old apartment building. He had followed the nearly invisible trail from the alley and ended up here. He entered the building and moved from room to room, finding nothing but corpses. Each floor was the same until he finally picked up the trail again on the fifth floor. He moved slowly down the hall towards a door on his right hand side. As he approached he heard another door open from behind. He quickly turned, ready to fight, but he was staring at an elderly woman.

"Hey you! Stay away from Johnny's apartment," the old woman said.

Hawkshaw lowered his fists and walked towards the woman.

"Ma'am you are in grave danger here. I need you to evacuate the building now," Hawkshaw commanded.

"I'm not going anywhere.. Say aren't you that bird guy from the news? Yeah, you are him! Wow a real live super hero," she said.

Hawkshaw approached her slowly, trying not to startle the elderly woman.

"Yes ma'am, I am Hawkshaw from the Guardians of Earth. I need you to come with me," the hero said calmly.

"Why should I leave my home "

"Can't you smell the horrible stench? Everyone in this apartment building is dead," Hawkshaw said.

"Well I can't smell very much with these sinuses and the medicine I take really… wait. Did you say everyone is dead?" she asked, terrified.

Hawkshaw nodded, then watched as the old woman's eyes rolled up into her head and she passed out. He was quick enough to catch her. Then he lifted her up and turned to carry her down the hall but found himself staring directly into the blank face of the Black Razor. He held a giant black broadsword raised high.

"Here, let me help lighten that load!" Black Razor said.

He swung down, cleaving the elderly woman in two. Blood sprayed in Hawkshaw's face but he instinctively jumped away from his attacker. The move saved his life as Black Razor moved in for the killing blow. Hawkshaw sprinted into the old woman's open doorway. Black Razor looked down at the body of his neighbor.

"I'm sorry Mrs. Garner. You were the only person who was ever nice to me here. Hawkshaw will pay for this," he said before running into the apartment.

Black Razor rounded the corner and stepped right into a left jab followed by a right hook from Hawkshaw. He stumbled back but quickly regained his footing and refocused his power into a black katana. Hawkshaw turned and ran into the kitchen.

"Come back here and die!" Black Razor screamed out.

He sprinted into the kitchen and attacked but Hawkshaw was ready for him, holding a butcher knife from the table. Black Razor's overhead strike was easily blocked. The two danced a deadly ballet of strikes, feints and parries. Black Razor pressed his attack but Hawkshaw's superior training and skill outmatched him easily.

"Why don't you just give up," Hawkshaw said.

Black Razor was angered by the taunt and struck from an off balance stance. Hawkshaw used the opening to grab Black Razor, knee him the stomach then throw him head first into the wall. The wall gave way and Black Razor tumbled into the bedroom of the next apartment. Dazed, he lost concentration and the black katana disappeared from his hand. He stood, shaking his head and tasting blood in his mouth. He saw Hawkshaw come through the large hole holding a small taser.

Black Razor began to concentrate his power and form a knife when Hawkshaw fired. A single wire shot out and stuck into his shoulder. It sent wave after wave of high voltage shocks into Black Razor. He tried to fight it but ended up on the floor screaming out in pain. Hawkshaw let up for a moment then squeezed the trigger again. Another scream erupted from Black Razor.

"I could easily kill you but that would make me like you, and I'm not a murderer," Hawkshaw said.

Something came over Black Razor and he stopped screaming. Hawkshaw pulled the trigger but Black Razor fought through the pain and came up to his knees. He shook from the electricity coursing through him but his eyes flashed with a black energy.

"Murderer? You dare to call me a murderer!? What about the countless innocents you and all the other so called 'heroes' murder every day?" Black Razor said as he struggled to stand. "WHAT ABOUT THEM?"

Hawkshaw continued pumping the voltage but took a step back into Mrs. Garner's apartment and replied.

"If it weren't for villains like you then we wouldn't have to..."

"SHUT UP!" Black Razor raged, then stood to his feet. "You were there the day Power House picked up my parent's car and used it to smash Elephant Man to death. Did you or any other damned 'hero' stop and think about my parents who were in that car?" Black Razor said as he grabbed the wire in his shoulder.

"I didn't know, but that doesn't justify..." Hawkshaw started to say.

"No, you didn't know and neither did Power House or Lightning or Lady Terra and that's why every last one of you are going to die!" Black Razor screamed.

Fueled by a deep rage, Black Razor's entire body became encased in a glowing black energy. He walked towards Hawkshaw and everything he touched disintegrated.

Hawkshaw dropped the taser, pulled several capsules from his belt and threw them towards Black Razor only to watch them disintegrate. Finally realizing the futility of attack at the moment, he threw down a smoke capsule. The apartment filled with thick white smoke. Black Razor heard a window smash at the back of the apartment and knew that Hawkshaw had made his escape.

As the smoke cleared, Black Razor's rage drained from him and the radiating energy with it. He ran back into the hallway and retrieved the two bags of C-4 he'd stashed. He smiled knowing he had made one of the Guardians of Earth turn tail and run. Now he was on to phase three of his plan.

***

"I'm Gloria Escamilla and this is a Channel 9 Action News emergency broadcast. We are cutting into your regularly scheduled program to bring you tragic news. Tonight in downtown Rockhaven an explosion ripped through the city's main police station. It's unclear at this time if this was a terrorist attack. We're taking you live to Mitch Bradley who is downtown outside the remains of the RPD building. Mitch what can you tell us?"

"Well Gloria, the fires are still burning and as you can see behind me here, the entire four story police headquarters is gone. The speculation that I'm hearing from the first responders is this had to be a terrorist attack. It seems there were multiple explosions set at key structural points that brought the entire building down in seconds. This has caused massive casualties and as you can see the rescue teams can't get near the ruins to even check for survivors with the fire still burning out of control," Mitch paused for a moment, looking off camera. "Wait, I'm being told there is a survivor who is coming over to speak with us. Detective Frank Carmon here made it out alive. Detective, how did you survive and who would carry out such a heinous attack?"

Frank looked quite disheveled as he came on camera.

"I was out back behind the station on a break. That's the only reason I survived. As far as who, it was the Black Razor. While I was out there I saw him running from the fire exit on the West side. I started to take after him but fell down and that's when the whole place went up. When I woke up Power House was there and I told him what I'd seen. He said that he would stay in the city until Black Razor is taken care of," Frank said.

"There you have it, we have an eye witness stating that the Black Razor is responsible for the bombing. He is officially the most monstrous villain Rockhaven has ever had. Lucky for us the Guardians of Earth are here and have vowed to stay until he is brought to justice. I'll turn it back over to you Gloria," Mitch said as he signed off.

***

"This is pretty messed up stuff Hawkshaw," Power House said as he took a swig of a mini bottle of liquor.

Hawkshaw sat staring at a table littered with dozens of high quality pictures of Black Razor. He had taken them with the camera built into his suit during their fight.

"Why just photos, Hawkshaw? Where's the video?" Power House asked.

He finished the mini bottle of liquor and tossed it across the room into the waste basket.

"Nothing but net!" Power House said.

Hawkshaw rubbed his temples and waited for his counterpart to bring his attention back to their discussion.

"No video because you said you had the equipment when we left and you didn't," Hawkshaw said in an annoyed tone.

"Oh yeah. Sorry about that man. You always want to bring all of this stuff and we usually don't need it," Power House replied.

There was a knock at the door and Power House zipped over and opened it. A blur sped past him but he already knew before he turned around who it was.

"Hey there Lightning! Did you get everything?" Power House asked as he shut the door.

Lightning was sitting in a chair drinking a soda. He held up the large laptop.

"Yup, one super laptop linked to the Guardians universal database right here for old Hawkie boy."

"Come on Lightning, don't mess with me," Power House said.

In the blink of an eye the laptop was in front of Hawkshaw, opened and turned on and Lightning was back sitting in the same chair holding up a bag of greasy tacos from a fast food chain a few states over. Power House used his own super speed to snatch the bag and grab another small bottle of liquor from the mini-bar. Hawkshaw shook his head then pulled up files and info on the laptop.

"Thanks for bringing the laptop. So here..." Hawkshaw said then was cut off.

"And thanks for the tacos!" Power House cut in.

Hawkshaw took a deep breath then continued on, ignoring Power House's interruption.

"Okay here it is. Black Razor is actually Jonathan Norris Goldman, born September thirteenth 1977 to Robert and Cheryl Goldman. He dropped out of high school in the 9th grade, started dealing drugs and ran away from home. He got busted a few times but didn't do much time behind bars. Then it looks like he joined the South Rockhaven Stranglers."

"Isn't that the name of the gang that Black Razor slaughtered a few nights ago?" Power House asked with a mouth full of taco.

"Yes. Now according to some sketchy info here it looks like he left the Stranglers about five years ago after having some medical issues. Let me check medical records. Okay, looks like he saw a lot of doctors but no one could figure out what was wrong with him. The final records are from a Dr. Slovack and state he thought Jonathan was developing some type of energy based super power. There was supposed to be a follow up visit but it never happened because the day it was scheduled Dr. Slovack was killed in a fire that burned his entire medical practice to the ground," Hawkshaw said.

"Wow, what are the odds the doctor's office burns down the day this guy is supposed to go back for a check up? Craziness," Power House said.

"The odds are beyond calculating, which leads me to believe he was murdered by Jonathan to try and cover up his new super powers. One year to the day a small time super villain shows up in Rockhaven called the Black Razor. He's been operating in Rockhaven for the past four years," Hawkshaw said.

"Why didn't we ever hear about this guy?" Lightning asked.

"Because he did just enough to stay off our villain list. He had to have known the exact criteria to get on our list because his robberies stopped once he got within five of our limit. Then his killings stopped at exactly five below our limit as well," Hawkshaw stated then trailed off in thought.

"How could he have known our exact criteria? Only members of the Guardians of Earth know those numbers," Power House asked.

Hawkshaw typed furiously on the laptop and then paused. He sat back for a moment then spoke.

"Do you two remember when Sharp Shooter disappeared? Never mind I'll tell you, it was four years ago. To be more exact, it was one month before the Black Razor showed up in Rockhaven."

Power House and Lightning were now standing behind Hawkshaw, all of them silently remembering how they had searched for months but had never found Sharp Shooter.

"Okay Hawkshaw, you're good but how did you figure all of this out in a day and a half?" Power House asked.

"Do you remember how all of you laughed when I started recording our battles against super villains?" Hawkshaw asked.

Power House and Lightning both chuckled but stopped when Hawkshaw continued his explanation.

"When I fought Black Razor he said we killed his parents in the fight against Elephant Man. More specifically, the third and final fight where you, Power House, used a car to beat Elephant Man to death."

Power House quickly became angry and defended himself.

"You know damn well I was justified in killing Elephant Man. He had just crushed a school bus filled with kids. I did what had to be done to stop that child killer from ever hurting anyone again."

"Maybe you felt justified in killing Elephant Man but were you justified in killing the two people in the car you used to do it?" Hawkshaw asked.

Silence hung in the room for a long moment before Hawkshaw went on.

"I went back to the video of that fight and was able to pull the license plate from the car you picked up. By running that I had everything I needed on Jonathan Goldman aka Black Razor. So now we know who we're dealing with. We know why we're dealing with him. We simply need to draw him out so we know where he is."

"But if he hates us and wants to kill us, then why waste time killing an entire gang or blowing up the police station? Why not just come after us like he did Sharp Shooter?" Lightning asked.

"He killed the Stranglers because he knew it'd push his murder count past our limits and we'd come to Rockhaven. He blew up the police station to make sure we'd stay here. He brought his prey to his own hunting ground and made sure we couldn't leave. It's exactly what I'd do in his place," Hawkshaw answered. "I shouldn't have to say this but we're not dealing with your typical crazy villain here. This is a manipulative, calculating killer who wants the Guardians dead and doesn't care if he kills an entire city in the process."

Power House pointed towards the door then spoke.

"Lightning, go as fast as you can to every TV and radio station within a ten mile radius of Rockhaven. Have them run a message from myself and the Guardians of Earth. Tell Black Razor that we won't stop and we won't run. We'll be waiting right here in this hotel to take him down hard."

"Hold on a second. Don't say this hotel, we've already seen what this guy does in hotels. Make the message say that we'll be waiting in the central city park," Hawkshaw said.

The door opened and shut so fast it was impossible to see. Power House flipped on the TV and waited for the broadcast. After five minutes went by and several different channels were checked they began to worry. It should have only taken a few seconds for Lightning to reach the first TV stations. They both knew something was wrong and Power House was the first one out the door.

At the end of the hallway they saw Lightning's body lying in an awkward position. His decapitated head rested a good six feet closer in the middle of the hall. Power House was there in a flash and fell on his knees in a pool of blood.

"Lightning! No!" he cried out.

Hawkshaw immediately started processing the scene. He searched for clues and soon found them.

"It was Black Razor. Look here," Hawkshaw said.

Power House slowly stood up and wiped his blood covered hands on his cape. He walked over to where Hawkshaw had indicated. There were fresh cuts in the wood on either side of the hallway, a little below eye level.

"Black Razor must have used his power to create a razor wire across the hallway at neck level. Even if Lightning had seen it he wouldn't have been able to stop in time. From what I've learned, Black Razor would've needed to be nearby to..." Hawkshaw said.

He was cut off when Power House grabbed him and flew down the hallway at top speed. He held Hawkshaw under his arm like a bag.

"No more talk! You're going to show me where this scumbag lives. We're not waiting for him to come to us, we're taking the fight to him!" Power House said as he flew straight through the hotel wall and into the morning sky.

***

Black Razor peered from a supply closet at the opposite end of the hall. He watched as Power House grabbed Hawkshaw and flew straight through the wall. After waiting a few moments to be sure they didn't come back, he finally exited the closet. He walked down the hallway to the suite being used by the Guardians. He casually strolled into the door left open by the two panicked super heroes. He checked out a nearby table and smiled when he saw pictures of himself strewn about. He noticed the notes on each photo where Hawkshaw was studying his stances and strikes. He stacked all the pictures up then looked at the laptop next to them. He moved his finger across the touch pad and the blank screen turned on. The laptop was logged directly into the Guardian's Universal database and staring back at him was a picture of his driver's license. He flipped through a few screens and could see the Guardians knew everything about him now.

"Hawkshaw you're a tricky one," Black Razor said.

He closed the lid then looked around for something to carry everything in. He spotted a large bag sitting on one of the beds. He opened it and found it packed with street clothes, Power House's formal super hero outfit he wore when meeting world leaders and five thousand dollars in cash. He pulled everything out of the bag except the money, then stuffed the laptop and pictures inside. He noticed a bag full of tacos and tossed them in as well.

He swept the room for anything else and found one of Hawkshaw's combat belts in a nightstand. Black Razor put it on and the belt automatically sized itself to fit him. There were compartments filled with capsules, tools and other items. He smiled under his black mask, zipped up the bag then turned to go. On his way to the door he noticed the mini-bar and opened it up. He cleaned out the small fridge and put everything in the bag. When he walked out of the room he noticed Lightning's body down the hall. An idea came to him that would further knock his opponents off balance. Hawkshaw wasn't the only one who studied his enemies.

***

As the sun started to set, Power House flew back to the hotel carrying an angry Hawkshaw. They landed out front and walked through the large glass doors.

"You're out of control, Power House. Leveling the apartment building that Black Razor lived in accomplished nothing and put citizens in danger," Hawkshaw said angrily.

"I'm through listening to you Hawkshaw. This guy cut off Lightning's head and tortured information out of Sharp Shooter; then did only god knows what to him. Enough is enough. I'll put an end to him."

Hawkshaw stopped abruptly and grabbed Power House's arm. There before them was a gruesome sight in the middle of the lobby. In a large leather chair was the body of Lighting, dressed in Power House's formal outfit. Lightning's head had been placed in his own dead hands.

"Where's all the hotel staff? Quick, search the hotel and let's pray they're still alive somewhere!" Hawkshaw ordered.

Power House disappeared in a blink. Hawkshaw knew it'd only take five to six minutes for him to search the entire building.

He inspected Lightning's body and noticed a piece of paper hanging from the mouth of the lifeless head. He approached cautiously and removed the note.

"Dearest Hawkshaw, it was nice knowing you. Sincerely, Black Razor," Hawkshaw read aloud.

Instantly he turned around towards the front doors. There stood Black Razor wielding none other than Sharp Shooter's magnificent sniper rifle. Before he could react the glass doors shattered inward. The special high caliber uranium oxide tipped bullet hit Hawkshaw square between the eyes, throwing him backwards into Lightning's corpse. The chair tumbled over backwards and Hawkshaw's body continued on another five feet before coming to rest against the front desk.

Black Razor knew the gunshot would bring Power House so he tossed the deadly rifle down and sprinted away. Power House would soon pay but not before every other member of the Guardians of Earth died first. He smiled knowing he had taken care of the most dangerous of the Guardians by killing Hawkshaw. Only Lady Terra remained and it was time to start the final phase of his plan for revenge.

Power House heard the gunshot down stairs and even though it'd been years since last hearing it, he knew that the shot came from Sharp Shooter's special rifle. He flew down the stairwell in a blaze and came into the lobby only to see Hawkshaw's body lying several feet away from the overturned chair and Lightning's headless body. Power House rushed over and saw blood everywhere. He knew that Hawkshaw was gone. He screamed out in a rage that shook the entire building. Suddenly a beeping noise went off on his wrist band. He looked down to see an emergency summons beacon sent from Hawkshaw's laptop to all Guardians. He tried to figure out why a summons beacon would be going off now. Then it came to him.

"Lady Terra! She has no clue what she's walking into."

He looked back at his band and saw that the summons was coming from the central park. He flew as fast as his power would allow towards the park.

***

"Hawkshaw, where are you?" Lady Terra called out.

She stood by a park bench in the middle of Rockhaven Central Park. On the bench was Hawkshaw's laptop transmitting the emergency summons but he was nowhere to be seen. She reached down and hit the end key to shut off the beacon. A violent explosion enveloped Lady Terra, throwing her into the air. She screamed as she landed awkwardly on her shoulder several yards away from the charred park bench. Blood trickled down her nose, her ears rang and she couldn't move. She closed her eyes and when she reopened them standing over her was the Black Razor. He held a large black battle sword.

"You… you're Razor.. Black Raz..." Lady Terra mumbled weakly. "Wh.. why?"

Black Razor knelt beside her, the large sword disappearing then being replaced by a wicked looking dagger.

"Because Lady Terra, you were there the day Power House murdered my parents and you did nothing to stop him. For that you must pay with your life."

He raised the dagger and slashed down for the killing blow that never connected. Power House flew in faster than light and grabbed Black Razor's wrist, lifting him several feet off the ground. Black Razor smiled underneath the mask even as Power House was crushing his arm.

"At last I meet the man who murdered my parents. Guess what Power House?" Black Razor asked.

Power House didn't reply. His eyes were filled with an unholy raging fire. Suddenly Lady Terra screamed out then stopped. Power House jerked his head around to see a five foot long blade protruding from Black Razor's other hand into Lady Terra's chest.

"I can use my powers with both hands, now it's your turn!" Black Razor yelled.

He reformed the long sword into a knife then jammed it into the side of Power House's head but the blade simply bounced off. Power House slowly looked back at the Black Razor.

"Die!" Power House screamed.

He threw Black Razor a hundred feet to the side, knocking over a large oak tree.

Black Razor tasted blood and stood up just in time to be hit by Power House flying at full speed with both fists extended. He cart wheeled end over end backwards until he landed near a swing set. He lay there a long moment hearing a thumping sound. At first he thought it was in his head then he realized they had finally come. He stood and pointed upwards at the approaching helicopter.

"Channel 9 Action News, Power House. I've been waiting for them to show up. Wave at the camera big boy because the world is going to watch one of us die tonight."

Power House never stopped his approach and as he got into range he threw a vicious haymaker.

"NO!" Black Razor screamed out.

His body became encased in black flames and a crackle of energy reverberated through the air. He moved quickly and with both hands caught Power House's fist, then jerked the hero forward and flung him into the metal bar of the swing set.

Black Razor pounced on the downed man, punching him over and over in the face with the raging black energy flowing around him. Power House took punch after punch but was finally able to shove Black Razor off and regain his feet. He kicked him hard in the head, then went to kick him again but this time Black Razor grabbed his leg and dug his energy encased fingers into the skin, muscle and bone. Power House screamed out and grabbed Black Razor by the neck and flung him straight into the air. He looked down at his ripped open leg and felt pain like he'd never felt before. He tried to take a step but stumbled as his leg didn't respond.

"What did you do to me you fiend?" Power House yelled out.

There was a thud off to the left of Power House where Black Razor had fallen. He limped towards the villain when suddenly a bright spotlight was on him. The news chopper above had illuminated the battle ground and had cameras trained on him. He ignored them and struggled over to Black Razor. As he approached, Black Razor sprung from the ground and grabbed Power House by the throat and focused his energy there.

Power House was stunned by the surprise attack and he struggled to breathe as the burning hands clenched around his throat. He began punching Black Razor over and over in the ribs and stomach. There were loud cracks as ribs snapped under the mighty blows. Black Razor gave a mighty head butt to Power House, dazing him briefly, then squeezed harder. Power House felt his life slipping from him, when suddenly Black Razor released him.

The two battered men stood no more than a few feet from one another. Black Razor held his shattered ribs and tried to stay conscious.

"You killed the only two people in the world that ever meant anything to me," Black Razor said.

He reached up and pulled the black mask from his head. Blood ran from his nose, mouth and ears. One eye was swollen shut. He removed his gloves, then reached down and removed Hawkshaw's combat belt.

"You killed my dad Robert Goldman and my mom Cheryl Goldman. Now you can go ahead and complete it by killing me, Jonathan Goldman," Johnny said.

Power House limped over and grabbed Johnny by the throat.

"With pleasure you little, worthless piece of trash. You are nothing but a waste of humanity and your parents deserved to die for spawning a vile person like you," Power House spat.

Then with a force more tremendous than a thousand pound bomb, Power House landed a punch that shook the city for miles around. He laughed maniacally as Johnny's body went slack in death. He screamed and threw the defeated villain so hard that his body flew out of sight. Power House took several deep breaths and finally cleared the rage from his mind. It was over.

"Are you proud of yourself?" a voice came from the darkness.

Power House turned to see Hawkshaw walk from the shadows.

"Hawkshaw? But you were dead. He shot you with Sharp Shooters gun."

"When Sharp Shooter went missing four years ago I developed a new type of fabric for my suit that could stop uranium oxide tipped bullets. Since we never found Sharp Shooter or his rifle, I planned for the possibility that someone else would," Hawkshaw explained. "Now answer the question. Are you proud of yourself, Power House?"

"What's that supposed to mean, Hawkshaw? I did what I had to do," Power House answered.

"Right. You did what you had to. Just like always."

"That's right, and if you weren't dead then why'd you let Lady Terra walk into his trap and die? Why didn't you help me out instead of slinking around in the shadows?"

"Thomas Jefferson once said that the tree of liberty must be refreshed from time to time with the blood of patriots and tyrants," Hawkshaw replied.

"What the hell is that supposed to mean?"

"It means you've been so far out of control that you've blurred the line between patriot and tyrant. You've created your own rules, justified killing not only the bad guys but anyone else who got in the way. It had to end. Justice needed to be refreshed and Johnny Goldman has done just that."

"You're twisted Hawkshaw, and besides, he didn't kill me," Power House said.

"You are correct," Hawkshaw said, then raised his hand and pointed.

Power House turned to see a group of cameramen and reporters. Then he looked up at the news copter circling overheard. Hawkshaw leaned in close and whispered.

"He didn't kill you physically, but he killed your spirit and everything you ever stood for. Every single victory you ever won over the past twenty years is gone," Hawkshaw said then continued after a short pause. "You are a dead man."

Hawkshaw walked away and disappeared into the shadows, leaving Power House behind with his head hung low and the curses of the gathering crowds.

GALLOPING DICK
BY ANTHONY MALONE

I woke up in a ditch. Across the muddy track that was the
Great North road the doxy from the mail coach was screaming and
closing fast were the shouts of righteous men. My plan had failed.
Turpin lived, my horse had bolted and that rum Duchess was
giving me an earache. I pulled myself up into a sitting position
and gazed at the wreckage of the overturned coach, suitcases and
trunks scattered everywhere. "You!" a voice cried and I turned to
see a sprawling coachman with a face like thunder scrabbling for
his flintlock. Not much you can do in a situation like that except
run and so it was, in a most undignified manner, I cut loose and
limped away thinking this was what you got when you tried to
hold up the most famous mounted robber in all of England.

You'd think the sight of young John Palmer twitching at the
end of a noose would have put me off mounted robbery for good,
but that's not accounting for my Nancy's wicked charms. She had
crooked teeth and hair the colour of mouldy hay but she meant the
world to me even though her love of musical theatre cleaned me
out of tin on a regular basis. Aye, musical theatre and even
though chaunting thespians weren't to my taste I had betimes been
driven to mounted robbery to pay for the seats Nancy loved so
much. Bless her heart, she thought I worked in the City, and I had
a mind to keep it that way. That said, the only thing on my mind

as I limped the last mile to the White Hart Tavern was some shepherd's pie and a warm fire. In fact I was still so addled by the throw from my horse I entered too swiftly through the door of the Tavern, caught the pocket of my coat on the handle, yanked it free, lost my balance and made my entrance into that great fraternity of rogues and villains sprawled on the floor amid sawdust and ale.

The White Hart that evening was filled with waggoners, carters, trampers, whip-jacks, beau-traps, some obvious pad-borrowers, a brewer from Truro, and a lost-looking parson going table to table drumming up God's holy trade. The innkeeper – a burly growler named Hewertson – spied me getting to my feet from behind the bar and bellowed "Oi! Ferguson. Stop treating this place like a mail stop!" and strode out brandishing a crumpled note. In a trice, he'd spun me round, grabbed the scruff of my neck and started shoving the paper down the back of my shirt to shouts of laughter from all around. I wriggled and yelled at this but not one person stepped forward to help me and when he was finished he pushed me away and I darted for the furthest corner. "Galloping Dick!" some wag cried triumphantly and the place erupted into laughter at my expense. Scowling, I slid into one of the wooden booths closest to the fire, nodded curtly at a shadowy figure across the table and helped myself to swig of his ale. "It's no good," I hissed at him out of the corner of my mouth. "It can't be done."

The fellow opposite was a shady-flash dandy in a fustian frock, a finely combed periwig and a pair of pumps that smacked of blunt. Jerry Abershaw was his name and I had recently approached him with a view to riding with his gang of rogues and sharing in their greater profits. Not for fun, mind, but to fund Nancy's theatre tickets more easily. Abershaw had been open to this idea but had set a price of his own. "Well now, Dick, here's the rub. The boys will want proof of your credentials, like. Any buzzard can hold up a coachload of fusspot actors. You come back when you've apprehended your namesake, that cattle-stealer and house-breaker, Richard Turpin. Then we'll talk."

It sounded simple enough, which showed how much I knew. It had turned out apprehending Turpin meant suicide as sure as Sundays meant sermons and right then in the White Hart as the glasses clinked and the low murmur of chatter grew around us I told Abershaw to his face he was mad if he thought it possible. By flickering firelight I described how after three weeks skulking in the woods waiting fruitlessly for Turpin to show up, I had thrown caution to the wind that very afternoon and stopped the mail coach, demanding a place on board thinking it the perfect place to lie in wait for a villain like Turpin. Unfortunately, in the melee caused by my sudden appearance from the woods, my pistol had discharged, the horses had reared and I had been thrown senseless into a ditch as the coach overturned. Those horses scared so easy. In fact it was a good thing the passengers hadn't had their wits about them or I would have swung for sure.

Abershaw chewed on his pipe and said the basic idea was solid but he didn't want to hear excuses. The greater the risk, the bigger the reward he said but I shook my head emphatically. What I wasn't telling him was that I knew as long as I had the love of good, kind Nancy, I didn't need his gang of villains. I'd find the money for her theatre tickets – and my debts, and for a place for the two of us to live – one way or another, but I'd do it alone and with less risk of Nancy finding me out. So I tipped my hat to Abershaw, said "thank'ee but no thank'ee" and cheekily finished the rest of his ale. He left soon after.

I flopped back in the booth then, well-pleased with this turn of events and only irritated by the scratchy ball of paper Hewertson had shoved down my back. Twisting and turning I pulled it out, flattened it on the table and cast an eye over the delicate writing. Much to my surprise the writing was Nancy's:

"I know your secret," it read. "Go to the devil."

In a lifetime that has included far too many unpleasant surprises, I can think of few nastier shocks than that moment. It hit me like a blast of icy water. So Nancy knew the truth! This was shipwreck! That lovely girl was the only thing that made my wretched life worth living and I beat at the table with my fists and cursed most foully. Aghast, I lurched sideways out of the booth, righted myself with a twisted foot but staggered into a table of elbow shakers, their shouts and cries following me as I reeled out of the tavern and into the cold night air.

Amid swirling mist I stole a black gelding with a star on its forehead from the livery behind the inn and soon I was thundering over the heath, my waistcoat flapping as my mount surged up the long, rising incline towards Wimbledon village. I could hear the thud of the hooves, see the clods thrown up from the wet turf and feel the wind in my face as the trees flew past but all I could think of was Nancy and my terrible luck and why it was I always seemed to hurtle from one disaster to another in life; never winning, never succeeding, always failing. I reached Wimbledon in record time and when my horse's hooves skittered over the cobbled stones I jumped down, wiped fresh tears from my eyes, and banged my fist on the wooden door of Nancy's lodgings praying to God her note had been part of some evil dream and that lovely girl still thought I was something big in the City.

"Ugh!" Nancy exclaimed on seeing me and slammed the door in my face. I knocked again, hearing muffled curses, then a third time, eventually rewarded with the contents of a chamber pot flung at me from an upstairs window. Sopping wet I pledged contrition and assured her of my continued ardor but she would have none of it. In a way, I protested, it was her fault I had fallen so low; she shouldn't have been so wretchedly enticing but she just squealed at this and slammed the upstairs window so hard the building shook. Some burly types appeared then and I knocked one down which caused a tremendous uproar, a constable being summoned and it was a near thing I wasn't hauled up before a magistrate which would have been the end of me for sure.

A smooth sea never made a skillful mariner but what is a man to do when the woman he loves abandons him on account of his history of violent robbery? Sit and pick posies? I stumbled through the streets of Wimbledon that night without a clue of where I was going or what I would do and in fact barged into two hams flouncing out of the side of the theatre who turned their noses up at my sodden state. Without thinking I snarled at them and relieved them of their purse and that, God bless 'em, paid for a much overdue plate of shepherd's pie at the local Tavern. Indeed, I later overheard gossip that the two stars of the play had been so unmanned by the experience the performance had had to be cancelled and I knew Nancy would be sorely dismayed by this and wondered why such a thing did not happen more.

Well, it did happen more; out of spite, I admit but over the next few days and weeks I turned a pretty penny frightening actors out of their wits and relieving them of their purse. In fact I would have continued on to a nice sized fortune if left alone except for one morning on the Great North road I drew back the scarlet curtain of a coach window, growled "Hand it over, Banquo!" and found, instead of the usual assortment of blubbing actors, none other than Jerry Abershaw grinning back at me, his flintlock cocked, a triumphant grin on his face. Abershaw roared with laughter when the wind unmasked me and said he would never have credited it – so Galloping Dick was the one responsible for persecuting the acting fraternity! Whatever next?

I gaped and he laughed and he explained some patron of the arts had put up a reward for the capture of that horrible rogue who was terrorising her favourite actors and Abershaw had realised all he had to do was ride with the local thespians and wait for me to show up; in fact he'd gotten the idea from me. "This villain invaded our coach without permission!" protested one of the actors but Abershaw just knocked him out with his pistol and roared at the others to be quiet. He turned back to me and I observed bitterly if my idea worked so well Abershaw could apprehend Turpin himself now and take all the glory.

"Turpin swung twenty years ago, my friend" Abershaw said. "You aren't half one for fooling."

I was silent. Abershaw said if I laid off the hams he'd pocket the reward and I could ride out with his men but suddenly that didn't seem so attractive a proposition. I couldn't help wondering what the reward would be if I turned Abershaw himself in and what Nancy would say if I returned to her as hero and man of wealth. It wouldn't involve chamber pots, that was for sure. The coachman caught my eye and nodded towards my flintlock and suddenly I remembered something I had learned from my recent misadventures: those horses scared so easy. So I smiled at Jerry Abershaw, said "thank'ee but no thank'ee", and – thanking God for the gift of plans come to naught – I raised my pistol in the air and fired.

LIFE IN A BOX
BY E. CRAIG MCKAY

Section 1: Gros Morne Park in winter

Sarah was lying inside what could well become her coffin. The temperature was 20 degrees Fahrenheit. It had seemed like a good idea at the time.

The element of surprise is important. This would certainly surprise her target.

Preparation is important too, but all her well laid plans had been scuttled by George's last minute change of routine. She could have, perhaps should have, aborted her attempt to kill him then and there. But she hadn't.

Now she was lying, curled up, starting to freeze, inside a wooden box used by park maintenance to store a mixture of gravel and sand to use on the roads in winter.

Her field of vision was limited. A small crack between two boards allowed her to watch George's car and the path he would likely take back to it. If he came back down that path she would be able to push open the lid and have a clear shot at him from within thirty feet. Even if he came back another path on this side of the parking area he would be no more than sixty-five feet from the box. But there were other paths which would let him approach from the far side which would give him a chance at cover if she didn't take him with the first shot.

If he returned on this side of the car, before her limbs had become cramped and her fingers stiff with cold, he would be an easy target with a handgun. 'Time was of the essence', as lawyers were fond of saying. She would give him half an hour more before calling it off for today.

She had planned to take him out with a rifle at short range along the cross country path he usually skied. Today he had chosen another and she had improvised. She had her Walther .380 inside her right-hand mitten keeping it and her hand as warm as possible.

She was starting to regret her creativity. It would have been so nice to sit in her warm car waiting for him to come back. Then she could step out of the car and act like a helpless woman with car trouble.

"Could you help little ol' me with my car, sir? It won't shift into gear."

Surely he would have come over full of male pride. It would then have been simple to put a bullet through his thick skull. 'Well, easier to think inside the box than out of it, I guess' she chided herself. 'But, if he doesn't come back within another 30 minutes I'm out of here.'

She tensed as she heard a sound coming from near the box, but out of her sightline. It was close, very close.

Section 2: Dexter is small, but we call it home

Sarah had not expected to be boxed in. It had all started in her home town, Dexter, in upper New York State. Sarah was at the family sporting goods store, doing year-end inventory, when her father, Erik, called her the day after New Year's. The broker had sent an offer.

"Where is it and when?" she asked.

"ASAP in Newfoundland."

"Where?"

"A big island off the east coast of Canada," he told her. "Want to see the details?"

"I'm coming over."

Sarah hung up and went to check on Google Earth. Sure enough there was a big hulking island out there. It was a province of Canada.

She had heard 'Newfie' jokes told by people up at the cottage in Oliphant Beach. To judge by the jokes, the whole province was filled with people who spoke with a funny accent, spent most of their time fishing or drinking, and seemed unsophisticated.

She had restrained herself from informing the people telling the jokes that to a person from New York City they all seemed to exhibit those same qualities themselves.

Sarah wondered, not for the first time, why it was that people all seem to look for some other group to poke fun at. Every group you could think of had a target for their jibes or smart remarks. Certainly lawyers were a group that got their share of abuse. Her personal favorite was: *"Question: What's the difference between a dead skunk in the highway or a dead lawyer? Answer: In front of the skunk there are skid marks."*

As she drove back to the house she considered the special aspects of a hit in Newfoundland (actually the name was Newfoundland and Labrador, she'd learned from the internet, but few people used the full name). One factor was that the Newfoundland section was an island and difficult to get to during January except by airplane. The other section, Labrador was always difficult to get to except by airplane. That meant that any guns which would be needed would have to be obtained locally.

Getting guns in Canada was always a little more difficult than in the U.S. She wondered how difficult it would be in Newfoundland.

Another consideration would be the 'stranger in town' aspect. Sarah would run a danger of standing out. On the other hand, it would depend where the hit took place. Newfoundland seemed to be mostly rural and Sarah was a country girl. She knew that in a small town anyone from outside the town would be a 'stranger'. She could be one of many.

When she sat down with her mom and dad, she discovered that the target lived in an isolated region within an isolated area. George, the proposed target, had a holiday home in a small town which was surrounded by the wilderness of Gros Morne, a Canadian national park.

The target was actually American, from Detroit. He had a cabin in Newfoundland; a place called Woody Point. According to the maps they consulted it was a small town not actually 'in' the park, but the park was on three sides of it and an inlet of the ocean on the north. Apparently George went there every year from mid January for about four weeks for skiing and basically getting away from business.

"Cross country or downhill?" Elizabeth asked. "If it's cross country, Sarah could catch him somewhere isolated."

"The file doesn't say," Erik responded, "but I'm thinking it is probable that he does cross country. I'll check with The Broker."

Sarah was using the internet while the family considered the offer. She had brought up a screen on Gros Morne and discovered that they had a lot of trails for cross country and even talked about "backcountry" skiing which would provide an excellent opportunity.

Sarah was an excellent skier and would be in much better physical condition than the 48-year old George who spent most of the year smoking and drinking while running his loan shark business in Detroit.

"I like the assignment," said Sarah. "I'm looking at a website here that indicates that the Gros Morne Park has a lot of trails and lots of wilderness. It looks like a good place to isolate a target. My only concern is how I would get a suitable gun or guns there."

"I'll contact The Broker and check that out," Erik told her. "What would you like?"

Elizabeth and Sarah were huddled in front of the monitor and comparing notes.

"I'd want a light carbine, no scope, bolt action, something compact. Light in case I have to ski with it, and with a reliable action in cold or wet conditions," Sarah told Erik.

"Good criteria," he agreed. "How about a 788 Remington in . 243 caliber? Similar to the one we have in the shop."

"Exactly," Sarah replied enthusiastically. "If The Broker can get one of those and a Walther PPK in .380 ACP as back up, I'll be happy".

Elizabeth was looking at a picture of a PPK on line. "Do you like the PPK because James Bond used one?" she teased. "Or is it because they're so small?"

"It's a great gun," Sarah responded. "It will fit in a purse or a small pocket. You can even carry it in your hand without it being noticed. I was sure glad I had it with me last summer in New York."

The last was out of her mouth before she could stop herself, but both Erik and Elizabeth responded with surprised looks.

"What happened then?" Erik asked and Elizabeth turned her full attention on Sarah.

Sarah tried to make light of it. Although both her mother and father knew she could handle herself, they had natural parental concerns.

"It was just some guy who followed me when I left the restaurant last August. He was persistent, so I had to shoot him. It was no big deal," she assured them.

"I never liked you being alone in New York," Elizabeth said.

"Well, things happen everywhere, mom. At least I'm prepared."

There ensued a discussion about travel. They agreed that it was best to drive into Canada and take a flight from Ottawa or Toronto to St John's, Newfoundland. The flights were more regular and there would be no hassle at customs since it would be an internal flight.

She would rent a car in St John's, preferably four-wheel drive for the long drive across the province to Gros Morne. The Michelin route planner calculated the driving time from St. John's to Woody Point at almost eleven hours. The population in Woody

Point was listed at 400, so Sarah would probably have to search for accommodations.

Erik was able to confirm with The Broker that the specified guns and 25 rounds of ammunition for each gun would be available for pick up in Clarenville, a town on route to Gros Morne.

After a bit of searching for flights and car rental the contract was accepted. Erik negotiated an extra $5,000 to cover expenses.

Section 3: Newfoundland and Labrador

Sarah drove to Ottawa to catch a flight to St. John's NL. Whenever possible she liked to avoid using her passport when going on a job. It was bad enough that she had to show it going through customs when driving up to Canada at Thousand Island Park. She had joined Interstate 81 near Fisher's Landing and had crossed Wellesley Island and entered Canada by the Ivy Lee Bridge.

Ottawa is reputed to be one of the coldest national capitals in the world. It was certainly cold in the parking lot of the Ottawa International airport. The good news was that the airport is not a major hub, so it is relaxing to fly in or out of.

Her flight to St John's was aboard an Air Canada plane. Sarah flew a lot. It struck her how similar all the airlines seemed.

Upon arrival in St John's she rented a four-wheel drive vehicle. She discovered that studded tires were legal here in winter. That might come in handy where she was going.

She took a room in St John's for the night and went over her plans.

The drive across to Woody Point would take about 11 hours. Sarah was always careful to keep her speed at the legal limit. When you carry guns and kill people you don't want to attract attention. Locals had warned her that moose could be expected to lumber out onto the highway at any moment. At up to 1200 pounds and seven and a half feet high at the shoulder, they should be avoided.

Clarenville was the stop to pick up the tools they had ordered from The Broker's contact. She decided that she would drive to Clarenville in the morning and then drive as far as she felt comfortable before taking a room. She would like to arrive in Woody Point rested and ready. She had brought her cross-country skis and serious outerwear. The Broker had confirmed that George skied cross-country and had given directions to his cabin.

She chose to skip breakfast to get on the road. Two hours out she discovered that service centers are not a feature of the TCH, Trans Canada Highway. There is basically only one road across Newfoundland. She passed a couple gas stations on the other side of the highway, and before she saw a place to stop for breakfast she was arriving in Clarenville. She'd seen a lot of pretty country, and lakes, and rocks. She had been told that the number of moose in Newfoundland was the same as the number of people. She hadn't seen any moose and since leaving St. John's she hadn't seen many people.

Clarenville was a major center. She had two hours to kill, so to speak, before meeting up with her gun contact. She asked one of the locals for advice and against her own instincts went for a late breakfast at the Irving Gas Station restaurant. She was wrong; the local was right. She had a great breakfast of bacon, eggs and toutons. Toutons are Newfoundland's answer to biscuits. They are basically pan fried bread dough, served with molasses. The toutons were tasty and the rest of the breakfast was good home-style cooking with bottomless cups of good coffee.

Sarah was in a good mood when she met the gun supplier. That was good. He was 40% amateur and 60% annoying. The guns were both used and the PPK had only one magazine. She wanted to try them out but was told she would have to find a place outside of town to do that. The salesman didn't know how to handle guns himself. He actually pointed the pistol in her general direction at one point and she never saw him make one safe.

She decided that she didn't have many options here. She paid the price, which was too high and took her guns and ammo down the road to test them. It turned out that the rifle fired a little left, but good enough. The .380 was in good condition; it felt good in her hand and the action had been well cared for.

It was just past 12:00 but the winter sun was rushing toward the horizon. The road was better than she had expected and she set her sights on Deer Lake for her next stop. The town of Deer Lake was at the north end of Deer Lake. That made sense. The odd thing was that there are no deer in Newfoundland. Go figure.

The road took her through long stretches of forest and provided vistas over lakes and streams. As she approached Gander she had a long view down the lake and wished she could be here in summer with a boat.

When she topped up her tank in Gander she parked and went into the Tim Horton's donut shop. Horton was a Canadian hockey player who had lent his name to a chain of coffee and donut outlets before his untimely death in a sports car. The sports car was really hot, a De Tomasa Pantera, which Tim had moving more than fast enough when he failed to make a corner while driving through St. Catharines, Ontario. The coffee was good; the donuts were donuts.

Sarah checked into a B&B in Deer Lake and went over the file on George again. Often his targets were drug dealers or fringe lowlife who had crossed someone. George was a small time loan shark who had put some heavy pressure, including a broken nose, on a businessman who was into him for thirty thousand. George had not realized that the businessman was connected. The connections had ordered the hit.

George qualified for Sarah's personal list of acceptable targets. She considered herself a professional in all senses. She was her own judge of whether a target deserved to be taken out or not. George did. Sarah made these decisions before accepting any contract. Right or wrong, it was a decision she could live with. Some proffered contracts didn't make her cut list.

The Broker had once sent a semi-political assignment which Sarah had refused. She agreed that many politicians were sewer rats, but she thought the electorate should decide who to toss out and who to reward with their vote.

She started to think about eating.

This trip was turning into a real culinary experience for Sarah. At the recommendation of her landlady she ate at a Roadhouse called Jungle Jims. Unfortunately it was the same old, same old. Decent fast food and draft beer. It was busy inside, considering Tuesday was a slow night for most restaurants. They had a chicken wing and bucket of beer special which seemed to be drawing them in.

Section 4: Parks provide a chance to relax, and to meet people

Wednesday morning was clear and crisp. The drive into and
through Gros Morne Park was uneventful, though she did note the
increased number of moose warning signs. Woody Point was as
small as she expected. She found George's cabin and decided she
would probably be better off taking him out away from town. Too
many windows looked out over the flat terrain for her to feel
confident of not being seen.

She checked into the Seaside Suites, where she found the
accommodations very comfortable. Her suite, called Tablelands
Suite for a reason she never quite understood, was actually fairly
luxurious.

Woody Point seemed to focus on summer for most of its
tourism. They made a great deal about boat trips and the walking
trails. Sarah noticed a couple cars with ski racks and engaged one
of the couples in conversation in the coffee shop. She learned that
there was downhill skiing available nearby, but that snowmobiles
and cross-country skiers used the park trails. Sarah already knew
that George often used a groomed trail at Trout River Pond, but
that he also did some backcountry skiing.

Over the next week Sarah shadowed George as
inconspicuously as possible. As long as he didn't know she was
following him, it didn't matter if he saw her. He didn't know her
and he wouldn't be identifying anyone after she finished with him.

George was regular in his habits. He got up late. Never out of
the cabin before 10:00 and there was no sign of him sitting inside
before 9:00. He was not an avid skier. He spent about one hour

to one and a half per day on the groomed trails at Trout River Pond and showed no inclination at all to go off the tame trails into wilderness skiing. Sarah would have to catch him alone somewhere near or on the trail. She spent five days watching and decided to hit him Monday. There would be fewer people on the trails then. Monday was Martin Luther King day in the U.S. but she didn't think that would be a factor here.

She could ski out behind him and pick him off near one section with a drop-off along one side. With any luck she could tip the body onto a spot where it wouldn't be noticed until the spring thaw.

Section 5: Praxis involves putting theory into action

Monday morning found Sarah parked within sight of George's cabin. If his routine held he would come out just after 10:00 and drive away from where she was parked toward Trout River Pond.

She would follow at a distance, park after he did and overtake him on the trail on skis.

That plan turned to rat shit as soon as he failed to make the right turn which would take him to Trout River. He seemed to be heading toward the exit from the park at Wiltondale.

Then, before he got that far, just past Glenburnie on the Bonne Bay Road, George pulled off into a public parking area which was shielded on the road side by a row of trees. Sarah had to drive on by and then turn back further up the road. She did a drive by and spotted George heading off down a trail on foot.

By the time she could turn around and come back, he was out of sight down one of three paths.

She had to make a choice. She could call it off for today and start again tomorrow. She could head off down one of the trails and hope to meet up with him. Or, and she thought this was a plan, wait here until he came back out. She had already checked out of her room, so she wouldn't have to head back to Woody Point. This was actually a better location if she could make a clean kill.

There were two cars in the parking area in addition to hers and George's. She wondered if there was someplace out of sight from which she could watch without being seen.

Then Sarah had a really stupid idea. It seemed good at the time. But it was really a bad idea. There was a big wooden box, apparently used to hold sand, beside the entrance to the rear section of the parking lot. For some strange reason which she could never understand later, she decided that it would be a good place to hide. It had a series of wide cracks which she could see out of and it was less than half full of a mixture of sand and crushed stone.

Thirty minutes later she started realizing how foolish this decision had been.

Section 6: Back in the Box, Where's George?

Sarah heard the noise getting closer. It almost seemed to be coming towards the box.

What if some park employee was coming to scoop out some of the sand-salt mixture? It would look pretty strange to find her curled up on top of the pile. Luckily the gun was still inside the mitten. She would just have to smile sweetly and say she was playing hide and seek with some friends who must have given up and gone home. It wasn't actually illegal to hide in a box. It was just very weird.

On the other hand . . . .

What if it was George who had somehow seen her climb in here 45 minutes ago and was coming back with a shotgun?

'Okay, here's the plan,' she decided. 'I'll keep the glove on and smile if it's the employee, and shoot George through the mitt if it's him.' There would be some deflection of the bullet on the way through the woolen mitten, but not a significant amount given that she would be firing at a separation of three or four feet.

She prepared to move, but the sound, which had passed right beside the box moved past it. She peered through the crack and clearly identified George. He was three feet away and walking toward the car.

Sarah pulled off the mitten and used her left hand to lift the lid.

She reared up onto her knees and swung the muzzle toward George's back.

He heard the lid open and spun around in time for her to see his startled expression as she squeezed off a shot into his body mass. He jerked back and she fired again from her crouching position in the sand. George went down hard. A .380 doesn't have knock down capability. She must have made serious contact.

She held her position for a moment. She could see his right hand and the left was under his body. He was not moving.

Slowly, keeping her eyes fixed on the inert body, she climbed out of the box onto stiff legs. There was no sign of life, but she would take no chances. Without shifting her attention, Sarah moved to her left to circle the body until she had a clear view of the head. She carefully put the next shot though the centre of the skull.

Now she could spare the time to look around.

Her first concern was to check for witnesses. There was no one in sight and she could hear nothing going by on the highway.

One of the weaknesses of her hiding place was that she could not check the area to make sure it was clear before taking George out. Hindsight being always 20/20, she realized now what a stupid idea it had been. 'Well, the result was alright; just don't ever use that approach again,' she resolved.

She had fired three rounds. She glanced down and saw a spent cartridge which she picked up. She walked over to the sand box to close it and spotted the other two brass casings. It was worth a couple seconds to scoop them into her pocket. She closed the lid and turned back toward George's body.

Still no one in sight. It took less than a minute to drag the body to the edge of the parking area and tip it into a ditch. It would be nice to move his car to somewhere it wouldn't be noticed, but that would be complicated and not worth the risk.

She walked to her own car, started it and drove back out the short, tree-lined entrance to the main highway. She turned right and headed back toward the park entrance near Wiltondale. She dumped the rifle at the edge of the woods near East Arm and the spent shells and Walther went into the water as soon as she found an isolated spot where she could do so.

One of her main concerns was the scarcity of roads. Even though she was now mostly clean of all traces of the hit, the Trans Canada Highway was the only way back to St John's.

It wasn't until she reached Gander that she felt as if she was out of the woods, although technically the whole island seemed one big forest.

Next stop, Dexter.

OFFERINGS
BY FRANCES PAULI

They fed her to the maze. It swallowed her whole, its silence eating away at her memory. The black walls stole her name, until the more she wandered the twisting corridors, the less she knew herself, the less she remembered and the less she lived.

A sigh escaped. It echoed against the walls of her soon-to-be tomb, taunting, ringing back through total darkness. The emptiness breathed with its own life.

How long had it been since she'd seen her hands? She knew that blood caked between the wrinkles of her palms, knew they'd been torn raw against the miles of rough stone. Her knees were in worse shape.

The passageways had narrowed and forced her to crawl more often than not. Now each step brought agony and a new desire to simply stop and fade away - to become a permanent part of the maze. Her bones might satiate its hunger, could spare some other soul the same fate.

Had she deserved it, this punishment? Had her crime been so great? The details slipped away with each shuffling step. There had been a crime, she knew. At the time it seemed insignificant, even justified. She'd spoken out of turn, had failed to go where someone led, had stood up to the wrong person. She snorted, sharp and haunted by the mazes echoes. The punishment yawned around her, unjust. No one deserved this.

She kicked at the wall and risked further injury. A stone skittered ahead, its clatter ringing through the dark tunnel. She frowned and squinted after the sound. She shouldn't have been able to see it, shouldn't have made out the bouncing trajectory or caught the faint outline of the pebble where it stopped. Still, somehow she saw. Many, many steps ahead, the darkness thinned.

She refused to believe it. It would be a crack, a small fissure or another impossible chimney placed within the maze to torture its victims with false hope. But her instincts forced her forward. Some fight remained despite all the failures. This time, the light miraculously brightened, and the pathway widened and sloped downward.

Fresh air assaulted her, and her lungs screamed for it. The passage turned, and the stone before her flared, lit from some unknown source. She stepped into it, stopped at the top of a flight of steps and cried as her eyes adjusted to a sun that they'd forgotten.

Finally, her lungs laboring to devour all the air they could hold, she took one tentative step down. When the world didn't shift out from under feet, she took another, and another until she half stumbled and half slid toward the bottom.

She fell the last few steps and lay sprawling before the mouth of the maze. The pain was insignificant - she lived. She lived and lay only inches from grass and sunlight. She might have remained there for days, reveling in her survival.

The instinct intervened again, eventually. It drove her to rise and take a gentle step forward. She leaned against the stone opening and let her eyes decipher what lay beyond her prison.

A sprawl of growth reached outward from the cave's maw. The grass glowed emerald in the sunlight. Stone cliffs ringed the glade, cliffs that may or may not reveal a passage or any escape. She didn't care. Here, now, she knew light and air and the scent of water flowing somewhere nearby.

She wobbled out into the open and examined the high walls. Recessed into the granite to her right, half a story above the grassy floor, a stone façade broke the cliff's surface. Shadowed pillars stood in defiance against the natural face of rock. They supported a triangular pediment, chipped from the stone base and marking the significance of the entrance below.

A rough stair wound up the cliff to the opening, and she took this without hesitation. If there was a power that moved her now, it had dwelt here for longer than she'd known life. It had plucked her from the black maze, and she happily yielded to its seniority. She stepped without thought, climbed effortlessly to the temple entrance and collapsed before it.

The stone pressed a cool comfort against her cheek. The platform where the pillars rose had been ground as smooth as glass. With each long breath, her limbs grew stronger, pulling some ancient strength from deep inside the stone until she rose without shaking or pain.

The pillars stood before her - twenty feet of polished granite guarding the secrets of the shadows beyond. High above, the pediment loomed, its original features worn by time and wind so that only fragments could be seen. She spied the twist of muscled limbs and the sharp curve of hooves. Amidst the arching of feathered wings, the trace relief of a profile remained - a relic of whatever gods had been served by its creation.

She turned from it, a surge of curiosity beckoning her toward the recess beyond the façade. Whatever lay in this space, whatever power slept in the dark corners, had been her savior from the maze's deadly embrace.

She took two long strides past the border of the pillars, and the darkness engulfed her. The strength that she'd gleaned from resting at the entrance grew in her. It swelled with each step deeper into the bowels of the temple. Her body glowed with it.

Here was sanctuary. Here was the power to survive, to thrive, and to lash out at all who had opposed her. Within the depths of her mind a foreign voice whispered, *Here!*

She paused. She shook her head gently and tried to remember who had ever opposed her.

Here, the voice promised. *Here are the answers.*

She took another step. Her eyes gradually adjusted to the shadows, and the room behind the pillars revealed its secrets. The dust of ages lay thick upon the floor. Arachnid weavings curtained the walls. The spiders themselves had long since shriveled into desiccated husks, but their trappings billowed overhead and to either side of a mammoth throne.

Here!

A crack split the statue seated there. The crumbled features twisted to rubble around the scar, leaving only the suggestion of the crowned face, the waterfall of one broad wing, the lap, knees and taloned feet draped in a rippled sheet of marble. The hands resting on the throne's arms had been severed by another fault just below the fingers.

Sit. The voice whispered louder, just a touch insistently. *Sit here.*

She stood at the base of the throne and craned her neck back. The knees rose beyond her head. The folds of stone skirt flowed around them and disappeared over the lip of the seat. She felt strong enough to heft herself upward, to scramble over the warm sculpture and pull her own body into the statue's lap. It proved an easy undertaking.

Though she was not a small woman, she looked like a child seated on the giant skirt. She could have sprawled across it and slept comfortably. Instead, she dangled her legs over the edge, reached her arms wide and touched the stone to either side of her. Heat flared there.

Here is power.

Strength rippled under her fingers. *Here!* It burst through her palms and vibrated through her arms and shoulders. Muscles relaxed to its passing. Aches and bruises faded as it flooded her torso, legs and feet. *Here is power.* The voice whispered as the hum of it rose into her neck, burned across her face and erupted from the crown of her head. *Here.*

She drank it in, swelled with the flow until she could feel each tiny hair along her arms raise, each nerve ending shiver anxiously. The world blazed. She'd wandered too long in darkness and here was light, and warmth, and safety.

Rest, the voice encouraged. She had more than earned the comfort of sleep. Curling across the giant lap, she fell easily away from consciousness. *Sleep.*

***

She woke slowly, twisted the kinks from her slim neck and stretched her mighty arms wide. Glorious power hummed in her bones. Life pounded within her. Her eyes blinked as she savored the pulse of it. Her limbs ached for movement. Her wings twitched.

Slowly. With some effort, she put aside the restlessness, took time to breathe and to survey her domain.

Beyond the temple, the emerald growth had nearly overrun the courtyard. *My courtyard,* she reminded herself. The entrance to the maze remained open but was strewn with rubble. Dust and errant grasses choked the once bright tiles. *Disgraceful. Unforgivable.*

Her vision stretched farther to the cliff walls and the slim passage that led from her sanctuary. Though she remained firmly seated against the marble chair, her vision wandered. She saw the vines clinging and twisting up the smooth stone. She saw the gash of a recent landslide and the debris piling around the passage entrance.

The narrow cleft itself had not been blocked. It wound through the range of peaks surrounding her and opened on the plains beyond. *Unused. Un-walked and forgotten.* Anger flared deep within. *Shameful.* Someone would pay for this.

She tried to reach them then, but her wings failed her. Even her sight refused to stretch beyond the narrow cleft in the rock. A futile attempt to reach over the walls left her exhausted once more. *Sleep, then.* She sighed. Her strength would return to her soon enough.

She slept, and woke, and slept again. With each shift her limbs felt stronger, her power surged to be released. But an odd calm had crept inside her. A stillness within yearned quietly for the victory to come, yet bade her wait, wait and linger a moment longer.

She watched the sun come and go. She saw the moon change shape. She waited. *Just a little longer.* Her wings flapped freely in emphasis. *Soon.*

The next time she woke, all patience had left her. Her veins buzzed for movement and she twitched to be free again. She launched without delay, bursting from the throne and out the temple entrance in a blur of feathered fury. *Free, free!* She screamed into the wind, rose without effort above the granite cliffs and hurled herself across the heights beyond.

Past these lay a vast plain, bathed in harsh sunlight and nearly devoid of life aside from the sparse and hardy grasses that waved across its breadth. She knew this place. The warmth of noon burnished her plumage as she sailed high above it. The wind of her passage supported and lifted her gently over the miles of yellowed ground.

The horizon to either side of her blurred and flashed green where, far in the distance, the plain broke into forest and life teemed once again. She ignored this and shot like an arrow deep into the empty waste ahead. *Justice! Vengeance!* She called the mantra to herself, diving closer to the quickly passing surface below.

She was nearly there. The village would come into view, sprawled at the edge of the plain - crude, and ugly, and fashioned from mud. It clung to the edge of the river like a tick, feeding off of the water's lifeblood as it grew fat and swollen with stolen riches - riches that had once been justly passed on.

There had been a time of balance. Sandaled feet had carried bounty many miles across the wastes. Carts had come, wreathed in flowers and smelling of resin smoke and spices, to hover at the temple entrance. Tribute had been paid in kind, in honor for a thousand moons and more. *Justice.* She chanted with each long wing stroke.

Below her the horizon broke, but it was not the snaking glint of river that caused her to pause and shift her flight upward. How many generations had it been since the people here had lain their gifts upon the temple steps? For the first time in her furious flight, she knew a flash of doubt.

A city rose at the plain's edge. Spires of white towered on the riverbank, and a smooth wall ringed the expanse of buildings. There were no mud huts here. There were waving flags of fine silk. There were horses, groomed and shod and lightly gaited. There were ships.

Shameful, horrid ships.

Crops grew beyond the walls. Their rows and parcels made quilted patterns from above. There was abundance here, wealth and more, and nothing flowed across the plain to lie before her. *Forgotten.*

She dove closer, spied the moving forms of the people. They swarmed through the buildings like a plague, unchecked and unconscious of their debt. She tried to count the generations in her memory, but she'd slumbered far too long. How many years' tribute had been missed? She calculated what was owed her and knew rage again.

Shameful. They'd pay what she deserved. *What price is worthy of such insult?* She circled the spires, watched the people who had forgotten her, and considered them carefully. *Value? Status? Power?* Her sight ranged far and deep into the crowded towers. She searched and stretched and knew fatigue again.

There! Just before her strength failed, she had it. *This one would suffice.* With one final surge she marked the mind below that she would know it again. *Rest.* Her wings longed for slumber once more. The temple pulled at her, and she drifted passively back to its embrace. *Tomorrow.* She heaved an ancient, satisfied, sigh. *Tomorrow.*

***

She felt him instantly when she approached the walls again. He came without thought. He came easily and mounted on a worthy steed. There were no flowers, no ribbon woven in the mane or tail, but it mattered little. The animal was, no doubt, appropriate for his status.

She pulled gently, allowing him some freedom to wander, enjoying the game more than she'd expected. If he strayed too far toward the wooded horizon, she nudged the mind carefully back on track. If he paused or made to turn for home, she sang within his thoughts and teased him gently on his way again.

It was a slow, delicious process. Anticipation wound like satin robes around her, like the silk ribbons that would have been tied to each basket of fruit, each barrel of fish and cask of honey that should have been offered at her feet. She could smell justice riding with him.

She allowed him to pause at the foot of the peaks, let him slow and linger on the pathway winding toward the cleft. He was too savory to rush, wrapped in fine garments and insignia of rank and privilege.

The horse snorted and tossed its chiseled head at the entrance to the passageway. The man touched it gently on the neck and pressed his heels in. They came closer. She could hear the ringing of hooves against stone from the throne itself. She shivered. *Here.*

They passed the cliff walls. They entered the sanctuary, wading through the growth without concern. The horse stopped before the temple steps and snorted. *Here,* she whispered to it. *Wait.*

The man dismounted, landing gracefully on the grass, hers now. He moved without thought, and she led him expertly across the wide courtyard, one confident step at a time, directly toward the entrance to the maze.

"No." She felt her lips move, heard the word ring harshly from her own throne. *Silence!*

In the courtyard, the man paused and shook his head. She nudged him forward. The maze beckoned. Another step and he stood on the tiles.

"STOP," the life inside her argued.

Silence, silence. Keep moving.

"NO!"

The scream poured through the shadows around the throne, spilled and echoed past the columns and down the wide steps. She followed it far more slowly. Tearing herself from the throne and sliding over the carved knees, she stumbled to the floor with little grace. Her own limbs quivered and threatened to fail her.

Stop! The other voice chased her. *Return! Here!*

She could feel the strength abandon her. It drained away with every stuttering step she took toward the pillars and the light beyond them. Fatigue replaced it, and terror. The voice assailed her, *Traitor! Infidel!*

The sound of flapping wings beat at her, but they were ancient wings, carved in stone and broken now. She fell forward into the column, clung to it for support. *Return!* the voice demanded.

"NO!" The cries faded to a whisper as she crossed the threshold onto the lighted steps. She had nothing left in her. How long had the power sustained her without food or water? She staggered forward. Her original wounds screamed for attention once more, and she collapsed, tumbling down the stairway.

She woke to the sweet taste of water. The man's face crystallized above her. A whisper of rage replied, *Infidel.* It faded rapidly as he pressed a skin canteen to her lips again.

"Drink." His brow furrowed. "You're nothing but bone and breath." Concern laced his kind voice. She squashed a second wave of anger and drank deeply.

Return here.

Every cell in her body burned for liquid. The man rocked back on his booted heels and watched her drain the canteen.

"Where did you come from?" he asked.

She paused, swallowed and pointed one finger at the maze's gaping mouth. He nodded grimly.

"What's in there?"

"Death." Her own voice sounded foreign, pathetic in her ears. *Fool,* the other hissed. *Traitor.*

"And in there?" The man continued, pointing above her to where the temple still beckoned. She could see it in his eyes - the curiosity, the longing.

"NO!" She was too frail to scream, but her tone moved him. She could see the shiver cross his features as he turned back to her and nodded.

"This is a dark place," he said. "My people worshiped here, long ago when we were young and superstitious."

She nodded. She knew it all already.

"What's your name?"

She could find none to give him. She'd had a name, one that she only needed to remember. Perhaps with time, and far from this place, it would be hers again. "I don't know."

"Well, then." He eyed her intently, measured her against some inner judgment. "You've saved my life, and my people will welcome and reward you for it."

She knew this too, could see the silk flags over the high tower that was his. She knew what and who he was already. *What is that against what you have traded away?* But the other voice already faded without her life-force to sustain it.

Her broken body had no strength of its own, and the man was forced to carry her from the temple. He did so delicately and with great care mounted the animal, laying her across its withers. She would heal in time.

As the horse picked its way through the cleft passage, she thought what a fine creature it was. The pale silk of its mane danced just next to her cheek. She would own such an animal, perhaps. When she did, she'd be certain to keep ribbons tied, like offerings, into the long hair.

UPPING THE ANTE: A PEEK INTO THE LIFE AND TIMES OF SNAKEJUICE SAM DENISON BY JOHN ANGLIN

Old Snakejuice Sam was one low down varmint. He was the type of fella that made cutthroats look like choir boys and desperados look like deacons. It was said when Snakejuice was born his mama's heart plum gave out because she had brought such a mean baby into the world. His pa raised him up in the hills all alone. In fact that is how he came by the name Snakejuice. He was raised on a mix of goat's milk, moonshine, and a touch of rattlesnake venom, so the story goes. Sam was so bad he shot his own pa dead when he was just four years old, just for sassing him. Yup, that Snakejuice Sam Denison was one bad hombre.

Just the sight of him was enough to make most folks know they wanted to be far away. He wore a wide brimmed old farmer's hat. He took it off a scarecrow just before setting the crops of a whole county in Kansas on fire a week before harvest just to see if the corn would pop. Some would say Snakejuice had a lazy eye. He would tell you the other was just extra keen. He had a broad smashed up nose as crooked as the Rio Grande it had been broken so many times. His face was covered in stubble as course as ten grit sandpaper.

He wore an old poncho that reeked of sweat and other things best left unmentioned. Across his chest he had a bandolier filled with shells. On his belt he wore a two gun rig. His left hip held a 32 caliber 7 shot British Bulldog. He loved watching that 7th round catch folks by surprise. On his right hip was a custom made double barrel sawed off twelve gauge with an ivory hilt that had the word thunder carved into it. His worn snakeskin boots had seen better days. He wore one spur on his left foot. The right one was probably still sticking into the rib of Snakejuice's last horse. The one he rode now was an old swayback mare. Snakejuice didn't like horses and they didn't care too much for him either.

Snakejuice sat on the ridge looking down into the valley. The small town below was Willow Springs, where the territories judge was suppose to be. He planned on being done with his business here and back on the trail by the end of the day. He chomped down on the cigar he had been masticating all morning, leaned over and spit a nasty glob of tobacco juice right onto a patch of wild flowers. He prodded the horse into motion heading down the trail into the valley.

William Hensley waved to the townsfolk as he rode by on his handsome bay stallion. A spotless cream colored hat was tipped to ladies old and young alike. A big bright smile was flashed to one and all. Sheriff William's badge gleamed in the morning sun as he rode to the edge of town. William was a good man. He wasn't an overly bright man, but he was a good one. When he got to the edge of town he saw the stranger coming down the ridge. That man didn't look so good. It didn't take long for William to recognize Snakejuice from his wanted poster. William decided to wait for him. It seemed he was going to get to do some sheriffing this morning.

Snakejuice studied the man waiting in the road as he made his way down the switchback. That was a lawman if Snakejuice had ever seen one. He smiled to himself. Nothing made Snakejuice happier than starting out his day by shooting a lawman. He ambled the rest of the way down the ridge in a cheery mood. When he got within hollering distance he called out, "Morning sheriff!"

William replied, "Good morning."

He looked Snakejuice over as he approached. He wanted to make sure he had the right man. Snakejuice stopped a few feet in front of him and William was sure it was him.

"You're Sam Denison aren't you?" William asked.

"Yup, that's me," Snakejuice beamed.

"I'm afraid I'm going to have to ask you to hand over your guns and come with me," William said matter of fact.

"Is there a problem Sheriff?"

"I'm afraid there is a matter that needs clearing up Sam. I'm going to need those irons now," William replied.

"Well sure sheriff, I want to clear up any misunderstandings right quick. I ain't one for having doubters."

Snakejuice slipped the bulldog from his holster nice and easy. Gripping it by the barrel he extended it hilt first to the sheriff. William smiled at Sam's reasonable response, ambling his horse forward to relieve Sam of his pistol. Just as fast as a duck on a junebug Snakejuice had Thunder in hand. The crack of the 12 gauge peeled down the main strip just like the hog leg's namesake. William flew from his saddle. His bay reared and raced off out of town.

Snakejuice hopped off his horse with a chuckle. He looked down at the mess of a sheriff. His nice cream colored hat was quickly becoming burgundy as the pool of blood spread in the dirt. Snakejuice picked up his pistol shaking his head. Lawmen were so gullible. He saddled his mare and headed for the saloon down the street knowing that eyes were peeking out from behind curtains. Snakejuice didn't mind, it wouldn't be the last killing of the day by his reckoning.

He reloaded both of Thunder's barrels as he rode down the street. He lashed his mare so that if she strained real hard she would just barely be able to get to the water trough. When he strode into the saloon he gave it a quick once over as he stepped up to the bar. Other than a couple fellas playing poker the saloon was empty this early in the day. The barkeep was sweating profusely and slightly shaking under Snakejuice's gaze.

"Whiskey," Snakejuice demanded.

The barkeep poured him a shot, getting most of it in the glass.

"Leave the bottle," Snakejuice snarled, making the barkeep jump back.

The small man nodded quickly, putting as much pinewood as he could between himself and his newest patron. Snakejuice grinned an ugly rotten smile at the man and tipped back the whiskey, draining the shot without so much as a blink. He felt the barrel under his chin just a split second before the shot was fired. Blam!

"Yeeehaawwww!" the young man hooted. "I did it! I killed Snakejuice Sam Denison! Ya'll remember you were here the day the Cripple Creek Kid killed Ol' Snakejuice."

He spun his shiny colt back in his holster. The fringe from his buckskins danced as the kid twirled back over toward the poker table. For the second time that morning Thunder cracked. Yup, a storm was brewing, Snakejuice reckoned. The kid flew through the fancy plate glass window onto the porch. Snakejuice stumbled forward, pulling the Bulldog. He looked down on the youth through the shattered window and fired all seven rounds into the Kid. Snakejuice reloaded and holstered his guns watching the unmoving men in the saloon. His face bloody, gore leaking out from under his chin, he made his way back to the bar.

"Somebody oughta told that boy 'bout counting chickens," Snakejuice slurred, a strange wet whistling sound accompanying his words.

He took a hefty slug off the whisky bottle with about half of it spilling from the hole in his jaw.

"Jumping Jesus that burns!" Snakejuice exclaimed.

"You go fetch the doc," he pointed at one of the other men at the poker table. "And ya better be quick or else these other two are going to be asking the Cripple Creek Kid just what he was thinking."

The man nodded and scrambled for the doors. The other men looked like they were desperately hoping their fellow didn't split on them. The barkeep huddled behind the bar. Snakejuice whipped out a bandana and held it under his jaw. He probed the hole under his jaw line with his tongue, sending a fresh wave of pain cascading through his head. It seemed like it took a month of

Sundays for the doctor to show up. Snakejuice noted the absence of the fella he sent to fetch him and reminded himself to save the craven a bullet if their paths crossed again.

Doc Forrest was in awe of the wound and how anyone could be so lucky as to get shot under the chin and have the bullet fly out their mouth only chipping a tooth and missing bone, tongue, and arteries. It had him dumbfounded. Snakejuice's request was only slightly more disturbing to him.

"That's right Doc. I said cauterize it," Snakejuice whistled. "I ain't got time to be layed up in no sickbed, nor time fer no stitches. You ain't knocking me out either. I'll take two more swigs of this here rotgut then you are gonna do it or I'm gonna plug ya."

Snakejuice waved the Bulldog for added incentive. Doc Forrest needed no such reminder. He preferred to remain intact and unplugged.

"It's going to hurt like the devil and once it's done there won't be anything for it later," Doc Forrest said as he heated his small forceps that he figured would do the trick.

"Just get to it Doc," Snakejuice grumbled as he took his second swig off the now mostly empty bottle of whiskey.

The remaining men in the Saloon looked on in part amazement part horror at the events unfolding before their eyes. Doc Forrest waited till the forceps were red hot then without so much as an 'are you ready' turned and popped them into the bullet hole. The smell of seared flesh wafted in the air. Snakejuice pounded the bar like a chain gang working on the rail. Doc looked at the wound.

"Well that should do it. It stopped bleeding, but you really should take it easy for a couple days," Doc suggested.

"I got one bit of business to attend to first then I will try to heed your advice Doc," the whistle seemed to be even more pronounced now that the wound wasn't bleeding.

With a tip of his hat to the doc Snakejuice turned and walked out onto the deserted street. He made his way down to the courthouse, leaving his mare tied to the post in front of the saloon.

Snakejuice walked up to the courthouse and kicked open the doors. A mousey looking clerk let out a squeal as he dove under his desk. Snakejuice smiled. Nothing warmed his heart like striking terror in folks. An office door flew open.

"What in tarnation is going on out here?" Judge Reed hollered before his eyes landed on Snakejuice who had Thunder in hand and a mixture of saliva and blood leaking out what Snakejuice was beginning to think of as his blowhole.

Judge Reed grimaced.

"What do you want?" Reed asked hesitantly.

"You the territory Judge?" Snakejuice whistled.

Judge Reed steeled himself.

"I am."

"I'm here to collect this reward," Snakejuice said, pulling a wanted poster from under his poncho. "Says I'm worth eight hundred dollars."

Judge Reed looked baffled.

"I don't think anyone has ever tried to collect a reward by turning themselves in."

Snakejuice sauntered over to the judge.

"You do have the money don'tcha? I heard this here courthouse was where all the territorial monies were kept."

Snakejuice smiled wickedly. Judge Reed looked a little nervous.

Snakejuice continued. "Ya know I reckon maybe that reward oughta be a bit more seeing as how I just killed the sheriff this morning, and I suppose they might even jump it up a bit for the youngster that fancied himself a gunslinger."

Judge Reed looked upset and scared all at the same time, his face turning as red as any barn on the prairie.

"But I figure what will really drive up the offer is killing a judge."

Judge Reed's face turned to one of horror as he realized what Snakejuice meant.

Boom!

Yup, a storm was coming and its name was Snakejuice Sam Denison.

THE GENERAL OF THE SIX-LEGGED LEGIONS
BY FRANK ROGER

Listen! Do you hear that noise? Could that be them? Are they on our trail, are we doomed?

Or maybe I'm simply being carried away by my imagination? But then again, what do you expect in circumstances like these? We all know what we're up against.

Well, I was asked to give an overview of the whole story. Why me? Well, I am a journalist after all, I was among the first to cover this particular chain of events as I happened to be around when it started to unfold, and few people have knowledge surpassing mine about the man who's central to the story.

So I'll start right at the beginning. Here we go.

<u>Humble beginnings</u>

I still remember the first time I met "the General". It was a sunny Sunday afternoon and I was strolling around in Heybourne Heights, my home town, as my attention was drawn to a group of children on the sidewalk. As I came closer, I saw they were watching a man sitting on the pavement in their midst, but I couldn't see what held their interest.

"What's going on, kids?" I asked, and a five-year old boy looked up at me and answered.

"This man has trained ants. They do what he tells them to."

"Really? I'd like to see that," I said, and inched closer for a better view.

There were indeed ants crawling around, lots of ants, and I could tell right away they were not moving at random as ants usually seem to do. They were moving in formation, like soldiers in a military parade, and I failed to see how this trick was being done. The man who was supposedly responsible for this was simply sitting on the pavement, studying the ants in intense concentration without saying a word. The ants now formed semi-circles that moved away from each other, and suddenly they remained motionless, all of them at once. No single ant moved one more step.

The man lifted his head and spoke to his awe-struck audience.

"Now pay attention. This is the grand finale."

He looked down again, staring at the ants as if he was in contact with them. Then the ants stirred into action again, moving in different directions. At first it seemed as if they were dispersing, but it quickly became clear they were arranging themselves into a number of shapes. When they were all in place, they stopped in their tracks, and to my amazement the ants now formed a series of letters. My amazement grew as I noted the letters read ANTS RULE. Was this a joke? Or just some kind of trick?

The man leaned back, sighed as if he was worn out and said, "That's it, kids. The show's over. Bye."

The ants broke up their formation and dispersed, and this time they moved as ants usually do. The kids ran away too, picking up their games where they had left off. Presently I was alone with the man.

"I'm a bit tired," he said. "I need a break. And a dollar or whatever you're willing to give me."

The man looked like a typical homeless person, living on the streets and performing tricks to have some kind of income. I gave him a dollar, and asked him how he did the trick I'd witnessed.

"It's not a trick, really," he said. "You see, I've got special powers. I can get into these critters' minds, and make them do as I tell them. These insects have a hive mind, you know. I can work my way into it, and control them. These ants you saw here aren't trained. They just look as if they are. Actually they're obeying my commands. When they form those words, they're not aware they're forming words, they don't have a clue as to what those words mean, they simply scuttle over to where I tell them to go. But people think I'm performing tricks. Well, so be it. Thanks for the dollar. I hope to see you again. Now please, I'd like to rest. I need it. This thing wears me out. The concentration, the probing, imposing my will. But I'm getting better at it. Goodbye, pal."

He crawled over to the wall of the nearest house, leaned back and closed his eyes.

I looked around. The ants had disappeared, apart from a few still creeping around. The kids were playing off in the distance. I was alone, and decided to let the man take his little nap. I walked on, hoping I would see him again, performing another crazy trick.

And maybe I should ask him some more details about those special powers of his.

Two days later I saw the man again, during my lunch break. He was performing his trick with the ants again, and this time he had attracted a bigger crowd, kids as well as adults. I quickly walked over and noticed that he was doing a variation of the "show" I had already witnessed. When the ants finally formed the letters, the audience reacted with surprise, understandably, and people started asking questions and talking to each other. The man didn't reply, just said he was tired and would appreciate a few bucks. He got a few dollars from the adults, and then the crowd dispersed.

I hung around until I was alone with him, handed him a dollar and smiled.

"I remember you," the man said. "Thanks for the money."

"How are you doing?" I asked.

The man nodded. "I moved a little closer downtown. I seem to attract more people here, and not just kids. Kids watch me do my stuff but don't pay me. I'm getting better at this since I decided to take it more seriously, and I hope I'll make some money with this thing. Anyway, it's all I'm good at."

"How long have you been doing this?" I asked. "And how does it work? And, by the way, what's your name?"

"Call me General," he said, in all earnestness. "I had a special bond with animals, and especially insects, since I was a kid, but lately I set out to improve my skills. I figured I could do more than I used to. It seems to be working. I can't give you any details. I hope you understand."

"Professional secret, right, General?" I said, laughing.

He nodded. A thought struck me.

"I'd like to ask you a favour. You see, I'm a journalist, I work for a local paper here, and I'd like to do a short piece on you. Would that be okay?"

The man stared at me, without saying a word. He was probably thinking about any positive or negative consequences a newspaper article might have on his ambitions.

"If you do a decent piece," he finally said, "it could be a good thing for my shows. Maybe I'll attract some more people, make a few more bucks. So maybe I should go ahead with it."

"Thanks, General," I said. "Don't worry, I'll do a decent piece. You won't regret this. Can we meet sometime tomorrow? I'll take a few pictures of your act, ask you some questions. Is that okay with you?"

"Fine," the General said. We parted company and I went to my office to prepare the article. That was the beginning of the General's media career.

Gathering the troops

Little did I know my short piece on "the General" would be but the first chapter of a long story. I had taken some pictures of him, staring at his "flocks" in utter concentration, and of the ants forming those dreaded words, and had written a short feature on this "local talent" who deserved more attention. I had avoided any sensationalism, such as references to "animal telepathy" or "a supernatural circus act", as some colleagues might have done, and thought the article did the man justice.

I saw "the General" again on and off the following days, usually busy entertaining increasingly big crowds with his ants, and on one occasion with a swarm of wasps, graciously flying around him in arcs and loops, performing a sort of miniature air show, truly a stunning sight. I noticed the man was getting more money with his act, and deservedly so, and people kept asking how he did all this. He still refused to answer these questions, so naturally people started to propose and discuss theories, none very plausible, mostly random guesses at best. Either they assumed magic was involved, whereas some were convinced the insects had been "trained".

I wasn't surprised to find articles about the man in various other papers and magazines soon afterwards, and some of these went straight for the sensationalist approach. "Mysterious man works magic on ants." Or: "Psychic commands armies of insects." I wasn't even too surprised when I saw the "General" appear on TV for the first time.

It was a show on a local TV station presenting all kinds of freaks and weirdoes with "special gifts", and although the "General" fit that bill, I feared that his appearance on that program might hurt his ambitions rather than help him. Basically he performed the act he did on the streets, making his ants march in a neat formation, regroup in semi-circles and even do a dance-like number ("the ballet of the ants" the emcee exclaimed ecstatically), and rounded off the proceedings with the insects forming their by now familiar slogan.

The audience went wild (but then it did after every act), and the emcee thanked the "mad insect magician" for parading his "army of ants" in front of a live audience. It was the first time that I heard the General's insects referred to as his "army", a term he must have liked, as he used it ever since.

In the weeks afterward, I noticed several more pieces about the "General" and interviews with him, and he popped up on a few more TV shows. His fame was rising, and in one newspaper article he stated that he no longer did his act on the streets, as he reached more people on TV and made more money that way.

Barely a month later, I discovered to my surprise (although admittedly it was a logical progression) that the General had his own weekly TV show. For this program people were invited to bet money on his ability to make his ants, wasps and other insect "armies" do whatever the bidder challenged him to. The General would then rise to the challenge, and perform the trick, somewhere "on location" (it wasn't specified where exactly, but I often recognised the rural area around Heybourne Heights), with a camera crew shooting the entire act, in some cases even live. Each TV show presented two such "manoeuvres" of the General's "armies", and invariably the General won the bet.

At first these "manoeuvres" were rather simple, straightforward affairs, where the General was asked to make his hordes of insects assume really intricate shapes or perform complicated choreographies. Soon, however, the challengers started to outdo themselves and systematically went for bigger and bolder things, often involving insects in vast numbers. The General accepted the challenges, but constantly asked more money for his shows, and things kept evolving this way.

For instance, in one show I watched a man challenge the General to "save" his wife, sitting in a leaking canoe afloat in the couple's swimming pool. I saw the General arrive, clad in black and looking rather ominous, and take position at the rim of the pool. Mere moments later, hordes of big red ants appeared, rolled themselves into balls, dropped into the water and moved slowly toward the sinking boat. Still more ants joined the gathering "army", and all of them swam towards the "victim". The balls of wriggling ants all clung to one side of the boat, and pushed it steadily to the rim of the pool. The woman screamed, but it wasn't clear if she was afraid of the sinking boat, the prospect of landing into the water surrounded by ants, or perhaps if she was merely "acting".

Seconds before the canoe disappeared under the water, the woman climbed onto the pool's rim, raised her arms triumphantly, as if she was responsible for her rescue herself, and walked off. The camera moved to the General who rose to his feet, smiled and made the V-sign to proclaim one more victory of his. Sadly, we didn't get to see how the ants got back out of the pool. For all I know, they all drowned.

On another occasion, the General was challenged to liberate a number of squirrels, trapped in wooden cages that had been set on fire. A rather similar scenario ensued: the General arrived, a morose expression on his face, and crouched down. Swarms of wasps followed in his trail, attacked the cages and started gnawing at the wood, inexplicably ignoring the flames that should by all accounts have driven them off. The squirrels darted out of the cages just as the flames leapt up higher, and as the last one fled to safety the wasps lifted off too, a huge cloud blown away on the wind.

In both these cases, and the other ones I watched, it was clear the General was responsible for the actions of the insects. There simply could be no other explanation. Ants don't descend into pools to push boats ashore, and wasps don't attack burning wood, unless some "force" orders them to do so. This force could only have been the General's will.

The last example I mentioned led to some formal protests from animal activists, which the General discarded on his TV show as "totally unimportant rambling from misguided souls who fail to accept the General's authority". It was not clear to me whether this was said tongue-in-cheek or not.

Around this time the General's fame and fortune were definitely on the rise, and I wasn't really surprised to discover he was no longer a homeless person. His affluence had apparently allowed him to rent a house, rather old but still in decent condition, in the outskirts of Heybourne Heights, where he lived and no doubt practised for his "manoeuvres". When one of his "live TV performances" went awry, I decided to pay him a visit, hoping he would still remember me and be willing to do an interview.

The show that went wrong was one where he was challenged to stop a driving car, holding four people, before it reached a certain point. On the images viewers could see four men climb aboard a Land Rover, start the engine and drive off toward a place where a flag was posted. The car had barely advanced ten meters before it was caught in a rolling carpet of termites, and skidded to the side of the road. The termites washed all over their prey, attacking the tyres and possibly also the engine, as the car seemed to have trouble getting back onto the road.

A swarm of wasps descended onto the vehicle, looking for ways to get inside and join the attack. The driver finally got his engine running again, but a dozen meters further down the road the car ground to a halt, and three men flung open the doors and threw themselves onto the ground, desperately trying to get rid of the termites and wasps crawling all over them. It was abundantly clear who had won the battle, but it was also clear that this time the General had gone too far. He hadn't simply told his "army" to wreck the car so it couldn't reach its goal, but had sent his troops after the four men.

To everyone's horror, the fourth man was still inside the car, apparently too badly hurt to flee to safety. By now the General had withdrawn his troops and made his typical V-sign, but I had the feeling this victory might result in the General being court-martialled.

Later on I learned that two of the three men were only lightly injured, but the fourth man who had remained in the car was in bad condition and had to be hospitalized. In an interview on the TV news that evening, one of the victims stated he would take legal action against the General. That same night, I decided to try to arrange an interview with the General. I knew very well he hardly ever agreed to be interviewed, but I figured that if he remembered me, he might make an exception. It was a slim chance, but worth taking.

First Skirmish

I had phoned the General, and had left a message on his answering machine, announcing my visit and telling him to get in touch with me if he preferred another appointment. He didn't get back to me, so I went over, hoping my strategy would work and I would be allowed in.

To my relief the house was not "guarded" by insects, as I had more or less expected, and the General himself opened the door and shot me a questioning look.

"Good morning," I said. "Do you remember me?"

"Yes," he replied after a quick glance and a smile. "I remember you. You're the newspaper guy who did a piece on me when I was still doing my thing on the streets. And now you'd like to do a second piece, I guess. You want to check my progress, right?" he chuckled.

He held the door open, beckoning me to come inside, and added, "Welcome to my headquarters."

He invited me to take a seat on a couch, and the General pulled out a chair for himself. We were sitting in a rather ill-kempt and poorly lit room, with furniture put down haphazardly. Either the General hadn't had the time to clean up the house which had been unoccupied for a long time, or he simply didn't care. I was prepared to see insects, the General's most loyal troopers, all over the place, but not one creature could be seen. Apparently the General only summoned his troops when action was called for.

"You've made some impressive progress," I started off. "Not so long ago, you were a homeless man with hardly any prospects, hoping to get a few bucks for your shows on street corners."

"Yes," he said, beaming with pride. "I worked hard to develop my abilities, and it paid off. I'm making lots of money now, I'm living in a decent place, and I've got a bright future ahead of me. No one can stop me now. You've only seen the beginning of my career, mark my words."

I noticed the burning fervour in his eyes, the pride and self-esteem he was exuding. This was a man who was well aware of his talents, who knew where he wanted to go and how to get there. I could hardly believe this was the same man who had struck me as a wino, earning a meagre living on the streets with an act that had little more potential than to draw the attention of a bunch of kids for five minutes. How had he realized this transformation? And what did it mean for the future? What did he have in store for us?

"What is it you hope to achieve? Do you have an ultimate goal you're working towards?"

"My army is by now invincible," he said, focusing his eyes on something beyond me, perhaps a vision of his glorious deeds to come. "I've reached the point where I can achieve my wildest dreams, and no one can keep me from making them come true. My control over my army is still gaining strength, I can command bigger and bigger legions, and their loyalty is increasing. There is little doubt about the outcome of any battle that will be waged."

It struck me he was thinking in purely military terms. Were the successes the man had achieved getting to his head? Was he living some sort of power fantasy, did he see himself as a superhero out to conquer the world? Was his quick rise from nowhere to the status of TV celebrity driving him nuts? I decided to change the subject.

"Scientists have tried to analyse and understand your special powers, but have so far failed to come up with solid explanations. Your refusal to co-operate is not helping matters, so they say."

"Scientists," the General snorted. "They have no idea what I'm doing, who I am, what powers I possess. Their puny attempts to understand me are of no importance. Ignore their rambling."

"Aren't you afraid the authorities will try to stop you after your recent show where one person was seriously injured?"

"Afraid?" he exclaimed, suddenly furious. "Don't people realize who they're up against? And let me tell you, if the authorities dare to challenge me, they will meet the fate they deserve. And so will these animal activist morons who are constantly filing complaints against me. Who do they think they are? What do they hope to achieve with their foolhardy behaviour? My army will wipe them out. Make no mistakes about that. Now please, leave me to my business. Your questions are beginning to upset me. Don't make me do irresponsible things. Write your piece, put in whatever you want, as long as it's respectful. I need to be alone now."

He showed me out, the pride and enthusiasm I had seen replaced by anger and frustration. Was this man still behaving and thinking normally? Had he been serious? Was this a show he was putting on, a facade that was part of a strategy to enhance his celebrity status, or had I glimpsed the first intimations of hubris and megalomania? I figured time would tell, thanked him for his hospitality and left. I didn't write the piece on him, as the events that followed my interview changed everything.

The General's Fury

As I was having breakfast the next morning, I listened to the news on the radio and heard the newscaster say "We've just had reports come in about what can only be described as an act of terrorism, right here in Heybourne Heights. Late last night, the house of Timothy Ortiz was almost completely destroyed by a veritable tidal wave of termites that literally ate away at the walls and supports until the structure collapsed. Mr. Ortiz and his family had the time to leave their house and are in a state of shock, but not injured. As Mr. Ortiz is one of the animal activists who had repeatedly filed complaints against the so-called General for his shows in which animals are often badly treated, and as the termites displayed extremely unusual behaviour, the General is obviously considered to be behind this outrage. Meanwhile the TV station that aired his shows has decided to suspend these until the recent problem with the challenger who was badly stung by wasps has been sorted out. Possibly this setback sent the General into a fit of rage and led him to seek revenge. The police confirmed a full investigation will follow."

I had barely finished my breakfast as my editor called me on my cell phone, asking me to take a look at Ortiz's house, take some pictures and try to get some additional information from the police, or if possible from the General himself as well, since I seemed to be fairly close with him.

I drove over to the address I had been given and discovered I was not the only journalist who had been put on the case. The house was indeed in ruins, but the police kept us all at a distance too far away to take interesting pictures. I talked to a few colleagues, but learned little of value. I assumed that at this stage the police would not divulge much information either, so I headed straight for the General's "headquarters", hoping for a scoop.

As I arrived there I discovered everyone who approached was kept at a distance as well, not by the police, but by the General's private guards, swarms of wasps, patrolling around the house in thick clouds and attacking anyone venturing too close. There were only a few journalists, and as I conferred with them about what we might do, a police car appeared and stopped right in front of the house.

Swarms of wasps hovered high above the car, but showed no signs of hostility. Was the General inside, pulling back his troops so the police could come and ask him questions, or possibly arrest him? And what would happen if they opted for the latter? Would he surrender and accept his fate?

The moment the two policemen left the car, the wasps came sweeping down and attacked the "intruders". Within seconds, the two men were down on the ground, kicking and screaming and thrashing, totally covered by wasps. They didn't stand a chance.

We all looked in horror at the spectacle, realising two men were being killed here, knowing there was nothing we could do to save them and that any help we called for would arrive too late. As I turned away my eyes, I recalled what the General had told me the day before. No one would stop him. He was in full command of his army, he would make his dreams come true, and all the obstacles on his path would be removed. It was clear that the General had been serious. It was equally clear that he was now descending into madness, and that his dream might well prove to be a nightmare.

Did the General really believe that he could solve his problems by killing those two cops? Did he really think the authorities would consider the case closed and accept their "defeat"? Or was his power really as unlimited as he claimed it was, were his armies truly invincible in the literal sense of the word?

I was sure of one thing as I left the scene of the crime: I had witnessed the beginning of a gruesome episode in the General's career, not its end. The wasps took to the air, leaving two unmoving bodies on the sidewalk, harbingers of dark times ahead.

This means war

Although the General's TV show had been suspended indefinitely, his true media career was only getting underway, even if very different from what he'd had in mind. Unsurprisingly, the incident that had led to the death of two policemen had caught the attention of the media all over the country and beyond.

"Who is this man?" was the question most often heard. "What's the true identity of this self-appointed General?"

I did some research myself, and failed to come up with any hard data on the General. I knew he had arrived in Heybourne Heights as a homeless man, of course, who might easily have concealed his identity. But how could he have signed contracts with a TV station, opened a bank account and rented a house without revealing his true identity? The identities that I did uncover proved to be dead-ends, forged identities, convincing enough for the purposes they had been created for, but unreal all the same. The General had plotted his strategy well, and had chosen an appropriate nickname indeed. Or should I have said "title"?

The next day, the General was back on TV. Only now they were no longer shooting his shows, but rather his attempts at defense against the authorities. I would have liked to be present on the spot, but no journalists were allowed when the police returned to arrest the General. The risk, so we were told, was too high, and the forces of law and order preferred to work under 'controlled circumstances'.

The images shown on TV were shot from a distance, by a crew working for the police. A special unit was sent to the General's house, and the man was informed, presumably by megaphone, or possibly by telephone, that the two dead bodies in front of his house would be retrieved, and that he ought to surrender to the law. If he failed to do so, they would arrest him by any means necessary, including the use of force.

I watched as four figures, wearing full protective clothing, walked up to the house. They did not encounter any resistance, and were able to collect the two bodies. Did this mean the General had given up his fight, or was this merely a symbolic gesture, allowing the "enemy" to take away his "fallen soldiers", without therefore yielding any territory?

Nothing happened for a while. We were told the General had been given an ultimatum. If he had not surrendered at a specific time, they would come and get him. As I had more or less expected, the General didn't show his face. The camera zoomed in on the General's house, where nothing moved. Something did stir in the neighborhood, though. Small swarms of wasps and other insects flew on and off, and a voice-over commented that an unusually high number of red ants had been spotted around the house. The General was preparing his troops, leaving the initiative to his opponent, and would no doubt strike back unhesitatingly.

When I saw the special units, wearing protective clothing and armed with flame-throwers and insecticide sprayguns, along with traditional weapons, I was convinced the General's reign had reached its end. As soon as his "army" was wiped out, he would be defenseless, and surrender would be his only option.

Had I underestimated his special powers, or the troops themselves? Whatever the case may be, the men that marched toward the General's house, apparently fully prepared to do their jobs, scarcely had the time to realize what happened. One moment they were about to force their way into the house, and the next moment they were down on the ground, fighting a losing battle against an army of red ants, eating their way through their clothing, and wasps, arriving from all sides and entering their shredded clothing. Their arsenal of traditional and special weapons was left unused.

None of the special unit men returned. Six motionless bodies were left around the house after the General's victorious army had retreated. The General had won his first real battle, but did this mean he would also win the war?

That same day the local radio station received a message from the General. He informed the authorities they were allowed to retrieve the dead bodies, but any attempt to enter his house or physically harm him would be dealt with in an "appropriate way". It was clear to all what that meant. It was less clear how the authorities would deal with the problem at hand.

I must admit I failed to understand the General's reasoning. What did he hope to achieve by killing off the men sent to arrest him? Did he believe the authorities would simply give up and let him have his way, shrugging off the casualties as "collateral damage"? Did he really think he could get away with murder? Didn't he see he was only making matters worse for himself?

At this point the General had the attention of the international media. News items about his "insect crusade" could be seen on CNN and the BBC, although few camera crews managed to get close enough to shoot valuable footage.

The authorities came up with a new strategy, one that should not lead to more casualties and ought to solve the problem quickly. The whole neighborhood of the General's house was evacuated, and insecticides were sprayed all over the area in the hope of exterminating the General's loyal army and thus render him powerless. No images were shown of this operation, so we had to rely on the information given through official channels.

The day after the "target area" had been "disinfected", a reconnaissance team was sent to check the area for insects. The four men cautiously inspected the surroundings, and reported they saw nothing suspect. They were about to return to their stations and tell the regular forces of law and order to proceed with the next phase of the plan, as they fell prey to the tireless jaws of a multitude of ants and the stings of an armada of wasps. Needless to say, the men didn't stand a chance.

Later that day the General made a phone call to the police, telling them they were idiots if they thought he would allow his troops to be slaughtered, and any men that would be sent to get him would meet certain death. Later that night, an NBC TV crew that had ventured too close was attacked by bees. Fortunately they managed to pull away in time, and only suffered some minor damage.

It was clear now that the General was indeed in full command of his army, that he could control increasingly large numbers of insects, and that they no longer acted only when they were summoned. His control over the insect population was complete and far-reaching. His subjects now acted under the guidance of a human mind, and could no longer be considered or dealt with as mere insects. The authorities would have to adapt their strategy accordingly. Insecticides, for instance, would be virtually useless, as the insects withdrew from any "danger zone" as directed by their human mastermind. This army could only be vanquished by severing it from its command structure; the General.

The Army on the march

The authorities opted for drastic measures, logically enough. The public opinion was outraged by the death of a rising number of law enforcement officers, and there was considerable pressure to stop this insect madness. The international media covered the entire episode and openly criticized the total lack of efficiency displayed by the powers that be, and consequently it was very important for the authorities to deal with the issue quickly and successfully.

So the General was given another ultimatum. He had to sever all the links with his "army", and surrender, otherwise his "headquarters" would be besieged. There would be no further warnings. This operation would be carried out by the armed forces, not by local law enforcement officers, and the intent was to kill the General, not merely to arrest him. One might say that by doing so the authorities fell in line with the General's military thinking. The idea was not to apprehend a criminal suspect, but to eliminate a threat by force. It was hard to imagine how the General would counter an offensive with high-tech weapons, against which his six-legged army would be doomed, but yet he refused to surrender all the same.

The authorities reacted promptly. The General's Headquarters was fired at from a safe distance. Images were shown on TV of the attack, leaving no doubt of the army's intentions. The house was severely hit, and smoke rose in thick columns from various parts. The General's condition was unknown, but for now the authorities decided to wait. They did not have to wait for a long time. Barely an hour after the attack, huge swarms of wasps and armies of termites carried out successful retaliatory raids against the police headquarters and other official buildings in downtown Heybourne Heights. There were no casualties, but the damage was considerable.

The General's Headquarters might have been hit, but the General himself was not down for the count. The war was not over.

At this point Ed, my editor, urged me to make a phone call to the General, and try to arrange an interview.

"Are you out of your mind?" I asked. "The man is barely alive and you expect him to give interviews? And what makes you think his phone is still working? His place is almost in ruins."

"You'll find out if his phone still works when you try to call him. And maybe he still remembers you," Ed said. "Just suppose he does and would be willing to talk to you. It's an opportunity you can't pass up."

I had to admit Ed was right and made the phone call. I left a message on the General's answering machine, not expecting a reply. To my amazement, he did get back to me. The moment I picked up my cell phone and heard that voice say, "Mr. Malgoire, this is the General. You interviewed me a few times before, and I assume you're keen to do a final interview now, right?", I almost dropped the phone.

"Oh yes, I'd like to do another interview," I blurted out. "Are you all right? Your headquarters was badly hit."

"Yes," he said. "About half of my house is no longer usable. Unfortunately I was seriously injured, and there's no way to get the necessary medical treatment without jeopardising my tactical plans. I can't trust anyone, not even paramedics arriving here in an ambulance. It may be an ambush, they may simply turn me over to the police, and I can't take that risk."

"So what will you do?"

"I suppose I won't survive my injuries, and I've made all the necessary arrangements. Even when I'm gone, my army will continue its mission. I will win this war, even if posthumously. The power I have over my army has now developed to the point that I can exert a much greater control than I ever imagined possible. Let me put it this way, I can now mould the insects' hive mind like a computer programmer writing software that will function long after the programmer has gone. Do you see what I mean?"

"Not quite. What is your army supposed to do after your passing?"

"They will seek vengeance. The world will pay the price for the disrespect with which I was treated. I will die, but I'll leave a legacy."

"And what will that legacy be?"

There was silence for a few seconds as the General lapsed into thought. Then he said, "My final revenge. It's all that's left for me to do now. I've always been the loser, the dropout, the guy destined for the gutter. I was still a kid when everything started turning sour, and I wound up in the gutter all right. And then I discovered I had this gift, and I managed to nurture that gift until it allowed me to finally make something of my life, swap my empty present for a bright future. And once again those bastards spoiled the fun, they took it all away from me, turned me once again into a loser. But, you see, I'm a bad loser. I'll spoil the game for everyone now. Those who'll think they've won won't have much time to celebrate."

"What will this final revenge be like?"

"It will be sweet indeed, believe me. I'm busy all the time, briefing my troops, and it's going even better than I anticipated. They're loyal disciples, carrying out my commands with total commitment, and their numbers are swelling beyond belief. You see, I also instructed them to establish contact with other insect colonies, and pass on my sets of commands to them. Those new recruits will in their turn recruit yet others, and so on. My commands will also be passed on from one generation to the next. So my army will increase in strength and numbers exponentially.

While they attack enemy targets, they will convert others to the holy cause, until the sacred mission is accomplished."

"Enemy targets? The sacred mission?"

"The target is mankind. The mission is extermination. If I have to go, I'll go with a bang, and we all go. As I said, I'm a bad loser. Mark my words, dear Malgoire, man is doomed. There's an unstoppable force on the march, out to get you all. Resistance is pointless. Goodbye, Malgoire. Write up a nice piece on me. Your third and last one. Get it into print while there are still people around to read it."

The line went dead after a final chuckle, and I put down my phone. Ed would be happy when he heard I'd done an interview with the General. Until he read the piece.

Lots of papers and magazines, not to mention TV stations and news websites, had done background stories on the General's rise and fall (mostly without coming up with hard facts), and Ed naturally had wanted a scoop. When he saw my piece, he only published a heavily edited version of it, understandably enough.

The day afterwards it dawned on me that the General had been serious. Termites attacked a school in Heybourne Heights, and a dozen children were badly bitten. Other "targets" were hit by wasps, bees and other insects, and this time they destroyed vital utilities (we had no electricity for a while) and hurt people as well. One old man even succumbed to an especially vicious attack by wasps.

The authorities no longer hesitated. A special unit was sent to the General's house, which was shelled with heavy mortar-fire until it could be ascertained no one was left alive inside. The General was no more.

It quickly became clear, however, that dismantling the general command structure did not stop or even slow down the army. Early in the afternoon, the decision was made to evacuate Heybourne Heights. Everyone was transported in buses and army trucks to the neighbouring towns, where we were housed in schools, sports halls and other buildings. On TV we tried to keep up with what was happening in the field.

The authorities at first tried to deal with the "insect plague" in a traditional way; pest control. They soon found out this didn't work, as the insects didn't think and act like insects. They acted according to a strategy, devised by a human intelligence, and that made them a thousand times more efficient, more deadly, more fearsome, and virtually unbeatable. The late General's army also had the advantage of its numbers. Even if a certain amount of insects were wiped out, the army's numbers kept swelling. There was just no keeping track of how and where they were burrowing or flying, what exactly they were doing and how their activities could be thwarted. Usually their plans became clear when it was too late. On top of this, the critters tended to reproduce fast. The combination of insect power and human intelligence proved to be awesome.

As I was watching TV footage of an army truck, covered by ants and wasps and being reduced to a skeleton, I thought about the General's last words, spoken in his final interview. There was something I failed to understand.

Why had the General taken this military thing so far? Surely he must have known he couldn't win. Was he really convinced of his absolute power? Or, the idea struck me, had this intense and constant contact with the insect hive minds influenced and altered his own thinking, had there been a two-way exchange of ideas, had he stopped being completely human and rational? Had he been rational to start with, for that matter? After all, virtually nothing was known about his past. Perhaps he had a psychiatric history.

Or perhaps there was a secret, embedded deep in his mysterious past, that he could not bear to see revealed under any circumstance, preferring to die rather than to be exposed. Had he been a rational man, in the true sense of the word? What had his special talent really been, the capabilities scientists had failed to understand and explain? We'll probably never know how his mind worked. But we'll have to cope with his troops, still following their leader's commands after his death. Might there be any helpful ideas to be gleaned from that final interview I had the privilege to conduct?

A few days later, we were again evacuated. Two reasons were given. Firstly, the number of insect raids against humans, buildings and public facilities was increasing, with mounting efficiency, and so our safety could no longer be guaranteed. A substantial number of people had been injured or sadly lost their lives in those ferocious raids. Secondly, the authorities fought back with pesticides and other unidentified "special" weapons deemed appropriate for the occasion, and this could not be done in an inhabited area. During the large-scale evacuation, people were wondering when they would be able to return to their homes, in what condition they would find these, and if a return would at all be allowed, what with those "special" weapons being used.

Well, that brings us to the present. We're now being housed in a make-shift encampment, hundreds of which have been or are being constructed, as by now tens of thousands of people must be evacuated. We get reports on TV and on the radio about the "progress" that's being made in the war against the insects, but I'm under the impression we're just getting mildly positive and comforting news that's supposed to soothe our troubled spirits and avoid a wide-scale panic, rather than to keep us informed.

If everything's going well, why aren't we getting full reports, with video footage of mountains of dead insects and cheering "exterminators"? And why are they telling us our current housing is only temporary and we may have to be evacuated again very soon?

It's clear to me that an unstoppable force is on its way, and that our counter-attacks have little or no effect. I wonder if this armada of insects will indeed wipe out humanity. Can't the authorities stop them, even if this means resorting to nuclear or other unconventional weapons? Don't they have an arsenal at their disposal that can destroy the planet? (But can they use it without killing us off too?) Or will the six-legged legions march on, conquering country after country, until no man is left? Isn't there a chance that with the passage of time, they may "forget" the General's instructions, that his commands will fade from their collective memory, and their offensive will grind to a halt? Maybe I'm just clutching at the last straw, maybe I'm underestimating the enemy, maybe mankind is too ill-equipped to emerge victorious from this war against another species.

My editor Ed, whom I'm still in touch with thanks to cell phone technology, not yet rendered inoperative by the insect legions, asked me to write a retrospective on the General's "career", which will be posted on the website that's replacing our "former paper version" (Ed's description). So I wrote this, my fourth and maybe final piece on this topic.

And now I'm sitting back and taking a break. It's late in the evening and very quiet. Every time I hear a sound, a word spoken in the distance, a door slamming shut, the humming of an engine, the clatter of footsteps or the creaking of a door, I think the vanguard of the army is upon us.

It's probably just my imagination, but I sense that army is hot on our heels. As I said, it's very quiet now, but I have a premonition it will soon be even quieter.

THE PROFILER
BY JOANNE GALBRAITH

Richard met her in Fairfield Park. She lay on a bench near the bike trail, gazing up at the jewel-blue sky. A warm breeze, perfumed with freshly cut grass, carried her hair away from her pale skin in golden ribbons. Even in death he found her beautiful.

"Do we have an ID?" Richard crouched beside the woman and inspected her fingernails—French tipped and perfect, no hair or skin beneath them.

"We didn't find a wallet, Detective." Nathan, the head of forensics for Cree Hill, snapped a picture of her bare feet. They too appeared pristine, polished, with not a trace of grass or dirt on the soles.

"Any signs of a struggle?"

"None so far. The uniforms are still sweeping the periphery though"

"So the perp killed her somewhere else and carried her here. Probably a male." Richard scanned the jagged line of conifers surrounding the park, shading his eyes against the July sun. "There'd be lots of cover at night and this place is always crowded during the day. He's cautious, but theatrical. He wanted everyone to see her posed this way."

Richard had crawled inside the heads of so many murderers

the process had become second nature. A smile twitched on his lips. He'd always enjoyed puzzles.

"There's no obvious cause of death," Nathan said. "By the look on her face, I'd guess she knew she was a goner." He shuddered. "Creepy."

Richard leaned over the body, staring into vacant green eyes.

"She smells of wine and perfume, and her lipstick is smeared. She knew him, probably intimately." With a pencil he pulled from his pocket, he moved her collar away from her throat. "I don't see any puncture or ligature marks. My guess would be ingested poison. What's your theory?"

"If I had one I wouldn't have called you, oh guru of the dead." Nathan grinned, packing up his gear.

"Get the uniforms to canvas the houses near the eastern entrance. He would have parked on Kennedy Avenue—it's the closest street to the park. And don't leave yet."

"I've bagged everything there is to find."

Richard scratched his stubbly chin, smirking.

"I've heard that before."

"Hell," Nathan scowled. "If you find something I've missed, the drinks are on me tonight."

Laughing, Richard nodded.

"You're on."

While Nathan spoke to one of the officers, Richard searched the ground along the trail. A few yards away from the bench, he stopped and inspected a patch of matted grass at his feet. He followed a line of crushed blades and found a large boot print in the dirt. He waved Nathan over.

"Size twelve Timberlands, I'd guess. Bring your camera and a ruler."

Camera in hand, Nathan crouched beside Richard and squinted at the print.

"You're stretching here, Rich. Anyone could have made this."

"Do you really want to take the chance?"

"Fine," Nathan sighed and pulled the ruler from the back pocket of his jeans. "This doesn't count for the bet, though."

Richard returned to the bike trail. He held his arms as if carrying a woman, walked to the bench and leaned over the way the perp would have. His hair brushed the back of the bench and his knees pressed against the seat.

"Bring me a bag."

Pulse racing, Richard pulled on latex gloves and inspected the wood along the top edge. He lifted a section where the plank had splintered. Beneath, he found two black hairs, one with a follicle.

Nathan jogged back and held out a clear evidence bag.

"How did you see—never mind. You're scary, you know that?"

"If you say so." Richard dropped the hairs inside the bag. "You took samples of the paint on the bench, right?"

Rubbing a hand over his mouth, Nathan looked away.

"Uh—no, actually."

"No?"

Richard raised an eyebrow and lifted his knee to show the flecks of green paint on his grey dress pants.

Nathan groaned and tossed his hands up.

"Fine, you win. Drinks tonight at the Landry."

"Music, sweet music." Richard beamed as he returned to his car.

A week later, Richard arrived at headquarters just after four o'clock. After wading through the handshakes, he found Nathan in the forensics office.

"You called?" Richard flexed his jaw, trying to contain his amusement.

Nathan stood up behind his desk and held out a file.

"A lady in the house closest to the eastern entrance tipped us off about a guy with a Yankees cap carrying a drunk woman. Our vic's name is Cynthia Ross, a waitress from Vinnie's down the street. And get this—the perp is Vinnie, the owner."

"No kidding?" Richard leaned against the door frame and crossed his ankles.

"Yep, and you were right about the poison—he used cyanide. We found the baseball cap and size twelve Timberlands in his apartment, and the DNA from the hair follicle matched. I found jeans with green paint on the knees in the dumpster behind the diner." Nathan chuckled. "One of these days I'm going to figure out how you do it."

Richard's chest tightened, but he forced a smile.

"Don't bet your life on it."

"Yeah yeah, I'd lose. Hey, don't you eat lunch at Vinnie's? I thought I saw you there a few weeks ago."

"I eat there once in a while when I'm in the area."

"I thought so." Nathan shook his head and tossed the file back on his desk. "I guess we can't escape the psychos, even in our own back yard."

"You can't truly know a person, I guess."

"Just do me a favour and watch yourself, Rich. Think like a

monster long enough, and you'll become one."

"Duly noted." Richard's smile faltered.

Nathan headed for the door.

"Want some coffee?"

"Yes please. Cream and lots of sugar."

After Nathan disappeared down the hallway, Richard eased the door shut and listened for footsteps. Satisfied with the silence, he slipped on latex gloves and searched Nathan's desk. From the top drawer, he retrieved a pencil sporting a perfect bite mark and slipped it into an evidence bag. In the next drawer he found a comb, pulled several hairs from it and deposited them into the same bag.

Richard picked up the hiking boots in the corner, wrote the size and brand in his notebook and placed them back on the floor. Smirking, he tucked the evidence bag and his notebook into his pocket while gazing at a framed photo of Nathan's beautiful wife on his desk.

"Be seeing you."

ALONG THE OUTER RIM OF TITAN'S ANVIL
BY CHRISTOPHER STIRES

On the first day of the standoff, Prince Ulrich ordered his best guardsmen to dress in dark clothing and, after nightfall, to assault the stone cabin. The demons barricaded inside kept their promise. Twenty yards from the cabin, as the soldiers edged past a wagon, the demons opened fire with muskets. One guardsman was killed outright. The others, two of them wounded, crawled back to the perimeter sanctuary. When I arrived on the third day, the body of the dead man was still laying where he had fallen.

The rain continued its relentless tattoo as I rode my Appaloosa stallion up the muddy trail toward the Prince's tents. The storms had been coming one after another and had been pounding the principality of Zar since I had crossed its border a fortnight ago. Reports in the out-lying villages were that the River of the Seven Sisters had crested its banks in the eastern region and the mammoth Io River, in the south, was expected to do the same.

A whip-thin soldier, with rain sluicing from his helmet brim, stared up at me as I neared the royal tents.

"We heard you were coming," he said. "You are him, aren't you?"

"I'm no one," I replied.

"I pray you're him. We've captured demons."

I knew the look I saw on the soldier's face. There were over two hundred people surrounding the cabin and all the ones I had seen thus far had the same weary expression. The excitement and thrill of capturing the demons was gone. It had vanished because while the demons were caught, they weren't in custody. They were also warm and dry. The Prince's army, meanwhile, was standing in the rain and muck and doing nothing hour after hour except staring at the body of a dead companion. The army - except for a handful of professional soldiers - was mostly made up of farmers and shopkeepers. Zar had not been at war in over five hundred years. It was a merchant state and remained neutral during all of its neighbors' conflicts. These guards would not be considered professional soldiers in other armies.

Lightning cracked between storm clouds.

I sat on my Appaloosa and appraised the situation. The stone cabin was thirty miles north of the capital and the closest township was Gaul. The cabin - half below ground - stood in a clearing with fifty-plus yards of open ground on all sides. The walls appeared to be granite and the roof, dotted with broken arrows, was made up of hand-cut rock shingles. The windows were covered with thick, heavy shutters. Butted to the west side of the cabin was a corral holding four horses. Three saddles were lined beside one another, hanging, on the fence. Several bundles - food and gear I reasoned - were stacked on the ground near the gate. It appeared that the demons had been surprised while preparing to head out on horseback.

Smart plan.

Ten kilometers north of the cabin was the outskirts of Titan's Anvil - a million acres of mountain-and-lake wilderness. Once in there, it would take an Amazonhenge tracker to find them. No matter which direction they went, they would be gone.

Very smart plan.

My question was why demons needed muskets and horses and gear.

I dismounted, moved onto a rise then surveyed the evergreens and pines encircling the clearing and the cabin. There were only three saddle horses and one packhorse in the corral. On the ride up here, I'd been told that there were nine demons.

"Are you Novarro the Crusader?"

I looked over my shoulder as a handsome bull-shouldered woman in her late twenties limped toward me. She was wearing a long greatcoat and a wide-brimmed hat. As she trudged through the mud, she favored her left leg. It appeared that the knee was giving her havoc. It also seemed that she was used to and accepted the condition.

"Are you Patrick Novarro?" she repeated, limping up the rise to me.

"Yes," I replied.

"I'm DeQuinn Mercy," she said. "Got word yesterday that you were headed our way. The Prince would be honored if you would grant him an audience."

"You're the sheriff of Gaul," I said.

"And tax collector, m'lord."

I had heard her story. A few years ago, DeQuinn, representing the desolate Cimera Plains, had competed in the Decathlon in the Athenia games. The favorite in the event was Jason Mercy from Zar. The two tied in each facet of the contest. The fierce competition between these two could be felt every time they entered the stadium. Then came the final event - the running high jump. Jason won by the length of his toes. The crowd gave both athletes a standing ovation. DeQuinn and Jason were married a week later and returned to Jason's home village of Gaul. While camping in the Anvil, DeQuinn and Jason were caught in a mountain avalanche. DeQuinn's leg was broken. Jason was killed. The elders of Gaul asked DeQuinn to stay. She agreed and became the village's first sheriff. And tax collector.

I looked at the cabin.

"You were the first one up here, weren't you?"

"Yes. Tillerman has lived here for thirty years with his wife and three sons. When I heard what happened at the capital, I came out here with a couple of friends to check it out. Never figured anything would come of it."

"But something did," I said.

"The sons were preparing to saddle the horses when we arrived. Never got a chance to say anything. They saw us and rushed inside the cabin."

I nodded, picturing the scene in my mind.

"We all went for positions and fired a few rounds at each other," she continued. "Didn't hit anything I know of. Ferris stayed with me, Oliver went for help. He came back with some guardsmen. The Prince showed up the next day. The joke's on Tillerman and his sons. There was just me and Ferris pinning them in there. They could have stomped us with little fuss and been on their way into the Anvil before the guardsmen got here."

"How many did you see?"

"The three sons and the father. Saw him standing in the doorway as the sons ran inside."

"Four … I was told that there were nine."

"The tale is growing. I only saw four, sire."

I nodded.

"Tell me Tillerman's story."

DeQuinn flipped the collar of her greatcoat up.

"Tillerman is a horse trader," she said. "He's always been a horse trader - just workingman's stock. Nothing a noble or soldier would want. They're poor people. We've never had any trouble with the Tillerman clan until recently. Tillerman the Patriarch was telling anyone who would listen that Lord Amondo was a dishonorable blackheart who would steal from the angels themselves to increase his purse."

"Who's Amondo?"

"The richest merchant in the province."

"Why was Tillerman vilifying this merchant?"

DeQuinn sighed.

"A few months ago, Tillerman's wife left the family. She became Amondo's maid."

And thus the blood feud began.

I looked at the cabin and corral again. I noted that the horses were huddled calmly together under the eaves of the cabin.

"Why aren't those animals crazed? They haven't eaten in over three days?"

DeQuinn cleared her throat, glancing down at the mud.

"I've been feeding them."

"You have?"

"Yes. Had some hay brought here and every day, about mid-day, I walk out there and feed them."

"Tillerman agreed to that?"

"Yes. I go unarmed and someone inside watches me the whole time but I don't do anything except feed the horses and they let me be."

"Tillerman won't let you collect the dead body but he'll let you feed the horses."

"He likes the horses."

"Interesting." A notion began to take hold. "So, DeQuinn, how did we end up here?"

DeQuinn told me the story. A few days ago, Tillerman went to the capital. He attempted to see his wife. Forced his way into the Amondo household; intended to drag the wife back to their home. Amondo had his guards rough Tillerman up and pitch him, battered and bloodied, back into the street. Witnesses said Tillerman's wife saw it all and laughed. She jeered that her life scrubbing Amondo's chamber pots was a thousand-fold better than the miserable life she had with him.

I shook my head. How sad, how cruel.

DeQuinn continued.

"The next morning the bodies of Amondo and Tillerman's wife were discovered in the house's library. Their throats had been slashed and they had been staked through the body. No one in the household heard anything out of the ordinary during the night. Nothing."

"No one heard anything," I finished, "and only a demon can murder without making a sound."

DeQuinn scanned the people surrounding the cabin.

"Ask any of them. We have captured demons."

I walked the Appaloosa toward the tents.

I'd heard the legend about Zar during my travels. It was said that a changeling demon lived among the people here. That it moved about in human form unnoticed, unrevealed. It snatched the breath from newborns and memories from the elders; it ruined the dignity of good men and women with rum and promises of easy fortunes.

"I came to Zar," I said, "because I was told that a demon resided here … all demons know at least one passageway to Hell."

"Yes, we have our demon legends and stories," DeQuinn replied. "You have my sympathy, Crusader. I know what it is like to find your soul-mate then lose them."

I did not answer. She did understand. There was nothing else to say on the matter.

"Shall I present you to the Prince?" DeQuinn asked.

"Yes."

She hesitated. Pondering.

"Ask, DeQuinn. Just ask."

"Is it true, Crusader, that Satan himself gave an oath that you would never be harmed by him or any of his minions?"

*   *   *

I have met Satan.

Twice.

On the first occasion, his appearance was so terrifying that it nearly edged my mind into the abyss. He moved untouched past fire geysers and shredding bramble thorns and with each step crushed to powder the skulls and bones that littered the ground beneath him. Formless and bewitching creatures hovered in his mammoth shadow. They were the siblings Fear and Madness, Horror and Sin.

On the second occasion, he was beautiful. No artist could ever hope to capture the seductive allure of the banished angel. Rich blond hair feathered around his chiseled-perfect face and down to his massive shoulders. His eyes were deep indigo-blue and his mouth firm and inviting. A gossamer, fire-yellow tunic was molded over his lean, muscled torso and arms; ice-black breeches cloaked his long legs. Demons, hundreds of them, crouched at his feet with bowed heads.

Satan hates and despises me.

I defeated the Griffin Vampire at Shankur and the necromancer of Camd'n Rin. I have sailed the River Styx and returned physically unscathed. I saw the destruction of the demon sanctuary at Ananyas and bested the Beast of Lyoness.

Satan has placed a bounty upon my head.

I am a hunter and I am the hunted.

My life was not always so. Once I was a quiet scholar of books and letters. A blade, let alone a pistol, had never crossed my palms.

I was blessed. The angels in Heaven were envious of my life. This was because Lenore was my bride and she loved me. Yes, I was indeed blessed.

Late one winter night however, a highwayman attempted to steal my meager purse and, during the robbery, my heart was pierced by the outlaw's blade. As I lay dying, no doctor or shaman able to save me, Lenore bartered a covenant with Satan. Her immortal soul for my life and for me to live the remainder of my years without harm from Satan or his servants. Satan examined my insignificant life and agreed.

It is said that no demon or angel could have imagined the warrior I would become.

Except Lenore.

She now stands at Satan's side and cheers each time I defeat the Underworld's minions.

I have met Satan. He keeps my loving and beloved Lenore. I will not rest until I can free her.

*   *   *

Prince Ulrich was sleeping. The on-going siege of Tillerman's farm had exhausted the fourteen-year-old monarch.

As the Prince was awoken, DeQuinn introduced me to the merchant Amondo's younger brother, Edwin. I had learned over the years not to make judgments based on first impressions. I had been wrong too many times when I had. Still, something was amiss about Edwin and the few words that passed between us left a sour taste in my mouth.

I also noted that DeQuinn's demeanor changed when she saw that Edwin was waiting inside the Prince's tent. Her posture turned stiff and her sentences became short and curt.

With the merchant were his two bodyguards. I would later learn that their names were Wilson and Math. I knew immediately that these ronin were from the Daarmoor region. They wore the short broadswords and chain-mail vests that were common in the army there. Both carried a Cordoba flintlock pistol in their belts. Wilson had a large brass armlet covering the bicep of his right arm. Thieves, deserters, and laggards were branded on the bicep before being turned out of the army. Both of Math's ears were notched. That, along with dismissal from the army, was the Daarmoor punishment for being drunk on duty.

Someone should warn Edwin about the trustworthiness of his bodyguards. That someone would not be me.

Prince Ulrich, dwarfed by several advisors, smiled as he approached DeQuinn and me. He was a small, slender boy with a freckled face and thick red hair.

Edwin stepped toward the Prince, to speak to him, but Ulrich waved the merchant back. It was clear that Edwin was not pleased that an untitled commoner was being received before him. He barely contained his scowl.

DeQuinn and I bowed as the Prince reached us.

"Your majesty, may I present Patrick Novarro," DeQuinn said.

Ulrich held out his hand.

I started to kiss his signet ring as was the custom in this kingdom.

Ulrich pulled his hand back.

"No, no. Greet me as you would a fellow warrior."

He held out his hand again. I placed my forearm along his and grasped him around the elbow as he gripped me. We shook and a wide smile appeared on Ulrich's face.

His advisors applauded.

He pointed at the pistol holstered on my hip.

"Is that the revolver pistol designed for you by the great gunsmith of Shankur?" he asked.

"Yes, your majesty."

I drew the pistol and handed it to him. The Prince examined it closely.

"I have never seen a revolver pistol before. It is an impressive and frightful creation." He returned the pistol to me. "Walk with me, Crusader. You too, DeQuinn."

The Prince moved to a rear opening in the tent and gazed out at the cabin.

"You must be honest with me. I will never learn if all I hear are compliments. The other day my advisors praised my bowel movement."

I chuckled.

DeQuinn quick-glanced at me. I'd broken a royal rule it appeared. But Ulrich smiled again.

"No one in my court laughs when I make a joke. Not until I laugh first. You did. We are friends already, Crusader."

"We are, your majesty," I replied.

"When we arrived, I had my soldiers surround the house," he explained. "The door we see is the only door but there are windows in the other walls. All are covered with heavy shutters. All are being closely watched and all who were inside when we arrived are still inside."

"Very thorough, your majesty."

"We do not know how stocked the house is with food supplies. They could have enough to last them for weeks or even months."

"That is possible, sire."

"My attempt to talk them into surrendering was rejected. The elder Tillerman called out that he would not receive a fair trial. My personal assurance that he would was met with silence. My plan to swarm the house under the cover of darkness failed and cost the life of a brave soldier." Ulrich sighed. "I would prefer not to lose any more lives in our capture of the Tillerman clan."

"You could take your people home, your majesty, and let Tillerman and his clan go. My guess is that they would head into the Anvil and never return."

"My brother's murderer must pay for his crime," snapped Edwin from behind us.

Ulrich turned and gazed evenly at Edwin. Edwin lowered his head.

"My apologies, your majesty, for my outburst. My emotions overcame me."

Ulrich looked back at me.

"Murder, whether of noble or of beggar, will not go unanswered in Zar as long as I am monarch."

I nodded.

"A question about the attack. When the clan fired upon your soldiers, sire, did they shoot at the same time or was the shooting of the muskets spread out?"

"What difference does that make?" Edwin growled.

A shocked murmur moved among the advisors.

"Why are we listening to this drifter, your majesty?" Edwin continued. "When the cannon arrives from Quantero, we will end Tillerman's defiance and send the demon murderer to Hell."

I knew it was best not to speak. But.

"No one saw Tillerman inside your brother's house a second time. No one saw the murders take place. There are no witnesses that he actually committed the crimes he is accused of."

"I say he did. That is enough for all. Are you challenging me, drifter?"

I smiled.

"I lack the skills of a tarot reader or politician, m'lord. If I'd challenged you, you wouldn't have to ask if I had."

The veins pulsed on Edwin's neck.

"No one talks to me in that manner any longer."

"Stop." Ulrich raised his hand between us.

Behind Edwin, Wilson and Math stepped closer to him. Wilson drummed his fingers on his pistol. DeQuinn rested her hand on my shoulder.

"Master Edwin," the Prince said, "because of your grief, I have allowed you some latitude in my presence today. But my leniency does have its limits."

"Please, pardon me, your majesty," he responded quickly.

Ulrich turned to me.

"Disrespect to my people is disrespect to me, Crusader."

I bowed.

"I ask humbly for your forgiveness, my lord. It's no excuse but I am uneducated in the ways of court and ask for guidance so that I do not unintentionally offend."

Ulrich heard the words "unintentionally offend" and clearly understood my meaning. He decided not to explain the words to Edwin.

"DeQuinn will assist you with proper court protocols, Crusader." He looked back at Edwin. "You may retire and regain your composure."

Edwin bowed. He and his bodyguards moved away from us.

Wilson looked at me and nodded. This was not over he seemed to be saying.

Ulrich studied the cabin again.

"You wouldn't have to ask if I had. I may say that the next time I meet with my council. I can already picture the looks on their faces."

I remained quiet. This time.

The Prince pointed at one end of the cabin then at the other as he thought.

"Four or five shots were fired from inside the house."

"I believe the shots were spread out and not fired in a volley, your majesty," DeQuinn said.

"I agree. Single fire. What does that tell you, Crusader?"

"Perhaps nothing. I am just gathering as many facts as I can."

"I've devised a new plan to get the Tillerman clan to surrender. My hope is that it'll succeed and I won't have to use the cannon," he said. "My plan is that I'll create a diversion. While the clan is watching me, a volunteer will sneak onto the roof of the cabin. That person will drop a smoke mortar into the chimney then cap it. The smoke will fill the cabin and force them out. I would like your opinion of my plan."

"I believe that would force them outside."

"Am I mistaken or do I hear a but in your response?"

"If I may, your majesty," DeQuinn replied, "there is a good chance that the clan would exit but they could come out shooting."

"Yes." Ulrich sighed, disturbed by the possibility. "Three lives have already been lost and it appears that more will be lost no matter what I do."

"Perhaps not, my lord," I said. "With your permission, I'd like to go talk to Tillerman. I'll need two unarmed volunteers to accompany me."

"Unarmed volunteers?"

"While I speak with Tillerman, they will retrieve your fallen soldier. I would consider it an honor, your majesty, if you would safeguard my pistol when I go to the cabin."

"Two is not necessary," DeQuinn said. "I'll go with you and I can carry the body by myself."

"You're needed for a different task."

"What task?"

"I need a witness to my conversation with Tillerman. So tell me again when you feed the horses?"

* * *

The rain had stopped as I joined DeQuinn and her two companions, Ferris and Oliver. We were all unarmed.

Several yards behind us, Ulrich watched intently. Edwin stood beside the monarch and the Prince's advisors and guardsmen surrounded them both. I noted that Wilson and Math were not among the gathering.

DeQuinn lifted a bundle of hay onto her shoulder.

"A short while ago, we received word from the capital. Two servants now claim they saw Tillerman inside the Amondo's main house after midnight."

"Of course they did," I said.

"I asked about. Amondo had no wife or children. His entire estate and business goes to his younger brother."

161

"How fortunate. Now no one will speak disrespectfully to Edwin any longer."

"Yes. And he will no longer have to live on the meager stipend Amondo gave him."

I nodded.

"Shall we go?"

We four sloshed across the saturated clearing toward the cabin. I could tell that Ferris and Oliver already regretted their decision to volunteer. They were perfect for the task given them. Neither was a hero or a fool. They would do what they'd been asked to do and no more. Or less.

DeQuinn separated from us and headed toward the corral.

We continued toward the wagon. Each step in the clinging mud was a chore. There would be no swift run across this ground. Oliver slipped and fell to his knees. One of his boots had been sucked off his foot by the mud. Ferris retrieved the boot. He did not jeer or make jest of his friend. Both solemnly watched the cabin door and windows looking for rifle barrels to appear. But no movement came from within the cabin. One of the horses whinnied as DeQuinn neared with the hay.

We three reached the wagon. Ferris and Oliver moved slowly to the body of the dead soldier.

"Tillerman," I called. "I ask to speak with you. We are not armed."

The door of the cabin cracked open.

"Go back or I will fire whether you are armed or not," Tillerman said. "We have nothing to talk about."

I motioned to Ferris and Oliver. They lifted the body of the soldier.

"I did not mean to kill the soldier," Tillerman called. "I aimed for his shoulder and missed. For that I am sorry."

"I accept your word on your intent."

Ferris and Oliver carried the soldier back toward the tents.

DeQuinn slipped inside the corral with the horses.

"You have the soldier's body," Tillerman said. "There is nothing more to say."

"There's plenty to say. First, you and your sons aren't demons."

Tillerman did not respond.

"Second, your sons escaped three days ago into the Anvil. DeQuinn had the front of your cabin covered but not the back. They went out the rear windows and out to the saddle horses hidden in the trees. You have accomplished what you set out to do. You kept the Prince's army here. Your sons won't be found unless they want to be so they are safe."

The door opened wider.

"Come forward. Keep your hands where I can see them."

I moved toward the door. The inside of the cabin was dark and filled with shadows. I could not tell where Tillerman was.

"I did not kill Amondo or my wife," he said.

I stepped down into the doorway.

"The Prince will listen to you. He has given his word."

"The Prince is but a boy. He still believes in honor and justice. He has not yet learned about the black heart of men – how they can do evil then lie about it and get others to do their evil bidding for them."

"On this we agree. Man doesn't need demons to entice him to wickedness, he does quite well on his own."

I stepped inside the cabin and stopped beside a table. Slowly, my eyes adjusted to the dim interior. Tillerman stood across from me with a rifle tucked in the crooks of his arms. Four other rifles, primed and loaded I assumed, were scattered around the cabin near windows.

From the corner of my eye, I saw DeQuinn's shadow cross over the cracks in the corral window shutter. She was listening.

"I did not murder them," he repeated. "But how do I prove I did not? I was there that day and I threatened both of them. I did kill the soldier. I would rather die in my home here than choking for a day on the gallows. The capital hangman is not a master of his profession."

I stared at Tillerman. Something was amiss about him.

Outside, I heard voices calling out but their words were unclear.

"If you allow it," I said, "people will believe you murdered Amondo and your wife and the true murderer will win out."

"How do I prove I did not?"

I studied him. Then I saw it. He was holding the rifle in his arms. I knew what was amiss. I knew and could prove that he didn't murder Amondo and his wife.

I stepped closer to the table. In the middle was a bowl of apples. Picking one up, I juggled it in my hand. Then I tossed the apple to him.

Tillerman was startled but he still, without dropping his rifle, caught the apple in the crook of his arm.

I nodded.

"Did a horse break the bones in both your hands? How long has it been since you could hold a fork and spoon?"

"I can still shoot my rifle. That finger works fine."

"But you cannot grip a knife," I said. "Your wife and the merchant were murdered with a knife. Put the rifle down and come with me."

Tillerman did not respond.

"Restore your name for your sons."

Tillerman, at last, lowered his head then nodded. He stepped to the table.

"Novarro!" DeQuinn yelled from the corral.

I spun about, dropping low as I turned.

Wilson and Math moved into the doorway with their pistols raised. They fired.

The rounds thudded into Tillerman's chest. He gasped and collapsed to the floor.

Math retreated into the muddy yard as Wilson reloaded. Even the best marksmen need at least fifteen seconds to reload.

Fifteen seconds. A long time.

I grabbed the rifle leaning against the wall near the door, cocked it as I aimed and pulled the trigger.

It misfired.

Wilson laughed as he finished reloading.

I jumped across the room and grabbed the rifle the dead Tillerman still held.

From a kneeling position, I aimed the already-cocked weapon as Wilson aimed at me.

I fired first.

The round nailed Wilson between the eyes, just above his nose, and exited the back of his skull. He fired into the ceiling as he went down.

I jumped to the doorway.

And I saw it all.

Math stood ankle-deep into the mud. He had given up reloading his pistol and drawn his broadsword.

From the corral, DeQuinn raced across the yard to him.

Math swung the sword at her. She blocked his swing with her left arm then punched him squarely in the midsection with her right. Then she followed with a quick left and another right to the face. Math grunted and the sword fell from his hand as he swayed but - rooted in the mud - remained upright. DeQuinn spun completely around and hammered Math with a sweeping high kick to the side of his head. He dropped unconscious, his jaw clearly broken, to the ground.

The rain began to fall again as I sloshed from the cabin to DeQuinn's side. Across the clearing I saw that the Prince had my revolver pistol aimed at Edwin while he ordered his guardsmen to arrest the merchant. Edwin could be heard saying he had not ordered his bodyguards to attack the cabin. Ulrich plainly did not believe him.

In the next few days, all would come to know about Edwin's treachery. He met his fate on the gallows executed, as Tillerman had said, by a hangman who had not yet mastered his profession. It was said that he was hanged four times before it was done right.

The Tillerman sons never returned to Zar. But the horses they raised in Titan's Anvil became much sought-after mounts throughout the kingdoms and frontier.

For the long reign of Prince Ulrich, he was always known as an honorable and just man. He was well admired by his people, by both noble and commoner, until the end of his days. The high regard was deserved.

"I'm glad you are unharmed, Crusader," DeQuinn said. "I didn't see the cowards until they'd reached the cabin."

"Being mortal has its limitations. I suggest you sink your boots down into the mud before it is seen that you are standing above it."

DeQuinn quick-snapped her head toward me. Then she lowered her feet down into the mud.

We didn't speak for a long moment.

Finally it did.

"I did not harm DeQuinn and Jason," the demon said. "I was following them as they traveled in the Titan's Anvil. I admit that I intended to wreak havoc upon them. But the mountain avalanche occurred before I could. They knew it was coming. There was a crevice to hide in but it was only large enough for one. Both pleaded with the other to use it but neither would. They perished embracing each other."

I nodded. I understood.

"I had never seen such thing," it continued. "I had heard the story of the Lady Lenore and you but I did not believe. I was overcome with sadness at the couple's demise. I had never felt that emotion before. Petty mortals such as Amondo and Edwin I recognize and understood but mortals like DeQuinn and Jason I did not. I decided to take DeQuinn's body and make it my own. I wanted to walk among other mortals and see if more such as them existed."

"And?"

"There are others. Many more. And I was surprised that I formed a friendship with Ferris and Oliver. Knowing them has brought me happiness and pleasure. Those emotions still feel strange but I savor them. Some day I hope to experience love for myself." The demon sighed sadly. "I shall miss the sensual delights of inhabiting this female body. I'll miss living among these people. I have learned much from them."

"Then why leave? You're no longer what you once were. The people here are safe from your old ways."

It stared at me, confused.

"I have no proof that you are a changeling and I rarely participate in gossip. Never had the knack for the art." I turned the collar of my coat up against the falling rain. "Is there an inn in your township where we might share a meal? Perhaps Ferris and Oliver can join us."

"The doorway," it said, "I once used between this world and the Underworld no longer exists. I cannot help you with your quest."

"Then I continue my search."

I started forward. DeQuinn stepped beside me.

"One day, Crusader, you will find a passageway into Hell. When you do, send word to me. I would be honored to ride at your side to free the Lady Lenore."

We shook hands as friends do.

I knew that one day I would send word to DeQuinn to accompany me into Hell to free Lenore. I knew I would.

LRRH2011
BY ROB ROSEN

"LRRH2011." It was her online name, one she'd used successfully for well over three years now. That day, like all the rest, the send button had just been pressed and she had only to wait the briefest of seconds for a reply. It was, of course, her picture that drew them in; young and sweet and innocent, her dimpled chin tilted downward, her large doe eyes open wide, staring intently into the camera, watching, waiting, and oh so eager. Come and get me, they seemed to say.

"Suckers," she whispered, with a bored shrug.

"BBWolf." The name blinked on her screen in a bright green, Times New Roman font. "Cute pic," the message read. "That really you?"

"Oh, it's me, all right," she replied, a knowing smile spreading wide across her face. "And even cuter in person, or so I've been told."

"Yum," BBWolf typed. "Good enough to eat."

She smirked, her fingers caressing the keyboard, her hands moved hummingbird-fast. "Eat, maybe. Good is debatable."

"LOL." The letters flashed. Needless to say, she wasn't in a laughing mood, out loud or otherwise. At least not yet. "And I *am* hungry," he quickly added. "Ravenous even."

"Too bad," she typed. "Kitchen's closed for the night. On my way out the door to grandma's house. I'm hooking up the cable to her PC today. Poor Granny, doesn't know a thing about computers."

The bait changed from time to time, but the response was generally the same. Throw out the hook; there was always some sort of lowlife catch to snag onto.

"U R in luck," came the anticipated reply. "Geek Squad ex-employee here. PC specialist. Can help. For free."

Her smile rose up, turning ever northward. Same old story. Helpless little girl, a babe in the woods. Or so it would seem. "Gee, free? It must be my lucky day," she wrote back, the words careening around the Internet, quick as lightning, hitting their target like a bullet between the eyes.

Another flashing response appeared. "Yep, free. Just for you. Special offer. What's the address?"

She could practically feel his hunger now, hear the snarl, pulsing off her computer screen. Her fingers paused above the keyboard, hovering, deciding which letters and in which order to select. So many options. So many. "No strings attached?" she asked.

No pause on his end, however. Then again, there rarely ever was. "Small strings. Thin strings. Strings light as a spider's web. Bring me a basket of goodies for my services. It's all I ask for in return."

"Good deal," she typed. "The address is…"

But the message was suddenly blocked. Lost in the ether. An unexpected turn of events, to be sure. "Webmaster Woodsman," appeared the words in brilliant cautionary yellow. "No addies," came the admonishment.

"Bug off," BBWolf responded.

"Yeah, bug off," LRRH2011 echoed, her smile vanishing in the blink of an eye, her lips pursing tight as a drum. "Nobody asked you."

"No addies," the webmaster repeated, the words filling the screen in a size 72, bold, italic font, flashing like a firefly's ass. "It's not allowed on this server. Not safe."

Now LRRH2011 did indeed laugh. "Hey, Prince Charming, knight in shining armor, help appreciated, but not necessary. Granny needs cabling. Find a different distressed damsel to rescue," her fingers furiously typed, and then, "BBWolf, the addie is now on MySpace. Basket is already packed. See you in sixty."

And with that, the screen went black as coal, dead as night. BBWolf had been on her radar for some time now. And he wasn't getting away. No sir, no how. She licked her lips. After all, he wasn't the only one who was hungry. Then it was off to Granny's house, skipping in girlhood glee all the way there, basket swinging from the crook of her arm, heavy with its hidden load.

The house was unexpectedly dark upon her arrival. Dark as pitch. The lights were usually on, blazing bright, attracting those nasty moths to its flame. She crept up to the side and peeked into the window. A shadow moved across the bare wood floor. Then two. Close shadows. Practically side by side.

"Uh oh," she muttered, grasping the basket good and tight for reassurance. "BBWolf is not alone. Two against one. Really, so not fair." Strangely, the smile returned, plastered to her pretty face. The odds, after all, were still in her favor, all things considered. "Goodies," she whispered, patting her stash. "Just like you asked for."

Cautiously, she climbed up the stairs to the front of the house. The latch was open, the door ajar, squeaking as she pushed it open. "Granny?" she uttered, her voice hesitant, meek, not her own. Not by a long shot. Timid, after all, was never her thing. "Granny, are you home?"

"In here," came the response, high-pitched, crackling with fire and brimstone and all things very un-granny like. "In the computer room, dear."

She entered, the floorboards creaking beneath her shoes, the sound echoing in the tight space around her. The only light came from her left, the blue from a screen, casting a pale moon-like glow. Ominous. Cold. She followed it to its source. A lone figure sat in a chair, a blanket draped over its head and body, fanning outward like a shroud.

"Granny, are you okay? Why are all the lights off?" she asked, her breath lodged in her throat, a lemon-sized pit forming in her belly. Something was off, different than normal.

"Not all of them," came the near-whispered reply. "The computer's is enough to see you by, my dear. And look how nice you look. Good enough...good enough..."

"To eat?" she giggled, despite the direness of the situation. "So I've been told." Repeatedly and often.

The figure growled, baring yellowed, jagged teeth. "Come closer, dear. Let Granny get a better look at you."

She inched in closer, closer still. "My, Granny, I do believe you're drooling."

The figure twitched. The voice deepened. "Just eager to kiss you, my dear. Kiss your tender, young skin. Come closer, dear, and let Granny give you a great, big kiss."

A muffled sound came from beneath the blanket; a slight tremor shook the center of it. "Your stomach is growling, Granny. Lucky for you, I brought a basket of goodies." She patted the basket, her smile beguiling.

The figure's growl turned to a groan, sending a sickened chill down her spine. "First the goodies, then the kiss," he told her, licking his chops.

Her heart beat even faster, racing in her chest like a runaway train, the sound roaring in her ears. She reached into the basket and felt the cold certainty of what lay inside. Her fears were allayed. Two against one? No matter; her *one* was good enough. Always enough.

"Granny," she said, staring at the monitor. "You know, those computers can be very dangerous. People hide in waiting on the other side of the connection. Bad people behind innocuous names. *Big, bad* people, in fact."

"Predators in search of prey," the figure rasped, standing up so that the blanket shifted and dropped. "*Hungry* predators." On the floor, sitting cross-legged and trembling, was a man with a gun pointed at his head, the shiny black of it barely discernable in the computer's dim light.

"Now come give Granny a kiss or the webmaster gets it."

She stared down at her would-be rescuer, surprised that such a man still existed outside of fairytales. She smiled, her heart again fluttering. Almost melting. Almost. "Let him go. I'll kiss you. As much as you like. *He* can even watch, if that's what turns you on." She sidled in closer, her face contorted into a mischievous grin, her own proverbial fangs now bared, the doe eyes now sly as a fox's.

The man above kept the gun pointed at the man down below. All in all, it was a good place for it to be. Better than pointed at her, at any rate, she figured. He stared as she approached, rapt in awe, in amazement, in lust. Her mouth parted, as did his. She drew ever nearer, until her breath could be felt on his neck. He shivered, moaned. Her hand rose and stroked the side of his head. Not soft and warm as he expected, but cold, hard, steely.

"Goodies," she purred, pulling the trigger.

A burst of light flooded the room, as did the nearly deafening boom. The standing man was standing no more but was now crumpled in a heap on the floor, the crimson pooling, flooding around him.

"LRRH2011?" the only man in the room still alive asked, his voice wispy, faint.

"The L is for Lieutenant," she responded. "And I thought I told you, I don't need rescuing."

He stood up on wobbly legs and managed a weak smile. "That picture you use, I thought you were a little girl."

She laughed, putting the gun back in the basket for safe keeping. "I was, when it was taken," The laughter grew, her eyes suddenly aflame. "But I'm all grown up now. Wolves don't like adult flesh, you know. Too *tough*."

His laughter echoed hers. "Good word for it. And thanks for saving me."

"Thank you yourself. For trying, at least, to rescue me."

"At *least*," he repeated, with a heavy sigh.

"Well, Woodsman, some girls just don't need rescuing. Some girls are fine and dandy all on their own." She paused, taking him in. In fact, he was pretty nice to look at, now that he finally stopped shaking. "But keep trying. *This* girl appreciates the effort." She smiled and walked him back outside. "And a happy ending," she added, coyly, her red cape fluttering in the crisp autumn breeze. "Isn't that how all good stories end?"

"Or begin," he replied, a smile so big and bright as to put the sun to shame.

"Ah," she said, with a grin of her own and a spring to her step as the two of them walked away from the house. "You mean, the stuff that happens after happily ever after. I always wondered about that. Are lessons learned, straw houses rebuilt with brick? Evil step-sisters kicked to the palace curb?"

"Dwarfs go out and hire a housekeeper, gingerbread house oven gets replaced by a microwave?" he added, his arm brushing hers, a spark riding up both their backs like wildfire.

They reached her car. "Need a lift?" she asked, tentatively.

He shook his head, a frown now evident. "Mine's just down the street." He paused, unsure of what to do next, the circumstances behind their meeting so strange. "But, um, thanks, thanks again for rescuing me."

"No problem," she replied, getting into the car and rolling down the window. "And thanks for *almost* rescuing me." She waved and slowly pulled away, a pang in her heart despite having just met him.

He waved in return and hollered, "Next time, for sure!"

She watched as he grew smaller and smaller in her rearview mirror. "Next time, huh?"

175

Her car sped away, back to her house, back to the grind. What choice did she have? It never ended, really. The wolves were always out there, always on the hunt. She turned on her computer and scrolled around, searching. It didn't take long to find another one. She wasn't surprised. The same address was given as before, the previous mess already cleaned up, she was certain. That's just how it worked.

Though this time was different.

She got there before him, the house dark, empty this go around. As she had guessed, nothing but a bleached stain remained from her last visit. The computer was left on, though, the place dead quiet. She logged in; the quarry was nowhere to be found, no messages. "I'm waiting," she typed, anxiously, her hand resting on her basket. "Goodies are getting cold." She laughed, more out of nerves than anything else. The job must've been getting to her, she figured.

Ten minutes turned to twenty. "Maybe this one learned his lesson already," she said, getting up and walking to the kitchen. "Lucky me." She opened the cupboards; they were bare. "Guess that luck of mine ran out. Maybe next time I'll carry around some real goodies, just in case." Her stomach growled. She opened the fridge. A box of baking powder and a shiny red apple were all she could find inside.

She shrugged and grabbed the fruit, flicking it in the air before catching it in her upturned palm. Sitting down, a polish with her cape, she sunk her teeth in, the juice spraying and then dribbling down her chin. Her stomach settled down a bit. And then just as quickly erupted. She dropped the apple onto the floor. It rolled across the linoleum, coming to a stop against a waiting foot.

"Who, who are you?" she gasped, her hand clutching her belly, the pain overwhelming as she fell out of the chair, her body landing in a dull thud.

"You killed my son," growled the crone, moving within an inch of her writhing body. "Now it's your turn to die." The withered, old hag kicked her, cackling all the while.

She stared up in a daze, her eyes clouding over, the room in a spin before everything started going dark. *An apple,* she thought to herself. *Oldest friggin' trick in the book.* The light shrunk to a pinprick. Then the sound, a blast, a sudden bright light before the nothingness enveloped her.

Stupid friggin' apple.

A new light woke her, 100 watt bright. She scrunched up her eyes and yawned. "Am I dead?" she managed.

"Not just yet," came the surprising response.

Her peepers popped open. "You?" she gasped.

"Webmaster Woodsman, at your service." He smiled and stroked her hand, the warmth returning to her aching limbs.

"How?" she asked, her stomach still in knots, the pain thankfully receding.

"Told you," he said, with a smirk, "no addies."

She smiled, despite herself. "Prince Charming came to my rescue yet again?"

He nodded, reaching into his coat pocket, holding up the remnants of the apple she'd eaten. "Got it out just in time. Lucky for you, I know the Heimlich." He blushed, though his eyes remained locked on hers. "And mouth to mouth."

That's when she remembered the last sound she'd heard. "And how to use a gun, I take it."

Again he nodded. "That's some goodie basket you got there." He moved in, their faces suddenly an inch apart. "Guess that makes us even now, huh?"

She reached up and put her hand behind his neck. "Not quite." She pulled him in, their lips colliding, meshing as one, that spark of theirs turning four alarm fire hot. She sighed and stroked his head, then pulled away, just an inch, his breath warm as a summer's day. "See, I know mouth to mouth, too," she whispered.

"Go figure," he whispered back.

"Yeah, but don't go too far. I feel an after coming on. And, wouldn't you know it, it's one of those happily ever ones."

"Ah," he chuckled, brushing his lips against hers, the kiss soft as a cloud, "those are the best kind."

WHARF WARS
BY ETHAN NAHTÉ

No one had seen Minsky in two days, which was very unusual. He had a way of showing up always at suppertime, lunch or breakfast. Didn't matter where you were or what was going on in the world around you, if it was time to eat it was time for Minsky to come sticking his nose into your business. His nose twitching and sniffing the air was almost like its own separate entity.

Sniffing the air was exactly what Tomas was doing at the moment. Minsky had a certain odor about him that was always detectable whenever he was around. So detectable that he was like some of those people who wore too much cologne or perfume that you could track for an hour after they had left the building, totally unaware that they were wreaking havoc on the sinuses and allergies of others. Minsky's scent wasn't on purpose. It was just part of who he was.

So Tomas was starting around the usual places, waiting to hear word, find a clue or catch wind of Minsky. This meant going down to the restaurant district not too far from the wharf. Common sense would say that to find a buddy who had a certain smell the last place one would want to be looking would be around the aroma of food or the fish boats but that was where Minsky could generally be found.

The rest of the gang was helping, as well, but Tomas was the best tracker they had. If he couldn't find someone then the odds of anyone else having success was close to nil. Some would call it a gift but often Tomas would call it a curse considering the times he found a buddy a week, a day or even a minute too late. Then again, best to find a friend even if they were dead than to spend eternity guessing their fate. He just wished that the dreams that came with the old memories, the ones that would jar him awake so suddenly in fright that the hairs on the back of his neck would be stiff enough to hang Christmas ornaments off of on a windy day, would go away and let him sleep for long uninterrupted periods of time instead of a quick cat nap here and there.

The rest of the gang had spread out and were canvassing the area over ten city blocks wide and more than a mile deep. There were a lot of hidey holes that Minsky could've been stuffed in if he were the victim of foul play and it would take a lot of time. They weren't searching further because there were no recent signs of their rivals. On any given day there would be at least one sighting of an enemy gang member or some hard visual evidence that they were around. Even throughout the restaurant district one could at least depend on hearing a hapless patron scream when they saw the ugly mug of a rival gang member. It was almost a given…but not over the past two days. Tomas didn't like it one bit, but it also stirred a sixth sense to let him know that they were being toyed with and Minsky was being kept somewhere nearby. The question was would he be found dead or alive.

Sounds of a scuffle broke out at a nearby restaurant. Screams and shouts broke the stillness of the dank evening air. Tomas peered through the window of the joint but quickly lost interest. It wasn't the enemy and it wasn't Minsky.

He turned and made his way down a narrow alley; a sick, sulfurous light flickered in a random seizure. As Tomas passed beneath a broken fire escape the scent finally hit him. No doubt about it, Minsky had definitely made his way through here within the past twenty-four hours. Tomas looked down upon the grime and sandy mud, searching for another sign. Sure enough there was Minsky's footprint. It led deeper into the alley, an unlit path that Tomas knew with certainty led to the heart of the projects. No good was going to come of this, of that he was sure.

Though it was a risk that could alert the enemy Tomas let out a wail that was the signal to those close by that he had found the trail. He would have to rely on them passing the message and hopefully one or two of them being as good at finding him as he was at finding their comrade. Odds were he would be going this one alone but there was no time to go track down reinforcements. It may be too late already but, to Tomas, every second counted and he'd hate to be even one second late if he could make a difference in Minsky's survival.

He shot off into the darkness. The night sky was cloudy but in the city that meant that the light pollution just glowed from the bottom of the low cloud-cover. It gave a dim lantern-like glow to the streets, even here in-between the wet bricks and amongst the stench of the maggot-infested dumpsters and the pools of various fluids that rankled the nose and was better not to think about as one foot then another passed through them, trying to keep pace with Tomas' heart rate as he followed the scent. He could hear his pulse pounding in his ears but between those drum-like throbs he could start picking up voices echoing off the narrow walls somewhere nearby.

He took a chance, running in the direction of the large storm sewer at the end of the alley. The closer he got the more the voices picked up. He had already seen three lookouts on the roofs above and knew that they had signaled his coming. No sense in trying to stay hidden and quiet. Not that that was really Tomas' style anyway. He had always been able to hold his own even with an opponent twice his weight and height.

As he came to the T-intersection between buildings he looked down the east end. A more stable light flickered off pools of sooty water and running sewage. An old boot that still had a portion of a foot gnawed off just above the ankle jutted out from beneath an old cardboard box. Odds were the remainder of the owner of that foot was nothing but bones, if even that, hidden beneath that box with hundreds of scummy little footprints trampled all across it.

Minsky was nowhere in sight, but Kalambran and his army of degenerates were in force. It wasn't all of his troops but it was enough. There upon a makeshift throne a few feet above the drainage he sat, a smile on his grotesque face and a bone, possibly from the "box man," being held like a scepter. He was truly delusional, which made him all the more dangerous.

"Well, well, well, if it isn't our old friend Tomas. Let's give him a big cheer for finding us, eh, lads." This was followed by a raucous din of pure delight. He did not waver nor did he belie his thoughts of hoping that the noise would be heard by any of his gang and help them in finding the two of them. His poker face remained solid as stone.

"How could I not have found you, Kalambran? I just had to follow the stench of urine and trash."

He smirked and then gave an uproarious laugh, "Oh my, my. The bravado you exhume. Yet it took you two days to find us."

Tomas didn't want to give him the upper hand. He maintained his façade as he walked in a little closer. "It didn't take me two days to find you and your scum. We were of a mind that Minsky had found him some tail somewhere and was out enjoying himself. I'd hate to interrupt someone's pleasure when I'm surely not their keeper."

"But you are interrupting someone's pleasure, but only by a degree." Kalambran motioned to his left and some of his boys began rolling back a large trash can. "See, I was taking great pleasure in torturing your fat little buddy. But I'm willing to forgive that now that you're here and I can have at you. Besides, Minsky seems to have tired of the game."

He looked and saw Minsky, tied with piano wire by all fours as well as another wire garroted about his neck. His tongue hung out between a couple of missing teeth. He was matted in blood and spoiled food substance. The wires were all cutting deeply into him and seemed to be the only thing holding him up.

"Minsky, can you hear me?" he said without trying to allow too much alarm into his voice. Minsky's eyes lolled up, almost to the whites, and he gave his friend a slight smile.

"You...you came for me. Save yourself, Tomas. I'm done for."

He was smacked a couple of times by one of Kalambran's toughs. Kalambran called a halt then turned back to Tomas. He was within six feet of his foe by now, but the circle of thugs was blocking his egress from all points behind and above.

"I'm willing to bet that this isn't what you expected," Kalambran said.

Tomas glared, ready to pounce upon his sorry ass.

"You probably thought it would be your friend tied up with only a couple of bruises, myself and maybe four or five of my guys holding him captive. I'm not that stupid. I wouldn't hold the position I commandeer if I were."

"I thought you only held that position because the rest of your gang was too stupid or too cowardly to do anything on their own. Most of them are lucky that breathing is autonomous or they would fall over where they stand."

A mirthful laugh escaped his sharp teeth. "Oh you kill me!"

"Soon enough."

Kalambran continued laughing. "Of course I had no guarantee it would be you that I would attract but the odds were in my favor. I mean we all know how great a tracker you are, don't we? But as you can see," he gestured to the surroundings, "I'm expecting a much larger war than just you. Maybe not this evening but if I hold you prisoner then the rest will surely come."

"And for what purpose have you orchestrated this demented scheme?"

"Such a vocabulary. That's one of the reasons I admire you more than most of those hairballs. You can track; you have some class and a smattering of education. You are almost too good to be a cat. And because of that I will tell you. Your gang has controlled the docks and most of the restaurant area for long enough and you're not even worthy. Such finicky eaters. There is so much that goes to waste that you pussies won't even eat, much less consider touching. Why not leave the spoils to those of us whom would truly feast upon mankind's leftover treasures?"

Weapons now extended and in plain sight, Tomas stepped forward.

"Ennhh! Not so fast, meow-meow," Kalambran commanded with a gnarled finger. "Another step and your friend gets it. You act so brave as though you believe you have nine lives or something."

Tomas looked at his old friend and saw that life had all but fled his body. His breath wasn't even short and rasping any longer. It was shallow and almost nonexistent. He managed to lift his head just a bit and give Tomas a slight wink from a swollen eye. "Kill the rat bastard," he said with his last breath.

It's hard to say whether he died before the wire sliced through his neck or not. It mattered not as Kalambran smiled upon the beheading of his captive and Tomas the Tracker lunged forward, leaping into the air to remove the enemy's head. A wall of bodies flew in between them, blocking the buck-toothed target who was yelling for Tomas to be beaten down but to be kept alive to draw in the other cats.

Tomas slashed, kicked, clawed and bit his way free of the multiple paws grabbing at him, trying to punch his lights out along with a few kicks to break some bones in the process. Bodies smacking the wet pavement got everyone's attention, all commotion coming to a brief halt. Heads turned skyward and against the hazy backdrop of illuminated clouds were the silhouettes of threescore felines, green eyes glimmering.

One large Maine coon landed directly behind Kalambran. "We're here, you rodent."

Kalambran swiped at Brogan's mouth but only clipped his whiskers. The rest of the cats came flying off the rooftops, landing on the fat, cushy bodies of the rats, crushing some of them in the process. Tomas had already sliced through the jugular of two rats in front of him when he saw that Brogan was being rat piled in an effort to protect Kalambran.

Tomas charged the huddle. Kalambran sensed his attack and dodged to the side. The momentum of Tomas' claws ripped the head from the rat Kalambran had sidestepped behind. Tomas' body slid into the pile and dislodged the heap from the top of Brogan who was spitting a rat with a snapped neck from his mouth while he had three others pinned below him.

The battle within the alley was noisy. Echoes of squeals and hissing pulsed across the waters and off the bricks. Trash cans being upset and pounced upon clanged loudly. Cries of mercy from rats who sought shelter in a dumpster, only to be trapped by a group of cats, were ended with the sounds of ripping flesh and pieces of bodies being slung against the metallic sides. There would be no mercy for the trap that had been laid or the death of Minsky. He was like that jolly old uncle that everyone loved no matter how young or old one was.

Brogan smashed a rather large rat aside, taking half of the rodent's nose and mouth off in the process. Tomas leaped over them to the escaping Kalambran. He was heading for a chink in the wall that would be a tight fit for him and impossible for any of the cats. Tomas scrambled across the asphalt, stepping in an old baby diaper. He flung a nasty paw out and pierced the disappearing hindquarter of Kalambran, pegging him to the ground. He tore and fought, trying to get himself loose even if it meant losing his tail. Tomas tried to shift his weight to hold him down better and sink his claws deeper. Nips and scratches assailed him from all sides as he hung on for all he was worth.

"Keep your grip," Brogan yelled. With a caterwaul the attackers all around Tomas fled or died in their tracks as Brogan and a dozen others came to his rescue. Most of the other rats throughout the alley had either been killed or scrambled away as fast as their smell feet could carry them. A couple of cats had died but only a few had serious injuries. The surviving rats that had been on top of Tomas were forced into a fallen trash can and held at bay.

He clamped down even harder on Kalambran and dragged his stinking, flea-infested lump of lard out from the crack. Great King Rat was gasping for breath and bleeding severely from where Tomas had pierced him. The deposed leader turned to face Tomas, snarling. The great tracker smacked him across the face, letting one claw connect and slice through his right eye. He screamed.

Tomas backed away and let Brogan step in. "I believe with your one good eye you will get to see your boys run the gauntlet. You know what that is, don't you, Kalambran? Answer me!"

"Yes," he said with a weary voice. "All of you smelly cats line up on each side and take a swipe at us as we run through the gauntlet."

"Very good. You're almost correct."

Some of the cats gave Brogan a questioning look. Kalambran did not venture to look up.

"You said 'we' you waddling, fat ball of putrescence. You are going to get your life's wish, what you've wanted from me since our early days as petty foot soldiers in this battle. I'm going to give you the docks."

Kalambran looked up with a mixture of amazement and vague terror.

"Put him at the end of the gauntlet so he can see each and every one of his followers run through it as far as they can before death overtakes them."

This they did, tying him with the same piano wire used on Minsky after his body had been reverently taken down. They placed Minsky's body and head in a box and would carry it home with them to be buried with a couple of fresh fish to see him on his way.

Kalambran's head was held aloft and his one good eye open, forcing him to watch as each of the surviving rats was torn and slashed to bloody ribbons. They pleaded for their miserable lives and reached out to their leader at the end of the line, hoping he had some plan to save them in the end. He gave them no hope and he shed them no tear. He was heartless and emotionless. The world he so wanted to dominate was for him alone. The other rats were just a means to an end and a way to feed his ego.

Finally, Kalambran's moment came. He was dragged by the piano wires, almost getting loose on one occasion when one of the wires around his forepaw cut its way through, leaving a bloody stump. True he may have bled to death, but that wasn't to be. A sharp set of claws stung him underneath the shoulder to maintain a hold while the other cats dragged him along.

There on the wharf the smell of fresh caught fish and shrimp poured through the misty veil settling in for the night. The planks where difficult to see in the on-setting fog but even more difficult in some of the areas enshrouded by shadows cast by the crates stacked alongside. The humans were taking a break for the moment in a building, laughing, drinking coffee and smoking while waiting for the next ship to come in. By the sound of the air horn it wasn't too far out.

Brogan and Tomas watched as Kalambran was tied to a rubber tire on the side of the dock. Still he made no sound. Despite the blood loss from his paw and his eye he was still quite alive, just defeated.

"There you go, Kalambran," said Brogan. "A nice view of the shrimpers and cod boats bringing all kinds of goodies for you."

Lights cut through the fog along with the churning of engines. The heavy fall of men's feet came out onto the planks as they prepared to tie down and unload the incoming boat. The cats scattered to the tops of various crates, out of the way of the humans and away from the sides unless they took an accidental dunking.

"Ahoy," a voice yelled out from the boat. Kalambran looked up to see the port side of the boat come floating in. The letters on the side grew larger.

"Save me," Kalambran squealed. The boat crushed him into the side of the tire, grinding him into a smear down its side.

"What was that," asked one of the dock workers.

"Just a rat that got caught in the wrong place," laughed another.

Tomas looked at Brogan, "Guess he did have some feelings after all. Kept them bottled up pretty good."

"His cork has been popped now. Let's grab a couple of fish and have a toast to Minsky."

Down to the beach went the procession, far enough away from the tides. The cats took turns digging a hole. They buried their friend, fish and all, and then sang a few rounds in more than a few keys simultaneously. Cats pawed and played with fiddler crabs popping up out of the cool night's sand. Minsky would've loved the feast.

THE THIRTEENTH TREE
BY JJ BEAZLEY

> *...what dreams may come*
> *When we have shuffled off this mortal coil,*
> *Must give us pause.*

This melancholy reflection is made by no ordinary mortal, but a Prince of Denmark - tortured by grief and the need for vengeance, teetering on the edge of insanity and musing on the state of death.

But what of the dreams of more mundane folk? The factory worker living in Birmingham with only the form of his local football team to concern him, the stockbroker settled comfortably in the Home Counties, or, in my case, the freelance photographer living in a quiet spot on the Northumberland coast with few real cares apart from the insecurity of never being sure that the next commission will come in soon enough to pay the rent?

And what are dreams anyway? Philosophers, mystics and scientists have been offering various explanations for as long as there have been philosophers, mystics and scientists. Are they merely part of some cerebral activity to be explained away as electrical impulses in the synapses? Maybe that is the mechanical explanation, but what drives the mechanics? As you go deeper into what proves to be a very deep question, you have to wrestle with the capricious and elusive workings of psychology. And then, deeper still, you are ever faced with the final question: what is reality? At that point you reach the edge of a continental shelf, and before you lies an abyss of unfathomable depth in which logic, as it is usually perceived, has little or no place.

My dreams, at least those I remember, are like everybody else's: vague, disjointed, full of contradictions and distortions – usually explainable as the reworking of things that have happened to me in real life. But one dream was very different. That one was clear and logical, and seemed to be a viewing of events happening in real time. And what I learned the following day confirmed that either the most unbelievable coincidence had occurred, or that dreams can be much more than mere synaptic flashes.

* * *

It happened three years ago, when I was that freelance photographer living in a quiet spot on the Northumberland coast at a place called Dryburgh Bay. I had rented an old farmhouse that had become vacant when the tenant farmer, finding it increasingly difficult to eke out a meagre living from the poor land behind the dunes, had decided to retire. The land had been leased to another farmer in the vicinity, the outbuildings were up for sale, and the previous occupant had moved out to live with one of his daughters in the city.

Although Northumberland is in England, I had felt from the outset that there was nothing "English" about the landscape – at least, not English as I understood the term. I came from the Midlands shires where the land is a fertile patchwork of well-manicured fields, dotted here and there by tidy black and white dairy cows. This landscape was very different.

The poor soil made the grass dull and lifeless, sparse tufts of marram struggled to colonise the sand dunes, and the cows were a strange, straggly bunch of all sizes and colours that looked as though every genetic misfit of their kind had been brought together in one place. Even the light had a piercing clarity that made the starkness seem all the more stark.

I had moved there in late March and, during my first night in the house, had been woken in the early hours by a cacophonous din. It had been the sound of the roof slates clattering loudly in a gusting easterly gale coming off the North Sea. The following morning I had looked out of the window and felt a profound sense of being in a foreign country.

The front of the house faced south and overlooked a narrow lane, beyond which was a dull, green-brown vista comprising poor grassland and marshy areas with pools occupied by waterfowl. It was the same to the north behind the house. To the east was the cold North Sea, fringed by sand dunes that rose to the height of a house in places, protecting the wetland behind them from the high spring tides. The lane ran west for about a mile up a shallow hill to a village called Waddington where it joined the main coast road.

The village was something like the civilisation I was used to. It had trees, cottages, a pub, an old church and a post office. I used to walk there several times a week to post my mail and gaze at the familiar plants in the cottage gardens.

It took me several months to get used to living there, but I did eventually find an uneasy peace with the place and came to respect its wild and unkempt air. Freelance photography can be an irregular and insecure occupation and I would sometimes go without work for weeks at a time. I used the empty days to discover this new and unfamiliar landscape on foot; sometimes walking on the dunes to watch the seabirds dive for fish, sometimes following the slow meanderings of the waterfowl on the pools, and sometimes marvelling at the shifting levels of the beach and the ever-changing colours of the sea - from electric blue on a calm spring morning to near-black when the onshore wind blew and the eastern sky took on the slate grey of an approaching storm.

I found an old ruin too, standing alone on the rough scrubland behind the house. I learned that it had belonged to the Knights Hospitallers during the Middle Ages, and was now quiet and empty apart from the occasional owl standing proudly on top of the stark masonry, hooting mournfully.

My walks up the hill to the village were different; they were sojourns into a more comfortable world. On one of my first visits I took a stroll around the church. It was a simple structure with no transepts, chancel or lych gate like those found in the village churches of the midland and southern shires. It had no tower to speak of, just a simple open bell cote so typical of Northumberland. The heavily weather-worn stone in parts of the structure attested to its age, and the pattern of the older windows was early gothic.

I went inside, but found it simple and unspectacular. I came back out and read some of the gravestones. What stories they had to tell. Whole families wiped out in the space of a few months, siblings dying many years apart but always at more or less the same age, two men who appeared to have been brothers, but who had the same Christian name and died within a year of each other. It was fascinating stuff that kept me engrossed for an hour or more.

But the really interesting feature lay on the eastern edge of the churchyard. It was an open, airy spot and almost constantly bleak. It overlooked the poor farmland running down to the sea and caught the force of the cold, damp easterlies that kept us living mortals needing several layers of clothing even in the warmer summer spells.

Running along the unfenced fringe of the church's land were twelve poplar trees. They were arranged in what amounted to a perfectly straight line and were equally spaced, apart from a gap in the middle between the sixth and seventh. There the gap was twice that between the other trees, as though a thirteenth should have occupied the space. What struck me as odd was the fact that nothing grew in the vacant spot; no grass, no weeds, nothing. There was only barren brown earth. During my years as a landscape photographer I had visited and photographed many churches and churchyards, and had never seen such an arrangement of trees before. I was intrigued and gave some thought to possible explanations.

The most obvious was suggested by Leonardo's painting of the Last Supper – twelve disciples sitting on one side of the table with Jesus in the middle. Presumably, some devout soul had planted twelve trees to represent the apostles and left a full space in the middle to represent the risen Christ. I was happy enough with that and thought no more about it until I met the vicar a couple of weeks later.

It was a sunny day in late spring. For once, a southerly wind was keeping the onshore breeze at bay and it was unusually warm down by the coast. I needed to send some mail and so I took a stroll to the village post office. As I made my way home I walked past the entrance to the churchyard. I saw a man in a clerical collar walking down the path towards the gate, and thought it would be interesting to find out whether there was a known history of the planting of the poplars. I waited for him.

He seemed an approachable sort and I stood aside as he unlatched the gate and came out. He smiled at me in that welcoming way that you have a right to expect of vicars. I introduced myself and came straight to the point of my interest. He told me that there was no official record of when they had been planted or who had been responsible, but the presumption was that the trees represented the twelve apostles and the gap the risen Christ. That was the view held by the local diocese. I was pleased to have guessed right. He seemed to hesitate slightly, and then said

"There is another explanation and that one *is* in writing. But it's highly fanciful and not something the Church likes to dwell on."

He looked uncertain for a moment and then continued.

"Oh, why not? I've been dying to tell this story ever since I read it when I first came here five years ago, and you're the first person who's ever expressed an interest."

As we stood there on that warm, late spring day he told me of a document contained within the parish records. The story it told was fantastical enough to make it safe to relate, he said. No one would believe it in this rational age. As far as I remember the exact procession of his words, this is what he told me.

"Back in 1693 the vicar of this parish was a man with the delightful name of the Reverend Jeremiah Jellicoe - his grave is round by the south wall, but the inscription's all but worn away now.

"During the autumn of that year there was a bad storm which lasted several days and the church roof suffered some damage. The Reverend Jellicoe called in the workmen to effect the necessary repairs and went up into the roof space to assess the damage for himself. Among the dust and rubble littering the floor he found an old leather pouch which contained a folded document written in Latin. The good Reverend was a Latin scholar, as all the clergy were in those days, and he had no difficulty translating it.

"What he read must have put the wind up him a bit. It wasn't only the common herd who were more superstitious in those days; the clergy were ready to see goblins and demons in every dark corner too. Apparently he gave the document to the bishop but made an English translation first, and that's the version that's contained in the parish records.

"The document had been written by a priest called Hugh de Ferrer in 1284. At that time the building was actually the chapel to a manor house which stood nearby and Hugh was the chaplain. The narrative begins in the year 1282.

"As well as being the chapel to the manor house, the church also served the local parish and, one Sunday evening, Hugh was in the confessional - it was Catholic then, of course - when a man

stepped in and confessed to having provided the local lord, a
powerful baron called Sir Guy de Menton, with his six-year-old
son to use in a sacrificial ritual. Apparently there had been a few
disappearances among the children of the locality stretching back
several years and they had been put down to the wild animals that
roamed these parts in those days. The peasant's confession told a
different tale.

"It seems that Sir Guy was a Templar Knight and the leader of
a thirteen-strong group of like-minded knights from the county
who were deeply engaged in hermetic practices, some of which
involved the ritual sacrifice of young children. I'm not claiming
this to be right, you understand; this is what the document said.
According to the peasant, this was where the children had been
disappearing to."

I had to interrupt at that point. I had always thought of the
Templar Knights as paragons of virtue, wearers of the red cross,
the embodiment of medieval chivalry. My childhood veneration
for the gallant knights of Old England had never fully left me and
I was inclined to scoff at some silly story that claimed they
worshipped the devil and murdered children.

"Well, don't write the story off just yet," said the vicar. "I'm
not what you would call an authority on the Templars, but I know
there are some suspicions regarding the true nature and purpose of
their organisation. They were formed during the twelfth century,
ostensibly to defend pilgrims on their way to Jerusalem. It's true
that their device was the red cross and that they had a reputation
as tough and worthy warriors, and I dare say most of them were
probably devout, God-fearing Christians. But there is a belief that
their function as defenders of the faithful was, or at least came to

be, a cover for something darker. Some believe they were a front for a secret society which more than merely dabbled in the black arts. The same belief surrounds the Masons, who claimed a connection with Solomon's temple in Jerusalem. Some modern writers have suggested that there was a link between the Templars and the Masons.

"At some point, early in the fourteenth century I think, one of the French kings – Philip the second or third – had the Templars disbanded. Slaughtered some of them, tortured many more and confiscated their lands and wealth. There is some mystery over the true reason for such a brutal purge and there are many who claim that it wasn't just about the politics of wealth and power. There are plenty of books on the subject. Anyway, back to the story.

"Poor old Hugh was at a loss to know how to handle this astonishing confession. He had no reason to disbelieve the man's story. Lying in a confessional was beyond the bounds of credibility in those days, and why would anyone want to make up such a story? He also had no reason to think that the man was insane. Furthermore, the confessional was sacrosanct so he couldn't tell anybody about it. And who would he tell anyway? The authorities? Sir Guy *was* the authority in these parts.

"He considered seeking the advice of the bishop, but he knew that the bishop was a strong supporter of the Templars and feared for his position and even his life. According to the document, he agonised over his predicament for a whole week before deciding on a highly unconventional course of action.

"There was a hermit living in a cave, a little way up the coast at Warkworth. He had, apparently, a somewhat ambivalent reputation; some said he was a holy man, while others believed him to be a pagan magician. Stories of his magical prowess were common in the county, but his actions were said to be generally benevolent and he was left in peace by both the peasants and the local gentry. Hugh decided that he would be worth a try. Being a poor man, the hermit wasn't likely to be in with the Templars and his magic just might be real - and powerful enough deal with the problem. Direct confrontation obviously wasn't an option and Hugh was desperate.

"So Hugh paid him a visit. Not that easy in those days, of course. The roads were far from safe even for a priest, and Warkworth must have been a full day's round trip on horseback. And he had to go alone as the whole business needed to be kept secret. To make matters worse, the cave was on the other side of the river from the road and the weather was particularly bad, so Hugh had some difficulty persuading the ferryman in the nearby cottage to row him across.

"He records the interview briefly, saying that he felt an increasing sense that beings or forces from another realm were close by – he could almost feel their breath on his face, he says. Whether they were benevolent, diabolical or merely disinterested he was in no position to tell. He felt severely unnerved by the atmosphere, and the darkness didn't help. There was no light in the cave except what little came in from the narrow entrance. All he could see of the hermit was a shadowy figure seated in the corner and wearing some form of long, hooded garment like those worn by monks. He also says that he never saw the man's face; he kept it turned away from Hugh's gaze the whole time and it would probably have been too dark to see very much anyway.

"To protect the sanctity of the confessional, Hugh told him the story in general terms, and the hermit – Hugh never names him – agreed to help. He told Hugh that he would need something personal from each of the knights and, to help him achieve this, he gave the priest a potion of herbs which was to be poured into their vat of wine. This would knock them out for several hours and it would be safe to cut a few wisps of hair from each man. He said that he would arrive to do the deed when he judged the time to be right.

"As the chaplain, Hugh had free access to the house and had little trouble in doing as he had been instructed. He kept the fragments of hair safe, fearful all the time that he was acting in a manner seriously unbecoming of a good Christian priest.

"Two weeks later there was a knock at his door late at night. Hugh says that the sight of the hermit in the doorway, lit this time by a single candle, unnerved him somewhat. He describes him as being unusually tall with wild, unkempt hair and a deadness in his eyes reminiscent of a corpse. The hermit said very little, just explained that it had been necessary to come late so as not to be seen in the vicinity. He demanded a promise from Hugh that he would not disclose his involvement during his lifetime and asked for the hair fragments, which Hugh gave him. Then he turned and walked away into the darkness.

"Hugh didn't know what to expect and admits to having severe misgivings at the prospect of expecting anything at all. He was, after all, a younger son of a genteel family himself, and admits to feeling uncomfortable at the thought of entering some dark conspiracy with a wild cave-dweller against people who were, in effect, his own kind.

"Anyway, life in the village went on as normal until a month later. Hugh says that this was significant as the moon had been dark on the night of the hermit's visit and it was dark again on the night that Sir Guy had some sort of a seizure. The doctor was sent for, and Hugh was called in to administer the last rites as the doctor thought he might die. He didn't. He made a complete physical recovery within days, but was never the same again mentally. He was listless and pale, all his old aggressive energy had drained away, and he had no will to do anything except wander restlessly around the house and sleep fitfully for up to twelve hours a day.

"Then the visits started. Some of Hugh's parishioners were employed as retainers at the house and they told him that the visitors included the King's men, Lord Percy and some of the friends and family of Sir Guy's twelve companions, none of whom had been seen for several weeks. Sir Guy stared emptily into the fire during all the questioning and denied any knowledge of the whereabouts of his erstwhile friends. The investigation eventually petered out and Sir Guy continued to live a reclusive existence in the manor house.

"Hugh was both intrigued and disturbed by the disappearances and predictably laid the explanation at the feet of the hermit. Although his sensibilities as a man of God made him reluctant to discover that he had been instrumental in the workings of some magical art, his curiosity persuaded him to make the arduous journey to Warkworth again to question his collaborator.

"The hermit refused to tell him anything, other than to state that he had done what he'd needed to do: separated the acolytes from their fountainhead and made sure that it would stay that way.

As long as Sir Guy and the twelve knights were kept apart there would be no further trouble. That's what the priest had wanted, and that's what he had got. No further explanation was needed.

"And that's what Hugh had to be content with. The knights were never seen again and there were no more incidents of children disappearing."

As the vicar paused momentarily, I asked him where the twelve trees came into the story.

"Well," he said, "that's the interesting bit, and it's what prompted Hugh to write the whole thing down for posterity.

"Two years later, in the spring of 1284, Hugh looked out of his window one morning to see Sir Guy walking up and down in an agitated manner along the eastern edge of the churchyard. He says that the old man had his hands clasped in front of his chest and appeared to be talking to something on the ground. At first he assumed the old knight's behaviour to be nothing more than the latest manifestation of his disturbed mental state, but was interested enough to look for himself after the lord had retired back into the house.

"He was surprised to find two lines of strong young saplings growing up out of the rough grass. The two groups of six saplings formed a perfectly straight line but there was a patch of barren earth between them where a thirteenth would have completed the set. He looked over at the house and saw Sir Guy staring back at him with a look of hatred that made his blood run cold. It was the first sign of anything other than apathy that he had seen in the old man's face since the day of the seizure. He felt sure that Sir Guy now knew what had happened to his friends, and that the look betrayed a hatred for Hugh and a consuming desire for revenge. The following day Sir Guy collapsed and died.

"The rest is a matter of historical record. Sir Guy had never married so he had no heirs. Lord Percy claimed the estate but never did anything about the land and buildings and, as was common in these parts, they fell into decay and the locals helped themselves to the masonry for use as building material. The foundations are still there I suppose but, to my knowledge, the site has never been considered important enough to be worth excavating.

"Anyway, Hugh wrote everything down and hid the account in the roof space expecting, no doubt, that it would eventually be found long after he and the hermit were dead and buried. And that's what happened."

I asked whether Hugh had confined himself to a straightforward narrative, or whether he had offered any logical explanation for these events

"Not really," said the vicar. "The whole thing reads like the work of a man shaking his head and shrugging his shoulders through the whole account. He does say at the end, however, that he prays to God that no tree shall grow in the spot during his lifetime, so he must have believed that there was a connection between the twelve trees and the missing knights."

It was a fascinating tale, told with enthusiasm and a fine recollection for detail by a skilled story teller. But, of course, I didn't take it seriously. I thanked the vicar for his time, exchanged a few pleasantries, and made my way home down the winding, treeless lane that ran to the sea. I took my usual evening stroll along the dunes, had dinner, and spent the evening trying to find something worth watching on the television. I gave up and spent the rest of the night before going to bed musing light-heartedly on the vicar's tale of medieval magic and skulduggery. I half expected to dream about Hugh, Sir Guy and the wild hermit that night, but I didn't. That was to come another night, a good six months later.

Why that night? I don't know. Was it some sort of anniversary? Were the planets in the same configuration as they had been on that day in 1284 when the trees had, apparently, magically appeared in the churchyard?

I had been to Warkworth by then and seen a cave on the far side of the river from the path that runs upstream from the castle. I had discovered that it was still called The Hermitage, and wondered whether it was where Hugh had conducted the fateful interview.

But I hadn't been near the place in months. So why that night? Whatever the reason, I had the most vivid and realistic dream of my life. At least, that's what the sceptic would believe it to be, although I'm sure that it was something of rather greater substance. Whatever it was, the memory of it now is as strong as ever and it is causing me to face an agonising decision, the like of which I wouldn't wish on anybody.

It was late in the year. Christmas was in the air and I had watched an adaptation of an MR James ghost story on the television. Perhaps *that's* why the dream came that night. I'm clutching at straws. This dream wasn't the usual fitful, disjointed affair populated by gypsy children, haunted ash trees and runic curses. This one was rational, sharp as a razor and very frightening. This is what I "dreamed."

I was standing in the field just a dozen or so yards downhill from the two groups of poplar trees. I saw that the moon was full and every detail of the scene was clearly visible. I had a strong sense of really being there, in real time. I was aware of having gone to bed as usual and felt surprised at suddenly finding myself in a frosty landscape, hearing the wind in the trees and feeling its cold breath on my body.

I felt confused. My gaze wandered restlessly along the line of the twelve trees. I felt a sense of expectation without knowing why. Suddenly they started to glow. "Glow" isn't quite the right word, but I don't really know what is. They took on a sort of luminescence which caused me to blink several times, attempting to clear what I assumed was some visual aberration.

The trunk of each tree cracked and opened, and out of each one stepped a figure - a female figure, naked and hairless apart from long, dark cranial hair blowing listlessly in the light breeze. Their bodies were pure white, as though they had never seen the light of the sun. Each was slightly different than the others, but alike enough that they might have been sisters – rather like twelve examples of the same species of tree. I remembered Orpheus' first meeting with his beloved Euridyce and how her beauty had led him to follow her to the very depths of Hades. Was that what I was seeing, the tree nymphs of classical legend?

They started to walk in my direction, but I saw that their gaze was directed beyond me. I turned and saw a man walking up the hill. I didn't recognise him, but I saw that he was aware of the women. He came to within a few yards of me, and yet was obviously unaware of my presence. He only had eyes for these naked beauties who were forming a tight circle around him.

The man was young – no more than thirty in my estimation - and dressed in modern clothes. He had a shotgun in his hand, which might explain why he was in the field and not in the lane on the other side of the hedge. Perhaps he was a farmer's son, out shooting rabbits. I had no idea. I'd never seen him before.

But I saw him now. I saw the look in his eyes, a mixture of amazement and expectation as the women surrounded him. One of them moved close in front of him and pulled him gently to his knees. He looked around at the others and smirked childishly. He was clearly enthralled and in no condition to see anything beyond their naked bodies full of erotic promise. The woman removed his coat, his sweater, and his shirt. I stared in amazement until a movement caught my eye and I swung around to look again in the direction of the poplars. Twelve very different figures were striding purposefully towards us.

I recognised them from countless pictures I had seen in books: medieval knights in mail and surcoats, each with a bold red cross on the chest. They looked tough and imposing as they marched, twelve abreast, down the shallow slope. As they drew closer I saw their faces, lined and weather-worn, with the ravening look of wild animals in their eyes. Those eyes were terrible: hard, cruel, devoid of humanity - the eyes of a pack of wild dogs closing for the kill.

I felt gripped with fear, but fascinated at the same time. I could see them as clearly as I see my own hand now, but I was still struggling to decide whether it was a dream or not. Could they see me? The thought sent a shock of panic down my spine. My question was soon answered. As they passed close by, the nearest turned and looked directly at me. He said nothing but his intense stare made words unnecessary. "Keep out of this," it said. "Don't interfere." The instruction was redundant. I was held rigid; there was no question of interfering.

As the men approached the poor wretch on his knees, the forms of the women became indistinct until they were mere wisps of vapour which floated swiftly back to the trees. Having watched their retirement, I turned back towards the half-naked man still kneeling on the frosty grass. His eyes carried a different sort of expectancy now; they held a level of terror that most of us, thankfully, never have to experience.

Two of the knights moved swiftly and took hold of his arms. A third placed one dark, leathery hand over his mouth and the other at the back of his neck, stifling the man's pitiful protestations. I looked at the shotgun that lay on the grass where he had dropped it. It was too late to hope that it might be used in his defence. He was held firmly by three men to whom brutality was obviously second nature. I was certain that it would have been useless anyway.

They dragged him roughly up the slope towards the line of poplars. All but one of the other knights rushed to the spot in the centre of the trees and began to scratch away the earth with their bare hands. The remaining knight stood close by and removed a vicious dagger from a scabbard on his belt. The victim was laid on his back, struggling wildly but held firm by his captors. The dagger was plunged it into his chest and dragged downwards to open a cavity. The knight thrust his hand inside and wrenched out a bloody, steaming mass which he looked at triumphantly for a few seconds, before throwing it unceremoniously into the newly-dug hole. The others scraped the earth back into place - and they were gone.

There was silence. The suddenness of their disappearance stunned me. I had been both enraptured and appalled by the scene that had been played out before my eyes. But now there was only an eerie stillness, nothing else - or almost nothing. A body lay contorted on the frosty ground, its head thankfully turned away from me. I dread to think what a look must have been in its dead eyes.

I awoke in my own bed in my own bedroom. Blue sky filled the window, and I rose to look out on a clear day bathing the frosty landscape in wholesome light.

Some dreams we disregard as soon as we wake up. Others persist and nag at us for hours or even days. This one did more than nag. It was too real, and I felt sickened and shaken. At that point, however, I still chose to regard it as just a dream.

I didn't go out that day, not even for my customary walks on the dunes. The dream hung about me like a heavy weight and my thoughts returned to it repeatedly. I couldn't shake off the sense that I had really been in that field and really witnessed those horrific scenes. I felt uneasy at the prospect of going through the door. I didn't exactly expect to see a sword-wielding maniac intent on my destruction, but the sense of horror was still strong enough to keep me erring on the cautious side.

By eight o'clock I was feeling restive. It wasn't like me to stay cooped up in the house all day. I decided to pay a visit to my nearest neighbours, a middle-aged couple who lived in another old farmhouse a quarter of a mile up the lane.

Fred Coulton was a local man who had built up a small building business, and his wife Wendy was an affable sort who came from Newcastle. She liked to regale me with tales of life as a "proper Geordie" when she was a girl. They had befriended me shortly after I had moved in and were more than happy for me to pop around every so often. They liked me to tell them what I had learned about their county from my researches as a photographer, and I needed an occasional break from the emotional austerity of living alone and doing a solitary job.

That night I wanted to tell them about the dream. I felt the need to tell *somebody,* and they were the only friends I had made during my short spell in the North East. But I hesitated. I hadn't told them the story of Hugh and the hermit as I had felt that it was somehow confidential, even though the vicar hadn't expressly said so. To relate the dream would have meant telling the whole story from the beginning and I just wasn't in the mood for talking at length. I had, however, told them the story of the twelve trees shortly after I had met them, during one of our chats about the oddities of the county. Fred was about to use it to thrust a sharpened lance through my self-imposed wall of silence.

Our conversation wasn't flowing easily and I'm sure they could tell that my mood was guarded and distant. After one of several uneasy lulls, Fred suddenly took on the air of a man who had thought of something to say to break the clammy silence. He looked at me and said

"Oh, I know what you might find interesting."

If words can have a power that is verging on the palpable, these were at the top of the league.

"You know that spot in the churchyard that you told us about once, the one between the trees where nothing grows? They found a body there this morning."

My chest felt as though it had been struck by something heavy. My heart began to thump and the back of my neck turned cold.

"A body?"

"Mmm. Graham Ferrers it was, Arnold's son; owns the farm down the road behind the dunes. Only twenty eight. The postman saw him lying there when he went to collect the mail from the box. Police were there for a couple of hours, apparently."

"What did he die of?" I asked foolishly, my sense of shock sidestepping the obvious fact that the cause would probably not be public knowledge yet.

"Don't know," said Fred. "Some of the old lads from the village stood around the whole time and said they couldn't see any marks or blood or anything. They heard one of the coppers say it must have been a heart attack. Can you believe it? Twenty eight! Makes you think you're living on borrowed time."

I think Fred expected this revelation to start the conversation moving but it didn't. Looking back on it now, I feel that I should have been full of questions, pressing him for more information. But the workings of the human brain are often at odds with what you later think they should have been, and the effect of this startling bit of news only made me more guarded. The conversation lapsed again and I went home earlier than usual.

I really didn't want to go to bed that night. The details of the two dramas were too coincidental for comfort, and the similarity in names hadn't escaped me. Surely the medieval "de Ferrer" would have evolved into the modern "Ferrers." Could there be a family connection going back to Hugh? Was the revenge motive part of this sordid picture? I became intensely conscious of the fact that I was a witness – the only witness. But that wouldn't matter to supernatural beings, would it? Or would it? I didn't know. My thinking was muddled, unfocused. Fear has that effect. If it did matter to them, I didn't relish meeting them in another dream.

And so I sat in my armchair, pondering uncomfortably on the meaning of such transparent synchronicity. I drank a lot of Scotch, which had a mercifully numbing effect on my agitation. At about four in the morning I went to bed.

I woke up late with a bit of a headache but a sizeable sense of relief. No nocturnal sojourns - or at least none that I remembered, and that would do. I felt better, more logical. I decided that I probably wasn't in any danger, that the whole thing might just be an almighty coincidence and there was nothing I could do about it anyway.

For the next few weeks I busied myself with the task of trying to get work from book and magazine publishers. A sharp recession was hitting the publishing industry and my regulars weren't putting out many new commissions. I wasn't having much luck and I was beginning to get depressed. I could see the end of my career looming and the dream went very much to the back of my mind.

Then Fred Coulton showed me a local newspaper that carried an article on the coroner's inquest into the death of Graham Ferrers. Briefly, it said that he had been found at the eastern edge of the churchyard, that he was stripped to the waist, and that a shotgun and some discarded clothing had been found a little way down the hill. His father confirmed that he had gone out that night to try to find and shoot a fox that had been troubling the hen sheds. The cause of death was cardiac arrest caused by an embolism. The obvious conclusion was that he had dropped the gun when the attack occurred - I remember thinking that the use of the word "attack" was unwittingly ironic - and it was assumed that he had struggled up the slope in an attempt to reach the village, but had died before he got there. No explanation was offered as to why he had removed his upper garments, but there was no reason to pursue the matter. The verdict was a formality.

I had to let this go; what else could I do? And I had my business to worry about. Spring, normally the start of my busy period, came and went with only a couple of half-day commissions that paid just about enough for one month's rent. My capital was draining away. Summer was completely dead and, by the middle of July, I was forced to join the ranks of the unemployed.

Life became tedious. Your activities are pretty limited when you're living in such a remote spot and dependant entirely on a single person's benefit. Even putting enough petrol in the car to do the weekly shop is a burden when the nearest town is ten miles away.

I became an expert in shoestring living. Socialising was out of the question and I became totally reliant on Fred and Wendy for company. In the autumn a friend from back home offered me a way out. He had inherited a terraced house on the death of a relative and offered to let me use it for a nominal rent. I didn't have much choice but to accept and, in early December, I moved back to my home town in the Midlands.

Northumberland soon became a distant memory. My new environment couldn't have been further from the old. The wild and stark beauty of the east coast was replaced by crumbling red brick, concrete and tarmac. The terraced houses were crammed together in a claustrophobic mass and the whole area was criss-crossed by streets that were too narrow for the lines of cars parked on both sides day and night. They only added to my sense of being closed in and dominated by the inert paraphernalia of urban life. There were no trees in this mortified environment, and the only wild flowers were the weeds that grew out of the gaps between the house walls and the paving slabs. The noise of people, internal combustion engines and hooting horns punctuated the brief silences all day long and for much of the night as well.

My only contact with Northumberland was the occasional phone call from Fred and Wendy. I was glad when they rang. If they didn't ring me for a couple of months I would ring them, even though I couldn't really afford to.

All the time they were speaking I would strain to listen for noises in the background, hoping I would pick up the rumble and hiss of the waves at high tide, or the infamous wind coming off the sea, or maybe catch the hoot of an owl somewhere close outside their window. They kept me in touch with a world that was open and airy and populated by the children of nature, living and dying by the cycles of the seasons. I really was glad of their calls - until yesterday. Now I wish they had let me go and forgotten that they had ever known me.

Yesterday I had a phone call from Fred. I was glad to hear from him as usual, until he told me his latest piece of news.

He thought I might be interested to know that there was a tree growing in the churchyard, in that bare spot between the two lines of poplars close to where Arnold Ferrers' lad was found dead. We talked about it when I lived there, remember? I shuddered slightly. The nightmare was back, alive and kicking.

"I suppose," he said with that gentle, Northumbrian lilt that makes everything sound so matter-of-fact, "somebody's planted it in memory of Graham. His parents probably."

Perhaps they had. Or perhaps there's a more disturbing explanation known only to me, the only witness. A game of revenge and resurrection played at some propitious moment by the souls of a dark alliance kept in enforced separation for seven hundred years. Fountainhead and acolytes reunited; the distant descendant of their tormentor being sacrificed to reverse the act of his forefather. Do I really believe that? I'm afraid I do. I had the "dream." Only I know what it was like to be there that night.

So what do I do about it? Make the trip to Northumberland and cut the sapling off at ground level? I've seen the men responsible for its genesis and I shudder at the thought of meeting them again. Maybe I'm wrong and somebody *has* planted it there, in memoriam, in which case I would be nothing more than a common vandal.

But I don't think I am wrong, so how do I reconcile my firmly held belief with the prospect of taking no action? How would I live with myself if one of the village children disappeared?

The fact that my belief could be totally fanciful should make it easy for me to take the soft option and ignore the whole thing.

I'm not made that way. I'm cursed with a strong sense of personal responsibility. The same objection applies to the other obvious option – sit back and hope the vicar will do the job.

I've been sitting here all day wondering how the evil energy contained within thirteen trees could translate itself into physical action. I don't see how it could; but I'm not an expert in such matters, so I can't be sure. Whatever the mechanics of the matter, the fact is established and cannot be ignored: the twelve trees have now been joined by a thirteenth.

The arguments go back and forth, back and forth, like the pendulum of a grandfather clock ticking me down to one form of doom or another. Which do I take, the devil or the deep blue sea? The decision needs to be made now. The power might not be unleashed until the thirteenth tree is fully-grown, but the bigger it gets the more impracticable it will be to do anything about it.

In the meantime I have felt it necessary to spend a few hours setting all this down for the record. If I do decide to back up my convictions with some courage, I'll need to move quickly before my resolve cools. There won't be time for writing then.

If something untoward should happen to me during the attempt, my story will be of no interest to the police or the pathologist and will be quite inadmissible in a coroner's court. But at least my friends will, if they feel so inclined, be able to interpret the circumstances of my misfortune in a more informed light. They might even feel moved to complete the job on my behalf. In all conscience, it is something I could not ask of them.

THE VILLAINY GROUP
BY T. SHONTELLE MACQUEEN

The room where five individuals sat in a small circle was a little dark and totally silent except for the clock ticking towards six in the evening. There was a slight rustle as one of the five adjusted himself on his seat, trying to find a more comfortable place to put his tail. Then all was quiet again. Four very different pairs of eyes evaluated the newcomer as the clock finally began to chime and the door was pushed closed with a soft click.

The newcomer shifted nervously in his seat and glanced around the room as the silence stretched out.

"So," said a man at last, "it appears we have a new member here today." He reached up to twirl his long mustache as he gazed at the newcomer in what was supposed to be an encouraging way. "Perhaps we should introduce ourselves. I am called Mustache, and I am here because I have an unfortunate problem involving, among other things, young ladies and trains." Mustache poured himself a glass of water and looked over to his left.

The wolf to Mustache's left ran his claws through his bushy tail. "I am called Wolf," he said in a soft growl. At least, the newcomer assumed it was a he. He'd had rather limited experience with wolves. "I'm mostly trying to cut back on some unhealthy eating habits." He ran his tongue along a collection of wicked looking fangs and glanced to his left.

A small green skinned woman sat in the next chair. She was wearing a bright floral hat and a yellow sun dress, and on her feet were a pair of heavy black shoes with curly pointed toes. "I am known as Witch," she stated, and the newcomer thought he might be sensing a theme somewhere. "I am here because I often feel strong desires to kidnap people and cook them or lock them in towers, and I'm trying to change."

Next to the witch, and to the right of the newcomer, sat a large troll. The troll looked over and smiled through an assortment of enormous broken teeth set in black gums. A huge pair of fangs hung down on either side of his mouth. The newcomer tried to hide a shudder. "I am Troll," said the troll. "I learn to fish."

No one else seemed to think this brief statement odd, so the newcomer just nodded politely and surreptitiously tried to slide a little closer to Mustache. There was an expectant hush as everyone stared at the newcomer. He poured himself a glass of water and took a long drink and then a deep breath.

"I am called Schemer," he started, not being slow on the uptake. "I'm here today because I can't seem to stop plotting. I make these brilliant, intricate schemes designed to topple businesses, governments, sometimes even small countries, but they never seem to work out. There is always some flaw that causes the whole thing to collapse. The last time it happened, I was almost killed by an explosion that went awry. I've only just fully recovered, and that happened over six months ago. It was when I was lying there, alone and in pain, on the floor of my subterranean lair that I really started to think." There were some sympathetic nods from around the room. "I thought, why is this happening to me? I'm a clever person. Am I sabotaging myself? Why does everything always go wrong? Then I thought, perhaps this isn't really what I want to do with my life. And that's when I decided to come here. I didn't know what else to do."

Wolf nodded slowly. "It seems like it always takes some kind of catastrophic event before someone realizes they need to change. I know in my case I was almost hacked to death with an axe before I recognized that I would have to make some changes in my life. Even now, I often find myself heading down that path again. I think to myself, surely it's ok to just watch the girl walking in the woods. Then I think, if I just follow her, that won't cause any problems. I'll just follow her until she gets where she's going. Sometimes I think I could just follow them and that would be enough for me, but it never works out that way. In the end, I wind up in some one's cottage, eating something I shouldn't, and it's all down hill from there." Wolf sighed and looked at the floor.

"Is there something you want to tell us about your week, Wolf?" Witch asked gently.

"Well, I don't know if I'm really ready to talk about it," Wolf replied. "It's just that the other day I was out and I just happened to see this girl skipping along through my woods. It's strange, you know. I used to have to hunt out girls to chase after, but now that I'm trying to stop they seem to be everywhere." Wolf paused and fidgeted with some fabric stuck under one of his claws. "Anyway, I thought maybe I'd just follow her for a bit, you know. Just to see where she was going. I told myself I was only making sure of her safety. The woods can be very dangerous after all." Troll snorted causing Mustache to frown over at him before

219

gesturing for Wolf to continue. "Well," Wolf said in a rush, "I was right behind her, and then she noticed me. She looked all frightened, and I guess I sort of panicked. I grabbed at her cloak, and it came off in my claws. She went screaming off into the woods, yelling about me like I was some sort of monster. It was awful. The cloak was made out of some kind of stringy fabric, and it took days for me to pick it all out of my teeth."

"And what was it doing in your teeth, Wolf?" Mustache asked archly.

"What do you mean?"

"Well, you said that you grabbed at her cloak with your claws, and then you said it was stuck in your teeth. So which was it?"

Wolf looked as if he might spring across the room and devour Mustache, but he didn't move. He just stared back defensively.

Troll snorted again. "Wolf ate girl," he stated flatly. "Wolf ate her. Ate her all up. Stringy cloak too." He smirked across the room at Wolf, which gave him a face like something from the nether regions of Hell. "Yum, yum, yum," he taunted, seeing how far he could push his luck.

"Well, how was your week then Troll?" Wolf snapped, obviously deciding a verbal rejoinder would be less hazardous than what he clearly wanted to do. "Any luck with the fishing? At least I don't eat goats!"

"Now Wolf," interrupted Witch sharply, "we don't judge one another here." Wolf snarled at her but kept quiet, lapping water out of his glass instead.

"One goat," muttered Troll. "Ate one goat." And he slobbered slightly onto the floor. "Ate three fish, though." For just a moment he sat up straighter. "Hate fish," he added, as if it was a kind of mantra. "Hate fish, hate fish. Fishy fish."

"Well, that's wonderful, Troll," Witch said, leaning forward and smiling. "Isn't it wonderful," she continued, poking Wolf with one of her pointy black shoes.

"Very good," he agreed, somewhat grudgingly.

"Yes," Mustache added. "We know how hard that must be for you, living near all those goats as you do. Have you thought about moving?"

"No. Like bridge. Lived there over 100 years. I can live there and not eat goats. Smelly goats," he added, drooling on the floor again and trying to cover it by taking a large gulp from his glass.

"No doubt," Mustache said. "Anyway, I wanted to say that I noticed your new bonnet, Witch. Very nice, I must say. A real change that."

"Oh, that," Witch replied, blushing slightly to a sort of purple color and taking a sip of her water. "Well, I just thought it might be ok to wear something a little different today. My black hat was dirty anyway. It's not permanent or anything," she added quickly.

"Of course not," Mustache said.

Witch was silent for a while, slowly twisting one of her pointy toes into the floor. "The thing is," she said finally, "the thing is, I still can't bring myself to free little Albert." When Schemer looked confused, she explained. "You see, Albert's the last child I have caged at home. All the others, I mean that were still alive, I let go over the past few months, but I just can't seem to release little Albert. He, he's stopped eating, but I still can't do it. I thought maybe if I started with something smaller, like my hat, I could eventually work up to it." She looked around hopefully, but the looks she was getting were skeptical. At last she sighed deeply as the clocked ticked towards seven. "It looks like Mustache is the only one here today who really had a good week," she said.

"Not really," Mustache said apologetically, glancing over at his untouched glass. "I'm afraid I poisoned the water."

A DWARF AT HIGH NOON
BY MARTIN T. INGHAM

It was raining in Selwood, a rare drizzle for the arid Nevada town. It was somehow fitting, Ron thought, as his horse trotted down Main Street beneath his stout form. The inclement weather mimicked his mood, and steadied his resolve. Such things he had on his mind, and none of them worthy of sunlight.

The foul climate didn't bother him, and it was a familiar scene from his childhood back east. Such a strange place, this western expanse. He wondered what his grandfather would have thought, had he known about this land called America. It was all a far cry from the dwarven subcities of Europe and Asia Minor, where his people had been forced to live underground for centuries. Here, in this brave new world, a dwarf could show his face up above, without fear of persecution—for the most part.

Despite the rain, there were people out and about. Businessmen, ranchers, craftsmen, and miners walked proudly, each distinct in their individual attire. A few ladies roamed the streets with stylish umbrellas, and Ron made sure to give them a wink in passing. They didn't seem to mind.

Most of the buildings were the same gray color, the shade of weathered wood, but one structure stood out, painted a distinct white. It was there that Ron was headed, the Lucca Saloon, which would determine his fate.

After hitching his horse to the rail outside, Ron sauntered inside the saloon, his chaps scuffing with each step. The swinging doors were no taller than his chest as he pushed through them and found the dingy atmosphere of the establishment. The kerosene lamps provided some illumination on a gloomy day, but not all of them were burning. The handful of midday patrons didn't warrant a waste of fuel.

With an undignified jolt, Ron threw himself onto a barstool near the taps. From the higher perch, he could look the bartender in the eye, and gauge his responses as only a dwarf could.

"Don't see many of your kind in here," the elf said with a snide inflection. He didn't match the profile of your average barkeep, looking more like a wealthy aristocrat with his silk shirt and neatly-styled hair. Most elves were like that; respectable to a fault.

"I'm looking for someone," Ron grumbled. "Fellow by the name of Vincent Lafayette. Maybe you've heard of him?"

The elf replied with a smile. "Oh, yes, I know Vint."

"Can you tell me where to find him?" Ron asked.

"Yes," the elf answered, but said no more.

"Well, tell me," Ron requested.

"No."

"What?"

"You asked if I could tell you, not if I would," the elf replied arrogantly.

"You dirty little sneak," Ron snapped, shoving a finger under the elf's nose. "If you know what's good for ya, you'll start talking."

The elf blinked nervously, as if he hadn't expected the outburst, and slid his left hand over an orb sitting beside the taps. A carefully practiced stroke of the glass ball produced a distinct glow, signaling the successful activation of the mystical device.

A bright flash of light appeared behind Ron, and he turned to see a new figure had arrived. The leather-clad individual with a long trench coat and badge pinned to his chest was easily identifiable.

"Sheriff Doliber," the elf greeted him.

"Solen," the sheriff replied, leaning an arm against the counter. "What's the matter?"

"This leprechaun spoke to me in a most threatening manner," Solen replied.

"Hey!" Ron exclaimed.

"See what I mean?" Solen added.

"Yeah, I see," Doliber replied. "You've been poking a bear, again."

"I beg your pardon?"

"You call the dwarf a Mick and wonder why he gets irate. Really, Solen, one of these days..."

The elf replied with a blank expression.

Doliber snapped his fingers, and the next thing Ron knew he was falling over, as the stool vanished from beneath him. Getting back on his feet, he realized it wasn't just the stool that was gone, but the entire saloon. He'd been teleported to the sheriff's office.

"Now we can talk," Doliber said, walking over to his desk.

"A mystic lawman?" Ron remarked as he found a chair.

"Journeyman Warlock, Delta Grade, at your service," Doliber replied as he lowered himself into a leather chair. "Cigar?" he asked, as he removed a pair of slender sticks from a box on his desk.

Ron declined, having never acquired a taste for tobacco.

"Yes, wizardry skills certainly help in this line of work," Doliber remarked as a mystic flame appeared in mid-air, lighting his cigar. "I've given most of the local businesses in this county a call-orb, so I can visit at a moment's notice. Now, what's your business here, dwarf?"

Ron sat in the creaky wooden chair in front of the desk as he replied. "Like I told the elf, I'm looking for Vincent Lafayette."

Doliber blew out a cloud of smoke and frowned beneath his mustache. "What for?"

"It's a personal matter," Ron said, reluctant to admit his reasons to the sheriff.

"Oh, I'm sure," Doliber said with a knowing nuance. "It's got to be personal when you want to kill a man."

"Who said anything about killing?"

"Empathy's another skill that comes in handy in my line of work. I can sense your hatred. You're looking for blood."

"You would, too, if Lafayette had killed your brother," Ron answered through his teeth.

"And you would be?"

"Boron Grimes."

"You're Darrell's brother?" Doliber asked with a scrutinizing stare. "You look similar, but that beard kinda hides it."

"You knew him?"

"Only in passing. He was an honest prospector, and while I wouldn't be surprised if Lafayette killed him, there's no proof."

"I've got all the proof I need, in here," Ron said, tapping the side of his head.

"Mind explaining?"

"Dwarf siblings share a psychic bond in some cases; nothing major, but when my brother died he sent his final thoughts through the ether, and I picked them up. I got a name and a face, and a whole load of pain along with it."

"What did you see?"

"Vincent Lafayette shot my brother in the back, twice, then rolled him over and put one between the eyes. I don't know why, but I intend to get an answer."

"That's going to be tough," Doliber said.

"Why? You intend to stop me, sheriff?" Ron asked.

"Actually, I'd like to help you. Lafayette's bad news. He's notorious for killing rivals in duels, and I'm sure he's left a few unmarked graves in the wild. If you want to challenge him, I won't stop you, but if you want to succeed you'll need my help."

"Why?"

"There's a reason he's such a lucky duelist, and it's more than just his shooting skills. Also, you should know he's half elf."

Ron groaned at the confirmation. He'd thought as much from the image in his brother's memory, but he'd been hoping it was just cosmetic. Going up against an elf complicated things, in so many ways.

"I guess that explains the bartender's attitude," Ron mentioned.

"Yes, they're a fiercely loyal race, and they have no qualms about bending the rules or breaking the law when it comes to protecting their own, even a half-breed like Lafayette. His outlaw gang—all of them elves—will support him to the bitter end. That's a dangerous thing, but with my help you could change all that, Deputy Grimes."

Doliber opened a desk drawer and retrieved a bright, silver badge from within. With a flick of his wrist, he tossed it at Ron, smacking the dwarf squarely in the chest. Instead of simply bounding off, the metal pinned itself to Ron's chest; all thanks to a little magic.

"I'm not interested in being one of your lackeys," Ron complained.

"You'd better be, if you intend to go against Lafayette. Shut up and listen to my plan, and maybe we'll stand a chance of delivering that justice you're after."

* * *

It was late afternoon on Friday before Vincent Lafayette rode into Selwood with his elvish gang. The rain was long gone, and dry air once more dominated the landscape, permitting a cloud of dust to drift in the wake of their Sand Mares. Looking more dragon than horse, the ghastly steeds thundered down Main Street, their clawed feet churning up bits of dirt with each step. They were far from graceful, but their speed was unmatched by any mammalian equine.

The saloon was fairly empty as the tall man with black stubble swaggered through the door, with enough sweat and stink on him to scare a starving vulture. The quiet room echoed his footsteps as he made his way to the bar and slid onto the stool in front of the taps.

"How's business, Solen?" Lafayette asked, reaching over to slap the bartender on the shoulder.

"Slow, Vint," Solen replied, pulling a bottle of aged whiskey out from under the counter. "Damned temperance movement's got too many folks abstaining. Curse those blasted Mormons!"

"Guess that leaves more for us, right, boys?" Lafayette cheered to his gang, who all grinned with mouths of stained and crooked teeth. These lawless elves hardly resembled their old-world brethren, but the ears gave them away.

Solen poured a double shot of fine Kentucky bourbon for Lafayette, then began filling mugs of ale for the others. He'd serviced these men for years, and knew their individual tastes.

"So, what's new?" Lafayette asked after downing his first double. "Anything interesting going on?"

"There was one thing," Solen remarked. "A dwarf stopped here looking for you the other day."

"Oh, really?" Lafayette asked, sounding less than surprised. "Bet we could guess what he was after."

"Hard time guessin' whose kin it'ud be, seein' how we's kilt so many of them midgies," one of his snaggle-toothed comrades opined.

A DWARF AT HIGH NOON

"So, what happened to him?" Lafayette asked the bartender.

"He was rude, so I had the sheriff haul him away," Solen said, pouring Lafayette another shot.

"Sorry I missed it," Lafayette replied. "Haven't had a good runt toss in months. You'd think they were avoiding me, or something."

The gang of elves laughed on cue.

"Speaking of avoidance," Solen mentioned, "your tab is getting heavy. With business the way it is, I hope you could make a partial payment... sometime."

Lafayette grinned and slapped the bartender on the shoulder again. "No worries, Solen. I'll have enough to square us up before I leave town."

"Are you sure? It's a very heavy tab."

"Oh, you'd be surprised," Lafayette said. "The claim we acquired from that Grimy midge a few months back, it's a literal gold mine. Soon as I visit the assayer's office, we'll be richer than a twenty dollar whore."

Solen raised his brows at the analogy, appreciating the full meaning. His ladies were only two dollars a visit, and they brought in a tidy sum for themselves and the house. He could only dream of the wealth one might acquire at ten times their current hourly rates.

"Speaking of which, is Tina available?" Lafayette asked.

"Indeed," Solen replied. "Like I said, business is slow... but I guess things'll be picking up."

* * *

Evening brought a modest crowd to the Lucca Saloon, as the working residents of Selwood came to eat, drink, and play games. Despite Solen's claims of poor business, things looked pretty hopping to Ron Grimes, as he walked in for the second time.

Every seat was filled, and the packed house concealed his movements as he walked to a corner table where quiet men played poker. Sheriff Doliber's mystic intel told him this was where he would find Lafayette.

"I'd shoot you in the back, but I don't do things your way," Ron said as he stood behind his quarry.

Lafayette tilted his head back, seeking the owner of the voice. "Oh, look, a midge," he said, turning around to face the man who stood neck high to the saloon chairs.

"You killed my brother," Ron said, trying to keep cool. Anger raged through him, enough to make him want a quick resolution, but he knew he had to do this a certain way.

"I've killed so many of you runts over the years," Lafayette bragged. "Which one was your brother?"

"Darrell Grimes."

"Sorry, I don't usually get their names."

"Two months ago, he was the prospector you shot."

"Oh, him. Yes, now I see the family resemblance. Though, all you midges look pretty much the same, don't you?"

"You killed him just for being a dwarf?" Ron asked, seeking an explanation.

"He was sitting on my claim, so me and the boys evicted him. But between you and me, I'd have killed him just for the fun of it."

"Your claim, indeed," Ron said dubiously. "You murdered him for his land, didn't you?"

"Now that's a damn lie," Lafayette growled. "You better watch yourself, midge." Seeking to end their conversation, he turned back to the card table.

"You're the liar here, Lafayette!" Ron shouted. "You killed my brother and stole his claim. I dare you to prove otherwise."

Lafayette jumped to his feet, knocking over his chair which nearly hit Ron. "You spit on my good name, you rot! You asked for it. Draw!" He set a hand on the Colt Peacemaker hanging from his hip.

"Hey!" a shout came from the bar. Solen rushed over, pushing past the apprehensive crowd. "You want to kill the midge, do it outside."

"Fine by me," Lafayette said.

One of Lafayette's henchmen tugged at his sleeve. "Say, boss, it's mighty dark out there."

Lafayette growled in frustration. "Alright, we'll settle it tomorrow, bright and early, assuming you've got the manhood!"

"At noon," Ron countered.

"Why wait?" Lafayette asked.

"I want to see you sweat," Ron said, walking backwards. He kept his face on Lafayette as he made his way out, fearing the bandit's bloodlust may outweigh his patience.

Once outside, Ron mounted his horse and rode down the street to the sheriff's office, where Doliber awaited.

"Everything's set," Ron said as he entered.

"I know," Doliber replied, having observed everything remotely on a magic mirror. He pointed a thumb at the sheet behind him, which displayed a real-time view of the saloon's interior.

"Nice trick," Ron said. "Are we ready?"

"I will be. Just make sure you don't miss tomorrow."

* * *

Dueling was currently legal in Nevada, but it was rare to have anything scheduled. Fights were usually spur of the moment, and concluded within minutes. In other circumstances, a good night's rest often sobered up rivals, allowing for a more peaceful resolution to disputes. This was not the case today, however, for both Vincent Lafayette and Boron Grimes were eager to see the other bleed.

The sun was high, and Ron looked at his large, bronze pocket watch, confirming the approaching hour. Two minutes shy of noon, and here he stood in the center of Main Street. A few riders trotted by, but most people were lined up on either side of the road, waiting to see the contest.

Lafayette sauntered out of the Lucca saloon and took his position, grinning all the while.

As the church bell rang noon, both men reached for their revolvers.

Ron yanked his old Remington out of its holster, cocked the hammer with the palm of his left hand and squeezed the trigger with his right forefinger, all in one swift motion. The thunderous crack of the shot filled the air, and a cloud of white smoke drifted out of the pistol's muzzle.

Lafayette didn't have a chance to fire before Ron's bullet sank into his flesh. Grabbing his chest in agony, he stumbled forward and fell over, planting his face in the parched earth. None of his gang came to his aid, but a lone doctor hurried over, took a look, and shook his head. With the medical opinion given, others from the crowd moved in to stare at the dying man and make their own assessments.

Ron walked over to his fallen opponent, hoping to confirm his accuracy. After pushing through the few dozen gawkers, he knelt down beside Lafayette and examined the half-elf's bloody shirt. It was hard to see where the bullet had entered, though the shot had obviously been on target.

"How'd you do that?" Lafayette uttered with his dying breath.

"Fair and square, that's how," Ron replied. He doubted the man was alive enough to hear him, but it felt good to say it. He had won. His brother was avenged, and this murderer would never kill again.

With the challenge over, Ron walked back to the sheriff's office, to see how Doliber had fared. He found the law man sitting behind his desk, smoking a cigar, grinning profusely as shouts of protest echoed out of the cells in the back room.

"Sounds like we have company," Ron mentioned as he sat down.

"If we didn't, you'd be dead," Doliber replied. "As I suspected, Lafayette's been rigging his duels, having his gang cast spells to deflect his opponents' bullets. I caught them dead to rights. Fixing duels like that makes it murder. They'll hang for it."

"Clearly, those amateurs were no match for a Warlock sheriff," Ron complimented.

"And their leader was no match for a real gunslinger," Doliber reciprocated.

"Lafayette was pretty lethargic out there," Ron mentioned. "Of course, knowing he could actually get shot might have sped him up a bit."

"I guess we'll never know," Doliber said as he snuffed out his cigar in a brass ashtray. "So, what are your plans now?"

"I figure I'll ride out to my brother's claim, see if I can find his body. After that, I might go prospecting."

"You do that, but keep yourself handy," Doliber said, putting his feet up on his desk. He leaned back and grinned at the dwarf. "You're still a deputy, remember?"

"Hey, that's not fair," Ron protested. "I never signed up for anything like that."

"You're the one who wanted justice. Accept the consequences," Doliber dug a silver dollar out of his shirt pocket and tossed it to Ron. "Here's your first paycheck. I'll call when I need you again."

"You do that," Ron said as he turned to leave.

COPS NOSE DOWN IN BLOOD
BY BARRY POMEROY

Driving recklessly, Eddy aimed for a town with the unlikely
name of Mactaquac. He was looking for a man named Sam,
who'd seen him kick a bum to death. Although he'd been on the
road for weeks, he was no closer to his goal. He had almost
unravelled the tangle of streets when he slammed on the brakes so
that the cop, hiding as he was under the cover of bushes on the
side of the road, wouldn't catch him speeding. Unfortunately, his
speed could not be arrested that quickly, or the cop had made note
of Eddy's driving, because the cop flicked on his light and tore
into the road, spilling dirt from the gravel edge and leaving a
cloud of dust.

Knowing he couldn't rely on the cop being crooked, Eddy
debated his options. He could pull over and just shoot the cop as
he approached the window, *serves him right for harassing drivers
minding their own business*, or he could speed up and hope his old
wreck, which was starting to misfire under stress, could get away.
Eddy elected to slow down and keep the car rolling, as though he
were looking for a place to pull over and didn't like the look of
the shoulder. The cop turned off his siren, but kept his lights on.
When Eddy didn't stop after a mile the cop flicked the siren back
on and swerved out into the empty road to force Eddy to stop.

236

Eddy had still not made a decision as to what he wanted to do, but seeing the cop beside him, commanding with his beefy hand, made all of his frustration at his increasingly hopeless search come out in one smooth jerk of the steering wheel. Fortunately for Eddy, both cars were approaching a small bridge over a shallow gully. To his delight, the cop car plunged nose down over the side of the bridge, and the smash as it hit the bottom was satisfyingly definitive.

Eddy pulled over on the bridge, and leaving his car idling, saw where the cop car had hit grill first into the rocks at the creek bottom, spilling its overfed contents into the stream before leaning and then crashing forward onto the cop. He watched for life in the one arm and shoulder he could see sticking out from the wreckage, but the gravel road was peaceful, now that the cop's motor had died. Eddy watched the slick spreading out in the stream, saw what he hoped was blood dirtying the stirred up water, and climbed back into his car.

He knew that even if the cop was dead, he had a few days at most before the rest, stirred up like a hornet nest struck with a stick, would stop every car on the road looking for dents and white paint. Eddy pulled over a few miles north and wiped what he could of the paint away, as well as kicked out some of the dents. He covered the recent nature of the accident with oil, knowing that the road would supply the rest of the camouflage.

True to his expectations, as Eddy turned west to Tracy and Fredericton Junction, dirt gathered in the creases and covered the door with a fine sheen of dust. He prowled towards the towns west of Fredericton, beginning to despair and strongly tempted to cut his losses and leave the province. "I've got the money to go," he argued with himself. "I've got enough cash to buy any place I want to live. What the hell am I doing here? If the guy hasn't ratted me out by now he ain't going to, and if he does, I could be gone."

Interpreting the silence of the road as a counter argument, Eddy mumbled to himself throughout the long day, marking on the map where he'd run the cop to ground, so he'd not accidentally return to the same road.

***

Eddy ditched his car near the US border, hoping to throw the cops off the scent. They would think that he'd crossed the border, like the famous killer who'd made national news as he was waved through by the US border guards even though he was covered in blood and carrying a gore-encrusted chain saw, hatchet, and sword. The border patrol had been thoughtless enough to let him in, so Eddy hoped that the RCMP, who had begun a country-wide manhunt, would come to the same conclusion.

Getting another car didn't prove to be as easy as Eddy first thought, and he finally had to settle for a motorcycle from a cottage as big as a house. Upon breaking in, he perused the rooms as if he were a homebuyer, infatuated with the open stair and loft, as well as the many rooms off the main floor that spilled around the pool. *Even my dope stash couldn't begin to pay for this*, Eddy thought, *and they call me a crook.* Finding the motorcycle had been a lucky accident. He had stopped to urinate beside the boat house, after checking for a boat, and had seen the gleam of chrome. The bike was an older Honda, but its key was still in the ignition and when he kicked it over it roared to life, belching the dark smoke of long storage.

Eddy spent a week in the cottage. He told himself that he was letting the heat dissipate, but in reality he was beginning to fear the extent of the manhunt he'd begun. He watched the TV in the living room, which was the only room that allowed a view of the roadside windows, and nightly he felt the noose tighten. He grew to resent the other news that was reported, such as the two minute spot on some special monkey that was stolen from a lab in Massachusetts, and a series of alien sightings in Maine.

Although Eddy revelled in the media's inaccuracy, as they supplemented their paucity of fact with wild fantasy, he flicked from one channel to another, watching for his hideout to appear on satellite TV, waiting to be surrounded. More than once he woke at night with a start, sitting upright in the bed, hands already upon him and his heart racing. He dreamt that he saw his own face, hauntingly distant and running, as a Cops episode was filmed around him. He saw himself die over and over, until he began to yell at the news' inaccuracies. "I'm here, you stupid bastards! In the mansion on the hill! You can't find shit!" The house echoed.

***

In the northern part of the province, Steve Mercer spent his days working with Crooked John, as he called him, and living in a one-room apartment beside a grocery store. Steve also made note of the news report about a police officer who had been forced from the road. Calling the station for details—which he was entitled to because of his posting on the highways—Steve confirmed the media's version. Some large metallic brown car, which would have its driver's side smashed in, had deliberately turned—according to the tracks—and pushed the pursuing police vehicle into the ravine where it had been found. The reported paint colour tweaked Steve's memory of the Chevy they'd pulled over less than a week before and he tried to remember the license plate.

The next day he tried to bring up the Chevy to John, but his partner was surly to the point of violence, so Steve contented himself with pressing the dispatcher for reports and keeping his eyes open.

***

When Eddy saw that his car had been found and the police had leapt exactly where he had expected he began to feel safer. The manhunt was extended to include New England, although the Americans objected that they would never let another murderer just walk into Maine, not after the derisive news of just a few years earlier. Upon seeing his car hanging from a tow truck, he half-expected his dreams to come true, to see himself on TV shooting from the back seat. But once the car was compressed into a news segment, Eddy felt dissociated from the long body of the Chevy, which looked reduced now that it had been parked in the woods for a few days. "Damn lucky that junkie stole it," Eddy congratulated himself. "Otherwise that would go straight back to me, instead of to whoever it was." Setting aside a momentary twinge of fear when he thought about all the cars he'd left behind, Eddy began to think about his own search.

Knowing that the cops were not looking for a motorcycle made him feel safe, and before long, Eddy was back on the road, driving from farm to town, from village to pulp mill, waiting for a sighting to let him know he'd arrived. He had lost a lot of his original anger, as well as impetus, and all he really had left was he had nothing better to do with his time. He liked driving the bike, and although he had some scars and burns from wiping out on the gravel on the corners of country roads, Eddy was even beginning to enjoy drifting the roads and seeing how people lived. He was window shopping for a life, not having ever developed one of his own.

***

Frustrated at his lack of involvement in the case of the cop who had been forced from the road, which he was even more certain had been bungled by whatever John's involvement was, Steve Mercer applied for a transfer to the southern part of the province. He was not alone in his desire, however, since every police officer in the country wanted to get in on the manhunt, so Steve had to content himself with taking a leave of absence and driving to southern New Brunswick. Absurdly reminding himself of the police movies and shows that had made him want to become a cop when he was a child, Steve prowled the back roads near the site of the accident. He even visited the fallen officer in the Fredericton hospital, where he lay in a coma.

Talking to local police as though he were just gossiping about a case that every officer had a right to be concerned about, Steve debated and dismissed the possibility that the suspect had left the province. "He's holed up somewhere," he said to more than one of his peers, and although they nodded in agreement, they had little solid evidence to offer. Steve examined the offender's car, looked at the contents of the ashtray and trunk, and came to other conclusions than the officers who had been through it. The car had obviously passed more than one hand since it had been stolen, so identifying its most recent owner was necessarily difficult.

***

When he asked casually after Sam's car at the Milton gas station while he was pulling a twenty from his wallet, Eddy was actually surprised that the attendant recognised the description.

"Green you say? Painted by hand?"

Eddy almost missed what the old man was saying, until it dawned on him that his search was drawing to a close.

"That'd be Liz's nephew. What's his name. Sam. Something like that."

Eddy confirmed that Samuel was the nephew's name, and as casually as he could, got directions to the aunt's house.

When he drove into the yard he didn't even have to pound on the door, for behind the screen door he could hear a high pitched and creepy elderly voice querulously demanding, "What do you want?"

Forcing himself to remain calm in the face of geriatric horror, Eddy told the old woman how he was a friend of Sam's and was in town and hoping to see him. *What happened to the good old days of just killing her if she refused to answer, of kicking in doors,* Eddy wondered while Liz fetched a map that showed where Sam was building his house.

Once he had the map, and had plotted out where Sam lived, it was late evening, and Eddy went back to the cottage as if he were going home. His plan was to return the next day and put an end to this business once and for all. He spent the evening cleaning his gun and reloading it with the bullets he'd bought in a local hardware store. When he fell asleep, he was already spending his money on an expensive house and Sam was long dead and rotting.

The sound of the car in the yard startled Eddy to instant wakefulness, although he'd spent most of the night scouring news channels for signs of himself. Moving by instinct, he grabbed his clothes and the money belt he'd made by folding a pillowcase. With his pistol in hand, Eddy slipped from the window his way of living had always made him leave ajar.

When the Jitneys pushed aside their damaged door and saw the mess made of the kitchen, they immediately went outside to their car. "We've got to call the police," his wife said, and her hand was already on her cell phone.

"Get the kids out of here. I'll stay and meet the police here. Don't worry," Tom added for his wife's concerned look, "I'm not going inside. I'll wait by the road."

Eddy was already cursing the loss of the motorcycle when he ducked under the low trees that divided the lots. Knowing he couldn't walk to Sam's, whose car he'd planned to steal, he picked the next easiest option. Pulling the wires from the ignition of an old truck the neighbors obviously ran only on the property, since it had no plates, Eddy pushed it down the slight slope and got it running before he had to turn onto the road.

Swerving to avoid her reckless neighbor, Sandra Jitney shushed the kids and then applied the gas and passed the truck, her mind only on the violation of their summer cottage.

Eddy drove straight to the road that led to Sam's land, but more than ten miles from his destination, the truck lurched to a halt and died. Although he had never been more than ordinarily superstitious, Eddy felt his luck starting to turn, and he touched the roll of money above his belt. He ditched the truck beside the highway, guessing a farm truck would not arouse suspicions beside the road. He crept into the quiet yard of a nearby house, hoping for another motorcycle, but humiliatingly had to make do with a bicycle, the only vehicle in the yard. Tottering from side to side, Eddy pedalled towards Sam's land, puffing from the unaccustomed exercise and cursing. "At the very least," he said to himself, "Sam should be willing to give me his car, after going through all this to kill him."

* * *

Even while Eddy was driving towards Sam's place, Steve passed him going west to the scene of the break-in. He'd heard the call come over the police band, so he responded, thinking that this was exactly the type of place the cop killer would hole up. More intent on his destination than his stated goal, or perhaps foiled by his lack of training, Steve didn't notice the missing plates on the passing truck, and gave its driver no more than a glance.

The Jitney cottage, a few hours later, looked more like a mansion to Steve, from the perspective of his tiny apartment. The children, reacting to their parent's stress and the disorder of their cottage, made the walls resound with crying. Steve introduced himself to the attending officers, who looked at him with more suspicion than gratitude, and then went to quiet the two boys. He distracted them by throwing rocks into the pond, aiming for the lily pads which had just begun to open their leaves in the early summer sun, all the while noting the forced door on the shed. When he led the boys to the shed, under the pretence that they could show him the motorcycle they'd told him about, Sam saw the signs of recent activity. He mentioned as much to the investigating officers, but they did little more than make a note of it for their report.

Frustrated, Steve left to begin his daily rounds of the back roads, looking for someone he wouldn't be able to recognize, driving a vehicle he didn't know in a direction that Steve would not be able to predict. Defeated finally, Steve reluctantly turned his car north. He was already dreading sitting on the highway with John, dreading the talk of women and sports, and John's sadistic urges to make the lives of those they were supposed to serve and protect as hellish as possible. Dreaming of an end to his maritime stint, Steve thought ahead to his next posting, which would surely be better.

***

Eddy was just entering Sam's road when he thought better of the bike. He took it to the side of Sam's lengthy drive, hid it in the bushes, and then proceeded on foot. He had his gun out and his roll of money felt heavy under his shirt. He was hot and sticky from the bike ride, and he was in a foul mood. Eddy needed coffee when he woke—as the Jitneys had discovered from the spills on their counters and floors—and until that first cup his thoughts were brutal and unformed. Woken with a start as he was, and forced into a farce of an escape, Eddy was in a murderous rage. "You're the whole reason I'm in this mess, you bastard," Eddy muttered to himself, "but I'll help you out with that."

Eddy stepped past the parked vehicles, looking them over proprietarily for one he might like to have, and then, deciding that the Honda was more nondescript, he approached the construction site.

"Sam," Eddy's yell was loud in the silent clearing. "I know you're in there Sam. I talked to your aunt."

Eddy was correct in his assessment that Sam would be easier to encourage into the open if he feared for his great aunt.

Sam stepped from behind the edge of the house. "What do you want?"

"Oh, come on now Sam. You know me. Don't you? I know you."

Sam knew who Eddy was as soon as he saw him, but once the admission was public Sam began to tremble uncontrollably. "I never saw anything. You can go back home."

"I came a long way to visit you, Sam. To see what you've done to the place. I can't just go away. Not without a real visit anyway." Eddy liked to play with his food.

Sam's awkward stance almost gave away the hammer he had in his rear pocket, and his fear of the man in front of him. Sam was pleading now that he had seen the gun in Eddy's hand and as far as Eddy was concerned that was the natural order of things. "Don't go whining to try to please me," Eddy began to sing, "you never tried to do before." Lapsing before his pop song was finished, Eddy began to explain his position to Sam.

"You gotta admit, Sam, you caused me some trouble. I've come all the way across the country, which I didn't do for the scenery. You're the only one who saw me, but I want to let you off the hook right now."

Framing his final protest, Sam contented himself with a head jerk that Eddy might mistake as a twitch of fear. *Stupid,* Sam thought to himself, *he certainly won't know what the hell that means.*

Eddy sensed that he was losing his audience, which concerned him enough to glance back to the house to look for reinforcements. That glance reminded him that he'd seen two vehicles, and only one Sam. Eddy suddenly had doubts about Sam's fear. He turned back to Sam, a snarl on his face as he aimed and squeezed the trigger.

His eyes almost shut, Sam took the hammer from his pocket. Faster than Eddy could react, Sam leaned forward and threw the hammer.

His head torn at the intrusion, blood spurting out from the multiple wounds, Eddy crashed first to his knees and then onto the ground. He gasped for a few long horrible minutes, and then lay still.

***

Once Sam had recovered emotionally and was prepared to deal with the mess in his yard, evening was fast approaching. Taking Eddy's gun, after carefully wiping it, Sam went to look for a vehicle, in case the murderer had brought an accomplice. Near the main road he found what must be the killer's bicycle, since it hadn't been there earlier. Sam repressed a nervous urge to laugh. *A killer on a bicycle*. The bike lay where it had apparently been flung when Eddy had arrived.

Sam shouldered it, and, after a brief glance toward the road, took it behind his house into the brush. "I'll get rid of it later," he said aloud. "I've got to deal with the other," to the empty clearing he gestured with his head towards Eddy's still body.

"I could just drag his body into the woods. No one is coming after him, right?" In his nervousness, Sam debated with himself.

"I don't think so," Sam replied. "But can we explain what happened to the cops."

"I don't think you can explain that hammer in his head. And they're not going to like it that both of us were living in Vancouver until just a few weeks ago."

"You're right," Sam reluctantly agreed with himself.

Sam dragged Eddy further into the woods, pausing periodically so he could scout ahead to find a place that he wouldn't ever want to see again. He didn't want his land to be full of reminders.

RAFAEL GARCIA MEETS THE DEVIL
BY ERIK SVEHAUG

The Spanish horse patrol was on route to Bodega on the Pacific. Rumors, then reports, had come to the fort beside St. Rafael near San Francisco Bay that other Europeans had been seen in the headlands around the mountain called Tamalpais.

The five leather-coated soldiers, their priest companion and the native servant stopped awhile to stretch their legs and barter food at a poor village. The missionary, mildly drunk, was still able to talk with the village elder in Bay area pidgin. The man had apparently seen nothing.

Private Rodrigo played with the kids. They got him into line with them in the field and passed a rawhide ball from one to the next, then faster, then two lines formed and raced to see who was fastest. They laughed; he laughed; no one used words, but they all cheered and yelled and slapped each other's back.

It turned into tag and racing through the woods. The Miwok kids were quick as deer and knew the paths, but Rodrigo's heart made up the gap.

A child yelled when a molting yellow Grizzly charged. Rodrigo shouted and raced forward, waving his arms. The bear broke his shoulder with the first swipe, then pounced down on him with both front paws, breaking ribs.

249

The village dogs and kids and the rest of the Spanish patrol came running at his screams. Private Joaquin raised his rifle. Corporal Garcia pushed the gun aside.

"You'll only wound it," said the corporal.

Private Olugio fired into Rodrigo's head above the ear. His scream cut off. His left hand stopped clawing the ground. The percussion froze the bear for a moment; the dogs rushed in.

Dancing and snapping, the skinny curs of the village harassed the confused Grizzly until he backed away and left toward the forest.

As his men rushed to Private Rodrigo, bleeding and twisted, Corporal Garcia shouted. "Murder and directly disobeying a superior!" Corporal Garcia was outraged, but confident. "Joaquin, Pepe, arrest Private Olugio at once. Remove his weapons and tie his hands. Someone tell these heathen to find Private Rodrigo's horse. And call the priest." No one left Rodrigo or even looked in Garcia's direction. They lifted Rodrigo sadly to their shoulders and let themselves be led by the children to the village.

***

Four days after the death of Private Rodrigo, the four remaining Spanish soldiers of the Bodega patrol had grudgingly but dutifully followed Corporal Garcia to the westernmost coast of the headlands. From a hill a few miles north of the Bodega community they had been watching foreigners. A palisade had taken shape around a group of buildings; additional tents and native huts filled a field nearby. They had noticed an organized competence, unlike the chaotic procedures of their own Presidio. The Russians were good-humored, even obviously warm, with their countrymen and civil, not at all unkind, with the natives. They liked to eat and drink. They liked music and almost all played instruments. Officers had fancy housing and married couples were separated from singles. There were apparently already mixed marriages (or at least convenient alliances) between merchant workers and native women. Maybe it was hard to feel threatened because it wasn't a military group they were watching.

A small group of short, ugly aboriginals kept to themselves after arriving on a schooner from the south, but seemed well treated. It was impossible to discern their tribe. The natives of the village outside the fort were mostly Koshaya Pomo, but included individuals from tribelets up the Coast, judging by clothing, as well as many Bay Miwok of Bodega, maybe even mountain Miwok and Yokuts. This place prospered. There was even a windmill for grinding grain, metal work, and stores of manufactured goods.

They were discovered during a lapse in vigilance. From his horse, a happy, well-fed Russian with a magnificent beard and moustache and passable Spanish skills had offered them their annual salary each month to learn to be merchants. None of the Spanish military in Alta California had been paid in nearly 8 months and even then only got a tithe toward what was owed. And the Russian could probably back up his offer. The men were tempted. After all, below them on a point of land, an actual fort had taken shape. "Rossia", he called it.

So tempted. Back at their base at San Rafael, near San Francisco Bay, their colleagues still lived in tule huts, helping to build the new fort like miserable natives, when they weren't out freezing their asses off scouting. Pants and tunics were in rags, patched over and over. Since they had to fight the cold and damp of autumn, stepping in and out of marshy ground, rot attacked their feet constantly. This seal-skin-booted Cossack offered them housing, hearth fires and winter clothing like his.

Very tempted. Red-faced at his own weakness, Corporal Rafael Garcia intervened. He yelled at the Russian, "Go back to your fort, you mackerel peddler. Go back to the Czar, you money-grubbing meddler. Go back to your country, before we make you swim home. You can kiss our horses' behinds, you snake. A son of Spain is not for sale. You men mount up."

Bravely spoken, thought Olugio, as he planted his feet for action. Nodding at Joaquin and Pepe, he grabbed the Corporal's right arm from behind and twisted it up between his shoulder blades. Driving with his feet, he brought the Corporal face first onto the pine needle strewn ground and landed on him with a thud. Garcia screamed once and bit off his cry.

Joaquin gathered up his superior's weapons, but Olugio said, "Wait a bit. Let's leave him something. It's a long way back."

So they chose to leave his sword, which they left across his lap. His hands, behind him, encircled the trunk of a tree in a reverse bear hug, bound.

The Russian led his three new employees and their four horses back to Fort Ross where they could wash up, eat, drink, and begin their language lessons.

Garcia considered his situation like the most detached tactician:

He was alive, bleeding a bit from forehead and cheek.

His arms were tied tightly behind him awkwardly.

The joints of his right arm and some ribs complained loudly.

He was thirsty and without water.

His sword lay across his lap, unusable.

His horse was gone.

The missionary would reach the rendezvous with his servant by noon tomorrow, three hours away on foot.

The construction camp at San Rafael was two days forced march away.

In the distance, the two-masted schooner was just leaving Fort Ross, deck piled with hides and furs.

His men could probably say "vodka" and "beet soup" and "piss on Spain" in passable Russian by now. He was alone. He would give no thought to revenge. He was alive. There would be time for revenge.

He tested the knots that held him, but he found his wrists had been lashed and didn't flex at all. Even if he twisted to the point of dislocating his shoulders it was unlikely to free him at the wrists. The tree was so big it didn't taper at all for 30 feet, so no slack would come from trying an agonizing climb. The bones of his wrists and hands were the weak link; if he broke or dislodged them, he might be able to slide free. Was there an alternative? The sword!

If he could dig a hole with his heel...

If he could get the hilt of his sword jammed into the hole...

253

If he didn't knock it over rotating his body to the other
side of the tree…

If he could center the blade on the ropes…

A thought raced through the fortified perimeter of his mind: I
could probably fix the point of the blade below my throat.

Suddenly, his clear analysis became certain defeat. He would
starve and die at this tree and the wolves would eat him. He
would pull his hands out in a pulpy mess and be an invalid and a
joke the rest of his life if he lived. If he did kill himself, he would
be damned and lose both his body to the beasts and his soul to the
devil.

Groaning almost mutely and sweating an acidic stinking
sweat, Garcia saw the devil roll the door away from the cave
leading to Hell and grin a yellow-toothed grin that sampled his
flesh and found it tasty.

"My God!" Rafael cried. "Save me! Holy Mother, save me!"

Suddenly his hands dropped to the ground at his sides as a
blade cut the ropes between his wrists. Olugio's face appeared
from behind the tree and frowned at him. The private kicked the
sword away.

"Strasvi, Corporal Garcia, strasvi! That's Russian. I've been
watching you for awhile. I've been a scout so many seasons now,
it's the way I am. And I saw something interesting this time. You
can cry! I had no idea you were so afraid of trees. Honestly, you
make me glad of my recent choices."

Olugio squatted facing his superior.

"Do you recall the recruiting patrol we made for the mission
last year, across the Sacramento River, Corporal? Down toward

Turtle Island? We brought the big group of native women and youngsters all the way back to Dolores."

"Rodrigo was with us. Do you remember? Of course, you do. He was making up his own names for all the different kinds of birds. I'll never again see an owl without thinking of the Archbishop."

Olugio stood with his back against the tree while Garcia struggled to get blood and feeling back into his leaden arms.

"What did you say on the way here, after he died? 'At least he could have died like a man'."

Olugio waited for a reply he knew wasn't coming.

"I'm not your executioner. You didn't even spare poor Rodrigo a bullet. If it wasn't for the local dogs driving the bear away, we wouldn't have even retrieved his body."

"The Holy Mother saved you today, by reproaching me. Maybe memory of your own panic will redeem your heart. I doubt it. If you live to see Lt. De Reche, you had better tell him we are dead, so as not to look for us, or I promise that every uniformed Spaniard in California will hear the story of you losing the battle with this tree."

Olugio strode to his horse and cantered away without looking back.

Garcia regained his feet and considered again the option of falling on his sword. The recent image of the Adversary with yellow fangs and the smell of that open pit He guarded turned his thoughts back toward living.

As he began the long walk back to camp, he tried to frame the report he would make to the Lieutenant. There were at least one hundred of them, all Miwok, I think, from several villages. They

killed Pepe from hiding, and then attacked from all sides. The
men fought bravely, but had no chance. They've probably eaten
the horses by now.

He stopped walking. Strasvi, he thought. Strasvi. The
language didn't sound too difficult. No, he had missed that
chance.

The redwoods towered above him. He shuddered a bit in the
fog that had settled in. He thought wistfully of his previous
posting in Baja California as a private, bored and sweating,
without another care.

He tried to keep his eyes on the trail and out of the trees and
plodded on.

***

Garcia found the native woman feeding the evening fire and
Brother Amoroso sitting on a nearby rock, wrapped in a mission
blanket. A green glazed cup was at his feet, a bottle nearby.
Yellow light from the fire played with the shadows on the canvas
tents. The trees around them grew and shrank with the wavering
flame.

The missionary looked up. "Did you bring game?" he asked.

Garcia shivered as he embraced the fire; he would have sat on
its lap, if he could. He shook uncontrollably now. His jaw
chattered.

"N-n-no food," he said.

Gradually, he told his story.

The priest was terrified. "Are they out there? Were you followed? What about us? Should we leave now? Why did they let you go? Should we put out the fire? Are they coming?"

The woman added some round cooking stones to the fire, since she would be cooking mush.

"Corporal, are we safe here?" said the priest.

Garcia saw that the priest was convinced and not inclined to administer the sacraments to bodies surrounded by savage killers. The soldier began to see an additional possibility emerging from this chaos.

Promotion.

Garcia was actually a careful, smart old dog, in planning, if not in action. When he was reasonably sure he'd reached his goal, he'd guard it, step away from it and circle it, see if anyone else was chasing it, make sure he still wanted it. He had learned by watching his disgraced father that achieving one's goals and actually winning something he desired sometimes changed a man. Changed his world. Sometimes in unexpected ways.

"They will not follow us," he said. "But I think we ought to demand their repentance with soldiers and neophyte-baptized natives from San Jose and the Presidio at Dolores. I can bring these cowards in for confession or meet their refusal with punishment," he said.

The woman handed them portions of smoked fish.

The priest stood still, clutching his blanket in front of his neck, studying a shadow shape in the trees to see if it was the enemy.

***

When the time was right, Sergeant Garcia, promoted for his bravery in action on the headlands of Tamalpais, led a group of soldiers and armed natives to a Yurok village northeast of St. Rafael. In the battle, with musket, saber and small cannon, two hundred surprised natives were killed, thirty-four of them armed with bows and hunting arrows. The remainder were women, children and the elderly. Sixteen teenagers, mostly girls, were brought back, tied together in a forced march of three days. There were no other survivors of the village.

His superiors promised him another raise and some fabric for a new uniform.

LOVE, SHE IS BLIND
BY EDWARD MARTIN III

There's not much that can make a man take a hard look at the kind of life he's led like staring directly down the barrel of a semiautomatic pistol in the hand of his most recent ex.

"Cynthia," I said calmly. "I can't tell you what a surprise it is to see you."

She tried to smile and I could almost remember what it looked like to actually see her smile, but then she did that thing she does right before she gets really angry at someone. She pursed her lips and turned her head slightly.

"Do you have any idea how hard it was to find you?" she asked.

"I'm sorry," I said. "It's been a little frantic these days. Been kind of under the radar."

"You disappeared," she said. "And frankly, I'm happiest if you prefer it that way. You're an ex for a reason, Paul. The only downside to that is that we had a little unfinished business and that's something that I just couldn't let go. Not yet. I have my reputation."

I tried very hard and successfully managed to not add any fire to the conflagration in my mind that was a conversation revolving around her reputation. Instead, I carefully and slowly opened my hands to show her that there was no mischief and asked "What can I do? How can I help?" although I knew exactly what it was that she was going to say.

"I want my money."

I took a deep breath. While there were and are many things about Cynthia that would drive any man insane, I had to give her this: she was always to the point.

"I figured that," I said. "That's it?"

"I learned a lot more about that job, Paul. I learned, for example, that you were not forthcoming with me on the complete value of the shipment, and that you did, in fact, make considerable bank off my efforts."

"I suppose you want a piece of that, too?" I asked.

"As strange as it might sound, no. I could try and work out what my piece would have been, but the fact is that I made a deal based on a flat fee, not a percentage. It's good to know that you were willing to screw me, and that helps me justify making sure you're not a part of my life anymore, but really, all I want is exactly what you said you would pay me."

She's also fair. Not too many people would insist on only their exact share when they had the gun and the drop on their ex. So she gets points for that.

"Okay," I said. "You're right. I'll get your money."

"And I'll follow you," she said. "Not because I don't trust you, but because I expect you to disappear again and it's considerably less likely when I am on top of your every move. No offense."

"None taken," I said. "But my place isn't really set up for visitors."

"I'm not visiting," she said. "This is strictly business."

"I understand."

Besides, it was a lot cooler in the house, and being cooler was suddenly very important to me. Cooler and darker.

I invited her in, and although I was chivalrous, she still insisted on me going first. Which is understandable, I guess.

"The safe is in the living room," I said. She didn't reply, but she didn't have to, it wasn't as if I had asked her a question. She followed me.

"It's dark in here," she said. "I recall you liking a lot of light, Paul."

"I used to, but things have changed. I like it a little darker now. And, well, my girlfriend likes it this way, too."

She snorted a laugh. "I hope she's a smart cookie," she said.

"No complaints so far," I replied. "But nobody's perfect."

"Then I hope that your imperfections are a fine complement to her imperfections," she said.

"That's very kind of you," I said.

"Money," she reminded me.

"Living room," I said. "Safe."

"Keep going," she said.

"Don't go into the kitchen," I asked. "It's really a mess in there."

"Not here for coffee and a chat. Just here for the money," she said, and then "You know, a lot of people have been enjoying furniture, Paul. Have you thought about that?"

"Well, yes, but we're just getting ready to leave," I said. "Moving. Sorry about the boxes."

LOVE, SHE IS BLIND

"I'm glad I found you now," she said. "It seems to be getting progressively harder to find you these days."

"Remember saying that's how you liked it?" I asked.

I was reminded that she didn't like being reminded of such things by the sharp poke of metal in my back.

"After you give me my money, you can vanish off the face of the Earth for all I care," she said. "I've got plenty of gigs lined up already."

The hall expanded out into the living room and I stepped to the safe.

"That's a gun safe," she said.

"What better place to hide money?" I asked.

"What better place to hide guns, too," she added. "After you finish the combination, I'm afraid I'm going to have to open it myself."

"Cynthia, are you suggesting that after all this, I would actually try to shirk my duty or even trick you?"

"Absolutely," she said. "And now that we're both clear on the expectations of the situation, get to opening that thing so I can get my money and be on my way out of here and into my new life without Paul Temple, thank you very much."

I did admire her directness.

Combination, combination…

"You don't have to worry about me seeing the combination," she said. "I really don't care at all, and I'm never coming back."

She looked around.

"Damn, Paul, it is nutty-dark in here."

"I put paper over the windows," I said. "I like it dark."

"Apparently. And so does New Girlfriend, right?"

"Right."

"It does not go well with the cathedral ceiling thing. I can't see shit in here."

"We manage."

"Manage to open the safe, please."

I spun the last number and stepped back.

"It's ready to open. You said you wanted to open it yourself."

"Thank you, I'm glad you remembered. Would you also be so kind as to step a few steps back? I have a broad category of things I can expect you to do and having you step a few feet away and still be where I can see you helps some of those be a little less likely."

I stepped back, and kept my hands up, palms raised where she could see them.

"Nothing up my sleeves," I said.

"That has always been a lie and you know it," she said, opening the door.

Inside the safe were my two pistols — polished 1911s from my father's collection — and my cashbox. Expertly, she flipped open the cashbox lid with one hand. She knelt down and dumped the cashbox on the floor and started counting out hundreds.

"This is going to take a while," I said.

"That's a shame," she said. "It would have taken less time to simply work all this out with me last year and pay me what you owed me instead of making me go to all the time and trouble of finding you and dumping money on your floor."

I was impressed at how quickly she counted out twenty-five thousand dollars in hundreds.

"You're running low, Paul," she said, as she stuffed the bills into her purse. "You might want to think about picking up another gig before you completely light out for the territories."

"I don't suppose you would be willing to help?" I asked. "Despite our differences in the past, I've found that you're pretty good in a pinch. And I'm willing to not let my personal feelings get wrapped up in our business relationship."

She shook her head. "Oh, I don't think so," she said, and stood up.

Just as she straightened out, a flash of dark within the dark struck.

I've heard a lot of different reactions, from screams to gurgles to growls and more. She only said "Hey!" loudly, almost indignantly.

Then her spine snapped.

Legs — thin, black, and steel-strong — crossed her chest and pulled her back. Her hands trembled, and the little semiauto she carried fell to the floor. I would have to deal with that later, I suppose. That's what gun safes are for.

Behind her, a shadow rose, and a body moved into view.

I have read very scientific sounding papers informing me that it's impossible for insects to grow as large as they do in horror movies. I can accept that they honestly believe this.

But, of course, they're wrong on two counts. First of all, she did anyway, and second of all, she's not an insect.

She dropped Cynthia, stepped over, and nudged my hand. I scratched along either side of her beautiful soft head. I stroked her and petted her and cooed.

One of her legs rose and petted the side of my face.

She doesn't blink, I know, but I like to think of her blinking at me when our eyes meet. Her eyes are absolute pitch black, but I swear there's movement inside them, that I can see her soul through those eyes. The big eyes, anyway. The little eyes are her hunting eyes. Best to not look too long into them.

"It's time, love," I said.

She tapped my face lightly.

"I know, and I'd love to, but Cynthia may have told someone where she was going. It's only a few days difference. We'll still use the trailer."

Tap, tap again.

"If you like, of course. We still have all the gear in storage. We shouldn't do it too close, though. Might have to drive westward a day or two."

Tap, tap…

"People get suspicious. The roadside attraction thing is a great idea, but if we're there longer than a few days, then people start remembering us and we can't have them remembering us. At least not up here in the States," I said. "Once we get past the border, things'll be a lot easier."

One last tap.

"I love you, too, beautiful," and I meant it. She knew I meant it — she could tell the difference between the feel of someone telling the truth and the feel of someone lying — but I've always thought it's a very good thing to hear.

She stepped back over Cynthia. Two of her legs lifted the body, and held it close. The other six easily kept her balanced.

I smiled at her, showing my teeth. She loved that.

"Besides, I think we're about out of room to store your leftovers, love," I added.

I swear, she winked. I know she doesn't, but I swear she does. She stepped back into the shadows.

"Wait!" I said. She stopped. I stepped close and pried Cynthia's purse from around her arm. "We'll need this piece," I said.

The two of them slipped away into the darkness for their private time and I put everything back into the safe and continued packing. I didn't like being on the move right now, but, well, you go where your heart takes you, I guess.

EQUILIBRIUM OF CHAOS
BY ADAM KNIGHT

The double-reinforced, steel and titanium doors closed with thunderous, metallic finality. Four foot thick concrete walls towered over me, so high I could not see the ceiling. Garish fluorescent lights lit my way but left plenty of darkness for the imagination. I wasn't sure what to expect in this facility, but I didn't expect it to feel so…lifeless. Sterile. The air in the hangar was cool, clean, and still. The last echoes of the sealed doors rang in my ears, like the doors of a tomb shutting on the dead.

I shook my head, trying to jar loose the image. Too poetic, I thought. I'm here for facts, for the truth. That's what journalism is all about, right? I turned to face my host. Trim and precise, Colonel Baldwin wasn't tall but gave the impression of being tall. His age, too, was misleading; the hint of gray in his buzz cut placed him anywhere between forty and sixty. His eyes and mouth revealed no emotion. Was he angry about giving me this once-in-a-lifetime tour of his top secret military facility? Was he honored? I wondered these things, but reminded myself of my assignment. This was no human interest fluff; this was the investigation that would vault my career into the stratosphere.

"Welcome to Hangar Eighteen," he said, his voice as flat as the walls. "You've seen the aircraft and land vehicles above ground. Now let me show you inside. Then you'll see there's nothing to the rumors you've been spreading."

He didn't mean me, personally. I haven't written a single word about Hangar Eighteen. But in recent weeks, the facility had been the twenty-four hour news networks' favorite bone to chew on. The fewer facts available, the harder they chewed. Speculations about strange weapons technology, conspiracy cover-ups, mind-control, and even more bizarre things were being irresponsibly thrown around without a shred of evidence. The Army allowed one national newspaper to send one reporter with a notebook—no camera, no cell phone, no recording devices—in for a personal tour with one high-ranking Army representative. Colonel Baldwin was the rep. I was the reporter.

"It's an honor, sir," I said, offering my hand for him to shake. He turned his back, walking the length of the concrete room in measured steps.

"This is the entrance to the deeper levels of the facility. The room appears empty, no?"

Bare floor, bare walls, as empty as an unused coffin. Colonel Baldwin walked over to the wall and I followed. He pointed to what appeared to be a chip in the concrete, no larger than a pencil eraser.

"Embedded in these walls are cameras, infrared sensors, voice recognition devices, and approximately twenty other instruments to identify every person who steps in this facility. This may be your first time here, Mr. Grant, but you are no stranger."

Fumbling with my notepad, I jotted down the information. Nothing shocking or revealing, but could make a good lead to the story. I tried to fight off the feeling of two dozen eyes on me.

Next to the steel door at the end of the room, Colonel Baldwin entered a string of numbers on a touchscreen keypad. A few seconds and subtle clicks later, the door opened. Expressionless soldiers in white Class B uniforms worked at computers, wrote notes, and sorted through files.

"This is our communication room. From here, we take in data and communiqués from other installations around the globe, and process that information to make it viable for statistical analysis. Said data and communication is then filed appropriately so as to render later analysis more feasible."

I scrambled to write down his words. When I finished, I reread it, then looked up.

"So, you gather information here, look at it, and then store it?"

Colonel Baldwin didn't smile, but I bet he wanted to.

"Moving on," he said, turning from me and walking down the rows, "Would you like an interview for your news story?"

"Sure."

The colonel stood by the desk of a lieutenant, a twenty-something young woman at a computer. I looked at the screen, which showed a U.S. map. I knelt next to the desk.

"So what are you researching?" I asked, notebook open.

"Weather data," she said. Her voice sounded like an automated recording. "See? A storm brewing over Illinois and Iowa."

I looked to where she pointed. Little green and yellow blips appeared over the Midwest.

"So this data, how is it used by the military on a larger scale? Does it relate to the operation of this hangar?" I asked, hoping that my story would be more than an expose on the use of Doppler radar. The lieutenant shrugged.

"I gather the data. Analysis is someone else's duty."

"I see," I said, pretending to jot something down. "And how is working in the Hangar? What's your typical day like?"

"Satisfying."

"Thanks," I said, snapping my notepad closed.

"Would you care for any further interviews?" Colonel Baldwin asked. I shook my head.

"I'd like to see more, if that's possible."

The colonel showed me a whole lot more of nothing. Maps, procedural manuals, storage rooms filled with old computer equipment. I began to feel insulted when he showed me the furnaces and the laundry, but I couldn't tell if it was a joke. Baldwin never smirked or even crinkled an eye. After walking a quarter-mile underground, I learned nothing I couldn't have found on a government website. We ended the tour in his office, the second room from the end of a long hallway. I asked to see the entire hallway, but Baldwin informed me that that was a restricted area. I sighed. I had a notebook full of crap.

Inside Baldwin's dull office, the Colonel opened a mini-fridge and pulled out a pitcher.

"Would you like some iced tea?" he asked. I accepted, not wanting any, but hoping it would coax some answers from him. He poured two glasses exactly three-quarters full, and set one before me. He sat behind his desk and took a sip.

"I find a little iced tea quite refreshing in the afternoon. It's one of my few indulgences."

"Oh. Yeah."

"Now, Mr. Grant," Baldwin said after another sip, "do you have any additional questions about this facility?"

I clenched my fist. Where could I start?

"Well, sure. Tons. I mean, I saw the planes above ground, and those wall cameras in the entrance were cool, but come on. I could've gotten more sensitive intel from my mom's nursing home."

"You understand, of course, that this is a highly restricted U.S. Army facility. There are some things too sensitive for civilian eyes. Personnel files and the like are confidential."

"I don't want to know where you went to high school or where your parents were from. You know what I'm here for, Colonel. What is it about Hangar Eighteen that everyone wants to know?"

"I'm not sure, honestly. Did you consider that there is nothing of interest here, that the intrigue about this facility has been fabricated? You have seen all there is to see."

"Spy technology!" I blurted out. "Never-before-seen weapons. Extra-terrestrials. Mind control, Colonel Baldwin, what about the mind control? What do I tell my readers who want to know about all those rumors?"

Baldwin shrugged.

"I suppose you'll tell them what you must."

"You realize," I said, leaning forward in my chair, "that your silence will only fuel the conspiracy theories, and the rumors will only spin further out of control."

"This is the United States Army. Do you think we're concerned what some little news rag says about us? We have a nation to defend."

"I hardly think my paper qualifies as a 'rag.' Look, if it's time for me to go, I'll go. But at this point, I guarantee that the phrase 'Colonel Baldwin was reticent to the point of being suspect' will appear in my article."

"That's a clause, not a phrase. As a writer, you should know better."

I rolled my eyes and stood up.

"All right then. I should leave."

"I'm sorry you couldn't find what you were looking for," the colonel said, standing as well. "But first, do you need to use the restroom? I have a private one here in my office."

I shook my head. I was already too busy crafting the venomous lines in my head to worry about peeing.

"If you'll excuse me, then."

Colonel Baldwin disappeared into a tiny room adjacent the office. I waited for thirty seconds, then a minute, then two. I looked around. He didn't even have photos on his wall. On his desk sat some unmarked folders, as well as an empty inbox. Taking a quick glance at the bathroom door, I peeked inside one of the folders. I saw the heading of the first page inside:

Surface Recon Reports for Moons of Venus: April 2010

I shut the folder and my heart started racing. Recon on other planets? If the Colonel knew this, he knew more, and I had to find the truth. With one final glance at the bathroom door—no sign of activity—I slipped out of the office and ran down the hall.

A small screen with QWERTY keypad was mounted on the wall. My pounding heartbeat thudded in my ears. As I approached the keypad, it lit up, asking me for the seven-character code. Shit, I thought. It could be anything. I looked behind me to be sure Baldwin hadn't left his office. The way was clear. My mind raced, trying to figure out seven character passwords. "Aliens"—too few letters. "Top secret"—too many. I tried typing B-A-L-D-W-I-N. Nothing happened. H-A-N-G-A-R-1-8. Still nothing. I cursed under my breath. I was seriously tempted to turn back and warm up my poison pen. What could Baldwin's password be? What makes that cold, uncaring robot tick?

I-C-E-D-T-E-A.

On a hidden, silent hinge, a panel slid away, revealing a metal staircase descending into a black chasm. When I stepped on that top step, the door automatically closed behind me. Lights lit up, illuminating my path further underground.

I never stopped to think, "Is this a smart move? How will I get out? What if I'm caught?" Ever since I was a kid, those questions never held me back from anything. I spent plenty of time in detention at school, and grounded with my parents, but I also could climb more trees than any kid into the neighborhood, hack into computers, pick locks, and do a lot more with firecrackers than manufacturers recommended. My snooping educated me about my dad's arrest as a teenager, my mom's abortion, my neighbor's drug business in his garage, and a hundred other hidden transgressions. It's not that I enjoy digging into the forbidden; it's who I am. Birds fly; fish swim; I rummage into shit I'm not supposed to.

The air grew cooler as I descended deeper. The metal stairs spiraled into the void whose bottom I could not see. Finally, hundreds of steps down, I reached the concrete floor. As my foot hit the ground, more fluorescent lights illuminated the large, circular room before me. Massive mainframe computers two stories high filled the room, whirring and blinking with trillions of calculations. I know computers aren't alive, but it was hard to believe these monoliths weren't thinking and watching as I walked among them. I took out my notebook and scribbled a couple observations, but words weren't going to do these house-sized computers justice. They dwarfed me on all sides, like the walls of a canyon or a well.

At the center of the room, I stopped short. The Earth—well, a model of it thirty feet in diameter—hovered above the floor. I approached slowly. I couldn't tell what supported it, what it was made of, or how it was suspended several feet over a glowing platform. When I was close enough, I reached out and touched the globe somewhere in northern Chile. My fingertip disappeared under the surface for an instant; the globe appeared to be a holographic projection. Immediately a scroll of text appeared in the air. "CALAMA, CHILE," it read, followed by some basic geographical information. Sadly, the words "RESTRICTED: CLEARANCE CODES REQUIRED" were superimposed over the rest of the text. I had no idea what it was yet, but I described it as well as I could in my notebook before moving onward.

I found a room with a single computer—just regular desktop sized, this time—in the middle, and a giant screen mounted to the wall. Onscreen I saw a pair of official-looking men talking in the center of some governmental office, seemingly unaware they were being filmed. "THE HAGUE" was displayed in the corner. Ten seconds later the picture switched to a different office, empty this time. It said "BERLIN." So this screen gave a video feed of high government meetings all around the world, I decided. I had to write this down. I thought this sort of surveillance might be a better fit for the CIA, but what did I know? I'm just a reporter. I'm not there to tell the military what to do, but I would tell the civilian world what the military was doing. The video feed switched over to the United Nations, then to Moscow, then to a bleak, gray, dusty landscape with a black horizon. "SEA OF TRANQUILITY," it said. Holy shit, I thought. We're getting video feeds from the Moon. Other feeds came through, from the Moon, from Mars, from Venus. From this room in this bunker, half a mile under the Earth's surface, the Colonel could watch any government meeting, any international deal be made, could watch dust storms on the surface of Mars. Readers would go nuts for this.

Another doorway beckoned me further. I couldn't think about turning back or getting caught. When you're into something as deep as I was, common sense and precaution don't even register. I needed to discover like I needed to breathe.

The harsh fluorescent light from before was replaced in the next room with a gentle, blue glow. At first I thought I was in a museum, or a house of mirrors. But it wasn't reflections of myself I stared into. Naked people were inside tall cylindrical cases, but the faces and bodies I saw were not human. Humanoid, maybe, but the craniums were too big and the jaws too small. Slender arms hung at the sides of pale green-gray torsos. The bodies were propped upright, strapped in place, and when I peered closer to look, I saw a hint of frost under two pinhole nostrils. A digital display on the front read "-130 CELSIUS."

My hands started trembling so hard I dropped my pen and pad. I went from one cylinder to the next. The grey men were frozen. Their heads were huge. They had no apparent genitals. Their feet were strangely small. I tried counting the bodies, but found I couldn't keep my mind under control. Fifteen, maybe? Twenty? I was getting lost and dizzy as I scrambled through the space-age catacombs. I had no camera but I furiously sketched one of the gray men on a blank page, trying to convey with drawing what my words could never show—the pure shock at seeing true, pure, indisputable evidence of alien life and human knowledge of it. I wasn't even thinking about my story now; I was thinking about the evolution of mankind.

I was at the limit. All of this was just too much. The fuses on my curiosity were blown; now I explored from sheer momentum and a mindless hunger to go deeper. I stood with my nose to the glass of one cylinder, looking into the blank black eyes of the gray man. I pressed my hand against the digital readout display and felt a sharp prick on my fingertip. I yanked my hand back. A bead of blood formed on the tip of the finger and I licked it off. A tingling, numb feeling spread down the finger and into my hand. I shook the hand and the arm, but the numbness spread like an instant freeze up my forearm, past the elbow to my shoulder, and then to my core.

Panic set in, but it was too late. My back and legs lost feeling and I collapsed on the ground. I was fully conscious—I could hear the hum of the cryonic tanks, smell the clean, sterile concrete, and see the alien bodies suspended above me. I just couldn't move, not even to wriggle my nose. It was then I knew I had gone too far, and had seen too much. All I could do now was wait for Colonel Baldwin to find me.

Did it take Baldwin a while to realize where I'd gone? Did he wait, just so I could lie on the cold concrete in a pool of my own terror? Well, it worked. My paralysis fed my fear, and my fear fed my anger. By the time Baldwin was standing over me, toeing me with his boot, I felt like a rabbit in the jaws of a wolf.

"Did you find what you were looking for?" he asked. Still, he didn't smile. I wanted him to gloat, at least. Revel in his victory.

"Since the neurotoxin will prevent you from moving or talking for a while, why don't you just listen? You've seen things you shouldn't have seen, things presidents aren't even allowed to see. You are undoubtedly confused.

"Those computers, for instance, orchestrate the functions of this world. I know the world seems scary and chaotic, but trust me; there is order. Every aspect of human life that isn't dictated by nature is operated by those computers. Overwhelming, right? Did you ever watch the stock market and wonder what makes prices rise and fall? It originates here. Market experts prattle on for hours about indicators and bear and bull markets, but just as casinos do with slot machines, our computer creates just enough of a hint of pattern to suggest predictability. That suggestion creates a whole industry of personal finance and causes grown men to run to their financial advisors for reassurance. The computer controls oil production, creates pop culture phenomena and trends, issues fabricated press releases to inflame one group against another...the permutations of what it does are incalculable to the human mind. In fact, we like to call the computer 'God.' That is a joke, you understand."

The harder it was to move, the more I felt my mind scurry around in my skull, seething to reply, to strike out at him. But there was nothing I could do. Baldwin began pacing around the room, weaving among the frozen alien bodies and stepping over me as though I was a fallen branch.

"Perhaps you ask why God—our God—doesn't simply create a string of events that will grant us...whatever we like. World domination, riches, what have you. That is the genius of God, however. God doesn't give us what we want. God creates an intricate network of events that appear random, but are in fact calculated, to help us achieve what we want.

"With our video feeds, we see into hundreds of 'secure' areas all over the globe. Much of this data is fed straight into God for processing. You saw, as well, our feeds from more exotic locales. Did you think our interests were limited to the national and the global? We watch the stars with the same interest we watch foreign leaders and pop music videos—they all feed into our future plans.

"And then this room. The wax museum. We call it this because everyone waxes philosophical here. It creates a shift of mankind's view of the universe that would be...disruptive to world order. We didn't kill them—they are all quite alive, in a state of cryonic suspension, frozen to be thawed another day—but we can't let them out, either. One was stranded in a town in Saskatchewan when one of their routine abductions went wrong and left the extra-terrestrial in some little girl's bedroom. Three were captured in a nuclear power plant and brought here. Many survived crash landings in Wyoming, Florida, Maine, Washington, and New Mexico. When their people discovered where the survivors were being held—here—they sent a rescue team, which we incapacitated and added to the collection. We only have the simplest understanding of their physiology, but our researchers learn while our staff keeps word of their existence silent."

Colonel Baldwin crouched in front of me. My brain wanted me to reach out and strangle him, punch him as hard as possible, but the command fizzled impotently when it reached my arm. Baldwin's face still betrayed no emotion. Either he had no feelings, and was inhuman, or was so supremely in control of that emotion that he appeared inhuman. His blue-gray eyes, which on most men would seem to be the windows to a placid, dreamer's soul, only made him look more robotic.

"You see, Hangar Eighteen is what Area 51 should have been, before that facility became a cartoon. With Area 51, the constant denial fed conspiracy theories. With Hangar Eighteen, you, Mr. Grant, have come in to investigate and reassure the world that everything is okey-dokey. That is critical to our plan.

"Many conspiracy theorists ask, 'Why does the government keep extra terrestrial life a secret when that knowledge could benefit mankind?' Let me tell you why. It could incur widespread panic. And contrary to what some might think, total panic is not desirable in a population that must be controlled. A little simmering fear, yes, but panic makes predictable people do unpredictable things. But do you know what could be worse than total panic? Unity. Imagine. All of humanity's little squabbles— the fight with the neighbor, companies competing, gang wars, nations slaughtering one another—would vanish under the altered perspective. Petty fights continue because they seem to be important. But when mankind learns that their little spats are microscopic specs of dirt in the mountain range of our universe, they will unite in brotherhood.

"We, in short, do not wish that. Discord is good for business, you might say. What would the military have left to do? What about the workers who build our fighter jets and missiles? How could we go to war for that dream of peace after the dream is realized? And beyond that-- what about the news networks with no conflict left to analyze? Police? Prison guards? Lawyers and judges? Our world would never survive a transition to a peace-loving utopia. So you see, Mr. Grant, we do not desire to take over the world. We do not desire to make it buckle before us. We desire to maintain the equilibrium of chaos that keeps man's attention on petty entanglements, rather than on what we are doing. But for this delicate balance to remain, you must do your part."

He reached out and withdrew my notepad from my breast pocket. He flipped through, nodding with little apparent interest at my notes and sketches. He slipped it into his own pocket, then withdrew an identical notepad—same color, same brand, scuffed to make it look well-used—and placed it into my pocket.

"That pad contains the notes for a perfectly salable, perfectly harmless news article that you will write about Hangar Eighteen. It will inform readers about the aircraft and weather balloons and ordinary satellites that we maintain from here. You will report that Hangar Eighteen is an efficient, orderly military installation with no more classified information that you might find at any other. You will earn your salary, perhaps even a promotion for your intrepid work.

"Perhaps you are saying to yourself now, 'But Colonel Baldwin, I have retained my own memory, and will write my news story from that.' Well, Mr. Grant, your memory is going to corroborate every detail in those pages. Come with me."

Colonel Baldwin stood up and began walking away, but then turned back to me. The tiniest hint of a smile—a sneer, really—played at the corner of his lips.

"Oh, perhaps you need assistance? Please, allow me."

As Baldwin hooked his arms under my shoulders and began to drag me away, I realized that Baldwin did have emotion. A little sadism and sarcasm were all I could detect in him, but strangely, I considered it a minor victory. At the end of the room, he reached another locked steel door with a keypad. He swiftly typed in the numbers, and the door swung open. Harsh light poured from it.

"I must give you credit—you showed above-average aptitude by deducing the entry code for the lower level of the hangar. But honestly, Mr. Grant, do you think a simple, seven-letter code would be all standing in your way? And if that were so, do you think I would so carelessly drop a clue for you in our conversation? Iced tea. Hah. You even fell victim to the most ridiculous lure—a conveniently placed folder on my desk with an intriguingly titled document inside. The planet Venus has no moons, Mr. Grant, but in your rush to find your precious truth, you devoured the bait. We could have manacled you and forced you down to this room, but it was, frankly, much easier to turn off our security, create a simple password, then let you walk here under the power of your own curiosity. You even had a few moments of self-satisfaction at your own daring."

My eyes had been temporarily blind in the bright light, but as they adjusted, I felt terror ripple up from my tailbone to my brain. At first I saw an electric chair. Damn it, I thought, he's hooking me up to Old Sparky. But there was too much equipment attached, too many sensors and computers. He dragged me— Baldwin turned out to be strong for a skinny old man—up into the chair, which was made of some plastic polymer. He tightened straps around my wrists, ankles, chest, and neck, and then secured a metal skullcap on top of my head. Now I understood why Hangar Eighteen was a tomb. It was a tomb for truth, which would lie preserved in these concrete walls, half a mile below ground, undisturbed and undisturbing.

Baldwin went over to the computer and began typing. I could hear the electric hum in the circuits attached to me. I supposed those were my new memories, waiting to be jammed into my brain.

"This will cause you no pain," he said, sounding clinical and inhuman again. "When you wake, you will have use of your faculties again. You will remember your informative, if somewhat disappointing, tour of Hangar Eighteen. Your little pocket notebook will help refresh you of the finer details. You will use your memories to write an article. You will remember exactly the truth we want you to remember, and nothing more."

TRAPPED IN AMBER
BY JALETA CLEGG

Sargandon brushed lint from his best robe. The counter spells woven into the black velvet crackled with power. He smiled, his thin lips curving upwards in unaccustomed movements. He slipped the robe over his head, smoothing it over his lean hips.

He posed in front of his full-length mirror, twisting to see every angle. Yes, the red lining glowed like blood, the black drank in light. He stroked the gold embroidery lining the collar and sleeves.

"Too gaudy?"

"Ye look like a vision of evilness, a true powerful sorcerer of the blackest arts." His faithful henchman, Blaine, squinted with his one eye. He smiled as he gathered up scattered articles of clothing, draping them over his arm. "A dream of loveliness, that's what ye are."

"What did you say?" Sargandon eyed him, suspicion in his dark eyes.

"Er." Blaine licked his lips, attempting to remember his last comment. He'd been thinking of Maude, down at the tavern. Not wise to let your concentration lapse around an evil overlord. "I quake in my boots at yer horribleness and decrepitude."

Sargandon flicked one hand. Magic seared the air around Blaine. The old, half-blind henchman squealed as he transformed into an old, half-blind squirrel.

"Choose nuts more wisely than you chose words." Sargandon returned to his preening.

The squirrel watched him with a baleful eye.

The evil sorcerer smoothed gel over his thick, black hair, slicking it back. He frowned at the effect. "Everything must be perfect today. I will not defeat my arch rival with bad hair." He licked one finger and sculpted his hair into waving curls. He nodded, pleased. His hair moved like a helmet, glued into a single mass.

He leaned close to the mirror, examining each pore on his face. He poked at a red blotch next to his left nostril. A single word of power and the spot vanished. His fingers pinched, plucking a stray hair from his eyebrow.

Sargandon raised his arms high, flourishing his wide sleeves dramatically. He watched his reflection, twisting to examine his back side. "Blaine! My belt!"

The one-eyed squirrel chittered. The noise resembled curses.

Sargandon rolled his eyes. "Oh, very well. You are forgiven. But do not make such a slip again." He snapped his fingers.

Power surged across the room. The squirrel stretched, changing into a one-eyed hunchback. He leered at Sargandon. "#%$*!" He spat on the floor.

"I said, fetch my belt. Or would you rather live as a goat?"

Blaine, a foul caricature of his former self, lurched across the room. He slammed open a closet door, retrieving a twisted rope of silver and gold spangled with crystals.

Sargandon looped the belt around his slim waist then smiled at his reflection. "Perfect," he murmured. "My triumph shall soon be complete. That wretched wizard shall learn the full extent of my powers."

He delicately lifted a knob of amber, holding it to the light. It glowed the color of honey. The weak imbecile, Gurandor, said amber was too delicate, too dangerous for magic. Amber twisted time. No wizard should touch it. Their Code forbade its use in spells. Cowards, all of them, afraid of the sheer power locked in the golden stones.

Sargandon laughed. Their silly wizard rules did not bind him. Decades of careful work and study yielded this precious stone, an impossible melding of amber, time, and power. Its creation proved that he, Sargandon, was the greatest sorcerer to ever breathe. Soon, Gurandor the Ninny would be forced to acknowledge him supreme. The most powerful wizard would bow and concede defeat, forced to his knees by Sargandon's undeniable superiority. He laughed at the glorious vision.

He clutched the stone in his fist as he strode from the room.

***

"Gurandor, my arch rival, today is the day you reap your just desserts."

"Does that mean you've brought cream jellies?" Gurandor carefully shifted his bubbling potion to the back of his work counter. Hours wasted, if it were spilled.

"You mock me, the Lord High Sorcerer Sargandon?"

"If it will make you feel better." Gurandor wiped sticky hands on the stained apron around his waist.

"Your impudence will no longer be tolerated. Let the duel begin!" Sargandon flared his wide sleeves, flashing the red satin lining. The gold trim along the edge sparkled, adding nicely to the effect.

"Not in my work room, please." Gurandor frowned. "How did you get in? My warding spells are unbreakable. You shouldn't have been able to surprise me."

"Silly wizard, always trusting your spells. You were not paying enough attention to your housekeeper. She was easy to bribe." Sargandon buffed his manicured nails on his black robe. "You're getting sloppy, Gurandor."

Gurandor sighed. "Bribing the help is not allowed under the Wizard's Code."

"You forget, I'm not a whiny, impotent wizard. I'm the Lord of Evil, Darkness Incarnate, Supreme Overlord of the Black Arts. I don't have to follow your foppish Code. I can do exactly as I please." He smiled his best evil smirk.

"I do hate it when you put on airs. You will have to pay the piper eventually. How much did corrupting Elspeth cost you?"

"One potion of youth, beauty, and sex appeal. A trifle, really. You should pick your underlings more carefully."

"You're one to talk. You hire incompetent buffoons, like Yurt who completely destroyed your Castle of Doom when he attempted cleaning the potion lab."

Sargandon sniffed. If Yurt hadn't perished in the blast, he would have lived the rest of his life as a rabbit in a cage of hungry weasels. "I never liked the floor plan anyway. My Fortress of Indescribable Torment is much more to my liking."

Gurandor held a bottle to the light, examining it closely. "Your fortress is a drafty heap of stone, if you want my opinion."

"I don't want your opinion. You live in a piggish hovel. You wouldn't know good architecture if it fell on you."

"At least I don't get chills walking to the privy. Did you plan to put them on the wrong side of the drawbridge?"

"A minor detail."

"And what do you do when you're under siege? Use the kitchen pots? The smell must be horrific." Gurandor ladled green syrup carefully into the jar.

"I've never been under siege. No one would dare challenge me. I'm too powerful. Today I prove it, once and for all." Sargandon cracked his knuckles. "Enough chitchat. Shall we begin? Where was I? Oh, yes. Gurandor, today you meet your doom!"

"Would you mind terribly if I bottled my potion first? I've been slaving over it for months." Gurandor held the bottle out. "It needs just another few minutes to finish cooling."

"No."

"Bother. Couldn't you wait? I do so hate wasting time. The recipe takes days to cook."

"Stop whining and prepare for your ultimate defeat."

"Can we duel out in the main hall? Just this once?"

Sargandon shook his head, his black hair moving as a single mass. He cocked his hands, fingers twisted in the opening moves of a spell.

Gurandor tried one last time. "Tradition dictates duels be fought in the main hall of the castle, not in the work room. Think of the magical backlash if your spell misses."

"I do not miss! Due warning has been given. Tradition has been satisfied."

"All right, then. Give me the speech about my imminent demise." Gurandor crossed his arms, leaning one hip on the workbench.

Sargandon chuckled. "You won't die, Gurandor. I have a much more devious end for you."

"You're going to talk me to death with bad clichés."

Sargandon's smirk died, replaced by an angry frown. "You will pay for your insolence, Gurandor." He cast the traditional opening spell of Magic Missile.

The bolt arced across the room. Gurandor nonchalantly flapped one hand, absorbing the dart. He twitched the fingers of his other hand. A fiery snake flashed into being, slithering towards Sargandon.

The Dark Lord stomped on its head with his Boots of Pain. The snake squealed before exploding in a cascade of sparks. Sargandon clapped his hands then spread his arms wide, his sleeves sweeping the remnants of magical snake into the air. Sparkling bits caught in the vortex he sent spinning towards Gurandor.

The white wizard snapped his fingers, calling up his invisible shield. The vortex howled as it split to the sides. Bottles and jars whirled on the raging wind, slamming into the stone walls. Glass smashed. Spells exploded in colored rainbows of raw magic. Reality shimmered. Strange shapes crept through the fog of power as it dissipated.

"Drat! Fifteen years work wasted! I warned you, Sargandon!" Gurandor removed a vial from a cord around his neck. He popped the stopper then poured the white powder into the air, his voice raised in an archaic chant.

Sargandon snickered in his twisted black beard. "You are a fool, Gurandor. Not even Vortigern's Blindness can save you now. I have a new spell." He raised his fist, slowly opening it to reveal the lump of amber.

Gurandor stopped mid-spell, eyes wide. "You harnessed the powers of amber? Impossible!"

Sargandon threw back his head and laughed. "Your fate, wizard! Trapped in amber for all time!"

"You're a fool, Sargandon. Magic and amber don't mix. Too dangerous. You'll pay for your presumptuous and imprudent act. Tampering with time is forbidden."

Sargandon tossed the amber into the air.

The stone caught the light as it tumbled, glowing like autumn fires. The spell stretched into the air, lazily spreading as the stone fell. Gurandor stared, mesmerized by the magic, his mouth open wide. The amber touched his forehead, clinging and spreading like syrup, until it encased the wizard in a thick skin of resin.

Sargandon smiled in satisfaction as he finished the spell. The amber hardened. Sargandon tapped on the shell. Gurandor's disbelieving gaze showed plainly. No hint of reaction or pain, no sign of breathing fogged the amber.

"You shall remain for all time, locked in your prison, preserved as a trophy of my superior intellect and magical skill. I have triumphed. You are defeated, Gurandor the Weak. You shall watch, impotently, as I rule the world." He clenched his fist, thrusting it skyward.

Gurandor's expression remained frozen.

Sargandon lowered his fist. "Drat. You can't hear me. You're trapped in time. No matter." He stroked the silky surface. "You'd look marvelous in my front parlor next to the Iron Maiden. I'll fetch my henchmen to carry you forth."

His dark robe swept dramatically through the lingering magical snake as he strode from the work room.

***

Sargandon spread his fingers on the wide stone sill. He stared unseeingly at the desolate landscape of burnt villages and dying swamps. The stench of rotting vegetation filled every sluggish breath of air. Sargandon sighed.

"Beltar, I'm bored," he complained.

"Yes, lord," Beltar lisped. He grinned mindlessly as he flattened himself on the mildewed stone floor.

"What is there to do?" Sargandon pursed his lips, his fingers tapping on the stone.

"You could burn a village," Beltar suggested.

"I've burnt every village at least twice already this year. It's no fun when only one peasant limps, screaming, from his home. The rest fled south a decade ago."

"Summon a dragon?"

"Last winter, five of them. They complained about the lack of royalty to eat."

"Attack the castle!" Beltar scratched absently at his armpits.

"This is the only castle still standing for a thousand leagues in every direction." Sargandon's fingers paused. "I could destroy it and build a new one." He shook his head. "I beheaded all my architects after they designed this Fortress. No one dares study architecture anymore and I'm all thumbs when it comes to sketching evil fortresses."

Beltar sucked his lip. "Rain of fire? Lightning storms? Evil gargoyles?"

"Child's play."

"Animated puppets? Doughnuts of Destruction?"

Sargandon raised one carefully plucked eyebrow.

"Pastry power. You told me about it once." Beltar nodded, his greasy hair bobbing around his face. "That new spell you were inventing."

"The spell had unintended consequences. It took me months to hunt down and destroy the nasty things." He shuddered. "Do you have any idea what a man looks like after bismarcks have fed on his flesh? Some arts are too dark even for me. No, what I really need, Beltar is an arch enemy, a rival, someone to give me a bit of a challenge before I destroy him."

Beltar scraped wax from his ear. "Aren't any wizards left. You destroyed all of them, great master. Incinerated them with your brilliance, that you did."

Sargandon twisted his fingers through his gelled beard. "Not all of them. Where did I put that amber statue?"

"The one with the man inside who's screaming like he saw his own ghost? Down in the storage pit."

"Fetch him forth, Beltar. I shall devise a counter spell. I shall release Gurandor and defeat him again." Sargandon rubbed his hands together, an evil smile twisting his lips.

"I must say, your darkship, it warms my shrunken little heart to see you excited about something."

***

"Put him there, by the fountain." Sargandon studied the effect. "No, he clashes with the tiles. Perhaps by the window."

Beltar grunted and strained as he heaved the enormous lump of amber across the marble floor.

"Careful, you fool! Even magical amber can break. I'd hate to have him split in half before I can wake him."

Beltar settled the amber near the window. He polished dust from the surface with his tattered surcoat. The face inside caught the light, glowing golden red in the sickly sunlight. Gurandor's mouth still hung open, frozen in that moment of time when the spell was cast.

Sargandon brushed his hand across the smooth stone. "Gurandor, my old enemy. You haven't changed a bit. Four hundred thirty-seven years, six months, fourteen days. It will be just like old times again. It may take a few years for me to find the correct spell. I wouldn't want to release you just to find you dead. I want you alive. You'll be patient, won't you?" The Lord of Evil cracked his knuckles. Power surged through the room.

Beltar scampered for the kitchens to hide.

***

The amber cracked, like ice shattering. Gurandor's stiff body toppled to the marble floor.

Sargandon prodded him with a bony finger, his face creased with concern. "Frozen in time, not dead in amber. I know I spoke correctly." He thumped Gurandor's bony chest.

Gurandor sucked in a breath, gasping like a fish as he arched his back. He coughed, spraying amber dust, before collapsing.

Sargandon stood, cackling evilly. "Gurandor, my arch nemesis. You have no idea how long I have waited for this revenge."

Gurandor pushed to his hands and knees, wheezing. "Seems like only a moment." His voice cracked and grated, like an old man.

"Would you care for a cup of tea? I've waited for so long, I can be patient a while longer." Sargandon snapped his fingers, almost dancing in his excitement. His robe swirled across the marble floor, gold trim sparkling.

Beltar scurried across the room, tea cups clattering on a tray clutched in his sweaty hands.

Gurandor used a nearby chair to pull himself to a sitting position. "Tea would be delightful. I'm parched."

Beltar set the tray on the floor. He busied himself pouring tea, adding the appropriate sugar and cream. He handed one dainty cup to Gurandor, the other to Sargandon.

"It has been so long, my old arch-nemesis. How are you feeling?" Sargandon sipped tea, one pinky extended.

"Like I've been trapped in a giant lump of amber. But I'm recovering." Gurandor sipped, then pulled a face. "I believe your cream has soured, Sargandon."

"It's sheep cream. The cows all died about two hundred years ago when I was experimenting with magical plagues. I sometimes

regret that incident. More sugar helps." Sargandon searched
Gurandor's face, seeking signs of his great power. The duel
would disappoint if it were too easy. He wanted a challenge, a
real struggle.

Beltar squatted on the floor between them, humming off key
as he rearranged the tea service.

Gurandor set his cup aside. "I see your taste in servants hasn't
changed. But you have. How long has it been?"

"Four hundred fifty two—What do you mean, I've changed?"

"How often do you dye your hair, what little is still left?"

Sargandon's hand crept to cover the balding spot on the back
of his head. "My hair is the same color it always has been," he
lied. He'd used every youth spell he knew, and a few he invented,
to cover the gray.

"You've put on a few pounds, too. But I hear that's pretty
much inevitable for older men."

Sargandon sucked in his gut, running his other hand over his
velvet robe. His belt had been a bit tighter lately but he blamed
that on lack of exercise. He'd been so involved in freeing
Gurandor, he simply hadn't taken the time.

Gurandor pushed to his feet, holding to the arm of the chair.
"You're getting old, Sargandon."

"I am not! Sorcerers do not age as normal men." Sargandon
stroked his beard. It was still full, dark, and nicely pointed. It
was also a fake, but Gurandor couldn't possibly tell. Nobody
could. Sargandon's eyes strayed to his reflection in the picture
window at the front of the room. Were those lines? "I'm as
young as I ever was. My vast powers are untouched."

"You're fooling yourself. Time is showing, Sargandon."

Gurandor flexed his fingers. "I, on the other hand, haven't aged a day, thanks to your amber spell. Shall we begin?"

"Begin what?" Sargandon frowned, then stopped. Frowning might deepen the wrinkles.

Gurandor straightened, stepping away from the chair. He shook dust from his robe. It sparkled like gold in the air. "The duel. It is why you broke the spell, isn't it? Or is your memory slipping, old man?"

"I am not old!" Sargandon stamped his foot.

"Gray hair, paunchy belly, wrinkles on your face, can't remember what you ate for lunch—definitely signs of old age."

"Now you're taunting me."

Gurandor smiled.

"Prepare to die!" Sargandon raised his hands, his robe flaring dramatically.

The spell arced towards Gurandor, a line of orange fire. Gurandor blocked it easily, deflecting it out the window. Glass shattered. A nearby swamp detonated with a dull thud.

Sargandon staggered, drained by the simple spell. "Breaking the amber spell must have taken more of my power than I thought. Perhaps we should reschedule for tomorrow."

Gurandor glanced out the window, watching the swamp gas burn. He wrinkled his nose at the stench of rotten eggs. "You've made a right mess of things. It will take me years to straighten it back out. No, I think we should fight this out, right here and right now. You challenged me, remember? Or is your memory slipping with age?"

Sargandon growled and flung another bolt across the room. It spattered harmlessly on the wall. He flexed his hand. Sparks fizzed from his thumb, an amber colored cloud sucking magic from his soul. "What spell is this? What have you done to me?"

"Nothing. You've done it to yourself, mixing amber with magic. I told you the consequences would be heavy."

"Reverse it or I shall be forced to destroy you!" Sargandon bunched his fist, gathering his magic, only he had none left. The amber dust drained him, pulling his stolen years away. He staggered to his knees, unable to stand. The spells preserving him faded one by one as his magic died.

Gurandor shook his head. "You did us both a favor, you know, when you trapped me. I'm still young, while you've grown old."

"You've tricked me."

"You did this to yourself."

"Tell me the spell that defeats me." Gray and white rippled over Sargandon's hair, bleaching away the artificial black.

"It's simple, really. You still haven't figured it out?"

Sargandon toppled to the floor, wrinkles sagging. He feebly pawed at Gurandor with one liver-spotted hand. "What power do you hold?"

Gurandor leaned close. "The one you gifted me: Time."

Sargandon sighed his last breath, eyes sliding closed. He sprawled on the floor, an ancient caricature of his former self.

Gurandor pulled the tattered velvet robe over Sargandon's face. "Time defeats us all in the end. It's a good thing your spell preserved me so well. This mess is going to take years to correct. Why must evil sorcerers always foul their own nests?"

He strode from the Fortress of Ultimate Evil into warm sunlight. The morass of magically created swamps showed the beginnings of dry land as Sargandon's power faded. Gurandor planted his fists on his hips as he surveyed the charred villages.

"At least you gave me plenty of time to set things right." He resolutely rolled up his sleeves as he strode towards the nearest village.

THE BETRAYAL
BY SHELLY LI

Sam saw no reason to resist at this point, and so he leaned back in his chair and let his surroundings wash over him. The spotless, cornerless white room, without windows and devoid of feeling. He knew that there were nano-cameras hidden all over the walls nonetheless.

The man sitting across the glass desk had introduced himself as Dr. Peter Kohl. A smile sat squarely on his face, a mixture of pity and repulsion.

But Sam didn't let this doctor, robotics psychologist, whoever he was, bother him in the slightest. He knew he couldn't escape his fate now, the conclusion drawn from the moment he killed Matthews, then the homeless man at the park, the grocery store boy, the fragile old woman at the spotlight, her younger friend sitting in the seat next to her...

He had lost count of how many lives he had taken.

But as he reflected back on the last few months of his life, his attempt to escape capture, the image of Matthews approached the forefront of his mind.

Matthews: his caretaker, his conversational partner, and his accident.

How was Sam to know that Matthews hadn't been like him, that Matthews would shut off when physical force was applied?

He sighed, wishing that RoboCorp could have coded the knowledge of human death into his system, and returned his attention to Dr. Kohl.

***

Robotics psychologist Dr. Peter Kohl stared into the robot's deep, humanly eyes, perfectly simulating focused emotions of pain and shame. Kohl had read up extensively on this case, this robot named Sam.

After strangling his owner to death, Sam had gone off on a rampage, killing twenty-two people before the police caught him at the cemetery, cleaning Tyler Matthews' gravestone.

Kohl looked down at the folder of papers in front of him, finding the best method to getting the answers he needed, so that he could deliver the root of the robot's malfunction to RoboCorp.

Since the killings didn't seem to have a pattern, or even a reason, Kohl couldn't attribute the malfunction to faulty programming at the factory. No. Something had happened after Tyler Matthews bought Sam, took the robot home, lived with him for over a year.

But RoboCorp's archives didn't show a single complaint filed by Matthews, or any complaint of robots of Sam's model.

So what had gone wrong?

"Sam, just to be clear here," Kohl began, "you do know that the consequence of your actions is deactivation, right? After a horrific debacle like this, there is no way we can reprogram—you know, fix—whatever is wrong with you."

"Yes, I know," Sam replied, a smile crossing his face. His humanly features were designed to make customers feel more comfortable, after all, more welcoming to the idea of a powerful, freethinking machine living in their homes. "So I assume you're going to ask me a few questions, put together an analyzation of my answers, and then cast me away. That's usually the procedure, right?"

Kohl nodded, taking down a few notes. One could tell a lot about a person by examining his robot—in Sam's case, Kohl expected his owner to have been a candid, yet bitterly sarcastic individual.

"So, I guess the obvious first question is: why did you kills Matthews?" Kohl asked. He looked up, watching something resembling sweet sorrow flicker into Sam's eyes.

"I didn't know that I could kill him," Sam said. Kohl noticed the robot's fingers curl into fists. "He was going to return me for the new model coming out, and, well, I thought I was more to him than a machine." Sam swallowed, his eyes, wet. "I became angry, and I wrapped my hands around his neck. I squeezed, I felt his pulse fluttering against my fingertips, and then I squeezed tighter."

The robot shook his head. "Why couldn't he value me as much as I valued him?"

Kohl fought to keep his answer to himself, but Sam voiced his words for him anyway. "You want to tell me that I'm just a robot," he said, his tone softening. "I'm a commodity of convenience."

Kohl didn't know how to respond.

"It's normal for humans to think like that, at least it is among all the people I've come across," Sam continued. "But you programmed me with emotions, and so I can't help but feel the way I feel. You gave me free thought so that I could grow and adapt to any surrounding. You even designed me to look like you, with this skin and these eyes... why bother making me look so human if you were just going to treat me as lesser than?"

Kohl paused a moment, digesting the robot's words. Then he said, "Sam, our race does a lot of illogical things, things that we can't ever explain."

"I've noticed. It kind of clashes with our programming. I've always wanted to ask why, but as I mature and learn more about human action, do things I can't explain either, I feel like I'm getting closer to the answer by myself."

Kohl took the opportunity to make a transition in the conversation. "So you killing Tyler Matthews... would you consider that an illogical action?"

"Do *you* consider murder to be illogical, Dr. Kohl?"

Kohl jotted down Sam's answers. "So how did you feel after you killed him?" he then asked.

Sam frowned and said, "Have you ever betrayed someone? Are you familiar with the crushing guilt that consumes you afterward?"

The words felt like a hot knife slipped into Kohl's chest. His thoughts began to separate from the present, parting like a curtain and bringing him back to the first time he had cheated on Sara. That feeling of threatening combustion returned, bruising, cutting.

"I'm familiar with betrayal, yeah," Kohl said. "But Matthews betrayed you first. He was going to return you for an upgrade." The words slipped out before he could stop them.

The robot gave him a half-smile, almost as if he knew what was going on inside Kohl's mind. The simple gesture, that which humans identified as commiseration, both nestled and amused him.

"Does it matter who betrayed first?" Sam said. "If you betrayed someone in order to get revenge, are your actions justified? Help me out—I am, after all, just a machine."

Against his will, Kohl's stomach knotted up, knowing that Sam was right. He had forgiven Sara for cheating on him the moment she had admitted to having an affair. His cheating—his continued cheating—had nothing to do with her one night of betrayal. He had cheated so that he could find a way to forgive himself for letting Sara's loyalty slip from his grasp.

After a few seconds, Kohl managed to blink away the memories of dark rooms and fake love and refocused on Sam. He wasn't sure whether or not he was mentally fit to continue the analyzation. This case seemed more entangled now than when Kohl had started picking at Sam's brain—or at least, the Com-chip that acted as Sam's information processing center.

"So if you felt so guilty about killing Matthews, then why did you run?" Kohl pressed on. This, out of every missing thread to this case, was the question he had wanted to ask the most. "Why did you continue to kill, to betray?"

At this Sam let out a chuckle that made the hairs on Kohl's neck rise to attention. "You said that you were familiar with betrayal, Dr. Kohl."

Kohl frowned.

"Perhaps you need to do some more self-examining." Sam tapped his fingers against the glass table, fast then slow, like he was rehearsing a song in his head. "After you betrayed whomever, you felt this crawling itch all over, did you not? You felt like you were on fire and that no matter what you did, you couldn't peel the feeling off of you."

Kohl struggled not to smile as an odd thought struck him. Now who was the psychologist here? Nevertheless he let Sam continue.

"After you betrayed once, did you betray again? And again?"

Kohl said nothing. His eyes wandered down to the notebook in front of him, and he suddenly realized that he had not been taking notes for the last few questions.

"Why do you betray continuously?" Sam said. "To lessen the importance of that first betrayal, distance yourself from the pain and guilt by scattering the betrayals across a wide net." The robot scoffed, looking away at the bare, white walls. "This is something I learned from human society, as I matured."

Kohl nodded and added, "Something illogical."

"Yes. But it is something that my emotions drove me to do, and the plan makes so much sense until you finish that second betrayal, and you realize that you're still burning with shame. You mentioned that these acts aren't considered betrayal if you were betrayed first." Sam's eyes returned to focus in on Kohl. "But when you love someone, truly love someone, being betrayed is an insignificant pain in comparison to the knowledge that your betrayal will crush that someone. And you would rather keep these secrets inside and let them tear you to pieces before giving voice to your actions and watching them hurt that someone. This is the price we pay for love, and it is a price we pay without regret." A smile crossed Sam's lips, so genuinely sad that it made Kohl forget who he was for a moment, forget their relationship as psychologist and machine.

The moment quickly passed, however, as Kohl began to snap out of this twisted robotics insight. Sam was just a malfunctioned machine that happened to say something that struck a chord in Kohl, nothing more.

Love. What does a robot know about love, about betrayal?

Letting out a deep breath, Kohl looked into the hidden camera behind Sam and motioned for the guards to enter the room.

Almost immediately, part of the seamless white wall caved away, and two men in uniform stepped in.

"Are you okay, Dr. Kohl?" asked one of the officers as they lifted the robot up from the chair. "You look a little shaken."

Kohl shook his head and faked a smile. "I'm fine, just going to stay here for a few minutes and finish my write-up. Can you escort Sam here down to,"—He paused as his eyes and Sam's locked—"deactivation?"

"Sure thing." And with those words, Sam and the two officers flanking him exited the room.

After the door closed, Kohl sat back in his seat and sifted through everything Sam had said.

It didn't make sense. Something had to have altered Sam's programming for the robot to snap like that. There was no way that Sam could have "evolved" into this deep a mindset about love, betrayal, guilt, pain.

Kohl reached up and rubbed the bridge of his nose, trying to clear this numbing cold from his mind. His thoughts returned to Sara again, then to all the secret rendezvous with various women, all that time spent with the warmth of another's body, pretending that he cared, pretending that he didn't…

He sighed and chucked his pen across the room. Now that he was all alone here, who was he trying to fool?

Sam was the embodiment of a human being, basking in—and at once suffering from—the same emotions. But yet the robot had been even more. Sam had understood the reasons behind his actions, and he did not regret, for his betrayals were performed out of love.

How does one analyze this, logically?

Kohl smiled and took out his cell phone.

Dialing the numbers, he then leaned back in his chair and counted the rings.

LOVELY INVENTIONS
BY A.C. HALL

Phase Four: The Inventor's Club

This wasn't going to be a happy story.

That was something Isaac Gray knew from the start. It wasn't going to be happy, or clean, or particularly easy to watch, but it was going to be a success. Of that he had no doubt.

He straightened his tie as he stood in the empty hallway in front of the bookshelf that wasn't a shelf at all. By all measurements he had no right to be here, in this place, on this night, but Isaac had never allowed that to stop him before. When told something was impossible, he immediately attempted it. When he failed he dedicated his life to figuring out why. When he knew why he then did whatever it took to grow strong enough to do the original impossible task. When that was done he moved on to the next impossibility.

Satisfied that his fancy suit was in order he reached forward and began touching some of the books. What would've appeared to be a random action by a passerby was in actuality the implementation of a very complex password. Books touched in a certain order, in just the right place for just the right amount of time until finally he heard the whirring of gears.

Isaac busied himself with fixing his short black hair as the bookshelf in front of him started to shake. A moment later it swung inward, revealing a dark staircase. He looked up and down the hall and when satisfied that no one was around he stepped inside.

Even a man like Isaac Gray became slightly unnerved when the bookshelf swung shut behind him, leaving him alone in the stone stairwell with almost no light to guide him. As he continued downward he began to hear voices and smell delightful foods. He smiled, his momentary fear subsiding now that he could hear the dinner party in the distance.

The stairs ended and Isaac found himself in a long hallway. It was lit by a single red light in the ceiling. The light was angled so it illuminated a heavy oak door at the end of the hallway. Isaac walked with a smile, enjoying the intrigue and uniqueness of the situation. He paused as he noticed words chiseled into the stone above the door.

Our inventions mirror our secret wishes. – Lawrence George Durrell

"Huh," Isaac muttered as he let the quote sink in.

After a moment of thought he continued on towards the door. He kept his eyes forward, not wanting to read the quote again. Isaac raised his fist to knock on the door but just as he neared it swung open slowly. Now the sounds and smells washed over him and he could practically taste the expensive wine, the exquisite foods.

Before him was a dimly lit room, barely larger than a closet. There was a nondescript door across from him but standing in front of it was a man in a tuxedo. His clothing was formal but Isaac could tell from the way he stood that this man wasn't someone to be taken lightly. He stopped, waiting to be addressed. After a moment of sizing Isaac up the man spoke.

"Papers?"

Isaac reached into his suit jacket and pulled out two sheets of carefully folded paper. These were the reasons he had been invited here tonight, his newest impossibility that he was oh so close to cracking. The man looked at the first sheet for some time, his eyes taking in the complex equations and statements that filled the sheet. He breathed in sharply as he realized what he was reading. Isaac smiled, getting the exact reaction he wanted. The man looked up at him and raised his eyebrows.

"You can really do this?" the man asked.

Isaac gently pulled the papers from the man's hand and offered a warm smile in return.

"Patent pending," Isaac said.

The man shook his head in disbelief as he turned and unlocked the far door.

"Enjoy your evening, sir," he said as he pushed the door open.

Isaac stepped through into a massive, beautiful chamber. It looked like it had been lifted right out of a castle or a cathedral. The ceiling was vaulted and there were gorgeous stone pillars reaching from the floor all the way up to it. A huge oak dinner table was situated in the middle of the room and the other guests, each of them dressed in fancy eveningwear, were milling around, chatting and laughing, glasses of wine in hand.

Directly in front of him was a small podium with a book sitting on top of it. Isaac approached it and saw that it was a guestbook. Stenciled into the top of it was "The Inventor's Club" and as he opened it he was surprised to see that each page was almost entirely blank. Aside from a date at the top of the page there was nothing written in the spaces below where guests were supposed to sign their names.

Isaac flipped to the page that had today's date written on it. It too was blank but there was a small X by one of the empty spaces on the page. He shrugged and picked up the pen that was lying beside the book. He signed his name in the space and watched as it immediately disappeared.

"Disappearing ink."

Isaac recognized the voice. It belonged to Harold Underwood, the man who had invited him to this gathering. He smiled as he looked up.

"Of course," Isaac said with a smile.

Harold was a man of a bygone era, as different as could be from Isaac. Inventing had been a business necessity for Harold, a way to get a leg up on his competitors. Isaac, as new as he was to the world of inventing, saw it more as an art form, a natural extension of his lifelong obsession to tame the impossible, to bend it to his will. The look of each man reflected these differences, with Harold looking stuffy and puffy in his oft-used suit and Isaac, with his perfectly kept goatee and piercing blue eyes matching up with a fashionable suit more likely to be seen on a Hollywood red carpet than at an underground dinner party.

Despite these differences the two men had taken an instant liking to one another when they had met just a short week ago.

Harold held out his hand and Isaac took it, careful to apply the exact proper amount of pressure fitting for such an occasion.

"I'm so glad you took me up on my invitation Mr. Gray," Harold said.

"Please, call me Isaac. And of course, how could I pass up the opportunity to take part in such a gathering?"

Harold released his hand and smiled. He followed Isaac's gaze, taking in the majesty of the room around them. He'd been coming to the gatherings here for over three decades and it wasn't until he watched a newcomer marvel at the large chamber that he remembered just how beautiful it truly was.

"Isaac it is. Are you prepared for an interesting evening?" Harold asked.

"Always," Isaac responded.

Harold put a hand on his back and gently guided him deeper into the room. Isaac was careful to take in every detail about the people he saw, knowing full well that some of them could be of critical importance to his current plans. As he was introduced to everyone there Isaac wasn't surprised that he recognized none of them. These were some of the greatest minds in the world, inventors of things that powered the planet, that made life as we know it possible, and yet they remained completely unknown, the hidden geniuses.

What they did was called "Impossible Science" by Harold. It was a term that immediately appealed to Isaac. He had been fascinated by the way Harold had explained it to him when they had met a week ago.

"Imagine that you're a peasant farmer in the Middle Ages, working in the field with your meager tools. Along comes a strangely dressed man holding a pistol. Of course, you don't know that it's a pistol, it just looks like an odd object to you. He fires the pistol at one of your cows, wounding it. You'd be bewildered and amazed, but upon learning of how it works, you would somewhat understand. After all, the idea of propelling deadly objects at high speeds is not uncommon in the Middle Ages, you've seen bows, crossbows, and ballistas. So while the science of the gunpowder may not make sense to you the overall concept of the pistol would be something that your brain accepted."

They had been in a small café and Harold had paused to drain his coffee before continuing.

"Now let's rewind, you're still a Middle Ages farmer, but this time the strangely dressed man approaches holding no odd objects. He simply points at one of your cows and then suddenly a blinding red beam of light shoots down from the sky and hits the cow, exploding it instantaneously. You'd be shocked, terrified, and even upon learning how it works you would still deem it impossible, unnatural. So when the stranger explains that there is a satellite in outer space, hovering above the world, and that it sent down a targeted laser blast to explode your cow, your brain simply can't accept it. You think it the work of God or the devil or some other dark magic."

Harold had paused then, seeing that he had Isaac completely and absolutely captivated.

"That is the difference between Experimental and Impossible Sciences. The gun is experimental, the satellite is impossible, at least in the example given," Harold had finished.

As he continued to be led around the room and introduced, Isaac wondered what it was that each of these people had invented. Harold had warned him that most were extremely guarded about their inventions, paranoid that they would be stolen or that their lives would be complicated if it became known exactly what they had invented. Even though he couldn't directly ask, Isaac tried to imagine what Impossible Sciences these people had mastered. If a laser satellite was Impossible Science in the Middle Ages, what then would be considered Impossible Science today?

It was clear from how he was being regarded that having a new person at one of these gatherings wasn't a normal occurrence. Obviously Isaac had made an impression on Harold with his proposed inventions, otherwise the man never would've invited him. A desire to know more about what invention he may be responsible for burned in the eyes of those who met Isaac as he finished making his way around the room and meeting everyone.

The time for the food had arrived and everyone took a seat at the table. Through the dinner Isaac kept mostly to himself. While he enjoyed the expertly prepared foods he studied those around him. Their conversations varied from philosophical discussions about the origins of the universe to a spirited debate about which was the best reality television program. What Isaac found even more fascinating than what was being said was the types of people saying them. There were heroes at this table, that much was clear. He could see it in their eyes, in the way they smiled, there were men and women in this room that had brought incredible gifts to humanity. There were also villains at this table, of that Isaac was certain. Their eyes gave it all away, the manner in which they sat, these were the inventors of dark and brutal things. It was these people that Isaac was most interested in.

One villainous looking man in particular had eyed Isaac through most of the dinner and as they moved on to cake and coffee the man finally spoke.

"I'm curious about something, Mr. Gray," the man said from across the table.

He was one of the only people in the room that Isaac hadn't been introduced to but he had overheard someone saying that the man's name was Castor Ileska. He looked to be of Romanian descent and spoke with a barely perceptible accent. He sat rigidly straight and wore a traditional power suit. His intense brown eyes were fixated on Isaac.

"If you promise to call me Isaac I'll gladly inform you of anything you wish to know," Isaac responded.

Most of the other conversations stopped now. They were all curious about Isaac and also interested in hearing what Castor had to say. The man rarely spoke, so when he did others usually listened.

"Harold has never brought anyone to these gatherings. You must've shown him something fantastic in order to pique his interest so," Castor said.

Isaac sensed the faintest trace of a challenge within the man's words. Before he could respond Harold leaned over and patted him on the back.

"Isaac here is something else, let me tell you," Harold said with a smile.

Under other circumstances Isaac would've appreciated the assistance but he wanted to play out the conversation with Castor.

He patted Harold and gave him a nod, then returned his gaze to the tense Romanian.

"Thank you Harold, but I think Castor was inquiring to the nature of my invention," Isaac said.

Even a man as hard as Castor knew better than to go against the rules of the club and he quickly raised his hand and shook his head as others around the table started to mutter. Harold had been right, asking about the inventions of others was serious business here.

"No, no, that was not my intention at all," Castor said.

Isaac smiled as he responded.

"It's no bother. As a matter of fact I have my work right here."

He reached into his suit jacket and started to pull out the two sheets of paper. Harold's hand flashed over and grabbed Isaac's arm, stopping him from revealing the papers.

"There's no need for that," Harold cautioned.

"Sincerely, I don't mind," Isaac assured him.

He tried to pull the papers out but Harold's grip tightened. The older man leaned in and whispered through gritted teeth.

"Trust me, you don't want to reveal your inventions here."

The rest of the people at the table were looking at them, half aghast at the break in their protocol and half captivated over what was happening.

"Please, let go," Isaac said.

Realizing that he was causing a scene, Harold reluctantly released his grip. Isaac cleared his throat as he pulled the papers out. All eyes were upon him as he unfolded them.

"My invention is broken into two parts, with the first and main part being love," he said.

A low murmur broke out as several people wondered aloud what he meant by this.

"Love?" Castor asked.

Isaac nodded.

"How can you invent that which already exists?" Castor asked.

"Sure, it exists, but is it defined? Is it something that you can explain, or map, or plan?" Isaac asked in return.

"Of course not," someone else chimed in, "that's the nature of love. It's mysterious."

"That's not entirely true," yet another person interjected. "There are chemical explanations that break down attraction and connection. There is science to aspects of love."

Isaac smiled slightly. The table was breaking out into spirited conversations on the subject. He sat quietly for a long moment and just took it in, a maestro at the head of his orchestra.

"Sure, there are some explanations available to us," Isaac spoke loudly, commanding the attention of the table. "They may explain the science of it but what about the act of falling in love? Does a dating book tell you how to manufacture it? Does a romantic movie train you how to make it happen?"

"Love happens many different ways Mr. Gray," Castor said. "It would be impossible to simplify it down to one reason that people fall in love."

Isaac held up the first sheet of paper.

"My invention would say otherwise, Mr. Ileska."

Everyone shifted in their seats to get a better look at the paper. He didn't want anyone as smart as these people getting too long of a look at the equations it contained so he lowered it after just a moment. Again a burst of interested chatter broke out about the things he was saying. Castor kept his eyes trained on Isaac, measuring him on many levels. Finally, the Romanian spoke.

"You mentioned two inventions."

It took a lot of self control for Isaac not to laugh out loud. He had found exactly what he was looking for in Castor Ileska.

"I did," Isaac answered, pausing to allow the rest of the table to quiet. "The second is something of a companion piece, if you will."

He held up the second sheet of paper.

"Crime of passion," he announced.

This caught some at the table off guard and they exchanged glances, suddenly unsure about what they were hearing.

"The two inventions together would be very powerful indeed," Castor said with a slow nod.

"You're quite right," Isaac responded. "On its own the second invention has its uses. A woman could cause her cheating husband to kill his mistress, for example. But it's when the two inventions are used in conjunction that they could be devastating."

He was commanding the full attention of everyone at the table now and loving every second of it.

"Use the first invention to cause a political leader to fall in love with someone. Then use the second to have that someone murder the political leader. You'd have a completely untraceable crime. You could change the world in the course of a few days solely through the use of my invention, the knowledge of how to cause love."

"And to subsequently tear it to shreds," Castor added.

These words hung heavy in the air and everyone quieted. Isaac nodded toward the man.

"If one so chose, then yes," Isaac said.

The silence stretched on for several moments. When the conversations started up again they were more serious, exploring the dangerous ways such a power could be used. A few of the people at the table eyed Isaac darkly, a confirmation that a few sharks swam amongst the group. But none watched him the way Castor Ileska did. The man's gaze was hatred itself, when Isaac locked eyes with him he could feel Castor plotting his demise, plotting how to steal the invention and take it for himself.

A kindly old gentlemen sitting nearby leaned forward and tapped Isaac on the hand to get his attention.

"Why love?" the man asked.

This was a question that Isaac would rather not answer but he was feeling powerful and in control and decided to indulge the man with an honest answer.

"The quote in the hallway, are you familiar with it?"

The man nodded.

"Our inventions mirror our secret wishes. It's a powerful statement," the man answered.

"Indeed it is," Isaac said. "As much as I'd rather not admit it, I guess it applies to this invention."

Isaac could feel the eyes of others on him now as he continued his conversation.

"You wish for love in your life?" the man asked.

Hearing it spoken out loud in such a way made Isaac uncomfortable. He tried to keep a smile on his face, tried to keep up a façade of control, but the smile slipped a bit as he searched for his answer.

"I have... difficulty accepting things that people say are impossible. I had a psychologist, a world renowned one, among the best on the planet, tell me recently that it was impossible for me to love anyone other than myself and thus impossible for anyone else to ever love me. This was in response to me telling him that I'd never truly loved anyone. He spoke of love like it was magic, indefinable, above definition."

Isaac paused and took a drink of his coffee.

"I found his opinions on the matter not to my liking and I set out to prove him wrong. This led me to my invention, which led me to be dining here with all of you wonderful people this evening."

"Why then did you also set yourself to deciphering the exact way to cause a crime of passion?" the man asked.

Isaac shrugged in response.

"It was a happy accident, the kind that science has from time to time. When working on my equations I happened upon a chain of experimental mathematics that led me to the crime of passion discovery. I thought it worth exploring."

The man's curiousity was satisfied for now and Isaac was thankful for it. He could feel someone watching him and glanced up to see Castor staring hard at him. The man looked positively bloodthirsty and Isaac believed that the man would gut him with a salad fork had no one else been in the room. The two of them stared for a while, Isaac with a smirk and Castor with a scowl. Finally, Castor spoke.

"These formulas of yours, these inventions, they are proven? You have tested them and they have worked?" the Romanian asked.

Isaac shook his head.

"In all truthfulness I must admit that I have not. I'll soon set into motion the process, however, and by week's end will have a woman who loves me, proving that the invention is sound," Isaac said.

Castor let out a cruel laugh and banged his fist on the table.

"Is that so? And who might the lucky woman be that will find herself bemused and transfixed by your equations?"

This was the one part of his plan that hadn't gone so well tonight. Isaac had hoped to see a woman among those gathered in the room, someone who might make a suitable candidate. But the only women present were older and generally not his type. He let his eyes wander around the room, looking for inspiration. A moment later he pointed and spoke.

"How about her?" Isaac asked.

Everyone turned to see one of the serving girls who had been walking by. She froze in place, completely confused as to what was happening and how she should react.

"Ha!" Castor said. "I could have five waitresses in love with me by the end of the week!"

There were a few chuckles and the serving girls cheeks turned red. Isaac shook his head and pointed again.

"Not her," he said. "Up there."

No one laughed this time. He was pointing at a long line of photographs that run just above where the serving girl had just happened to be walking. The photos were unmarked but Isaac had puzzled together enough about their meaning to feel comfortable using one for this purpose. They appeared to be some sort of recognition, a reward for being an outstanding inventor. The last four photographs were all of the same woman. She looked captivating, her eyes big and curious, her face beautiful despite the smudges of grease on it in several of the photographs.

"That's Elise Hargrove," Harold said. "She's one of the greatest inventors this world has ever known."

"She's very fetching," Isaac said. "I look forward to meeting her and putting to test my own invention."

Castor scoffed.

"A waitress may fall for your system of equations but I assure you, Hargrove will not."

That was the exact reaction Isaac had wanted. He needed it to be spoken aloud that if this woman were to fall to the invention then anyone would. Then he would be left with no doubt that it had really worked, that this particular impossibility had been conquered.

"We shall see," Isaac responded.

As the spectacle of the exchange faded people returned to their regular conversations. A few minutes later Castor left without bidding anyone goodnight. Isaac wished to leave too but leaned over to Harold before doing so.

"Is there another exit I could take?" Isaac asked.

Harold knew exactly why he was asking. Everyone in the room had seen how Castor was eyeing Isaac. They also knew that once Castor had set his mind to acquiring something he always got it.

"Pete is the doorman, the one who let you in here. He'll see that you get safely back outside the bookshelf. If you take a right out into the hall instead of a left you'll go deeper into the building, into the lesser used section. Go down past two intersecting hallways and then take a left. You'll find a fire exit there," Harold said.

Isaac nodded and started to stand up. He froze and then returned to his seat.

"That's the exact route he'll expect me to take," Isaac said.

After giving it a second of thought Harold nodded.

"I hadn't thought of that but you're probably right."

"The front door it is then," Isaac said.

He stood up and held out his hand to Harold. The man took it but shook his head as he looked at Isaac.

"I hope you know what it is that you've set in motion and how it is that you're going to stop it."

Isaac smiled.

"As do I."

After telling everyone else goodbye Isaac left the building, eager to move on to the next part of his plan.

Phase Five: Elise Hargrove

Finding Elise Hargrove was no easy task. Aided by Harold, Isaac had finally been able to track down where she was holed up, hard at work on her latest invention. In researching her, Isaac hadn't learned much. She was obsessive, a trait he could identify with, and brilliant, another thing the two had in common. But what she had previously invented or what she was currently inventing was unknown by most and not to be mentioned by the few that did know. The only thing that was clear was that she was thirty four years old, working around the clock, and hiding out so no one could find her.

Isaac hated showing up places unannounced so on the rare occasion that he was forced to do so he always came with a gift. He had a large thermos full of expensive coffee and two mugs with him as he approached the non-descript building in the mostly rundown section of town. All the other businesses on the block had long since closed their doors and more and more each month this area of downtown became overrun by drug dealers and homeless people.

He sat the thermos and mugs on the sidewalk and pulled out his lockpicking tools. He remembered when he had developed this particular skill.

When Isaac was fifteen years old, a neighborhood tough had tried to convince him and some other kids that a particular building in town was a secret bank where banks stored their extra money. He said there were no alarms since the banks thought it was secret, but the locks on the door made it impossible to break into. That word always set Isaac into action.

It had taken just a week to get good enough with a few rudimentary tools to pick the lock and get inside the building. Of course there was no money inside, just a vacant building in dire need of a good cleaning, some basic maintenance and a tenant.

But the lockpicking skill had served Isaac well since and had become even easier once he had obtained proper tools.

There were several locks on the door that he had to pick. He admired Elise's commitment to security, even if it had slowed him down a bit. Once the door was open he retrieved the thermos and mugs and went inside, being sure to lock the door behind him. A set of dirty stairs led down into a basement. He could hear the sound of hammering so he moved towards it.

The basement was large and filled with clutter. Isaac thought it looked like a mass grave for electronics, wires, scrap metal, and circuit boards were everywhere. There were tables filled with them, boxes filled with them, piles of them on the floor. On the far end of the room he saw Elise, hammering a thin piece of steel into shape with a mallet. He waited until she was between hits and then spoke.

"Coffee?"

She shrieked and jumped, then spun around, mallet held high.

"Whoa there, I come in peace!" Isaac said with a disarming smile.

She didn't lower the mallet. Elise looked like a human who had been raised in the forest by wolves. Her hair was frizzled, her clothes were layered with dirt and sweat stains, her skin was caked with grease and grime. But it was her eyes that sold the illusion, wild and wide.

"How long have you been down here?" Isaac asked.

Elise moved her mouth strangely, as if chewing on some food that wasn't there. After hearing a slight squeak Isaac realized that she was trying to talk. A few moments later she succeeded.

"Who are you?" she asked.

Her voice was scratchy and quiet, the mark of someone who hadn't spoken for some time. Isaac smiled as he answered.

"Isaac Gray."

"How did you get in here?"

He gestured up the stairs and chuckled nervously.

"It wasn't very gentlemenly of me but I'm afraid I must admit that I picked the lock on your door," he answered. "Don't worry though, it's very secure and I doubt anyone else will be bothering you down here."

Isaac paused and held up the thermos.

"I brought you some coffee, just as a way to say sorry for barging in. It might help with your throat."

He stepped forward but she tensed and raised the mallet higher. He stopped.

"Okay, okay, it's okay," Isaac said.

There was a table nearby with a little free space on it. He walked over to it and sat the thermos and the mugs down, then backed away until he was by the stairs again. She eyed him suspiciously but slowly made her way over to the thermos. She kept the mallet pointed towards him at all times. When Elise reached the thermos she opened the top and poured some of the coffee out onto a nearby slide. She then moved to a nearby microscope and placed the slide on it. Very quickly she put her eye to the microscope and adjusted some of the dials. After a few seconds she looked up to be sure Isaac hadn't moved, then returned to examining the coffee.

Apparently satisfied by what she saw, Elise returned to the thermos and poured herself an overflowing cup of the coffee. She drank it quickly, giving little regard to how much of it spilled onto her already filthy shirt. Once the mug was empty she refilled it and again drained it. Elise placed her hand on the table, steadying herself as the first coffee she'd had in over a month coursed through her. Many long moments later she stood up straight and again focused her full attention on her unwanted visitor.

"What do you want Mr. Gray?" she asked, her voice normal now.

"Please call me Isaac," he said. "I'm afraid the answer to your question is going to sound rather bizarre, but suffice to say that I'm hoping you'll help me prove the worth of my invention."

Her eyes cut over to where she had been hard at work before he entered. Isaac recognized her obsession, he admired it. She hated being interrupted, hated that he was keeping her from accomplishing her goal.

"You admittedly broke into my workshop. I could crush your skull with this mallet and suffer no legal consequences for having done so."

She was fiery and unafraid. Isaac liked that.

"You're correct. As a matter of fact, this area has been subject to a lot of crime in recent months, including more than a handful of break-ins. You could claim I was the thief of those other places and that you'd finally ended my reign of burglary terror. You'd make the newspaper, maybe even get a commendation from the local PD," Isaac answered.

His flippant attitude had disarmed her and she looked at him more closely.

"Seriously, who are you?"

"Isaac Gray. I was at the most recent meeting of the Inventor's Club. A man, Harold Underwood, invited me there because he was impressed with my proposed invention. And now I need you to help me make that invention a reality."

Elise shook her head as she answered.

"No, no way. My work here's very important. I've been at it for," she paused and looked around, "a long time. Too long. I can't be bothered with anything right now."

Isaac took a moment to examine the room more closely. He saw a pile of clothes on the floor, a refrigerator, a cot. She was living down here, working endlessly on her latest invention.

"It really should be no bother. As a matter of fact, if it works like I believe it will, you won't really have to do anything at all."

She looked back at her work and then to him. Her patience was almost gone.

"The idea is for you to fall in love with me," Isaac said.

"Excuse me?"

"My invention, in theory it is a surefire way to cause someone to fall in love. I'm going to use it on you to prove that it works."

Elise laughed.

"Is this some sort of a joke? Did Harold send you here because he thinks I've been working too hard?"

Isaac stepped forward. There was no smile on his face now.

"No Elise, it's no joke. I will use a predetermined series of equations and formulas and you will fall in love with me. I will lie to you, I will do whatever I must, and you will fall in love with me."

His sudden intensity frightened her and she again raised the mallet. She was about to speak when someone knocked hard on the front door of the building. Both of them looked towards the stairs, then back at one another.

"Did you tell someone where I was at?" Elise asked.

"No, of course not."

She moved past him, mallet clutched tightly in hand, and started up the stairs. Isaac followed her. The person knocked again, harder this time. Elise reached the top of the stairs and moved to a small barred window and peeked out. She quickly recoiled, hopeful that no one outside saw her.

"This can't be happening!" she hissed.

"What? Who is it?" Isaac asked.

"Castor Ileska."

Isaac's heart started pounding. He moved to the window and looked for himself. There were three burly men, all of them Romanian, standing near the door. They wore expensive suits and Isaac could see that at least one of them had a gun that was currently in a shoulder holster under his suit coat. Standing by a parked black sedan was Castor.

Elise flew back down the stairs and Isaac rushed to keep up with her.

"Why is he here?" she asked.

"He wants my invention," Isaac said.

She whirled around to face him.

"You led him here?!"

"I'm sorry, Elise, I didn't know I was being followed."

She turned away and began rushing around the basement in a frenzy. She was shoving components, notepads, everything she could get her hands on, into a large bag.

"Why don't we call the cops?" Isaac asked. "They'll come and see that he and his goons are trying to break in."

Elise scoffed as she continued packing things.

"Castor Ileska has diplomatic immunity. He can do anything he wants, the police can't touch him."

"Oh," Isaac said.

He was stunned by this and his mind raced for another way out of the situation.

"It's not you he's after, it's me," Isaac said. "I'll go out there and then he'll leave."

"You don't understand this man, Mr. Gray. If he breaks in here and sees what I'm working on, he'll not only kill you for your invention, he'll kill me for mine."

He let this sink in for a moment, then responded.

"Then we stop him from breaking in."

Elise paused and turned towards him.

"How? With a mallet and a thermos full of coffee?" she asked.

"We take away his reason for needing to break in," Isaac replied. "Is there a way to get onto the roof?"

"I think so. Why?"

"We get on the roof and make a run for it. Once we're a few buildings away we call out to him, draw his attention away from your workshop. They'll come after us."

She twirled her hair for a moment as she thought hard about his plan.

"There are a lot of unknown variables," she said.

"It beats staying here," Isaac responded quickly. "Pack what you need and let's go."

Elise knew that he was right, but she froze as she stared at her not yet completed invention. Every part of her life over the past months had been dedicated to it and the idea of leaving filled her with dread and sadness.

"You said it yourself, he'll kill us and take both of our inventions. At least this way we have a chance to stay alive and he never sees your invention," Isaac said.

Finally she started packing again. Every so often she would pause and again look upon her invention. The banging on the door upstairs was constant now. Castor's men were trying to break it down.

"We have to go. Now," Isaac said.

Elise looked at her invention one last time then turned towards him.

"I'm ready."

They rushed upstairs and past the main door. There was another staircase that led further up into the building and they moved up it quickly. The rest of the building was empty and in disrepair. The stairs felt rickety and unsafe, squeaking loudly as they moved up them.

The building was only three stories and they reached the hatch to the roof in under a minute. It was rusted shut and Isaac had to hit it several times before it finally swung open. He climbed out and then helped Elise up. While she looked to see where the fire escape was at Isaac crept over to the side of the building and looked down. Just as he had thought, the locks on the door were very strong and were still holding up against the assault of the Romanians.

Isaac moved back over to Elise and noticed the panicked expression on her face.

"No fire escape," she whispered.

He took a moment to look around and realized that she was right. Isaac turned in a slow circle, then pointed at the next building. She looked at it and then shook her head.

"It's too far."

He looked at it again. It was also a three story building, so the roof was even with the one they were on. However, the gap between buildings was quite wide, twelve feet by Isaac's fast estimation. He turned towards Elise and smirked.

"No problem," he said. "I'll go first and then catch you after that."

"Wait, Isaac…"

He didn't let her finish and sprinted towards the edge of the building. He ran with confidence and ease, recalling his time in college, when someone had foolishly told him that it was impossible for the school record in the long jump track and field event to ever be broken. After four months of training, not only had Isaac broken it, he had obliterated it, and his name still adorned a dust covered plaque in the athletics building on campus.

Isaac jumped and for a single instant let the feeling of freedom and flight wash over him as he sailed across the gap. He then focused in on his landing. His feet came down far clear of the edge on the other roof, his success never in question.

He turned back to Elise and motioned for her to jump. She was scared, but it sounded like Castor's men were getting closer to breaking into the building. She moved to the edge and threw her bag across to Isaac, then retreated and prepared her approach.

Isaac positioned himself at the edge of the roof and extended his arms. He nodded towards her.

"I'll catch you."

Elise looked like she was going to throw up but she started running towards the edge of the roof anyways. Her jump was awkward and ungraceful and Isaac immediately braced himself. She was short by over a foot and he had to reach out to grab her outstretched hand. She swung hard into the side of the building, letting out a grunt upon impact, but he had a strong grip on her and didn't let her fall. Isaac pulled her up and she collapsed on the roof beside him. There was a small trickle of blood running down her face.

"You okay?" Isaac asked.

She was breathing heavily but she nodded. He stood up and helped her to her feet, then the two of them rushed to the fire escape. They made their way down it and emerged into the alley behind the line of buildings. Isaac led the way and took them down the alley in the opposite direction of Castor and his men.

Behind one of the businesses they came across a white Cadillac. Isaac broke the driver's side window with his elbow and then unlocked the door. He got in and unlocked Elise's door but she didn't get in. He could sense her hesitation and rolled down her window so he could address her.

"If you don't trust me enough to get in, I understand," Isaac said. "I can take the car and try to distract them, maybe that'll buy you enough time to escape on foot."

She leaned down so she could see his face.

"I don't even know who you are," she said.

"I'm Isaac Gray..."

"And you're going to make me fall in love with you," she finished, her tone clearly calling into question his sanity.

"That's the plan."

Isaac looked down and set about hotwiring the car. He could feel her eyes on him and he talked as he worked.

"When I was in college I had a professor who really hated my guts. He drove a Jaguar XK convertible. One day I was walking across campus and he saw me, so he slowed down and leaned and said 'in your entire life you'll never be able to know the pleasure of driving a car as expensive as this'."

He paused for a minute as he pulled more of the wires out from under the steering wheel.

"I was dirt poor, so I was never going to be able to afford one, so I set about learning alternate means to get behind the wheel of one."

Isaac paused again as he made the final connection.

"I proved him wrong," he said as the engine roared to life.

Elise opened the passenger door and sat down. She looked over at him.

"Once we're away from here, you'll let me get out?"

"Of course. I'll drop you anywhere you want me to."

He pulled out of the alley and onto the road. They could see Castor and his men outside the building.

"Hey, Castor!" Isaac yelled.

The Romanian inventor turned around and saw the two of them. His men started to draw their pistols but Castor held up his hand to stop them.

"You'll never get my invention, Castor!" Isaac yelled. "Never!"

Castor smiled. It was a wicked sight to behold.

"You may want to ask your poor grandma what the consequences are of trying to keep me from getting what I want," Castor said.

"Grandma?" Isaac muttered.

"Yes, she played quite the game of cat and mouse, trying to tell us fifty different places where you might be."

Isaac looked at Elise, his eyes filling with tears.

"He wouldn't, would he?" he asked.

She stared at him for a moment, not wanting to answer the question. Finally she nodded. Isaac slammed on the accelerator, causing the large Cadillac to peel out before lurching forward quickly. He weaved through traffic without slowing down as he continued speeding across the city.

"She's the only family I have," he said as he sped through a red light.

Elise nodded her understanding and stayed silent as he got them across town in record time. He stopped the car outside a nondescript little white house and leapt out. Elise got out slowly, looking up and down the road for any sign of Castor's men.

Isaac rushed up to the front door and kicked it as hard as he could. It swung open and he ran inside.

"Grandma?" he yelled.

Satisfied that Castor's men weren't here yet, Elise went into the house, hoping desperately that they'd find Isaac's grandmother alive and well, even though she knew that it was a near certainty that they wouldn't. As she came through the door she saw a grisly sight. Isaac was on his knees in a pool of blood, cradling the dead body of an old woman. It looked as if she had been cut up badly, like she had truly suffered before she died.

Tears were streaming down Isaac's face and he was rocking back and forth, clutching the dead woman to his chest. As much as Elise hated to have to see this she hated what she had to say next even more.

"We have to get out of here, Isaac. Castor knows this is where we were headed, he'll be here any second."

He didn't respond, didn't even register that she had spoken. Elise moved closer, sick over what she was trying to do. She knew that no one deserved to be rushed through something like this, but they had no choice. She placed her hand on his shoulder and he looked up at her quickly, as if suddenly aware of her presence.

"I'm sorry Isaac but we have to go."

He stared at her blankly for a moment and then nodded.

"Okay, you're right."

Isaac gingerly laid the old woman down onto the floor, back into the pool of her blood, and stood up.

"I'll be right out," Isaac said.

Elise nodded and then exited the house. The Cadillac was still running and she got in the driver's seat. A moment later Isaac emerged from the house. His clothes were covered in blood and he looked like he was in a daze. She checked the mirrors, knowing that Castor could be pulling up at any instant. Isaac reached the car and she slammed on the gas even before he had closed his door.

Once they were clear of the neighborhood, Elise slowed down and looked over at Isaac. He was staring at the dashboard, his eyes unfocused.

"We need a plan, we need to figure this out," Elise said.

Isaac didn't answer. She hated to prod him but she needed help. An idea occurred to her and she held out her hand.

"Give me your cell phone."

He pulled it out of his pocket and gave it to her. She quickly dialed a number and waited for the person to pick up.

"Harold, thank goodness!" she said.

Harold Underwood was the closest thing she had to a friend in The Inventor's Club or anywhere else for that matter. The fact that he knew Isaac as well made him the most logical choice to turn to for help.

"Elise? What's happening? Why are you calling me from Isaac's phone?"

"It's Castor Ileska. Isaac found me at my workshop to try his foolish invention on me but Castor followed him."

"That's not good," Harold said.

"People are dead, Harold, this goes beyond 'not good'."

"Of course, Elise. How can I help?"

She paused as she changed lanes to go around a slow moving car.

"I don't know what to do. Isaac's, he's in shock I think, and Castor knows where my workshop is, I can't go back there."

There was a long stretch of silence before Harold answered.

"I can't get too deeply involved in this Elise, I hope you understand."

She had to bite the insider of her mouth to keep from screaming and cussing at him. Once she had stemmed off the immediate urge she spoke.

"Anything, Harold. Anything at all you can give us would be appreciated. You know Castor, he's not going to stop until Isaac's dead and he has his invention. Now that I'm involved, it probably means the same for me."

There was another long pause.

"I can't do anything to help you," Harold said.

"Dammit! Give me something! Some advice even!"

"Get out of town. Get as far out of town as you can. Stay off the radar and I'll," he hesitated, "once things calm down I'll see what I can do to help you."

"I need my invention," Elise said. "Is there any way that…"

"Impossible," Harold interrupted. "I'm sorry, there's just no way I could do that, not right now anyways."

Elise sighed and had to fight back tears.

"This one means a lot to you, huh?" Harold asked.

"More than you know."

She hung up the phone and set it on the seat beside her. Her mind was racing, trying to figure out the next move.

"You can drop me off somewhere," Isaac said.

His voice startled her.

"The only reason you're involved in this is because of me. People are dead because of me," he said. "I'm just a stranger who showed up and ruined your life. Just leave me somewhere and get yourself out of town."

He was dejected, his eyes still filled with tears. Elise watched him for a moment. Even though he was right, that he had been the cause of a very quick and terrible turn of events in her life, she didn't want to just throw him out of the car to fend for himself, not after the traumatic event he had just endured.

"No, it's okay. Let's just put some distance between us and Castor. Then we can figure things out," Elise said.

Isaac nodded and sat back as she steered the car onto the interstate.

Phase Six: On the run

After several hours on the interstate the two agreed to switch places and Isaac took over behind the wheel. The sun was going down and as he took them further and further away from town he could sense that Elise was growing despondent. She stared out of the window and remained silent as they continued across the rural countryside. Forty five minutes passed before Isaac finally spoke.

"Thinking about your invention?"

She winced slightly. After a long pause she nodded, not taking her eyes off the darkening world outside.

"It must be something important to have you this upset."

Elise turned to look at him now. She clearly didn't want to talk about this and just gave him a slight nod, hoping he'd get the point.

"I'm sorry, I don't mean to press you on it. I'm just trying to take my mind off what happened earlier. What I saw."

Her expression softened as he mentioned this.

"I understand," Elise responded. "I'm sorry, it's just hard for me to talk about this. Being forced to leave it behind when I was so close to getting it finished it…"

"It hurts," Isaac finished.

"I'm not trying to downplay the pain you must be feeling," Elise said.

"I know that."

She nodded but didn't say anything else. He wanted to ask her more but respected her wishes to stay quiet. Elise returned to staring out the window and as night fell Isaac kept them heading East. Two more hours passed and he saw the sign for a motel up ahead.

"If you're okay with it I think we should stop there for the night," he said.

Elise frowned as she saw how rundown the place looked but eventually nodded. Isaac steered them into the parking lot. They left the car running as he went in and paid in cash for one night. When he returned to the Cadillac he handed her the key to their room.

"Here's the key. You head inside and I'll go ditch this car and pick up a few essentials for us."

She took the key and nodded. Elise grabbed her bag and was about to get out of the car when Isaac spoke again.

"I know it's a bit of a delicate subject to bring up with a woman but if I may make one small suggestion…"

"Shower?" Elise interrupted, looking down at her stained and dirty clothes.

"If it's not too much trouble."

She got out of the car and he watched her until she got into their room safely. Isaac pulled back onto the road and headed towards a small town they had passed about ten minutes back. There was a tiny bus station there and he parked the Cadillac in the parking lot and got out. If anyone tracked the car they'd find it there and assume that Isaac and Elise had hopped on a bus.

He then walked to a nearby store. He arrived just ten minutes before they closed, so he did his shopping quickly. He had customer service desk call him a cab and after a twenty minute wait for the cab to arrive Isaac had the man drive him back to the motel. The whole trip took a little over an hour and he was ready for some rest when he finally got back to the motel.

They had only been given one key so he had to knock on the door and wait. For a moment he was left to wonder if Elise was still in there. He wouldn't have blamed her for taking off, but he was relieved when he started to hear the chain lock on the door being undone.

She pulled the door open and moved with it, using it to shield herself. He wasn't quite sure why she was doing this until he stepped inside and turned to look at her. She was wearing nothing but a dingy white towel that was wrapped around her, barely covering her. Despite his fantastic good manners, Isaac couldn't help but stand and stare dumbly at her. Gone was the grimy, filthy wild woman who had been holed up in a basement working around the clock. Here stood a sexy, full figured, completely clean woman. Her slightly damp brown hair cascaded down past her shoulders and her eyes shined a brilliant green.

Elise closed the door hard and the sound of it pulled Isaac back to reality. He quickly turned away and moved towards the queen size bed in the middle of the small room. Elise moved past him, careful to keep the towel from slipping. She sat on the bed and picked up one of the pillows and used it to cover herself.

"I couldn't bring myself to put those disgusting clothes back on," she said.

"I understand," Isaac said. "I didn't mean to stare."

She blushed slightly.

"It's fine. What did you get at the store?"

"A few things, but first I'm sure you'll want these."

Isaac reached into one of the bags and pulled out several articles of clothing. He placed them on the bed next to her. Two shirts, two pairs of pants, some socks, a new pair of shoes, and even a few pairs of panties and two bras. Elise was surprised that he had been so thorough and she slowly looked over all of the items.

"Do they look okay?" he asked.

After inspecting them for another moment she nodded.

"Actually it's all sort of perfect."

He smiled slightly. Of course it was perfect. Isaac had once heard a man complaining that his wife always wanted him to buy her clothes but that she hated everything he bought for her. 'It's impossible to please her no matter what clothes I buy', the man had whined to a nearby friend. That word stuck in Isaac's mind, and seeing as he was at a point in his life with very little going on, he introduced himself to the man and took up the challenge. He assumed a new identity and ran a large survey with women, finding out exactly what it was they looked for in clothing, getting deep into their process of what they chose to wear and why. A month later he learned a little about the man's wife and then went clothes shopping for her. The woman was thrilled, calling his choices perfect.

As he watched Elise pick through the clothes and decide what she wanted to put on right now he was glad to see that she was pleased with his choices. He reached into another bag and pulled out a comfortable pair of pajamas and tossed them to her.

"For you to wear tonight," he said.

She looked at them and nodded and he could've sworn he saw the slightest bit of a smile. They were as far from sexy as you could get, just a shirt and a long pair of pants, adorned with a cute moon and stars pattern and made out of a comfortable fabric. Elise went into the restroom to get dressed. While she was gone, Isaac pulled out a fast food burger he had picked up on the way back to the motel. He unwrapped it and stared at it longingly. He hadn't eaten all day and his stomach was growling and grumbling.

Isaac raised the burger towards his mouth.

"No!" Elise shouted.

She rushed to him and slapped the burger out of his hands. It fell onto the unsavory looking carpet. Isaac looked at her, waiting for her to explain what just happened.

"Trust me, you don't want to put that stuff in your body," Elise said.

"We don't exactly have access to organically grown food options here."

Elise walked over to her bag and unzipped a side pocket. She pulled out a small clear pouch that was half filled with a strange looking blue paste. She tossed it to him.

"Eat this."

Isaac turned it over in his hands, eyeing it suspiciously. He opened it and a powerful odor came rushing out. He crinkled his nose and looked over at Elise.

"It's a full day's dose of everything your body needs to survive. I made it myself."

He took one last look at his burger on the floor and then emptied the pouch of paste into his mouth. It tasted much like it smelled and it was a struggle for him to swallow it. After recovering from the ordeal, he realized that Elise was standing there staring at him, her hands on her hips. He was sitting on the edge of the bed, the only bed in the room.

Isaac quickly stood up and gestured towards the bed.

"It's all yours," he said. "I'll sleep on the floor."

She looked both relieved and apologetic. He spoke again before she could protest.

"You've been great today, despite the fact that I slightly ruined your life. Please, take the bed."

She nodded and climbed onto it. He got situated on the gross, uncomfortable floor and she flicked off the lamp, plunging the room into darkness. Several minutes later Isaac spoke.

"Elise?"

"What?"

"I really wish you hadn't knocked my burger into the floor."

She sighed before responding.

"I did you a favor."

"How exactly?"

She paused for several moments, then answered.

"Let's just get some rest."

The next morning they agreed to put one more day's worth of travel between them and Castor before putting together any sort of plan of action. They walked down the side of the interstate for an hour, towards a small farm Isaac had spotted the day before. Once there they hopped the fence and moved along it to the back side of the property. There they found an old broken down truck. It was barely visible from the road and looked like it hadn't been touched in some time. Isaac described it as "the kind of vehicle no one will come looking for" and so he and Elise set about fixing it.

Even though Isaac possessed decent automobile repair skills, Elise quickly took over and delegated him to keeping watch for the owners. Her mastery and understanding of engineering and mechanics was second to none, and within an hour she had the truck fully functional. The keys were inside, so they started it and drove it off the property via an unpaved back road. Eventually they made their way back to the interstate and were off once more.

Isaac took the first driving shift and quickly set his sights to finding some food. When he pulled off and got in line at a fast food drive through, Elise sat up and shook her head.

"Uh uh," she said. "No way. Get us out of here."

"Unless you can give me one good reason why I should drive away I'm going to order a cheeseburger and I'm going to eat it."

She sat back and nodded.

"Fine, go ahead and order it. Then I'll give you your reason."

Isaac ordered himself the biggest burger they had, then pulled forward and paid for it. After they handed him the food Elise directed him to pull around and park in a secluded corner of the parking lot. He did as she asked and once they were stopped she started digging around in her bag. She pulled out a strange looking microscope and then pointed at the burger.

"Pinch off a piece of the meat and hand it to me," she said.

He did it and she placed it on a slide and put it under the microscope.

"Look at it and tell me what you see," Elise said.

He placed his eye on the microscope and adjusted the knob to bring it into focus. Like anything, the meat didn't look appetizing up close but there was nothing out of the ordinary about it.

"Looks like hamburger meat to me," he said.

Elise nodded and reached over. She had a small lens attachment in her hand and she screwed it onto the tip of the microscope lens.

"Now look again."

Isaac did as she asked. He nearly jumped out of the truck as he saw the meat through this new lens. It was covered in tiny organisms. They looked robotic, but they swarmed all over the meat like ants. It caused his skin to crawl and he immediately threw the rest of the burger out of the truck.

"What the hell are those things?" he asked.

Elise tossed the small piece of meat on the slide out of her window before answering.

"Nanites. They're in everything we eat."

A chill ran through Isaac as he thought about this. He then looked back at the microscope.

"What was that second lens, the one that allowed me to see them?"

She placed the microscope back into her bag as she answered.

"I call it the Hargrove lens."

"You invented it?"

She nodded.

"How? How did you know to look for the nanites?"

Elise had been hoping he wouldn't ask this question, but should've known that a man like Isaac would connect the dots.

She thought about ignoring him, or about lying, but finally faced up to the truth of it.

"Because the nanites were my invention."

He fell silent upon hearing this. The parking lot was filling up with the lunch crowd so Isaac started the truck and pulled them back out onto the interstate. Elise was in a dark mood again, but he wasn't ready to just let the subject drop.

"What exactly do the nanites do?" Isaac asked.

Not even her fellow Inventor's Club members knew the extent of Elise's nanite invention. They knew it was big and worldwide, but even her closest acquaintances like Harold didn't know much beyond that. She looked over at Isaac for a moment, wondering what the dangers would be if she confided in him.

"We've got a long drive ahead of us," Isaac said, somehow sensing her dilemma.

She sighed. Maybe it would help her to let someone else in on the story, she thought.

"Do you ever get those thoughts, the ones that appear just in the very back of your mind?" Elise asked.

"Of course, doesn't everybody?"

"Most people, yes. Just the sudden thought, maybe I'll go see a movie today, or I think I'll call my old friend. When I envisioned nanites, I wanted to target these thoughts, but only in certain individuals. Murderers, rapists, these are who the invention was meant for. The nanites could be fine tuned, so that when a certain thought comes into the brain, like, I think I'm going to strangle that woman jogging through the park, the nanites can latch onto it and morph it."

"Are we talking mind control?" Isaac asked.

"No, the nanites can'tdo that. They can change the thought, not completely, but they can shape it into something else as long as it stays related to the original thought and stays consistent with that persons regular thinking. So instead of 'I think I'm going to strangle that woman jogging through the park', the nanites could make it into something less sinister, like 'I'm going to scare that woman' or 'I'm going to chase that woman'. It wouldn't make for a good evening for the woman, but at least she'd be alive at the end of it."

Isaac sat for a long moment, thinking about this.

"So how did the nanites end up in fast food?" he asked.

That was THE question, the one that kept Elise from sleeping at night, that kept her obsessed with her next invention. Telling Isaac these things had already made her feel better, but the idea of admitting to the last part of it made her sick at her stomach. When she finally did respond her voice was quiet and full of regret.

"The Inventor's Club is built upon disassociation, a separation between inventor and invention. Is the man who invented the gun a killer? The Inventor's Club says no, they create these things and let them loose into the world, completely unaware of how they'll be used and what they'll actually become."

She paused for a long moment.

"But J. Robert Oppenheimer, the father of the atomic bomb, he knew better. He said 'I am become death, the destroyer of worlds.' Too late he realized what he had done."

Isaac nodded slowly.

"And that's how you feel, too?" he asked.

"Not to that level, but yes. The government got control of my nanites invention and they sold it to the corporations. The corporations had their scientists specifically tune the nanites and then as a way of getting them into people, added them into food."

Isaac scratched at his head, suddenly feeling very violated.

"Yes, they're in your brain right now," Elise said.

He shuddered.

"What thoughts do they mess with?" Isaac asked.

"Have you ever had a craving for a Kansas Fried Chicken meal? Or a McDouglas burger?" Elise asked darkly. "Ever get that unscratchable itch to go shopping?"

The truck swerved slightly as he turned to look at her.

"You're kidding me," he said.

"I wish I was. I created the single most invasive form of marketing there is. You think that you're getting hungry, the nanites morph that into a specific urge to go eat at a specific place. You think you want to go do something, the nanites morph that into a need to see the latest Hollywood blockbuster. So on and so forth."

"That's... that's sick," Isaac said.

Elise looked out the window, not wanting to talk about it anymore. He got the point and drove them for many more hours straight until the sun was starting to set.

"Let's pull off and call Harold, maybe something has changed," Isaac suggested.

They found a payphone at a small gas station and poured plenty of quarters into it, then dialed his number. Isaac held the phone where both of them could hear.

"Hello?" Harold answered.

"Harold," Elise said. "It's both of us here. Please, tell us you have news."

He cleared his throat.

"I'm afraid it's not good."

Isaac and Elise shared a worried glance.

"Just tell us," Isaac said.

"Castor's going crazy looking for you two. You know this man, he's never been denied something he wants before, and he's not going to start now. But look, there are some things going in your favor."

"What's that?" Elise asked.

"Castor's convinced that the two of you split up, so he's got two different groups of people out there looking. They're not looking for a couple, so if you stick together you'll stay off their radar."

"Okay," Isaac said. "What else?"

"Castor's has to go back to Romania. Once he's out of the country he'll be out for almost a year. That will give me enough time to work with the people that I know and get you two clear of him. You just have to stick together and find somewhere to lay low until he leaves."

Elise had known Harold long enough to pick up on something in his tone of voice as he delivered that last statement.

"How long?" she asked.

Harold hesitated.

"How long until he leaves for Romania, Harold?" she asked again.

"Four months."

Elise couldn't believe what she was hearing. Her mouth dropped open but no words came out. Isaac answered for her.

"Four months?" he asked. "Are you serious, Harold?"

"I'm sorry guys, I know it's not ideal, but it's your only chance," he paused for a moment and cleared his throat. "Listen, we should really get off the phone."

"Wait," Elise said. "What about my invention? Is there any way you can get to it and…"

"There's nothing I can do," Harold interrupted. "I'm sorry Elise."

She looked devastated.

"Get into hiding, stay together, stay off the grid, and come find me in four months," Harold said, then hung up the phone.

Elise walked quickly back to the truck. She stared angrily out of the window as they headed back down the interstate and tried to fight back the bitter tears that were gathering in her eyes. After a half hour had passed, Isaac spoke.

"Your new invention is something that can stop the nanites, isn't it?"

She wiped her eyes as she slowly turned towards him.

"How did you know?"

Isaac shrugged.

"I know we just met but it just seemed like the kind of thing you would do. You were so upset over what that invention turned into that you want to stop it. It's very admirable," he answered.

Elise scoffed.

"It's not admirable. It's nothing," she paused and turned away from him. "It's all gone now anyways."

They came up with a plan to go to Rochester, New York and drove straight through, taking shifts behind the wheel. At almost every stop they made along the way Isaac made phone calls, but when Elise asked him about them he told her not to worry. For her part she remained depressed for the whole trip, lamenting the loss of her one chance to right her terrible wrong and rid the world of the nanites.

Isaac assured her not to worry about money and always seemed to have enough cash on hand to pay for anything they needed. They ditched the truck in Ohio and took a bus into Rochester. Elise noticed that Isaac was growing strangely excited as they got closer and closer and by the time he was leading her to the small apartment he had rented for them in downtown Rochester he was downright giddy.

"What's with you?" she asked, begrudgingly letting him lead her by the hand down the sidewalk.

He only smiled in response. When they reached the building they found that the elevator was out of order and they had to climb up to their eighth floor apartment. Isaac held up the key.

"Would you do the honors?" he asked.

Elise eyed him suspiciously as she took the key and unlocked the apartment door. It was larger than she had thought it would be, but bare of all but the most rudimentary of furnishings. When she flicked on the light she noticed a huge pile of things in the middle of the floor.

"What?" she asked quietly.

She dropped her bag and rushed into the room. The floor was filled with components, wires, and pieces of scrap metal. She dug through them for a moment, then spun around.

"Is this my invention?" she asked.

Isaac smiled and nodded.

"I had some highly specialized, discreet men who owed me a big favor. I had them get as much of your things from the workshop as possible and fly them up here."

"I don't know what to say," Elise said, tears forming in her eyes. "Thank you."

"It's the least I could do. I know there's still a lot to be done before it's ready and this isn't exactly the best workshop, but if you're willing to teach me a few things I think you'll find me to be a capable assistant."

She stared at him for a long moment, trying to find any sort of sarcasm, or malice, or dishonesty.

"You're serious? You'll help me get it done?"

Isaac took off his coat and tossed it onto the floor.

"Of course I'm serious," he said, stepping closer to the pile of parts in the floor. "Let's get to work."

Elise laughed, then nodded.

"Okay, let's do it."

Phase Seven: In hiding

The two and a half months that Isaac and Elise spent together in Rochester were among the best either of them had ever had. At first she had returned to an obsessive work schedule, but progress was slow with their limited number of tools. After a few days, Isaac was able to convince her that they had plenty of time and that they could fill the hours with more than just working on completing her invention.

Each of them introduced the other to one of their favorite hobbies. Elise shared her love of classic movies, none of which he had ever seen, and Isaac sheepishly admitted to his love of trashy romance novels. When she was done laughing at him, Elise had agreed to a trade. For every three classic movies he'd watch, she'd read one of his trashy novels. Their nights were spent watching movies like *Casablanca, Ben-Hur, Citizen Kane,* and *Blade Runner,* and sometimes they'd fall asleep together on the couch in the middle of them. During the day she'd begrudgingly read the novels, often throwing them at him from across the room when she'd get to a particularly ridiculous moment in the plot.

They discovered an organic market a few blocks away from their apartment and were frequent visitors. After Elise checked the ingredients to be certain they were free of nanites, they'd take turns cooking dinner, each enjoying sharing their favorite meals with the other. Every now and again Elise picked up more tools for them to use but they always seemed to get lost, leaving them with just the short screw driver and few other tools they had started out with. She theorized that the tools were getting lost in a sub-dimensional fold that overlapped with their apartment. Isaac wasn't sure if he bought it or not.

They had been there for two months before Isaac asked about the nature of the invention they were working on. Elise cringed. She had been afraid that he would ask and she looked at him fearfully, afraid that he would stop helping her, that he would leave once she told him.

"I can't take the nanites out of people but I can stop them from working altogether," Elise said, trying to ease into the explanation. "By sending out a pulse I can short them out and shut them down."

"How can you target a pulse that just goes after the nanites?"

She looked at him and shook her head. He was just too damn smart.

"I can't."

Elise watched as he put it together. She found it fascinating to see how fast his brain processed complex concepts.

"This pulse won't just take the nanites offline, it'll take down..."

"Everything electronic," Elise finished.

Isaac sat down on the couch.

"What about hospitals?" he asked.

"Hospitals and a few key military and government installations were contacted about a year ago by a company with a deal that they couldn't pass up. A new kind of insulation that's cheaper, cleaner, and five hundred percent more effective than anything else on the market. It also happens to be woven with a specially designed material that will block out my pulse."

Isaac looked up at her.

"You invented an insulation to block it?" he asked.

She nodded.

"I'm just sorry I wasn't able to get it installed more places. Time was of the essence though. People with pacemakers or other home medical equipment, they'll be the first to get help from the hospitals after the pulse. I don't want anyone to die because of what I'm going to do."

Isaac thought some more before asking his next question.

"Beyond knocking out the nanites, this thing is going to knock out what exactly?"

"Everything," Elise answered.

She turned away, not sure if she could handle seeing any sort of disgust or anger in his expression if it should materialize there.

"It's designed to not only fry anything electronic, but to do a full wipe of everything. So the computers that store the knowledge of how to create and operate my nanites will no longer have that information. And without my original notes, which I burned, they'll never be able to recreate them."

"So credit scores, banks, stock markets," Isaac started listing.

"Everything," Elise interrupted.

"You're going to set the world back sixty years," he said.

She searched every word for hidden meaning, scoured his tone for anger or disgust.

"In a manner of speaking, yes."

She turned back around and stared at him. He sat in silence for several minutes. Finally he nodded and stood up.

"Okay," was all he said.

Elise watched him closely, looking for signs that he was unhappy or afraid of the things she had said. But he just returned to working on the invention and never gave any indication that he felt negatively towards her or what she was going to do. She had feared that he would run for the door, but instead here he stood, helping like always.

They had been living together for two and a half months in the apartment in Rochester when they completed work on the invention. Isaac marveled at the size of it. It looked like an egg and was no bigger than a gallon of milk. He understood the way in which it was to work. The pulse was an ever amplifying wave, starting out with the tiniest of sparks. One circuit overloaded another, then jumped to a slightly bigger circuit. With each jump the power of it grew until it would eventually sweep through power grids in the blink of an eye. The whole process would take less than a minute.

But the idea that all of that, such a massive change to the world, would originate from here, this tiny little thing, blew Isaac away. Elise stood beside him, her arm hooked through his. She too just stared at it, relieved and elated to see it finished. They looked at each other and smiled.

"You did it," Isaac said.

He fell back onto the couch and she fell with him, keeping her arm entwined with his. She liked being near him, and loved the sound of what he had just said. It brought tears to her eyes but she didn't fight them, and soon they were rolling down her cheeks. Soon her greatest mistake would be righted, and even though it would mean a big change for the world, maybe it would be the best thing that could be done to help everyone refocus on the things that were important.

"We did it," Elise said, barely aware that she was running her hand up and down his arm.

Isaac noticed it and he looked over at her. There was an electricity where their skin touched, and their eyes locked. Elise found it hard to breathe, hard to think about anything. She leaned forward to kiss him.

At the last second Isaac pulled away and stood up quickly. Elise fell onto the couch where he had just been sitting.

"It worked!" Isaac exclaimed.

Elise was completely confused and looked up at him. Isaac reached into his pocket and pulled out two sheets of paper.

"I can't believe it actually worked!" he said as he unfolded them.

She sat up slowly, still not sure what was happening.

"Isaac? What's going on?"

He completely ignored her as his eyes ran over the calculations and formulas on the page in front of him. He laughed and shook his head as he read them.

"It worked. I did it," he said.

Elise was growing upset and she stood up quickly. She looked at the sheet of paper in his hands and her blood ran cold. It was his invention, the one he had mentioned when they first met over two months ago, it was his formula for causing someone to fall in love.

She recoiled, crashing into the couch and almost falling over.

"No, you didn't," she said. "YOU WOULDN'T!"

Isaac turned to face her.

"I'm sorry Elise, but I had to know that it wasn't impossible."

"No!" she screamed. "I know what I'm feeling, it's not fake. This is real."

"Of course it's real. It had to be real for it to work," he replied quickly, trying to make her understand.

She backed away further, wanting to put as much distance between them as possible.

"But... but... Castor..." she said, barely able to speak now.

"I told him about my invention at the Inventor's Club knowing he'd come after it. Knowing it would force us on the run together."

Elise stopped and tears started rushing from her eyes as another thought occurred to her. She was growing hysterical and had to force the words out between sobs.

"That woman. Was she even your real grandma?"

Isaac shook his head.

"No, she wasn't," he answered.

Elise backed away until she hit the table against the far wall where all of their tools and spare parts were kept.

"Oh my God!" she yelled.

"Elise, it's not as bad as it seems. That woman had cancer, she was dying a slow, lonely, horrible death in the hospital. She begged me to help her, she was so excited to go out in the midst of one last adventure!"

He stepped towards her.

"No!" she screamed. "Stay away from me!"

Her hand ran across the top of the table and she felt the small screwdriver. She picked it up and held it out like a knife.

"You're sick!" Elise yelled.

Isaac smiled. It was the most infuriating smile she had ever seen in her life.

"Is that any way to talk to the man you love?" he asked.

Elise's vision went red. She rushed forward. Isaac didn't move and she reached him quickly. She plunged the small screwdriver into his side and he cried out as he fell to the ground. Elise stumbled back onto the couch and sobbed as she realized what she had just done.

The pain jolted through him like currents of electricity and Isaac ran his fingers across the handle of the screwdriver that was still sticking into him. The reason he had chosen this particular tool, the reason that it was the only one he wouldn't get rid of while she slept, was because he had determined that it couldn't be stabbed into him far enough to do any lasting damage. But as another terrible wave of pain shot through him he began to think that he had misjudged that, that maybe she had been stronger than he had thought, that she had stabbed him deeper and nicked something important.

Isaac remained on the floor and Elise remained on the couch, crying ceaselessly. He still had his two sheets of paper in his hand and he tried to block out the pain as he looked them over again. Love, check. Crime of passion, check. He wasn't happy to have put Elise into such a state of disarray, and already his mind was working on ways in which to repair the damage he had caused her here today. But he also couldn't wipe the smile from his face as he looked over his two inventions. His two successful inventions. Another impossibility proven possible.

A sound in the hallway caught his attention and he focused on it. It was the sound of too many people trying too hard to remain quiet. Isaac knew instantly what it was.

"No," he said.

He fumbled in his pocket until his hand fell upon a lighter. He pulled it out and flicked it on. Every movement of his arm caused the wound in his side to hurt even worse, and he could feel far too much blood running out of him and onto the floor. But he focused his energy on the lighter, and held it up to the two sheets of paper. Soon they were engulfed and he was happy about it. He had gotten all he needed out of them and wasn't about to let them fall into the hands of anyone else, especially not Castor Ileska.

They had no reason to fortify their door so it took just one kick from the big Romanian to get it open. Castor and his Romanian bodyguards came sweeping into the room.

"YOU!" Elise screamed as she leapt off the couch.

The gunshot was the loudest thing Isaac had ever heard. It filled every bit of available space around him. He watched in terror as the bullet caught Elise in the lower abdomen. The impact sent her stumbling back onto the couch. Her beautiful green eyes were wide open as she felt of the wound. It was in almost the identical spot as Isaac's.

"NO!" Isaac screamed.

Castor laughed and walked over to him. He saw the burnt papers, little more than tiny shreds of black ash at this point, and shook his head.

"Pick him up," Castor commanded.

One of the men picked him up. The motion caused the screwdriver to move and more blood spilled out of him. Castor noticed the burnt papers on the floor, then turned to look at Isaac. Seeing the screwdriver in his side, the man laughed.

"You really did it, didn't you? Made her love you, then made her attack you. Then you burn your invention," Castor paused and shook his head. "This I just don't understand."

"It's not for you to understand," Isaac said, then looked over at Elise. "Keep pressure on the wound!"

Castor and his men laughed.

"I spent all this time tracking you down, came all this way expecting to find not one, but two inventions to steal. I'm sensing that this is to be a disappointing trip for me," Castor said.

Instinctively Isaac looked over at Elise's invention. It was on the table nearby. Castor followed his gaze.

"What have we here?" Castor asked.

Isaac used every bit of strength left in himself to lunge forward. He broke free of the Romanian man's grip and headbutted Castor as hard as he could. He then stumbled towards Elise's invention.

"Shoot him!" Castor yelled.

Isaac reached out and pressed the small button on top of the invention, initiating the pulse just as one of the men fired their pistol. The bullet caught him in the back of his shoulder and he again fell to the ground, a new round of pain rippling through him.

The lights in the apartment went out and then one of the men who Castor had left to guard the hallway spoke up.

"Boss! Look out the window, something is happening."

Castor moved to the window and glanced down at the street. The stoplight in the nearby intersection had gone off and several cars had wrecked into one another. People were yelling, some screaming, and he saw several of them running down the sidewalk.

"Perhaps it is time for us to go," one of the Romanians said.

Castor turned back around and looked at Elise, then at Isaac. He motioned for one of his men to come into the room.

"Want me to kill them?" the man asked.

"Check them first. Any chance we can just leave them to die from their current wounds?" Castor asked.

The man roughly looked them both over and then stood up and flashed a wicked grin.

"Most excellent idea sir. Their deaths will be horribly painful," he said.

"You're sure that they won't survive?" Castor asked.

"With the chaos breaking out in the streets, I'd say that the chance of them getting help before they bleed out is zero percent."

"You're certain?" Castor asked, always a man to double check.

"To survive from those wounds under conditions like these, it's impossible sir."

There was that word.

As the sounds outside grew louder and more serious Castor and his men started leaving the apartment. Castor scooped up Elise's invention, not realizing that it's one purpose had now been fulfilled. He cradled it under his arm as he left, not bothering to look back at the two wounded and dying people in the apartment.

Phase One: Survive

Isaac's vision blurred with each movement as he slowly crawled across the floor towards the couch. Elise was still breathing, but was starting to slump over. The words of Castor's thug rang out loudly in Isaac's mind. He had said it was impossible that they would survive. Isaac liked those kinds of odds.

As he reached the couch he pulled himself up. Elise's eyes were still open and she looked at him and frowned.

"They shot me," she said.

"I know, it's going to be okay. Just stay with me," Isaac told her. "I set off the pulse. Your invention worked."

She smiled weakly.

"It did?"

He smiled back and nodded.

"It did. Now let's get you up off of that couch and to the nearest hospital."

Every movement he made caused agonizing pain and it took every available part of his will and strength to keep moving, to keep trying to get them out of the apartment and somewhere they could get medical attention.

In a small corner of his mind a thought occurred to him. The idea that by risking his life to activate her invention he had put Elise's happiness ahead of his own. That in some ways and by some definitions, that was love.

He stole a glance at her, noticing that even as she battled back death itself she looked beautiful. A slight smile pulled at the corner of his mouth for an instant as he considered it, the fact that he loved her. He forced himself to push the idea into the deep recesses of his mind, an impossibility for another day. Right now he had to focus on the one right before him, how to keep them both alive.

That was a particularly vexing impossibility, almost as much as the one he had just filed away. But one thing that Isaac Gray knew was that he had never met an impossibility he couldn't conquer.

And he wasn't about to start now.

AUTHOR BIOS

JOHN ANGLIN

John Anglin is an aspiring writer
Living in North Texas. He has always
enjoyed fantasy and historical fiction.
He is a longtime tabletop RPG gamer.
One day he hopes to be writing for
Paizo Publishing in their Pathfinder
setting, Golarion. He is also working on a series based in his
own fantasy setting.

JJ BEAZLEY

JJ Beazley likes to think he's a bit of a
philosopher and a bit of a mystic. Mostly
he's just a bit of an eccentric. His two
favourite mottos are 'I don't
actually know anything' and 'There
are more things in heaven and earth,
Horatio, than are dreamt of in your philosophy.' He lives a
mostly quiet life in a small house deep in the English countryside
where he communes with the local cows and wildlife, and tries to
pretend that the twenty first century has nothing to do with him.
He has been writing speculative short fiction for seven or eight
years and has had twenty five short stories published so far.
He recently finished his first novel and is currently trying to find
an agent to take an interest in it. My blog, should anybody
be interested, is at http://jjbeazley.blogspot.com

JALETA CLEGG

Jaleta Clegg loves to tell good stories, usually with a big dash of silliness added. Her hobbies include crocheting Cthulhu toilet paper roll covers, quilting, and costuming. Her day job involves a portable planetarium, tarship simulators, and lots of School children. She lives in Utah with her husband, toothless old cat, and a horde of her own children. You can find more about her at http://www.jaletac.com or http://www.nexuspoint.info

CHRISTOPHER DONAHUE

Chris Donahue is an electrical engineer, former Navy avionics tech, brewer and writer. He has sold short stories to a number of small-to-medium press anthologies in horror, sci-fi, history, humor and combination markets. In addition to counting breasts, displays of kung fu and rolled heads as a one-time member of the Joe Bob Briggs movie review committee, he smokes a respectably spicy and savory piece of brisket. He lives in the Dallas area with his wife (and fellow author) Linda. They preside in relative peace over a variety of deadbeat critters.

JOANNE GALBRAITH

I'm an aspiring writer from Huntsville, Ontario, where I live with my husband and daughter. My bookshelves are full of tattered Stephen King novels, my original hero and the writer who first inspired me to put my wild imagination down on paper. After dabbling with the art of fiction for many years, I took a few writing classes and found a writing group who have helped me hone my craft and turn my hobby into a true passion. I now have two completed fantasy novels and several short stories currently under review for publication. Email address: joanne.galbraith@gmail.com Writing Samples: http://jgalbraith.scribblefolio.com/

A.C. HALL

Born feet first on a hot summer day in 1981, A.C. (spoiler alert: the initials stand for Aaron Charles) resides in his hometown of Fort Worth, Texas. He spends his days as a reporter for a local newspaper and his nights as a writer of fiction. He loves hanging out with his three nephews and the rest of his family and one of his proudest accomplishments is co-founding Hall Brothers Entertainment with his big brother Phillip. Other books written by A.C. are available at the Hall Brothers website and you can email him directly at freejenkins@gmail.com

PHILLIP HALL

Phillip resides in his hometown of Fort Worth, TX with his wife and three boys. He currently works as a project manager in the medical field. He is an avid reader of all genres of books but his true passion is for speculative fiction. He doesn't watch TV, instead he concentrates all of his time and energy on his family, writing, reading and creating. He loves music of every kind but is quite partial to progressive and power metal. His inspiration to create and write throughout his life has always been his little Brother A.C. Hall. Phillip is currently hard at work on more great fiction for Hall Brothers Entertainment. Feel free to reach out to him at plaskocordova@gmail.com

MARTIN T. INGHAM

Martin T. Ingham is a speculative fiction writer living in Downeast Maine, with His wife and three children. He currently has four novels in-print, and his short stories have appeared in numerous collections, including Pill Hill Press' "Patented DNA" and "Haunted" anthologies. You can learn more about Martin and read samples of his literature at http://www.martiningham.com

ADAM KNIGHT

Adam Knight is writer and middle school English teacher in northern New Jersey. His stories have recently been accepted for publication at Brain Soup, Halfway Down the Stairs, and Golden Visions Magazine. When not grading essays or toiling away on fantasy and sci-fi projects, he can be found running, reading, or struggling to play a heavy metal riff or two on guitar. (His story in this anthology was inspired by a Megadeth song). He is blessed with a wonderful wife who supports his writing dream, and with a dog and two cats who remind him when it's dinner time.

TONY LAPLUME

Tony Laplume was born thirty years ago, and began an early career of moving about New England, ricocheting between Massachusetts, Rhode Island, and Maine, the last stop of the tour, where he eventually contributed the comic strip "Newsroom" for the local school paper during his senior year. In college, where he eventually earned a Bachelor's Degree in English at the University of Maine, he helped found and regularly contributed to the literary journal Hemlock. Later, he wrote and self-published his first novel, The Cloak of Shrouded Men, and continued with a variety of other writing pursuits, which landed him in Colorado Springs. He can be reached at bandido@gmail.com.

SHELLY LI

Shelly has published multiple short stories in venues such as Nature, Cosmos Online, Robot, and more. Her novel of YA Fantasy, The Royal Hunter, is forthcoming from Philomel Books in Fall 2011. For more information, please visit: www.shelly-li.com.

T. SHONTELLE MACQUEEN

Shontelle MacQueen was born in London, England and lived in Europe, Scandinavia, and an assortment of U.S. states before settling in North Carolina where she is a licensed psychologist. In addition to professional publications, Dr. MacQueen enjoys writing short stories that often defy traditional categorization. She enjoys a variety of interests including music, martial arts, and spending time with her two young children. She is currently at work on her first full length novel.

ANTHONY MALONE

Anthony Malone's fiction has been published in, among others, Murky Depths, The Delinquent, Lowestoft Chronicle and his short stories are included in the forthcoming anthologies Best Of Murky Depths (2011) and Cup Of Joe (2010) from Wicked East Press. He has read at Short Fuse as part of the 2009 Coastal Currents Arts Festival, the London events writLOUD, Tales of the Decongested, Liars' League, Storytails and One Eye Grey's "Spectres At The Feast" event and recorded for London Link Radio. Guess what? He lives in London.

EDWARD MARTIN III

Edward Martin III is an award-winning filmmaker from Portland, OR. He adapted and directed an animated adaptation of H. P. Lovecraft's "The Dream-Quest of Unknown Kadath", produced "The Cosmic Horror Fun-Pak", wrote and directed a 10-minute comprehensive period adaptation of "Lord of the Rings", and is in deep post-production of "Flesh of my Flesh," a ground-breaking independent zombie action movie. He's also in development or preproduction for several other feature films, and a handful of shorts. Visit http://www.guerrilla-productions.org/ for more information.

E. CRAIG MCKAY

E. Craig McKay is a retired college professor. For years he's written non-fiction (wine, food and travel articles for Canadian magazines, and movie critiques for Canadian newspapers). His non fiction writing was also under the names James W. Marsh and Craig Gambarotto-McKay. He began writing fiction in January 2010. Publication pending for fiction and poetry in Dead Mule, School of southern Literature, short story in Renaissance, short story in Pink Narcissus Anthology. He lives in Newfoundland and Labrador, Canada during the summer and Almunecar, Spain in winter.

ETHAN NAHTÉ

Ethan Nahté was born and raised in Arkansas, mainly bouncing around between the Ouachitas and the Ozark Mountains. As a teen he played in a variety of bands; was published in school literary magazines; assisted the local college with their TV programs. For the next two decades he focused on a career as a professional journalist; published in over 20 magazines, e-zines & newspapers worldwide, and a television career with his work making it to network & cable TV. He also produced his own entertainment TV programs in the Dallas/Fort Worth, TX region interviewing several well-known celebrities. In 2009 he decided once again to take his fiction writing seriously. You can keep track of him at http://www.livenloud.net

FRANCES PAULI

Washington state author, Frances Pauli, writes Speculative fiction with a touch of romance. Despite a tragic predilection to paint, she discovered her calling as a writer sometime in her mid thirties. As a lifetime reader of Science Fiction and

Fantasy, the stories that clamor for her attention inevitably fall into the Speculative Fiction category. Frances maintains that the Romance is not entirely her fault. More information about Frances, her work, blog and free online serial, Space Slugs, can be found on her website at: http://francespauli.com

JOHN E. PETTY

JOHN E. PETTY, a freelance writer living in Lewisville, Texas with his significant other, Judy, and their ever-expanding menagerie of cats and dogs, is the primary author of Capes, Crooks, & Cliffhangers: Heroic Serial Posters of the Golden Age (available from amazon.com), about the serials of the 1930s, 40s, and 50s based on comic books, pulps, radio shows and more. He is currently pursuing a Masters Degree in Film Studies at the University of North Texas, and has published extensively on film and popular culture subjects in Big Reel, Films of the Golden Age, Classic Images, and more, and co-writes the monthly column Obligatory Fight Scene for The Comic Buyer's Guide with Jim Johnson. Previously, John worked as a radio talk show host, tarot card reader, comedy defensive driving instructor, sommelier, opera singer, and professional magician/escape artist, to name just a few branches on his twisted career tree. Visit www.johnepetty.com for more information, or send email to john@johnepetty.com.

BARRY POMEROY

Barry Pomeroy's PhD. was found at the University of Manitoba, although he refuses to let that be a limitation. He is an itinerant English professor, boat designer and builder, traveller, carver, sometimes mechanic, carpenter, and web designer. As a writer he is responsible for the novel Naked in the Road. "Cops Nose Down in Blood" is from his novel Malu.

FRANK ROGER

Frank Roger was born in 1957 in Ghent, Belgium. His first story appeared in 1975. Since then his stories appear in an increasing number of languages in all sorts of magazines, anthologies and other venues, and since 2000, story collections are published, also in various languages. Apart from fiction, he also produces collages and graphic work in a surrealist and satirical tradition. These have appeared in various magazines and books. By now he has more than 800 short story publications (including a few short novels) to his credit in more than 35 languages. Find out more at www.frankroger.be

ROB ROSEN

Rob Rosen, award-winning San Francisco author of the novels "Sparkle", "Divas Las Vegas", and "Hot Lava", has contributed to more than 125 anthologies in just about every genre imaginable. Please visit him at www.therobrosen.com

CHRISTOPHER STIRES

Christopher Stires lives in Riverside CA. He has written three novels – REBEL NATION (An Alternate History-Thriller) and THE INHERITANCE (Winner of the 2003 Dream Realm Award for Horror) are both available from Zumaya Publications (www.zumayapublications.com). TO THE MOUNTAIN OF THE BEAST (A SciFi-Horror/Western) was published by now-defunct Carnifex Press. DARK LEGEND, his paranormal horror novel, will be released by Zumaya Publications later this year. He has had over 70 short stories and articles appear in publications in the United States, Argentina, Australia, Belgium, Finland, France, Greece, the Netherlands, and the United Kingdom. "Along the Outer Rim of Titan's Anvil" is his fifth tale about Patrick Novarro, the Crusader.

ERIK SVEHAUG

Erik Svehaug works a day job at a picturesque Santa Cruz lumberyard with steam train tunnel and white cathedral on a hill and writes when he can seize the time. He loves his wife and two inspiring daughters and regularly walks the dog. His shorts and flash fiction have appeared on-line and in print, thanks to Bartleby-Snopes, the Linnet's Wing, and the Dead Mule School of Southern Literature, among others. Stories with a Marin County focus have also appeared in the Outlaw Chapbook from Bannock Street Press, Static Movement and Crispin Best's: For Every Year. Two of Erik's Micros have been included in Binnacle UltraShorts productions and he was a prize winner in the 2010 SuRaa Short Fiction Contest. He was pleased to be included in the "50 Stories for Pakistan" anthology. Published work blog: eriksvehaug.wordpress.com

ABOUT HALL BROTHERS ENTERTAINMENT

After 29 years of being brothers, Phillip (the big brother) and A.C. finally decided to do something productive with all the time they spend hanging out. Lifetime fans of both reading and writing fiction, the Brothers Hall have now brought their love of literature to life in the form of Hall Brothers Entertainment. By providing daily two sentence stories, weekly episodic fiction, holiday themed fiction on most major holidays, and two short story anthologies a year, Phillip and A.C. hope to give fans of fiction so much content that they can't help but come back to hallbrosentertainment.com several times each and every week. Not only does all of this appear free of charge on the website but the brothers publish many books throughout the year as well.

ABOUT THE COVER DESIGNER

Paul Milligan is an illustrator, graphic designer and sometimes
writer from Norman, Oklahoma (though his heart belongs
in Dallas, Texas). His comic book work has appeared in several
small press anthologies such as Young American Comics' Big Ol'
Book of BIZMAR, Space-Gun Studios Synesthetic and many
others he published himself while part of the Dallas-based creative
group, Stumblebum Studios. Recently he self-published God of
Rock collection as part of Indy Comic Book Week. Currently he
is the artist (with writer David Hopkins) for Souvenir of Dallas, a
semi-regular full-page comic appearing in D Magazine and is
hard(ly) at work on his first graphic novel. Paul is not related to
Peter Milligan, but he'll tell you he is if it'll help him get work.

HALL BROTHERS
ENTERTAINMENT

ORIGINAL FICTION ONLINE AND IN PRINT

DAILY TWO SENTENCE STORIES!

WEEKLY EPISODIC FICTION!

BI-WEEKLY SHORT STORIES!

ANTHOLOGIES & COLLECTIONS
PUBLISHED QUARTERLY!

WWW.HALLBROSENTERTAINMENT.COM

31449259R00216

Made in the USA
Lexington, KY
16 April 2014